UP WITH THE SUN

"Thomas Mallon has been America's premier historical novelist for a decade. *Up With the Sun* cinches the accolade. It's New York City in the aching eighties. The murder of show-biz bottom feeder/monster Dick Kallman and his male lover ramifies throughout the turmoil of the decade—in a stunning hybrid of Tom Wolfe's *The Bonfire of the Vanities* and frontline reports from a beleaguered gay demimonde. This book packs period pizzazz and heartbreaking intimacy. And, as always with Mallon—it's a page-turning blast." —James Ellroy

"In this funny, vicious tale of ambition and moral corrosion, Thomas Mallon turns his rapier intelligence and seismographic sense of the workings of power to the worlds of Hollywood and Broadway. Among imperishable legends and declining stars, he chronicles desperate competition and half-open secrets, the longing for the next new thing and the lure of the past. *Up With the Sun* is a novel as stark as a Greek drama and as delicious as gossip." —Garth Greenwell, author of *Cleanness* and *What Belongs to You*

THOMAS MALLON
UP WITH THE SUN

Thomas Mallon is the author of eleven novels, including *Henry and Clara*, *Dewey Defeats Truman*, *Fellow Travelers*, *Watergate*, and *Landfall*. He is a frequent contributor to *The New Yorker*, *The New York Times Book Review*, and other publications. In 2011 he received the American Academy of Arts and Letters' Harold D. Vursell Memorial Award for prose style. He has been the literary editor of *GQ* and the deputy chairman of the National Endowment for the Humanities. He lives in Washington, D.C.

thomasmallon.com

UP WITH THE SUN

THOMAS MALLON

VINTAGE BOOKS

A DIVISION OF PENGUIN RANDOM HOUSE LLC

NEW YORK

FIRST VINTAGE BOOKS EDITION 2024

Grateful acknowledgment is made to Alfred Music to reprint an excerpt from
"Hank," words and music by Johnny Mercer, music by Frank Perkins.
Copyright © 1965 by WC Music Corp., copyright renewed. All rights reserved.
Reprinted by permission of Alfred Music.

Photographic credits: *Everett Collection*: 176; *Photo by Earle Forbes*: 19 (left);
Photos by Friedman-Abeles © The New York Public Library for the Performing Arts:
128 (top: Paula Steward and Lucille Ball; below:
Kenneth Nelson and Rita Gardner), 159, 223 (top).

The Library of Congress has cataloged the Knopf edition as follows:
Names: Mallon, Thomas, [date] author.
Title: Up with the sun / Thomas Mallon.
Description: First edition. | New York: Alfred A. Knopf, 2023.
Identifiers: LCCN 2022011693 (print) | LCCN 2022011694 (ebook) |
Subjects: LCSH: Kallman, Dick, 1933–1980—Fiction. | LCGFT:
Biographical fiction. | Historical fiction. | Novels.
Classification: LCC PS3563.A43157 U67 2023 (print) | LCC PS3563.A43157
(ebook) | DDC 813/.54—dc23
LC record available at https://lccn.loc.gov/2022011693
LC ebook record available at https://lccn.loc.gov/2022011694

Vintage Books Trade Paperback ISBN: 978-0-525-56591-8
eBook ISBN: 978-1-524-74820-3

vintagebooks.com

Printed in the United States of America
10 9 8 7 6 5 4 3 2 1

For Lynn Freed and Patricia Hampl

Author's Note

Up With the Sun is a fictionalized rendering of Dick Kallman's life and death. It is inspired by actual events that have been considerably altered by the author's imagination. Some of this novel's characters never existed at all, and those that may have some basis in actual people are not meant to be factual depictions of those persons. The book's dialogue has been created, not reiterated.

Many people, over many years, spoke to me about Dick Kallman's life, associates, career, and murder. I am especially grateful to Kaye Ballard; the incomparable Carole Cook and Tom Troupe; Rita Gardner; Charles Kallmann; David Levy; Richard McCabe; Judge Patrick McGinley; Martin Newman; Robert Osborne; Rod Pleasants; and John Jacob Rieck Jr.

Leads, information, documents, and good advice came from: Stephen P. Barba, former president and managing partner of The Balsams resort; Donald Behr; Matthew Bogdanos and Karen Edelman-Reyes of the New York County District Attorney's office; Michael DiMaggio, deputy chief clerk, New York County Supreme Court; Gregory Goeckner, Hollywood Foreign Press Association; Val Holley; Arthur Makar; Jeremy Megraw and Andrea Felder of the New York Public Library; Mark Scherzer; Kris Stoever; and Benjamin Taylor.

The death in 2021 of Dan Frank, my editor and friend for twenty-five years and ten books, remains a source of keen sorrow. But at Knopf I have been solaced and splendidly served by the skills of both Edward Kastenmeier and Brian Etling. Dan Novack and Patrick Dillon were also invaluable, and I am once again grateful for the sharp eyes of Thomas Giannettino.

My agent, Andrew Wylie, and his unfailingly generous associate, Katie Cacouris, also have my thanks.

My deepest gratitude goes, as always, to Bill Bodenschatz.

UP WITH THE SUN

FEBRUARY 23, 1980

In one way, this whole story starts thirty years back. But in another, it begins two weeks ago, on February 7th, at the Martin Beck.

The first thing I remember from that night at the theater is the two fur coats: identical, huge, floor-length. I watched them coming down the aisle toward the pit, where I (the show's only musician) was still at the piano fussing with my sheet music a minute after the lights had come up for intermission. Those coats seemed to be moving toward me on their own, so all-enveloping I couldn't see anybody underneath, let alone guess who was wearing them.

He spoke first: "So how much are we going to lose on this bomb?" As if I were somehow in a position to know. She didn't say anything right away, but I actually recognized her before I did him: Dolores Gray, and what little of her was on view looked great. Fifty-five, maybe? Striking makeup, full lips. There was enough noise in the theater—mostly people smacking their foreheads and groaning about how bad this thing was: a musical version of *Harold and Maude*!—that I was able softly to play a couple of bars of "Here's That Rainy Day," her signature number from *Carnival in Flanders*, a show that inexplicably flopped about twenty-five years ago. Dolores Gray and Dick Kallman, who I now realized was the guy wearing the other coat, turned out to be great pals, both of them with a little money in the show.

"Dolores," he said, "this is Matt Liannetta."

My name is actually Liannett-o, but this wasn't a camp joke. Over the years Dick had often misremembered it—willfully, I thought, as if having retained it would diminish his status.

"Pleased to meet you," said Miss Gray. Throaty, and a bit grand. I wondered why her career had petered out so early. Married a rich guy, I think.

But it was Dick I had trouble taking my eyes off. I don't think I'd seen him in five years, and most of the memories I had of him went back closer to twenty or thirty, to his first big stage role, his nightclub gigs, and his early attempts at trying his luck in Hollywood. He had been, back then, what my daughter would now call "preppy." But standing there in the Martin Beck, two weeks ago? I couldn't get over him. I know it's the seventies—no, wait, it's already the eighties—but his getup was really out there. All I could see beneath the coat was a gold chain descending into an open mauve shirt.

"You won't believe this," he said to Dolores, "but Matt was the pianist for *Seventeen*."

"No," she said, with just the right degree of politeness and disbelief. You know: *Almost thirty years ago? Surely you were too young?*

"Yup, he was," said Dick, all false flattery, one of his habitual modes. Now, as in the past, the phoniness coming from him could seem more charming, more authentic, than sincerity would have been. I'd actually never seen Dick be truly sincere about anything, and if he'd started now, I think it would have repulsed me. As it was, he just nodded and smiled his big, overly expressive smile, as if he were acting in a silent picture.

"I *was* too young," I told Dolores. "Only nineteen. Three weeks into the show they replaced me with an older guy."

"So that's how you met Richard?" she asked.

Richard? Lah-dee-dah. But she clearly knew Dick's résumé,

whose first big item, back in 1951, was a Theatre World Award as Most Promising Newcomer. He'd played Joe Bullitt, a supporting role in that musical adaptation of what the playbill always called "Booth Tarkington's timeless classic."

"I was up at the Mark Hellinger that summer," said Dolores. "With Bert Lahr."

"*Two on the Aisle*," I said. "I saw it. A couple of times, in fact. Maybe even once with him," I added, pointing to Dick.

"And wasn't she *amazing*?" he asked.

I didn't know whether to fill her in on my other sporadic encounters with Dick—how I'd sometimes played for him in clubs, out of town, when we were still in our twenties. How I'd been asked, from time to time, to come around while he was doing great, like when he was back in New York on a break from touring the Bobby Morse part in *How to Succeed*. That was just before his brief pinnacle, the year he had the honest-to-God lead in a network sitcom called *Hank*. It was on on Fridays, one of the nights I got to have my daughter, and we'd watch the TV together and laugh. She was only five, but she understood the silly premise that put Dick into all the funny disguises.

No, I decided not to tell Dolores about my intermittent friendship with Dick, because, if I started, within a minute we'd be getting into his disappointing last decade, when his arc dipped and he was off TV except for the odd guest shot; was back to touring in other stars' musicals; and was finally doing crappy two-handers that never made it to New York. All this before he disappeared from show business altogether.

"We're partners!" he exclaimed, draping his mink arm over Dolores's mink shoulders. "Isn't that grand?" For a second I thought he meant partners in some awful Judy-Garland-and-queer-husband-number-four kind of way, but it turned out he meant partners in an antiques business. Which confused me, since post-showbiz Dick had already gone into menswear and, at least for a while, as I understood things, made a lot of money at it.

He was soon explaining the way he and Dolores operated—selling everything out of an apartment, which at that moment I didn't grasp meant *his* apartment. As it was, I had to keep looking around, a little nervously. Unless the stage manager knew this was Dolores Gray I was talking to, he'd want me to be out of the pit this far into intermission.

A little leather datebook came out of Dick's fur pocket. From it he extracted a business card: POSSESSIONS OF PROMINENCE, LTD. (I handed it over to Detective Volker a little while ago.) Leaning down, Dick stuffed it into the pocket of my opening-night tuxedo and invited me to "a little party on the twenty-first," at his place in the East Seventies.

My hesitation must have shown, because Dolores seemed to notice and overrule it. "Say yes, sweetie. Let him cook for you. Besides, from the looks of this turkey"—she cocked her glossy head in the direction of the stage—"you're gonna be out of a job by then."

———

And I am. *Harold and Maude* lasted four performances, two fewer than *Carnival in Flanders*. But I'm out of a job more than half the time, and it's not much to worry about: a few more private lessons for Brearley girls and some extra days as the auditions pianist across the river at Paper Mill and I'm fine until some other show comes along. In fact, subbing always suits me best. Favorite career experience? Filling in at *Mack & Mabel*, best failed show ever, over Thanksgiving weekend in '74.

I live at Manhattan Plaza, which if you don't know New York is a big clean high-rise Nirvana of subsidized housing for music and theater people near the western edge of Forty-Second Street. The whole thing is spacious and kind of grand because it was built as a luxury rental before the developer went belly up five years ago with the rest of New York, and the state got the bright, beneficent idea to snap it up. There's a waiting list to get in here that's longer than the one for Eton, and I count myself incredibly fortunate.

Some people say the city's starting to come back; I can't say I see much sign of it. People still talk about their muggings the way they used to talk about their operations. My own happened in Bryant Park two years ago, after I'd come out of the library, which can be a scarier place than the park: shorter hours and no money for books, though the drug dealers in the bathrooms keep their voices down in a way that would please the old ladies with eyeglass chains who used to shoosh you at the reference desk. I know, I know, I'm being nostalgic for the fifties, when I first started working in the city.

But now's not the time for my life story, not with Dick lying dead in the medical examiner's office, down near Bellevue, and his California brother—all this according to Detective Volker—staying at the Stanhope until he can arrange the cremation.

In that apartment of Dick's, at the other night's dinner party, there were at least a half dozen urns and vases fancy enough for him to be put in, though I suspect that if the furniture had been made to play *To Tell the Truth*, two-thirds of the supposed antiques would have had to stand up, admit they were fakes, and exit the premises. It's not that I have any expertise in such things, but a couple of other guys at the dinner did, and I could see what they were thinking: *What exactly is going on here?* Along with: *How soon can we leave?*

That afternoon I was giving a lesson down in Murray Hill. I stopped to buy a cake—I know, so Italian—before taking the M1 up Madison and getting off at the Carlyle, just around the corner from the address Dick had given me on East Seventy-Seventh. To kill a couple of minutes I went into the hotel lobby, just off the café, and sat down, recalling the time I backed Jo Stafford there; another nice memory, from way back when, before I was divorced. I wondered if tonight, after dinner, we'd all wind up at the hotel listening to Bobby Short. It would be like Dick to make a show of marching everybody in, telling us he'd been comped and then secretly paying off the maître d'.

My punctuality is an occupational virtue. All my life, afraid the curtain will go up before I get to the theater, I've set my watch ten minutes ahead and used two alarm clocks for an afternoon nap. So it was no surprise that I was the first guest to arrive at the apartment—or townhouse, I should say.

I was let in by a houseman called Tommy, whose full name is Pao Kao Liou; I now know the whole dramatis personae from the interview I just had with Detective Volker. Tommy's English was impenetrable, his smile nonexistent. He took my cake and my topcoat and sat me down in the living room, where there was no sign of Dick. The place was all showroom, no showbiz, not one piece of career memorabilia that I could see. There was something obvious and strange all at once about the space, as if you'd stumbled into Montgomery Ward's idea of Versailles. On two different tables sat laminated copies of a small, recent write-up about Possessions of Prominence that had run in *New York* magazine and which I guess I had missed.

I started reading about the Imari plates and the Reynolds oil sketch while Tommy got me a glass of wine. I was soon joined by two other arrivals—a couple, I supposed: Kyle Waterman, a designer, nice manners, Southern, in his thirties, pretty in a well-Cliniqued kind of way; and Fred Johnston, quite a bit older, also a gent, and apparently very rich. His family had gotten that way long ago by mining the exact kind of nickel that the government used to buy for making, well, nickels.

There was barely time for any nice-to-meet-yous before the three of us were back on our feet to greet another two men coming into the living room—definitely a couple, I thought, though probably not destined for permanence. The older one, Jack O'Rourke, lived on Gramercy Park and had that roasted, leathery Bill Blass look, as if he'd just stepped off a plane from Nantucket in July. The only one of us not wearing a tie, he introduced his lower-keyed friend as Jeff Mathis, "just like Johnny." Mathis seemed decorative and uncomplicated, though Detective Volker just told me that describing people as "decorative and uncomplicated" is useless, at least for police purposes.

Mathis rolled his eyes and said he'd been running an errand in Chinatown before meeting up with Jack and that there was some kind of traffic nightmare down there, thanks to a fund-raising appearance by Rosalynn Carter, who's trying to save her husband's job from Teddy Kennedy.

"I hope she gets eaten by a Chinese dragon," said O'Rourke, not because she'd inconvenienced his companion but because he's a Reagan man. I myself know nothing about politics but have always been sort of sympathetic to Carter, maybe because he reminds me of myself: slight and usually soft-spoken and just trying to keep warm in that cardigan sweater.

"I guess things in Washington never really change much," I said—my staggering contribution to the current-events discourse. "But did you see that Alice Roosevelt died yesterday?"

"Well," said O'Rourke, giving my shoulder a squeeze and quoting her famous pillow, "if you can't say something good about someone, sit right here by me." We all sat down, while Jack opined that even Joan Kennedy would be better than Rosalynn Carter: "At least the poor thing'll stay plastered."

Tommy, exasperated by all the overcoats he had to handle and needing help with the drink orders, shouted upstairs: "Mister Steven! Are here! Are here!"

Well, we *were* here, and I wondered: Is this *it*? No Dolores Gray? Too bad. And who is Steven?

Waterman and Johnston cast informed, dubious glances around the place as Steven came down the stairs: a nice-looking young man in his twenties, blond (perhaps with a little assistance), two open buttons on his expensive-looking shirt. Maybe something left over from Dick's menswear days? Steven seemed like someone who got up late but went running once he did.

"Ah!" said O'Rourke, raising the glass he didn't yet have. "The lady of the house!"

"Jack, give it a rest," said Mathis.

Steven smiled, good-naturedly, then set to mixing drinks as if he were studying for a chemistry final. As it turns out, he had recently finished law school. I watched him being teased by O'Rourke and still couldn't get over the idea of Dick with an official in-residence boyfriend. Steven's open, acknowledged status was as unexpected as the floor-length mink coat at the *Harold and Maude* premiere. I mean, I can remember when Dick was actually *engaged* to that rich girl in Detroit. Stupid, I know, to find the change so surprising: even *I* was once married, to a poor girl from Hartford even more naive about me than I was.

"Hi, everybody!"

Well, here was Dick at last, bursting through the front door of the apartment as if making his entrance on *Hollywood Palace* after a commercial break. No mink this time; just a conservative camel-hair coat that Tommy took from him. But the shirt underneath was open one button beyond Steven's, and I recognized the necklace from that night at the theater. He didn't bother with a drink, and as the rest of us got started on our own, I wondered if he might be high.

He launched into telling us that he'd just been "over on Beekman Place, seeing my ring man. Sold one! This guy likes to fondle the merch while I display it on my fingers. Creepy, I grant you. But this was no cheap piece of turquoise he bought. A nice little emerald. You've seen it, Steven."

Steven nodded, while Waterman and Johnston exchanged looks about the whole off-kilter feel of things.

"So what do you think?" Dick asked, sweeping his hand to indicate the whole ornate, antique-stuffed room. The question did not seem meant for O'Rourke and Mathis, who had evidently been here before.

We first-timers murmured that, yeah, it was amazing, impressive.

"It's a terribly, terribly exciting thing to be able to live with this kind of beauty," Dick said, quoting himself, I now realize, from that article in *New York* magazine. He began explaining how clients made an appointment, were given an unhurried tour of the premises, and then—

Jack O'Rourke interrupted him. "Dick, you didn't have *room* for a Calder in here. Not even a little one."

Dick let out his big road-company laugh. It seems that he had personally delivered a huge Calder gouache to O'Rourke's house on Gramercy Park a couple of weeks before—"a stunner I had on my wall for just four days," Dick swore. O'Rourke, who'd bought it sight unseen, now seemed, however slyly, to be questioning its provenance, and maybe even its authenticity.

"Tommy!" Dick cried. "Pao Kao Liou! Are we ready?"

Ready to eat? I thought. Already?

Before another five minutes went by, we were all consuming a lot of delicate, inventive Chinese food, and the conversation felt fitfully normal. Still, I would have been more comfortable with a couple of women there—not Dolores Gray necessarily, just anyone to lessen the predictable grind of double entendres arising from what the next day's *New York Post*, in a rare burst of accuracy, would call an "all male-dinner party."

There were also strange gaps and reticences.

"What do you do, Mr. Liannetto?" asked Fred Johnston.

I gave him the abbreviated version of my involvement with *Harold and Maude*, whose awfulness was beginning to achieve the legendary status of *Kelly*'s.

"Janet Gaynor!" crowed O'Rourke. "As adorable as my fifth-grade teacher."

She was, too. I told the table how I'd felt sorry for the show's seventy-three-year-old star, a perfect doll who'd had to do the hula onstage and at one point found herself literally up a tree.

"Was she in movies?" asked Steven.

A disbelieving clatter of silverware from the older homosexual brethren.

"Silent films," said Johnston, politely. I then offered the opinion that *Harold and Maude*, even live and onstage, would have benefited from an absence of sound.

"Well, not just silents," said Waterman. "Gaynor was in the original version of *A Star Is Born*."

"Oh, come on!" cawed O'Rourke. "This one's too young to remember even *Judy's* version." He copped a feel of Steven's right biceps.

But this is what I mean by gaps and reticences. Here was a moment for Dick, one of the greatest name-droppers ever, to mention that he'd been at Garland's 1961 Carnegie Hall come-back concert (so had I!), albeit a lot of rows back from the red-hot celebrity center of the audience. But he never said a thing. Which, given this crowd, was like dining with a half dozen clergymen and not mentioning you'd had an orchestra seat for the Sermon on the Mount. He just let the opportunity pass, issuing instructions to Steven and Tommy that kept the procession of little courses coming ever faster. True, it was a Thursday night, but I couldn't understand the rush. Or why I was there. Fred Johnston, with that fortune in nickels, was presumably a sales prospect, and Jack O'Rourke might still be good for another Calder. But me?

It seemed as if Dick had lost interest in his own party some-time between issuing the invitations and his guests' arrival. There was something listless about him; the usual brassiness could still be detected, but it felt as if somebody had stuck a mute into half of his seventy-six trombones.

"Mr. Kallman, this is delicious," said Kyle Waterman. And it was; but here, too, I felt something was peculiar. Dick was an absolutely tiptop cook. Not only, in my memory, did he always love to make the food for his guests; he liked to make it in front of them. "It's like being at fucking Benihana," somebody once whispered to me at a party Dick gave during his *Half a Sixpence* tour. He had learned his recipes as a boy, hanging out in the kitchen of the resort hotel his father owned. When we were all kids doing *Seventeen*, we'd stay out until two in the morning and then go back to his place, where he'd make scrambled eggs that left everybody prostrate with admiration.

I mentioned those eggs when Tommy set something eggy-looking down in front of us. Dick responded with a big loud empty smile, but not a word of reminiscence. Steven said he wanted to hear more about *Seventeen*, but Dick asked him to get up and fetch some Peking bowl that he wanted to show Johnston. I was by now pretty sure that—unless Tommy used to watch *Hank* on Friday nights—no one here except Steven and me had any idea that Dick had ever been in show business.

The phone in the kitchen rang. "Mr. K!" cried Tommy. "It's Jimmy!"

"Yimmy?" asked O'Rourke.

"Jimmy," Steven corrected him, with disapproval—not of the bad accent joke but of the caller.

"No," said Dick, firmly, to Tommy. "Tell him to come back later. I've got guests." Despite the instruction, it seemed clear that Dick had expected the call.

"Jimmy's twenty-one," Dick explained to us all, "and com-pletely fucked up. It's a *friend* of Jimmy's who wants to buy this. I'm expecting them to show up later tonight." "This" was the watch on Dick's wrist, a gigantic chunk of ostentation that looked as if it had been scooped from a gold mine by a steam shovel. He was expecting some guys to come over and buy it later *tonight*?

I pushed around the little dessert that was on my plate (Tommy never served my cake) and realized—I don't know if it was a bad kumquat or something else—that I wasn't feeling so well. From the kitchen I could hear Tommy washing up some of the dishes we'd already gone through. I could also hear *Quincy* coming from a little countertop TV in there, which meant that it was past nine o'clock. When I mentioned this to Detective Volker this afternoon, he commended my powers of observation. Aside from being a concrete detail, unlike "decorative and uncomplicated," my knowledge of the Thursday-evening television schedule seemed to mark me as a man of steady habits.

"Upstairs!" cried Dick, as if shouting "Charades!" We were all being dispatched to the second-floor "library" for after-dinner drinks, whose fast-forwarded production was in keeping with the rest of the evening. Steven did the honors. The space was awfully dark but basically another showroom. Certainly not a lot of books. Dick used to tease me for being a reader.

O'Rourke pointed to a TV and shared a sudden inspiration. "Let's watch Eric!" It was the night for the fifteen-hundred-meter speed skating, and while this was not a group of men that even knew a US hockey victory over the Russians would be considered an Olympics upset, Eric Heiden and his grain-silo thighs had caught everyone's attention all week. When my daughter, now a sophomore at Georgetown, had called the other night from school, she'd mentioned him and said, "Hot stuff, no, Dad?" She didn't mean his skating, either, and I thought that any minute she was going to ask if Eric was my type. Kids today . . . bless her progressive little heart.

I noticed that Dick now *was* drinking, straight vodka and pretty fast, too. It had started with the phone call. Between gulps he more or less ordered Steven to have a second cognac. His acting had always been so emphatic that you could have trouble guessing any of the subtler emotions he might be trying to convey. Right now I couldn't tell if he was nervous in a happy way or a dreadful one.

"We're going to be rich!" he said, spinning the watch on his wrist. "Or at least *you* are," he added, more softly, to Steven.

Tommy then called upstairs: "Mr. K, they here! Front door!"

"Yimmy?" asked O'Rourke, who was disappointed there'd been no takers for watching Eric. I didn't understand the fast arrival: had Jimmy and company been phoning from a booth up the street? The call couldn't have come ten minutes before.

Dick was rattled; this was *not* what he'd been expecting. He sat down at a desk, pulled open one of its top drawers, and extracted some tiny item he then put in his pocket. After that he kept his back to us, but he was clearly agitated and, even from behind, almost visibly *thinking*, trying to figure something out as quickly as he could. Johnston gave Waterman the high sign, and they got up to make their excuses. The younger man seemed worried that they would look rude, but I heard the older one reassure him in a whisper: "You can send flowers around, with an apology, tomorrow." (Which is just what he wound up doing, Detective Volker tells me, before he saw Friday after-noon's *Post*.)

Before I knew it, O'Rourke and Mathis were getting ready to clear out, too, not from exasperation but from boredom. "We're thinking of heading down to Rounds," said Jack, squeezing my shoulder. "Want to come along?" I smiled and took a pass. The idea of going to Fifty-Third Street and listening to Jack honk and squawk while we all watched the bar's floor show of hus-tlers seemed competitively awful with the thought of being the last guest here.

"Tommy!" cried Dick, turning around, acting perfectly cheer-ful about the imminent departures. "Lead them out through the back garden! They'll love getting a look at it!" It appeared evi-dent that Dick didn't want his dinner guests seeing whoever was at the front door. Or . . . who knows? Maybe there was a hydrangea for sale out back. He maintained a sunny we've-all-gotta-do-this-again-real-soon attitude and escorted the four men downstairs.

Soon afterwards I heard a loud, adolescent voice saying, "Mr. Kallman, this here's Dante." And then everything diminished to a murmur, as if Dick had shooshed the arrivals. Presumably they were going about their business.

"Tell me about *Seventeen*," said Steven, touching my forearm.

I laughed at the sudden change of subject, this earnest attempt at calm. I was relieved to be alone with Steven instead of Dick, and I imparted a few memories of 1951 at the Broadhurst.

"You wouldn't have been born yet," I added, sounding like O'Rourke.

He smiled, and tilted his head toward the downstairs. "He's not wild about the age difference. Not that he would want me any older. It's just that *he'd* like to be a lot younger."

"My favorite number in the show," I told him, "was 'How Do You Do, Miss Pratt?'" If it could keep me from having to discuss Dick's sexual psychology, I was even willing to sing a little of it: "'Beautiful dress, Miss Pratt, beautiful dress! / But you don't deserve anything less!'"

"Oh, God, *Seventeen*!" It was Dick, flying up the stairs, done with his business at both the back door and the front, keyed-up but managing a comical groan. "I *told* them there were still guests here upstairs! They didn't believe me, but they said they'd come back later."

I thought, now that it was just me and Steven, that he might relax for a bit, own up to his former life in show business, take it out like a family heirloom. But instead of joining me and Steven for a bit of reminiscence, or even a postmortem during which we could pretend that the awful, just-concluded party had been a success, he kept pacing and pointlessly straightening things, sitting down at and getting up from the desk. I noticed that he was still wearing that Hope Diamond of a watch. Hadn't Jimmy and his friends come to the house in order to buy it?

Steven, observing Dick's jitters, touched his finger to his nose by way of silent explanation. Was Jimmy really just Dick's supplier, making a delivery? Maybe. But if so, why invent the watch story? Nobody bothers with such a cover today; dealers come over in the middle of a party as if they're the delivery boy from D'Agostino's. And if the watch *wasn't* a cover story, why was it still on Dick's wrist?

He once more sprang up from the desk, ready to race down-stairs again. "Got to say goodbye to Pao Kao! He's heading home to Queens. Pow! Pow! Pow!" he cried, punching the air, making the sort of fast getaway he used to make in his sit-com. He certainly *seemed* coked up. I could hear him starting to fuss in the kitchen—pots clanging, cabinets slamming—after Tommy was gone. All this bustle must have continued for fif-teen minutes, during which I attempted to make conversation with Steven.

"So how long have you guys been together?" I inanely asked him, while trying to remember where Tommy had put my coat.

"About a year," Steven answered. He told me a little about law school and how he and Dick had met; he asked me about the various shows I'd done. I kept responding with polite follow-up questions and my own bits of information, however much I longed to be out of there. And then, finally, the phone rang again.

After answering it, Dick bounded up the stairs once more. His face was white. "They're already on their way back," he said, before frantically pouring himself more vodka. Even now he was stagey, but the desperation was undeniable. He stayed with us for thirty seconds before rushing back down to the kitchen.

"I really need to go," I at last said to Steven.

He nodded, and then asked, "Did they ever make a cast album of that show? *Seventeen*?"

They did—a fairly early LP. But when I thought of explain-ing to Steven how before then an album was really an album, a binder with slipcases for several different 78s, I realized it would have been like describing Grandpa's shaving brush, and I felt too sad and nervous to do it. "Why don't you say goodbye for me?" I suggested, heading to the first floor while there was still a chance to get out before Jimmy and his pals reappeared. I could hear Dick clattering around the kitchen again while I waved farewell to Steven at the top of the stairs. I was halfway through the living room and headed toward the closet that I hoped held my coat, but I was too late.

Dick came rushing toward me. He didn't try to stop me from leaving, but he gave me a crushing hug and opened his hand to reveal a tiny piece of jewelry.

"'Oh, Joe,'" he said, in a high voice, quoting the girl who used to feed him the cue for his big second-act number in *Seventeen*. "'Your fraternity pin! Your beautiful five-dollar pin!'"

This junky little prop that I must have seen with my own eyes twenty-nine years before: why did he want me to have it? I protested, but he insisted. He put the pin in my hand and folded my fingers over it. And ten seconds later I was gone.

And just now, a day and a half later, I've had my visit from Detective Volker. After a steady stream of questions, he had, like Columbo, "just one more thing" to ask: "Have you seen Dick's latest eight-by-ten?"

"A headshot?" I responded, idiotically.

"In a manner of speaking," he replied, putting the picture on my kitchen counter.

God almighty! I saw this ultrasharp black-and-white image of Dick, in one of those Louis XV chairs, wearing nothing but a pair of boxer shorts, one side of his head pristine and the other side exploded. The eye, the one he'd been shot through, looked like a tomato that somebody had dropped.

"Jesus Christ," I said, more a prayer than a curse. Even so, the photograph—taken about thirty hours ago, maybe twelve hours after I'd been sitting in that chair myself—seemed weirdly remote, like an old Weegee now being sold as art, along with the ormolu and jade and Fabergé eggs and everything else that Dick had on sale in the apartment.

Detective Volker tossed his business card down onto the photograph. It landed on Dick's face, covering up the black-and-white blood. From what was left visible you might have thought Dick had just dozed off in the chair after a midnight snack, unless you noticed, in the bottom right corner of the picture, a naked foot, and realized that it belonged to Steven, who'd also been shot dead. Detective Volker must have had a close-up of him, too, but he didn't show it to me. After a few seconds went by, he pulled the photo of Dick out from under the business card, like the tablecloth that gets jerked away in a magic act. And then he left, without even saying "We'll be in touch," the way I thought they were supposed to.

CHAPTER 1

JUNE 19, 1951

Dick Kallman is making his Broadway debut as Joe Bullitt in Seventeen. *Kenneth Nelson and Ann Crowley are playing the leads.*

Flahooley had flopped and no one was that sorry, except for Matt Liannetto, who was crazy about Barbara Cook. This was her very first show, and he'd stood in the back of the theater three times during the past four weeks just to hear her sing "He's Only Wonderful."

But the show had closed three nights ago, and *Seventeen* was taking its place at the Broadhurst, getting ready to open the day after tomorrow. Right now the theater felt like a house on moving day, one family's things going out the back door as the new arrivals' stuff came in the front. The noise exceeded anything reasonable for a day before dress rehearsal, but Matt, who had just become the show's pianist, didn't mind. His patience and concentration were always good, and he loved all the grandfather clocks and front-porch swings that were starting to fill the stage. The producers hoped to draw in everyone who longed for that simpler time they thought they actually remembered, or the childhood they thought they'd actually had. Recently turned nineteen, Matt had never had much childhood at all, and he'd gladly settle for this small-town fantasy of fifty years ago coming to cardboard life a few feet above the orchestra pit.

His off-time reveries ran to such gentle fictions, and he was probably the only person inside the Broadhurst, including the director up in the balcony, who had read "the original material." He had come upon Booth Tarkington's novel—falling in love with the author's name—five summers ago in the Astoria branch library.

There was no telling how long a run *Seventeen* would have. The notices in Boston had been good, but Matt hadn't been with the show up there, and two days of stop-and-start piano playing, during rehearsals that never quite became a run-through, hadn't given him a sufficient feel for the thing to make a prediction. The songs were pretty enough, but the show might get blown away like a puff of cotton candy by the street's big, brassy mainstays: *Guys and Dolls* and *Kiss Me, Kate* and *Call Me Madam* were all still going strong, and *The King and I* had come to the St. James a couple of months ago.

Surely Kenneth Nelson, *Seventeen*'s slender young lead, could be knocked flat by so much as a dirty look from bare-chested Yul Brynner. Only a few years older than the lovesick boy he was playing, Nelson now went into a second tremulous rendition of "This Was Just Another Day," the song that Tarkington's Willie Baxter is inspired to sing after meeting Lola Pratt, the blond minx who's come to town for the summer:

> *But my, oh my, oh my*
> *The same old sky*
> *Has turned a brand new blue . . .*

As Matt looked up from the score to the stage and saw Nelson's face, he experienced the flutter he always felt when one of these good-looking out-of-town guys with no New York accent came into his professional range of vision. He'd get tongue-tied and quiet, and they'd assume, incorrectly, that he must be hardboiled with city sophistication. This one, he'd heard, was from North Carolina by way of Texas. In fact, a redheaded friend, a somewhat older girl named Mildred who knew Nelson from Baylor, had dropped by earlier to pay him a quick backstage visit.

The director cut Nelson off two bars from the end and ordered the dancers to assemble for another go at the previous scene, which even now, after Boston, looked ragged. Any number of things were causing problems: the finale was a confusing business, and the closest thing the show had to an eleven o'clock number was a duet for two supporting players instead of a big solo for one of the leads. "After All, It's Spring" sounded fine, lovely even, but was so melodically predictable that when he was playing it, Matt felt able to look up from the score, however new it was to him, at least a half dozen times. In profile, the duet's boy, Dick Kallman, appeared almost as delicately handsome as Kenneth Nelson, but when Kallman faced forward and sang full out—his clear preference—he was good-looking in an entirely different and more familiar way. He had a fine, glossy New York kisser, the kind that made you wonder: Italian? Jewish? A less perfect Tony Curtis; magnetic and mischievous.

Kallman also had a stronger, more Broadway-ready voice than Nelson's. It was the voice of a *lead*, and Matt whispered as much to the first violinist when the director paused the duet after a flub by the girl.

"He tried out for Willie," explained the violinist, who'd been with the show from the beginning.

"Why didn't he get it?"

"You think *he* could play lovesick? If Lola Pratt refused *him*, he'd tell her to go fuck herself. Or he'd beat her to death with her parasol."

Kallman's performance in the duet so made up for his partner's that the director decided they could call it a day. As everyone dispersed, they heard Dick say to the girl, as if he were still projecting for the balcony, "I'll be ready for you in ten. Out on Forty-Fourth." You'd think he *was* Tony Curtis. She gave him a "Yes, sir!" smile.

"And how about you?" he called to Matt, who was packing up his music. The two of them had been introduced yesterday morning, during a lot of regulation chaos.

"How about what?"

"How about coming along? I'm cooking dinner for some of us at my parents' place over in Brooklyn. They're out of town."

———————

By "dinner" he didn't mean anything simple. An hour after leaving the Broadhurst, Kenneth Nelson and Matt Liannetto—along with Ellen McCown, the girl in the duet, and Paula Stewart, a girl in the chorus who also understudied the leading lady—were watching Kallman roast a chicken, prepare acorn squash, and roll out the dough for a blueberry pie. In the course of it all, he rarely stopped talking.

"She's no Ruth Gordon, wouldn't you have to say?" he asked the others.

Matt had seen Ruth Gordon scads of times around the theater district, and he knew she'd played Lola in a nonmusical version of *Seventeen* during the First World War. But he said nothing. Miss McCown and Miss Stewart both sported expressions showing worry that somebody should be knocking their own show's female lead.

But Kallman didn't care what the girls or the pianist thought. It was Kenny he was trying to provoke. Making the male lead criticize his female costar would put him in a vulnerable position, and Kallman wanted him to be as vulnerable as possible. For one thing, aside from playing Joe Bullitt, Kallman was Kenneth Nelson's understudy. And for another, Dick was secretly in love with Kenny.

Alas, Nelson didn't seem to know who Ruth Gordon was. So there was no invidious comparison to draw, and Kallman had to settle for making the boy from Texas look like a rube.

"Really?" he asked, while he ladled some blueberry filling into the pie shell. "Never saw *Over 21*? Never looked at the writing credits for *Adam's Rib*?"

Nelson couldn't say he'd done either.

"Ruth Gordon's a writer as well as an actress," Matt explained, as matter-of-factly as he could, trying to establish that there was really no reason anyone, inside show business or out, had to know who she was.

Kallman closed the oven door and Miss McCown changed the subject. "So how'd you learn to do all this?" she asked, gesturing toward the pots on the stove. "I can't even make toast." She had lived in cold-water flats for the last three years, ever since coming to New York from Tennessee and getting chorus parts in *Oklahoma!* and *Gentlemen Prefer Blondes*.

"See that place on the wall?" Kallman pointed to a picture in the adjacent dining room. "My old man owns it, up in New Hampshire." The watercolor, he explained, depicted The Balsams, in Dixville Notch, up near the Canadian border. A giant nineteenth-century resort on the order of the Greenbrier, it welcomed whole families for long summer stays. "I learned to cook in the kitchen. All the staff were happy to teach the boss's son anything he wanted to know. Mom and Dad have been up there since high season started." His four guests looked over at two framed photographs flanking the portrait of the hotel.

"Dad started out as a stunt flyer," explained Kallman, in effortfully casual tones, as if remarking that his old man had once sold shoes. "Long before he bought the hotel." Miss McCown appeared to be giving her host the benefit of the doubt, though this Brooklyn house seemed modest for a man who owned a huge resort. Both Matt and Nelson were sensing a flimsiness, or at least an elasticity, to some of Kallman's autobiographical pronouncements.

"Are you really headed to the Ivy League?" asked Nelson. The *Playbill* for *Seventeen* had come off the press this afternoon, with a cast note saying that Dick Kallman had spent time "prepping for Dartmouth at Tilton Academy."

"Nah," Dick answered. In almost a single smooth movement he pulled the chicken from the oven and slid the pie inside. "I thought a mention of Dartmouth sounded right for this little varsity-scale production we find ourselves in. The only place I'm going is *places*," he declared, with a smile whose high-wattage gall attained a sort of perfection. It filled his face as expertly as he'd filled the pie shell.

"Liannetto, could you bring the water glasses?"

The guests took their seats in the dining room, and Kallman informed them that the repast coming to the table was "a test drive."

"Are you going into the catering business?" Paula Stewart asked, cheerfully. "You make this sound like a backers' audition!"

"No," explained the host. "There's a gal from the *World-Telegram* I've got to cook for next week. She's the Teen Talk columnist, and her angle is 'Young Bachelor Who Knows How to Fend for Himself.'"

A couple of Dick's guests appeared to wonder whether the word "bachelor" could even be applied to a boy who had (or had not) just graduated from prep school. So Kallman shifted ground a little. "Of course our friend Nelson here knows all about big-time publicity." He was referring to *Life*'s upcoming spread on *Seventeen*, which would feature a few pictures of the male lead and Ann Crowley, his female costar.

Kenny managed a smile, but this mention of the magazine gave him no more confidence than the issue's impending appearance on the newsstand did. He looked down at the potatoes on his plate, beside the squash, and thought back three months to the job he'd had at a Woolworth's in Midtown, demonstrating a new electric peeling gadget. He understood just enough about the theater to know that three months from now he might again be shaving spuds over a sheet of wax paper.

Kallman's own trajectory, as he described it, was surefire and one-way. While his guests dug into the food—which even more educated palates would have deemed excellent—he began telling them about his multiple associations with Billy Rose. Last December he'd had a part, with lines, in a dramatic sketch that had aired on the old showman's new TV variety show, which had led to his taking a temporary job in Rose's office, just after his early graduation from Tilton, in January. "Just to get a little better acquainted with the business," he explained.

Nelson carefully nodded between forkfuls of chicken and

squash, while Matt tried to imagine Dick as an office boy. Miss McCown became entirely absorbed by Kallman's description of Billy Rose's Manhattan apartment, but seemed perplexed when he confided to the table that the impresario was these days "busted up over Fanny Brice." The fact that Rose had once been married to the singing comedienne, recently dead from a stroke, was unknown to her. It belonged to an entertainment era that felt remote to everyone here but Dick.

"Of course," Kallman added, "Billy's still busy having his affair with Joyce Mathews. You know, Berle's ex."

"Really?" asked Miss McCown.

Improbably enough, Milton Berle, the biggest star of the new medium Billy Rose had managed to enter, was the principal investor in *Seventeen*. Everyone at the Broadhurst was wondering if he'd show up for opening night.

"So," asked Kallman, "is that the enemy?" He pointed to his parents' television set, visible in the next room. "For you guys, I mean." He himself was immune to threats and confusion; he had things figured out.

The cocksure display was by now so overdone that Matt Liannetto began feeling a little embarrassed for him. "The question's above my pay grade," he said with a modest laugh. "I just worry about all those book shows playing Broadway. Each one that goes up seems to kill off three or four revues—and those are the real bread and butter for us piano men!"

"Not nightclubs, Matty?" asked Nelson, who was intrigued, grateful for a piece of showbiz knowledge that was coming from somebody's mouth besides Kallman's.

"For most guys, that's so," said Matt. "But I can't do too many nightclubs." He tapped his thin chest apologetically. "Asthma. The smoke is hard on me."

"You know the real problem with book shows?" asked Kallman, who took an ostentatious pause, just long enough for them to fail to come up with an answer. "The *book*. Look at *Flahooley*—a lot of anti-American junk." On its surface the story of a toy company, the now-shuttered show had satirized the current political witch hunts with songs like "You Too Can Be a Puppet."

"You sound like McCarthy!" said Paula Stewart.

The only questionable thing Matt had heard about *Flahooley* involved Yma Sumac, one of the singers: some said she wasn't really a Peruvian princess, as her press agent claimed, but Amy Camus (now spelled backwards) from Brooklyn. Matt found himself wondering once more about Kallman's New Hampshire prep school, and whether it might be the equivalent of Amy's Inca kingdom.

Kallman ignored Miss Stewart's remark about McCarthy. "Seconds on the squash?"

All four of his guests said yes, as they did to seconds on the chicken and to another glass of wine. They became so intent on eating that Kallman replaced his pleasure in quizzing them with the enjoyment of watching them consume what he provided. For its silent stretches, the little dinner party had an innocent, let's-play-house feel, the adolescents trying to ape adult behavior the same way they were sometimes required to, for comic effect, in *Seventeen*.

But with the clearing of plates came a return of Kallman's ringmaster voice. He proposed that they make a trip back into Manhattan for a nightclub show. "Can your lungs handle an hour at the Bon Soir?" he asked Matt, with a little more sadism than solicitude. "It's hardly the Latin Quarter, but it might put a little life into this evening. My folks caught Sinatra at the Quarter while all of us were up in Boston. All of us but Liannetto, that is."

Underlining the pianist's belated affiliation with *Seventeen* seemed an odd piece of pedantry, a pointless little swat. It left Matt unsure about spending another few hours with Dick Kallman. But thanks to the wine, he *had* gotten into a mood to go out tonight; in fact he'd been trying to work up enough of an attraction to Miss McCown to suggest that they drop in at Roseland's Tuesday rumba night.

Kenny put an end to Kallman's proposal by telling the host what he surely knew already: that his four guests didn't have enough money for even the Bon Soir's modest cover charge. "And you've already been generous enough," he added, in a way that made generosity sound distinctly oppressive. "Besides, I think the rest of us have nine o'clock calls." This time it was Kallman being excluded, with the implication that his later start time derived from his being peripheral to the show. The remark was a nice little piece of revenge, exacted by Nelson on Matt Liannetto's behalf, and the pianist's heart sped up when he realized it.

"Suit yourselves," said Kallman. "Coffee?" With a glance he directed Miss McCown to help him serve it, and once she'd given each boy a spoon, she began chattering about things she'd lately read in the columns: a rumor that the Windsors might be splitting; the suggestion that an illegitimate baby could be the least of Ingrid Bergman's troubles with Roberto Rossellini.

"It's the blind items that are always more interesting," declared Kallman. "Did you notice the latest one Earl Wilson ran?"

Kenny, who had never seen Wilson's column, said nothing, and Matt, who read it in the *Post* all the time, decided he wouldn't say anything, either. He didn't want to look like a sharpie in front of everyone—and besides, Dick Kallman would never credit him with any worldliness, not if he offered proof of dining with Walter Winchell every night.

"What did the item say?" asked Miss Stewart.

Kallman seemed to have it memorized: "'Which restaurant chain has been purging its New York branches of swishes?'"

Paula Stewart laughed at the word. Nelson said nothing. Neither did Matt, though he wondered if it might be Childs that Earl Wilson was hinting at. The one near Bleecker Street always seemed filled with older men who were that way, all of them watching the good-looking guy who flipped pancakes in the window.

"They're even a problem up at The Balsams," said Kallman. "A few of them each summer, arriving with trunks that are probably full of powder puffs. One of them sits in the dining room wearing more makeup than Miss Crowley does."

He'd managed to associate an unpleasant subject with *Seventeen*'s leading lady, but Nelson wouldn't take this bait, either. He pushed back his chair and said the meal had been terrific but that he really needed to start for home. Miss McCown was torn between a small fascination with Dick Kallman and her sense that she should appear professional before Kenny, to whom she was junior in position if slightly senior in experience. At last she said, "I guess that should be my cue." Nelson said he would see her as far as Grand Central. Miss Stewart said she would head out with them.

"Liannetto will stay and help me clean up," said Kallman.

Of *course* he would, thought Matt; no Italian boy brought up by his aunts in Astoria would do otherwise. But he wondered why Kallman hadn't given him a minute's chance to make the offer himself, wondered why everyone in Dick's audience continually had to be knocked off balance.

"Good night!" cried Miss McCown, as if exiting a party scene inside the Broadhurst's painted little paradise.

Matt waved goodbye to his fellow guests. He lifted his eyebrows to Nelson in a signal of gratitude for the oblique words of support—*I think the rest of us have nine o'clock calls*—and admitted to himself that he wasn't experiencing the faintest rumba of feeling for Miss McCown or, for that matter, Miss Stewart. As soon as they were gone, he walked over to the sink and started running the water.

"What are you bothering for?" asked Dick. "The colored girl will be coming in the morning."

"Are you sure?"

"That she's coming? Yes." A mild joke, but Dick's timing of it was split-second perfect. "Come have a drink."

He had gone into the living room with the television set—it was, in fact, the night of the week when Berle became monarch of the airwaves—but he didn't turn it on. He opened his parents' liquor cabinet instead, and took out a bottle of Scotch. "Single malt," he informed the pianist, while pouring the first of two glasses.

Matt watched him. It now *really* felt as if they were playing grown-ups, as if they ought to go put on neckties belonging to the elder, absent Mr. Kallman. He wanted to say no to the drink, to tell Dick he'd never had anything stronger than wine, not even at the couple of cast parties he'd been to. But Dick pushed the glass into his hand. "It'll help your breathing."

Matt laughed and took a seat at the other end of the sofa. "Okay." He clinked his glass against Kallman's and said, "To *Seventeen*," before taking a tentative sip.

"I guess," said Kallman, with a sigh of contempt for the show.

Matt had a second swallow of the Scotch and wondered how soon he could head home to his tiny place on Spring Street without seeming impolite. His roommate, a trumpeter who sometimes brought his girlfriend home, was out of town, and he was looking forward to a full night's sleep.

Kallman seemed lost in baleful reverie, and while he stared out over the coffee table, Matt thought of the parental pictures in the dining room. He assumed that Dick would soon ask about *his* family: the father who'd taught him piano but died when he was eight; his much older brother, killed in the war; and his mother, with worse asthma than his own, who'd years ago gone to live with distant relatives in New Mexico.

But when Kallman finally asked a question, it was: "So what do you think of Nelson?"

Wary of being drawn into the same kind of conversation that Dick had failed to ignite about the female lead, Matt answered cautiously: "He seems like a nice fellow."

"I'm sure he's a fag."

"I wouldn't know."

"I'm sure he's also a nice fellow."

Matt took another sip.

"But more to the point, how do you propose we drain the gas tank?" asked Kallman.

His guest looked puzzled.

When he saw that the penny wasn't dropping, Dick elaborated, with some exasperation: "Jesus, goombah, don't you ever get to the *movies*? I'm Nelson's *understudy*."

"Oh," said Matt, who at last realized that Dick was referring to *All About Eve*, which he'd seen three times last year: that scheme to make Bette Davis late for the theater and thus allow Anne Baxter to go on in her place. "You're kidding," he said, beginning to wonder if Kenny had been given a separate, poisoned portion of squash.

"Oh, relax," said Kallman. "Yes, I'm kidding. Sort of."

When it came to Kenneth Nelson, he'd been kidding the whole evening. All the jokes, all the superiority and expertise, all the stuff about fags: it had been for his own self-protection. The fact was, he'd been in love with Kenny from the minute he met him at the auditions. The feeling remained even after he lost the lead to him; it had stayed and grown all through the rehearsals. The day after tomorrow, on opening night, he planned to *tell* Kenny, to give him the little piece of jewelry that he was now clutching in his pocket. All of tonight's aggression, all its disdain, however naturally that came to him, was also his own way of not tempting the gods, of shoring himself up against whatever defeat might await him forty-eight hours from now.

And at this moment Matt Liannetto would be a distraction from the thrills and dangers that preoccupied him. Kallman took both their drinks and set them down on the coffee table. Then he undid one of Matt's shirt buttons: "Let's have a look at your poor wheezing chest."

CHAPTER 2

FEBRUARY 26, 1980

I don't know whether to call Le Moal a "boîte" or a "bis-tro." But it's a nice French restaurant on Third Avenue, between Fifty-Sixth and Fifty-Seventh, with a piano player who works even during lunch. A few too many glissandos for my taste, but the guy is pleasant and takes his job seriously.

Dolores Gray had chosen the place—summoned me there, really—during a minute-long surprise visit that she made to Manhattan Plaza on Saturday, not too long after Detective Volker left. The doorman called up, but by the time I got down-stairs she was gone, having decided just to leave her card. The engraved script—MISS DOLORES GRAY—was florid and girly-girly. So was the inked notation: *Le Moal, Tuesday, 1:00.* The restau-rant was just around the corner from her home address, also printed on the card.

So there I was, reading the paper while I waited for her to arrive. The Oscar nominations were out, and everything was *Kramer vs. Kramer,* which I hadn't seen and didn't intend to. The painful memories of my own divorce, back in '64, all involved how *nice* Lois had been—never once throwing in my face the real reason for our unhappiness. She's been dead for five years now—cancer—but I still recognize a lot of her, all of it good, in my daughter.

As I waited for MISS DOLORES GRAY to get there, I admit I got to feeling more and more excited—and more and more guilty, too, since this lunch was only taking place because of what had happened to Dick, who was gone not just from the world but from the papers, too, already squeezed out by more recent murders. His autopsy hadn't even been performed; it was scheduled for Saturday, a fact Detective Volker imparted during a follow-up phone call.

My excitement crested, and my guilt departed, as soon as I heard the piano player strike up "Here's That Rainy Day." I guess every time she comes into this place he gives her the same little tribute I did that night at the Martin Beck. And sure enough, there she was, letting the maître d' take her fur coat and storm boots, which he removed in a reverse Prince Charming maneuver, literally on bended knee, while she extended, one by one, a pair of even-now-excellent legs.

Her sort-of-familiar face and powder-blue Ultrasuede dress—Halston, I think—caught several diners' attention as she walked toward my table in the back, which had been booked under her name. She nodded hello to me as the maître d' pulled out her chair. No handshake, just a little smile, as if we were the oldest of friends and lunch were the most familiar of our routines.

The piano player headed into the last bars: "Funny, that rainy day is here." "Six performances," she said, referring to *Carnival in Flanders*. "That's only two more than your *Harold and Maude* wound up having. But at least I got that song out of it."

"Well, that and the chance to look at John Raitt," I suggested. My daughter really was changing me. Even a few years ago I wouldn't have made a remark that camp, that "out," in front of a woman—not even one from show business, used to a fairy flotilla traveling in her wake.

"You think?" she replied.

Maybe John Raitt wasn't that good-looking close up. I thought I'd pivot to another topic, but she wound up pivoting first.

"*Seventeen,*" said Dolores. "That's when you came down the street to see me and Lahr." So she remembered our conversation at the theater. But I still didn't know how she'd found me.

"'If You Hadn't But You Did,'" I answered, offering the title of her patter number as proof of my attendance at *Two on the Aisle*. She smiled at me, like she was the teacher and I'd just gotten a tough one correct in the spelling bee. But the smile faded fast, probably with the thought of how that show hadn't lasted either, hadn't provided her with anything like the huge London success she'd had just before, doing Merman's role in *Annie Get Your Gun*. Truth be told, she never really had another smash.

"Bert Lahr hated me," she said, taking the first sip of a cocktail the waiter brought without needing an order. "But he hated himself even more."

I didn't know what to say to that, so I posed a question: "Wasn't 'If' meant to be Kaye Ballard's number?" I'd heard the legend of how thirty years ago Mrs. Barbara Gray—a stage mother beyond Mama Rose—had snatched the song for her daughter somewhere between New Haven and New York. And Kaye left the show.

"I love Kaysie," was all Dolores said in response. She smiled over the rim of her cocktail glass. "I used to have spaghetti at her place on Sundays. Those were nice times."

I began to wonder if we'd even talk about Dick's violent death. Maybe we'd skip it entirely, and the conversation would keep hovering around her career, whose death had been less violent but still something painful and premature to its victim. She'd almost always gotten reviews that pointed out her superiority to the stuff she was stuck in. There was no doubt she'd had a lot of bad luck, and her face had never been her fortune. It was longish and a little horsey; her nose had been surgically overcorrected, in a way that added to the general difficulty. Even in the table lamp's forgiving peach light, I could see she was trying to hide her bad complexion with too much makeup. Movie directors who loved her voice and pizzazz tended to doll her up in crazy costumes, almost as a kind of camouflage. Or they kept her in the background, as in *Mr. Skeffington*, her first film, where she had a little turn as a nightclub singer. And sometimes they kept her out of sight altogether, like when she dubbed Marilyn's singing voice on the soundtrack album of *There's No Business Like Show Business.*

"Did you really lose *Mame* to Angela Lansbury?" True, I didn't have much of a segue for this, but I could tell that during the pause in our conversation she'd been mulling over her disappointments.

"Cupcake, I lost *My Fair Lady* to Julie Andrews!"

This seemed a little improbable, but I made sure my face registered solidarity instead of skepticism.

"Have the chicken," she said. "They're famous for it."

We waited for two paper-thin paillards to arrive, and she started talking about *Sherry!*, another flop, this one a late-1960s musical version of *The Man Who Came to Dinner*. By that time she was past forty, and the whole thing proved to be the same old story: a big buildup; a handful of performances; reviews that praised her and eviscerated the show.

"You know," she said, finishing off her drink, "there was one good line in that bomb: 'Broadway's been waiting for a really tragic musical comedy!'" She put down the glass. "Well, maybe that's what *this* is."

It took me a minute to realize that "this" was Dick, his whole life and death. I waited for her to say more, but she closed the door as fast as she'd opened it, and got back to *Sherry!*

"My entrance number was the title song. It was a good one too. My usual consolation prize." She went for a husky laugh, worldly and rueful. I might have been across the table from Helen Lawson. I couldn't recall the song, and this time she gave me a scolding look, as if I'd stumbled in that spelling bee.

She pushed my newspaper, still open to the entertainment pages, to the edge of the table, as if she could be wounded by the sight of every show listed in the ABCs. God, I found myself thinking, as just one of them entered my mind: what she might have done with *A Chorus Line*! As it was, she'd had to finish her career with numbers on the Red Skelton show and *The Bell Telephone Hour*, stuck inside those trumpet skirts like a toothpick inside an olive.

We started on the chicken in silence, but after a few bites, without looking up, she said, "I was supposed to see Richard at five o'clock on Friday."

I stopped chewing.

"I showed up right on time and saw that yellow police tape all over the door. Two cops told me to go home and wait to hear from them. I told *them* I owned the lion's share of the stuff that was in there! They gave me a funny look."

I gave her one, too. "You hadn't known he'd been killed until that moment?"

She shook her head. "I saw the *Post* headline on my walk up Madison. It never occurred to me that the 'Art Dealer Slain' could be *him*. I didn't even notice the little picture."

She could see what I was thinking: that I believed her but had been struck by how quickly her thoughts could turn from murder to merchandise.

"I suppose I was in shock, blurting that out to the cops. I don't know."

"Of course," I replied.

"I knew him for three years," she said, somehow marveling at the duration, as if three were the same as thirty. "Steven I only knew for a couple of months." She seemed not to like him much—or maybe just not the idea of him.

"When did you last see Dick?" I asked.

"I spoke to him over the phone on Thursday, just before lunch. He was telling me how we needed to get a regular porter or messenger boy."

I thought back to Jimmy, the kid who'd shown up at Dick's place on Thursday night: the "completely fucked up" twenty-one-year-old who, we were told, had been boyfriends with Dick's "big Mafia man" since he was fifteen; the one coming around with a friend who wanted to buy Dick's gigantic watch. Could she be talking about him? I somehow doubted Jimmy was somebody looking, or being considered, for steady employment.

Dolores stirred her coffee, and with an abstracted shake of her head she mused: "I thought *I* would be the only one of us who ever got shot."

I gave her my I-don't-understand look, which had been getting a lot of practice.

"I had a bullet in my lung for more than fifteen years," she explained, blending pride with matter-of-factness, as if finally able to claim the kind of long run that had eluded her on Broadway. "I was working a club in Chicago, eons ago, when I was way underage. My mother had lied to the owner and told him I was eighteen. When I walked out the door to go home one night, I caught one of the shots some guy was firing from a passing car. They fixed me up in the emergency room, but I couldn't get a surgeon to take out the slug until the early fifties. A little after *Two on the Aisle*, in fact. I was glad to get rid of it, though the thing never stopped me from belting." She took another sip of coffee. "See if Merman could manage *that*."

I later found out that every word of this ridiculous story was true.

Telling it seemed to shake something loose in her. She put her cup down on the saucer with a loud, unexpected clatter and burst into tears. "My beautiful Richard!" she cried. And then she covered her face with her hands.

I wondered if she had been in love with him, at least a little, with the help of some deliberate self-delusion.

She quickly pulled herself together. When her hands came away from her face, they revealed a show-must-go-on expression. She nodded reassuringly in the direction of the piano player, who launched into something peppy. And then she spoke to me very directly: "Hal Hastings once told me you're okay, Mr. Liannetto. I guess your name stuck with me because it's musical."

I was startled by the compliment. Hastings, dead for several years now, was a great piano man, and I'd been honored to sub for him a couple of times at the Persian Room. I told Dolores I was grateful for his kind words, but I was getting unnerved by the still-unspoken premise of this whole lunch. My mind began sending me questions like fast little eighth notes. What did she want from me? Help in finding whoever had killed Dick? Some new arrangements? A new fan?

She looked at her watch. It didn't surprise me that I was

expected to pay, no matter that I'd been commanded to come here. I've been around enough show-business names to know that this is the procedure, that their company and glamour are supposed to cover their share of the tab and tip. So I put down some cash beside the plate of tiny macaroons that the waiter brought with the bill. Dolores then waited for me to pull out her chair, and as she stood I was struck by how small, even delicate, she seemed without a helmet of stage hair and the armor of those trumpet skirts.

We stood beside the maître d's lectern as he fetched her coat. As he reverently restored Dolores's boots to her feet, I averted my gaze, turning it toward a signed photo of Ed Koch that hung near the front door. Getting ready to say goodbye, I wondered whether Dolores really had a husband, let alone a rich one with racehorses, as she'd told me back at the table.

Out on Third Avenue a college girl stood waiting with a leashed poodle: Dolores's dog, whose delivery to its owner had been arranged and timed in advance. The girl having conducted the essential business of the walk, Dolores could now have a purely pleasurable stroll with the poodle, a little excursion through the neighborhood, before heading home.

We started up Third and turned east on Fifty-Seventh, passing two Guardian Angels. They always look preposterous in those red berets, though they do make me feel the tiniest bit better, as if someone is at least making a *gesture* against the city's ever-rising mayhem. Really, how on earth are the police going to catch whoever killed Dick? These days there are more murderers than cops.

Dolores held the leash with her left hand and put her right arm through mine. The maneuver seemed half companionable and half regal, her starlike assertion that she merited a walker as surely as the poodle did.

"You're probably wondering why I got in touch with you," she said.

"Oh, no," I replied, carrying politeness to an inane new level. "I'm just curious as to how you found me."

"I saw your name and address in the detective's notebook, down at the station house on Friday night. I remembered who you were from that night at the theater, and I read Volker's handwriting upside down when he got up to fix himself a cup of coffee. Four packs of sugar! I told him he's going to wind up deader than Richard if he doesn't change his habits."

I laughed. "I wouldn't have had the nerve—to tell him that *or* to read his notes." I thought about her singing with that bullet in her lung, whereas I still let a case of asthma slow me down. "I guess I *have* been wondering why you contacted me," I added at last.

"I want you to look at his things with me. The cops say I can get into the apartment this Friday. In fact, they told me to make it my business to be there then."

This I hadn't expected.

"And there are a few other things I may ask you to do," she said.

We reached Second Avenue. She wanted to keep walking east with the dog, but I had a music lesson with a rich house-wife a dozen blocks south, and I needed to start heading in that direction.

"Meet me at his place on Friday," she said. "Three o'clock."

Her expression, under all the makeup, was hard. It told me that she was ashamed of crying in the restaurant and that there would be no more tears from her. Whatever feelings she'd had for Dick weren't going to make a chump out of her.

"I'll be there," I promised.

"Good. Richard told me you were a reliable person. Obliging."

I would have settled for "reliable." But it must have been that last word (uttered to her as they went back up the aisle of the Martin Beck that night?) that made her come find me on Saturday. This was a woman who needed to be obliged, con-stantly.

"See you Friday," I said, before starting down Second Ave-nue. Within a couple of minutes I was passing the boy hustlers in their usual spot, at the corner of Fifty-Third. Three or four of them, jacketless, were plying their trade, showing off their bare muscled arms despite the February weather. Just looking at them made me feel colder, and I realized that my winter cough was a little worse than usual.

CHAPTER 3

OCTOBER 29, 1953

> ### *DICK KALLMAN*
> ### *The Blue Room*
> ### *Shoreham Hotel*
> ### *Washington, D.C.*
>
> Dick Kallman impresses as one of the better young singers to come down the pike, with a solid future if he is handled properly and not rushed too fast. In style and voice, he resembles Eddie Fisher, although he still lacks the "heart" which gives Fisher's voice its special plus. However, Kallman is a youngster of 20 with plenty of time to pick up the extra polish and finish . . . In addition to voice, Kallman is a very attractive looking youngster with a pleasing manner.
>
> *Variety*, October 21, 1953

"What a town," sighed Kallman, tossing the trade paper across the dressing room to Matt Liannetto at the piano. "A friend of my brother, Charlie, is dating a girl down here, and *he* had to bring this all the way from New York. You can't find a newsstand in Washington that sells *Variety*!"

The singer's bass player, the third man in the dressing room, looked at him askance. The *knowingness* in Kallman's voice actually projected the opposite of whatever sophisticated contempt he seemed to be going for. He was too young to have earned the tone—never mind that DC probably had more out-of-town newsstands, complete with copies of *Variety*, than any other city in the country.

Through the wall the three young men could hear the flamenco shoe-beats of Roberto and Alicia, the dance team performing a supposedly "torrid" couple of numbers before Kallman's set. The singer's onstage time in the Blue Room was short enough that Matt had been able to accept this pianist's gig without having to worry his asthma would kick up.

Kallman read out the latest Julius La Rosa news from *Variety*. Arthur Godfrey, TV's folksy martinet, had during a live broadcast of his show fired La Rosa for a supposed lack of "humility," although the enormously popular singer was pulling down less than a thousand a week.

"The whole thing is a publicity stunt," Kallman proclaimed.

"How do you figure that?" asked the bassist.

"Because it's working for both of them. La Rosa will get a bigger record deal and a show of his own, and Godfrey just got interviewed on *Person to Person*. Murrow treated him like he was Ziegfeld."

Matt and the bassist exchanged a look. For all of Kallman's success hunger, there was something weightily obsolete about his show-business frame of reference, which had been constructed from all the big bands and crooners and ex-vaudevillians whose summertime bookings had filled his childhood at The Balsams. *Ziegfeld?* Really? Kallman mentioned him as naturally as he sometimes did Al Jolson, as if Jolson were still the competition to be reckoned with, instead of Eddie Fisher and the temporarily stalled Sinatra.

He now began talking about the Broadway experience he'd had this spring in *The Fifth Season*, a hit comedy. Dick had played Marty, a high-school football star who declines the chance to go to Princeton so that he can stay home and help out in his old man's failing dress business. Matt had seen the show and heard the story Dick was telling, but he didn't interrupt the monologue, knowing it was designed to impress the bass player, who standoffishly smoked a cigarette, trying to convey that he didn't want to get too chummy with two guys he'd by now marked out as fruits. When Kallman mentioned Dorian Leigh, the bombshell model who'd had a bit part in *The Fifth Season*, the bassist allowed himself to ask what she was like, if only to establish his own heterosexual bona fides.

"Very *approachable*," Kallman responded, with a boyish leer, trying to convince the accompanist that he'd made a successful approach himself. The bassist wasn't buying it any more than Matt was, so Kallman shifted into a little speech meant to illustrate his excellent career instincts. "Hit or no hit, a few months of that was plenty for me. All that old Yid-theater stuff revamped into English!"

Matt winced. Saying "Yid" instead of "Yiddish" was another pointless piece of mendacity, a crude assurance to the bassist, who had an Irish name, that Dick Kallman was no more a Jew than he was a *feygele*.

Beyond the dressing-room wall the rat-a-tat flamenco heels stopped and gave way to applause. Kallman took a look at the type-written list, supplied by the Blue Room management, of supposedly prominent people in the audience tonight.

"Symington?" he asked, sounding out the name, unsure how to say it. The senator and his wife were residents of the Shoreham. The roll of names also included a congressman and the head of a government atomic agency that Kallman, who knew far more about Julius La Rosa than about Julius Rosenberg, had never heard of. Matt, on the other hand, who grew up in a New Deal family, had for the last week and a half gotten a kick out of being in this hotel that had held FDR's first inaugural ball.

The management's list contained a single celebrity from out-side politics, a local actress whose name prompted no more rec-ognition in the three young men than the congressman's had. "Everybody's over at the Sheraton listening to Nanette Fabray," declared Kallman, as if only that could explain anyone's absence from his own show. Ever since arriving here with Matt, he'd acted as if Perle Mesta should be throwing him a party, and been crab-bing about the suite the Shoreham put him in—no matter that it had a fireplace and an excellent view of the park. He griped that there would have been something better on offer for talent at The Balsams.

"All people want is a little mercy," Kallman sighed cryptically, checking himself in the mirror. It was a line from *The Fifth Season*, and he figured that the bassist and Liannetto wouldn't know or remember its source. They also didn't know what had prompted its utterance. Kallman—who always had a horror of silence, or what he liked to call "dead air," to remind you that he'd done some radio—suddenly asked: "Have you heard any news about Half Nelson?" It was his nickname for the lead in *Seventeen*. Matt said nothing. He knew full well that Kenny had lost his job playing Henry Aldrich on TV, and Kallman knew full well that he knew it.

"He's not living on Beekman Place anymore, that's for sure!" said Kallman. "He's *nowhere*."

The bassist felt things getting a little fruity again—the shared history; Kallman's bitchiness—and he was relieved when Roberto and Alicia, in a burst of heavy breathing and sweat, came flying through the door of the single dressing room.

Kallman ignored them and just said "Ready?" to his accompanists.

After an interval long enough for the Blue Room's patrons to order another round of drinks, the three men gave the dancers some privacy and took the stage themselves.

For the opener, Matt and the bassist supplied Kallman with a bouncy version of "For Me and My Gal." The song had been composed during the First World War but felt even older, and Kallman's rendition of it exuded the winning nostalgia he'd practiced two years ago at the Broadhurst. The Symingtons, at the front row of tables, applauded heartily. They were unprepared for the emotive version of "With a Song in My Heart" that followed; Kallman filled it with a near-weepy excess, as if to make a point to his *Variety* reviewer: if "heart" was what he needed to show, he would outdo Eddie Fisher and go all the histrionic way to Johnnie Ray.

The impassioned interpretation made the Symingtons a little uncomfortable, but they didn't have to worry about making eye contact with the singer, who was delivering the whole number to a supremely handsome young man in the row behind them. Matt and the bassist, both positioned behind Kallman, didn't realize the single-minded projection until the number had finished, and whatever discomfort they felt about the singer's recklessness was soon dispelled by another lurch in mood: first, Kallman offered a bright-eyed bit of patter about growing up in a hotel ("the first telephone number I knew was for room service!"), and then a personal declaration to Washingtonians about how special it felt to be in the nation's capital during a time of such danger to the republic and its freedoms. Kallman's politics, insofar as he had any, derived straight from Walter Winchell; the enemies he cited were plainly foreign Communists and domestic pinkos, and he followed his little speech with a sonorous, eyes-toward-heaven rendition of Frankie Laine's current hit:

> *Every time I hear a newborn baby cry*
> *Or touch a leaf or see the sky*
> *Then I know why*
> *I believe . . .*

When he turned a bit in their direction, Matt and the bassist saw that Kallman was himself crying—as were a couple of women toward the back.

The set roller-coastered through four more numbers, with Kallman finishing to reasonably fervent, if perplexed, applause. Back in the dressing room his spirits seemed low, but they underwent a sudden elevation when the manager asked if a few audience members might come in to offer their congratulations. One of them, Matt saw, was the extremely handsome young man who'd been the recipient of "With a Song in My Heart." The bass player made a hasty, disgusted exit.

"This is Mr. Hawkins Fuller," the manager announced. "He's with our State Department's Bureau of Congressional Relations." Fuller locked eyes with Kallman for a crucial moment before introducing his colleague and apparent date, Miss Mary Johnson. The third member of their party, he explained, was some sort of government-in-exile representative from Latvia whom they were entertaining, a courtly middle-aged man with a difficult-to-pronounce surname.

"You were wonderful," Miss Johnson politely told the singer.

Even without the bassist, the dressing room was filled to capacity. And then an entertainment reporter, a young woman from the Washington *Evening Star*, arrived at the door. Kallman hoped that his unusual song "stylings," as *Variety* might put it, had paid off and sparked her interest. As he went to get her a chair, Fuller and Miss Johnson shook hands with Matt Liannetto.

"Remind you of anyone?" Fuller asked his colleague, while nodding toward Matt.

Miss Johnson explained things to the pianist: "He means a young friend of his. A very sweet fellow. I'm sure you are, too."

Kallman took this in with whatever attention he wasn't expending on the reporter. This Miss Johnson had seemed disapproving when he and Fuller connected with their eyes, but not in some jealous or moralistic way; in a worried, *protective* one. But protective of whom? Fuller seemed manifestly not to require anybody's safeguarding. Maybe it was the "very sweet fellow," whoever Fuller's friend might be, that she was concerned about.

Matt could sense Kallman wishing that this local reporter would magically turn into someone syndicated. You could almost photograph the surge of ambition, a kind of aura, that had erupted over him upon her arrival; his excitement was competing against, and mixed up with, whatever desire he felt for Fuller. "This won't take more than a couple of minutes—don't go away!" he called out, before he began talking to the woman from the *Evening Star*. "It's terribly exciting being able to entertain public servants like Mr. Fuller and Miss Johnson, who each and every day . . ."

The reporter nodded but didn't write anything down. "I'm actually here," she at last explained, "because I'm doing a story on Ann Crowley"—*Seventeen*'s star—"and I'm wondering if I can get a few words from you about her. She seems to be breaking through. She did Eddie Fisher's TV show last week and is off to test in Hollywood a few days from now."

For a second Kallman looked as if he might explode with rage—or just burst into tears. Matt thought it best to pretend nothing out of the ordinary was happening. "Well, I'm off to the last showing of *Roman Holiday*," he said by way of goodbye. "It's only a few blocks away."

"Maybe I can impose on Mr. Ezergailis to run me home," said Miss Johnson to the Latvian. It was probably, thought Matt, a request she often had to make when out with Hawkins Fuller.

"Off the record," Kallman told the reporter, "I think Eddie Fisher has already peaked. What would you say, Mr. Fuller?" The anger and arousal on Kallman's face were indistinguishable. They amounted to the same thing.

"I'll tell you later," said Fuller, with a wink.

CHAPTER 4

FEBRUARY 29, 1980

My one and only sex skirmish (a fiasco) with Dick, back during *Seventeen*, ended with his pulling my hair and calling me a
"good little cocksucker," which I doubt was true. The episode
ended abruptly, to his physical relief and my emotional one. "I
don't think you're the right guy for what I *really* could use," he
said with a smile, as if I'd given a creditable but still failing audition, for exactly what role I wasn't sure. I don't remember much
after he pulled up his trousers.

For all his dispatch, I came to realize that Dick's sexual nature
was baroque to say the least. A couple of years after *Seventeen*,
a dancer named Corrine St. Denis was being featured in *The
King and I*, and Dick managed to get his name linked to hers
in Winchell's column. Winchell's assistant performed the favor
in exchange for a blind item Dick supplied about one member
of *The Fifth Season*'s cast making a drunken pass at another.
The warped part of this is that Dick wanted me to admire his
craftiness in approaching Winchell's underling *and* to believe
in his involvement with Miss St. Denis, as if she were an actual
girlfriend instead of a beard. Toward the end of our conversa-

tion about it, I realized that he believed this himself, though at the start he'd *told* me she was in on the ruse.

What I remember most about seeing him at that time was that things always came back to Kenneth Nelson. Long after I'd gotten over my own little crush on Kenny—had replaced it with a next unspoken, hopeless one on somebody else—Dick would yammer on and on about him, running him down with a nasty intensity, hoping that he was back in Texas, unemployed and failed forever.

I've begun thinking a lot about these long-ago things, but today I had my summons ("Friday, three o'clock") from Dolores, whose proposals are never to be turned down, let alone on Leap Day. I agreed to meet her outside 17 East Seventy-Seventh, and I got there early. I sat waiting on the steps, trying to imagine the killers who'd walked up them a week before.

Soon enough a cab pulled up and Dolores stepped out in a bright-red look-at-me coat nipped tight against her still-youthful waist. The contrast between figure and face was striking, and it partly explained why she hadn't gone further in the movies than she did. Bert Lahr supposedly said her face looked like a golf course, "eighteen holes," a cruel exaggeration of what was really just an ordinarily unfortunate complexion—but still not a movie star's. The bone structure it covered was also too angular, almost fierce, to make for comfortable close-ups. The figure, like the voice, was to die for, but even the voice made for problems. Dolores was a belter at a time when belting was going out of style. If you listen to the dubbing she did for Monroe on the soundtrack of *There's No Business Like Show Business,* which I'd now done on an old album in my apartment, you can almost hear her struggling to muffle her sound into something that could plausibly have come up from Marilyn's whispering larynx.

"Let's take a walk around the block," she told me.

"What exactly is it that the police want from you?" I asked, as we started toward Madison.

"That Volker guy needs me to tell him if I can spot any stuff that's missing. You can do the same."

I understood the reasoning, of course: tracking the stolen

goods might lead to the killers. But I told Dolores that, having been inside the apartment only once, amidst a lot of uproar, I was unlikely to be struck by the absence of any object.

"You'll do" was all she said, like John Wayne in *Red River*. I began to realize we were walking around the block only so that she could be a few minutes late—a movie star's prerogative, even when responding to an order from a police officer.

Once Detective Volker buzzed her up to the second floor, he was annoyed to see me along for the ride. Barely polite, he seemed to share my own view that my presence would only confuse things.

He didn't offer to take Dolores's coat. "Have a good look around," he instructed her. "Don't move things too much, but you don't need to walk on eggs. The place has all been photographed and dusted for prints."

Dolores gave him a look to convey that she didn't walk on eggs in *any* circumstances. "I'd like to remind you, Detective: I *own* these things, or at least a 50 percent interest in them." Once she finished scolding, she smiled, as if performing the mood alternations of "Shall I Be Sweet or Hot," a song she liked to open with in clubs. Detective Volker, her junior by at least a decade, appeared immune to the vamping.

She walked into the dining room and got down to business. I followed. The table where last Thursday's guests had done their speed eating was now bare of even a cloth or a candlestick. Had Tommy been called in to clean up once the crime photographers finished their work? The eight empty chairs— two of which had been filled by the victims—looked like the set for some genteel mystery drama.

"Well," Dolores said, "*he's* still here." She pointed to a bust of Caesar Augustus. "By Clerici," she added. Whether she pronounced it right, I couldn't tell you. "And *she's* here too." She indicated a Joshua Reynolds oil sketch. "Her name was Mrs. Hoare. Can you imagine?"

"We're interested in what's *not* here, Mrs. Crevolin," the detective reminded her, using her married name, I thought, to invalidate her movie-star status.

Dolores quietly resumed what anyone would have to concede is a strangely difficult task: trying to earn a eureka by *not* finding something. She peered hard at every shelf and surface, and as she walked around, the silence lengthened.

"Mr. Kallman told you that everything was insured?" Detective Volker asked.

"Yes."

"Well, so far we've found no evidence—like, say, a policy—to indicate that."

Dolores flinched—just a little, nothing actressy. Her spoken reply, when it came, was calm and icy. "Richard did the paperwork and kept the books. Every so often he'd give me a duplicate set."

"Did they match?" asked Volker.

She didn't answer.

"That's okay. We'll tell you when we've been over them."

She moved slowly through the living room, and after another two or three minutes was able to say, "There are a lot of things I'm noticing—or *not* noticing: some Imari porcelain, some jade jewelry, and a silver necklace that used to be spread out on a velvet cloth over there. Plus a Louis Seize clock."

Had those articles been there a week ago? For a moment I thought I could remember the necklace, but now I wonder if my imagination wasn't being led, like a witness, or the pointer on a Ouija board.

I'd read that Dolores had trouble memorizing lines and lyrics, and having to construct and keep this list in her head must have added to the difficulty of the assignment. I offered her a pen and the small spiral pad I always kept in my pocket. Assisted by these items, she was soon walking around the room with a curvaceous confidence straight out of *The Opposite Sex*, the best of her movie musicals:

> *Why do men who should know better*
> *Gape at a well-filled sweater. . . .*

For a moment Detective Volker appeared susceptible to the siren song of her movements.

She didn't even seem nervous approaching the yellow armchair covered with a sheet: the piece of furniture on which Dick had been murdered. I could see a dark dried crust of what must have been blood on the edge of the blue carpet, and I imagined that the upholstered seat was still soaked with it. "Some of it dripped straight through to the basement," said Volker, who'd been following my gaze and inferring my thoughts. "A whole puddle."

No gun had been recovered, but the catastrophe a gun had created on this exact spot was so palpable that I expected the yellow chair to start clicking once Dolores, like some busty Geiger counter, got near it. Had three years of holding the title prop in the London *Annie Get Your Gun* made her fearless around firearms? Or had she become that way thanks to the bullet in her lung, that benign companion for fifteen years?

Whatever the case, she was dry-eyed today and gave no sign that her burst of emotion at Le Moal—"My beautiful Richard!"—was about to recur. She stood straight, right next to the yellow chair, as she finished her list and handed it to the detective.

"We broke open the safe" was all he said. He pointed to a landscape painting on the far wall. "It's behind that."

"What did you find?" asked Dolores, sounding less suspicious of police high-handedness than of some shady move by Dick.

"Surprisingly little," Volker answered. "A bunch of deeds for properties the Kallman family no longer owns. A few thousand dollars in three different foreign currencies. No jewelry or *objects*." He pronounced the last word hard, with a sort of sneer, as if refusing to say "objets," the froufrou term I suppose he'd become acquainted with during his week on the case.

"Well, there wouldn't be," Dolores responded evenly, reminding him that the whole point of Possessions of Prominence had been to put everything on display.

"There was no indication that the safe had been recently opened," Volker elaborated. "In fact, there was dust on the knob. Tell me, Mrs. Crevolin, if someone had held a gun to Mr. Kallman's head while asking for the combination, would he have given it to them?"

"Yes," she replied immediately, her firm tone seeming to add: "Don't be ridiculous." Even so, as if not wanting to picture that scene, she changed the subject: "May I look through his personal things? The closets and so forth?"

"Knock yourself out. We've already done it. And taken photos." He sat down in one of the less ornate chairs, making clear he wouldn't follow her upstairs.

Dolores looked in my direction. "Come on," she said.

Right behind her, I climbed the stairs of the duplex; we passed a painting of a horse. "That's Determine," she explained. "My husband won the Derby with him."

"Is he, I mean the painting, for sale?"

"Certainly."

I still didn't know much about her marriage, except that Crevolin was some kind of rich businessman who lived in California while she remained mostly in New York. Given how infrequently she worked these days, I figured that he—or maybe alimony—paid for her apartment here. "Are you divorced?" I asked.

"Catholics don't divorce, sweetie."

I could have pointed out that I was an exception to this rule, but as we reached the top of the short staircase, everything went out of my mind except for having been up here a week ago with Steven—sitting in the "library" during the last minutes of his life while Dick's coke-fueled havoc began erupting all around and below us.

"Everything's still here," said Dolores, already in the bedroom, pulling open a third and then a fourth dresser drawer. "What are they waiting for? Can't somebody call the Goodwill?"

I went to work on the bureau, making piles of socks and underwear on the bed, wondering if anything in them had been Steven's, while Dolores extracted shirt after shirt—beautiful Oxfords and some newer, eye-scalding disco numbers—from one of the closets. In the lowest dresser drawer I also found a big alligator scrapbook. A quick flip-through revealed clippings that ran from *Seventeen* straight through that *New York* article on Possessions of Prominence.

Dolores opened a second closet, one whose former lock had been visibly pried away, and began rummaging through what was tightly piled inside. I was looking for the mate to a lonesome argyle when I heard her cry out "Mother of Christ!" She flung one copy of *Torso*, and then another of *Honcho*, onto the floor behind her.

As gay porn goes, these two periodicals aren't very extreme, but the items that followed them onto the rug were specialized and pretty awful—objets I was glad Detective Volker wasn't here to see, even though I knew he must have glimpsed them already: a large cat-o'-nine-tails; a pair of handcuffs; and two rubber fists, apparently flexible, one black and one white.

Dolores breathed fast and tried to stifle a sob. "It's almost as big as what they used in *Destry*" was all she said, picking up the cat-o'-nine-tails. She was referencing the whips that Michael Kidd had had the cowboys crack during her big dance number at the Imperial Theatre, twenty years ago.

I wanted to tell her that none of this stuff was really *that* unusual—these days you never knew what you were going to find when somebody brought you back to his place—but a further gander at Dick's closet revealed a *quantity* of such goods that bordered on the alarming. I could see another whole tower of stuff, amidst which glistened a long, industrial-looking chain.

"Let's go back downstairs," Dolores ordered.

"And leave all this here?"

"Yes." She abandoned the shirts along with the paraphernalia.

Sitting behind a copy of today's *New York Post*, Detective Volker offhandedly called out: "Find anything interesting?"

"Some things for Goodwill," I explained, jiggling a big Bloomingdale's bag into which I'd put some of the underwear and socks. They covered the alligator scrapbook, which I'd decided, without letting Volker know it, to take for myself.

"Thank you, Officer," said Dolores, with great dignity, as we made for the front door. Opening it to leave, we discovered on the other side of it a figure who'd been just about to knock: a small woman, maybe eighty, with tightly waved hair and white-gloved hands.

"Who are you?" asked Dolores, as roughly as if the ancient little creature were a Hells Angel attempting a forced entry.

Unfazed and unsmiling, the old lady looked up and said, "I'm Zara Kallman. Dickie's mother."

CHAPTER 5

DECEMBER 28, 1954

Sophie Tucker, with a cross expression, looked up from her private booth in the El Rancho Vegas's Wagon Wheel restaurant. Tiny Zara Kallman had squeezed between two plastic ficuses that the hotel's management kept in position to guard Sophie's privacy. Teddy Shapiro, her pianist since 1921, was normally the only person allowed to approach, but despite her exasperation Sophie decided to grant this woman a lunchtime audience.

She had her reasons. Dick Kallman, opening for her here at the El Rancho, was a talented pain in the tuchis. He'd told her his parents were coming in for a couple of days and, crucially, she knew how the father had long catered to Jews—and even made the Christians like it—at the resort he owned up in New Hampshire. So she extended a meaty hand to this prim white-gloved lady in her woolen suit with the nipped-in waist. Sophie's own idea of daytime casual, even here in the air-conditioned desert, remained satin and corsages and diamonds as big as the Ritz—almost everything she wore in the act except for the feathered tiara, which gave her some height.

"So, what kind of son leaves his mother alone?" she asked, forcing herself to smile if not to get up. She motioned for Mrs. Kallman to have a seat.

"I've just arrived. I've been told that Dickie's out horseback riding."

Sophie summoned the waiter, and Zara Kallman ordered some Earl Grey tea, with precise instructions for scalding the pot and for how the whole thing should be steeped, stirred, et cetera.

While they waited for it, Sophie said, "Dick tells me you were an actress."

"Oh," replied Zara, with a demure laugh, as if being asked to recall something foolish, like a childhood pet rabbit. "That was so very long ago." She paused, her eyes modestly downcast. "My father, Mr. Whitman, a very proper Bostonian, didn't want me onstage, but he relented for a bit of light opera. I originated *Naughty Marietta*."

"Did you now?" asked Sophie, while thinking: *Wos a ligner*. She herself never forgot a marquee, and she'd passed the one at Forty-Fourth and Broadway for weeks on end in the fall of 1910, when that operetta premiered. This dame couldn't have been much over ten. When it came to the Kallmans, mother and son, Sophie concluded, the *schmegegge* didn't fall far from the tree. Uninterested in any fake corroborative details Zara might offer, she asked no follow-up question. "Speaking of opera, Dick and I are actually performing in the Opera House." She rolled her eyes and gestured toward the El Rancho's so-named performance space. "But since right now we're in the restaurant, I'm going to have a cream puff." The waiter took her request for one as he set down Mrs. Kallman's order, probably prepared from a Lipton's tea bag. "How about you, ZaSu?" asked Sophie. "A cream puff?"

"It's Zara. And I'm afraid I couldn't possibly."

"I let others watch my weight," declared Sophie, "so I feel

obligated to give 'em something to watch. You coming to tonight's show?"

"Yes, I hope to be there." She made it sound as if it were doubtful she could squeeze it into her schedule. And the accent! Some crazy Brahmin affectation, Sophie realized. In fact, she was certain—to call things by the name of the song she'd sung a thousand times—that this was a Yiddishe Momme sitting across from her.

"I'm hoping you've been satisfied with Dickie's work," said Mrs. Kallman, who it now seemed apparent had gone looking for Sophie to find this out, not because she was starstruck.

"Dick's doing a good job" was the headliner's measured evaluation of this oddball kid Billy Rose had sent her way. "But he's *too* good a fit in some ways. He should throw out a couple of these numbers from the twenties and stick to modern material. I *already* bring in the *alte kakers*. I'd like him to lure at least a handful of people under forty through the door."

The message, Sophie could see, was definitely registering, even if Mrs. Kallman pretended to be puzzled by the term *alte kakers*.

"He's got lots of pizzazz," Sophie assured Dick's mother. "But Jesus—" and here she let out a hearty, Soph-sized laugh—"it's like watching a circus midget, you know? Like an old person in a young man's body. I mean, he's scrumptious to look at, but it's a little eerie the way he comes at you out of another era."

Sophie could see that Zara was shocked at the midget metaphor, but even so, the woman's face expressed not what she was really feeling so much as a simulation of what she thought shock should look like.

"Where's your husband?" asked Sophie. "You didn't come here solo for a divorce, did you?" Another patented Soph-laugh; a rumbling one. "It's just as easy to get one here as it is in Reno, you know."

"Mr. Kallman has been summoned to Cuba—for a meeting with Batista himself, very hastily arranged. They'll be negotiating my husband's purchase of the Hotel St. John's in Havana's Vedado district. I'm now planning to join him just after New Year's Day."

The Hotel St. John's in Havana's Vedado district: the phrasing sounded like it came out of a brochure, but Sophie let it pass.

She took a big bite of her just-arrived cream puff and said, "Well, there's nothing like expansion." Until she clarified the remark, Zara seemed to think it was the setup for another joke about the entertainer's waistline. "I was speaking of your husband's business," Sophie explained. "How he'll be adding this new hotel to The Balsams."

"Oh, yes. Mr. Kallman has also owned the Savoy Plaza in New York, and managed—"

Sophie cut her off. "So what is Dick planning on showing you while you're out here?"

Zara betrayed no discomfort in making the conversational shift. "After he finishes working with you tomorrow night, he'll be taking me to the Sands." She made it sound educational and improving, like a day trip to Boulder Dam or the perimeter of the atomic-testing site.

"You can bet your son won't be able to take his eyes off the showgirls there." This was less a jest than an experiment; Sophie wanted to observe Mrs. K's reaction. It turned out to be a tasteful shrug, designed to convey that boys will be boys and to preclude any further discussion of the subject.

"The owner at the Sands spent twelve thousand bucks on the girls' costumes," Sophie informed her. "More than he was paying Danny Thomas, which burned up the Lebanese no end! Maybe he can take it up with St. Jude. He's always talking about him."

"I'm never comfortable discussing money," said Zara, taking a sip of her tea. "I was brought up that way."

"The only thing rude about money is not having any," pronounced Sophie, who would bet that this one across from her had started out without a pot to piss in. She took a gander at a little pin from last year's coronation that Zara was wearing.

"Oh, yes," said Zara, realizing what the Last of the Red-Hot Mamas was noticing. "Mr. Kallman gave me that. He brought it back from a trip to London."

"I did a command performance for Queen Mary and King George in '26."

"How extraordinary."

"She was a mean cunt. But I got the idea for my aigrette from her." She patted the top of her own head and let Zara take two more sips of tea before suggesting, "You ought to go get your beauty nap. So you can really enjoy Dick tonight."

"That's a good idea," said Mrs. Kallman, impervious to insult. She patted her mouth with a napkin, extended her hand to the legendary performer, and departed through the Wild West interior of the Wagon Wheel. Sophie watched the little tailored figure disappear into the sound of the slot machines in the Nugget Nell lounge, and conceded to herself that there was something oddly formidable, maybe even mysterious, about this tiny fake.

For the next quarter of an hour Sophie did business over the phone that the maître d' always brought to her booth. She spoke to New York and was just being connected to the El Rancho's owner when Dick Kallman entered the dining room. To judge from his clothes, he looked about as likely to have been out riding as Zara did to have played Naughty Marietta. Sophie, who had told only tactical lies her whole life, marveled at the compulsive mendacity of Mother Kallman and son. She gestured for Dick to sit down while she proceeded with her phone call to Beldon Katleman, the hotel's proprietor, ordering him to resume the sale of Israeli bonds outside the theater after tonight's show. He'd stopped it on Christmas Eve, as if afraid to commercialize the Christians' holiday and as if somehow unaware that two-thirds of his Christmas-night audience were Jews fleeing the tinseled oppressiveness of the goyim's big day. Well, it was now the twenty-eighth, and he was damn well going to start selling the bonds again, if Sophie had to man the table herself.

"Worse than Lou Walters at his place in Chicago," she told Kallman, with a laugh, once she'd won the argument and hung up the phone. "Lou didn't want me hawking my memoirs in the lobby of the Chez Paree. But I got my way and we patched things up."

"You met my mother," said Dick. Sophie only now noticed his stricken look.

"Yeah."

"It's gone," he said, underlining with a sort of stammer what Sophie took to be half-real emotion. "The hotel."

"Well, *hasta la vista*, as they say down South American way." She assumed that Alvan Kallman's bid for the St. John had just fallen through in Havana.

"No," said Dick. "The Balsams." His mother, evidently over-coming her inability to talk of money, had just informed him that the senior Mr. Kallman, owing six hundred thousand dollars to the federal government's Reconstruction Finance Corporation, had been forced to let go of the New Hampshire property at an auction held in the upper lobby of the resort's main building. "Where I used to play with my brother, Charlie!" Dick informed Sophie. The place had sold for $192,000, to a local millionaire who'd invented latex gloves. "It happened months ago, and my mother's only now decided to let me know! I suppose she thought it would be less of a shock to tell me in person than over the phone."

Sophie doubted it, but before she could agree for politeness' sake, the boy was snapping back toward brightness and brass. "I guess change is the law of life!" he averred. This first-time visitor to Vegas was soon showing Sophie that he knew it all: "I hear that Bill Moore is getting ready to give up the Last Frontier—all those Navajo blankets and stuffed heads will be getting the heave-ho for something new and improved." Turning his head to survey the El Rancho's low-rise rusticity, and trying to hide what Sophie could see was nervousness, he remarked, "I wonder how long *this* place will stay the way it is."

Sophie had seen the town explode over the last half-dozen years—the advent of the Thunderbird, the Flamingo, the Sahara—but she remained loyal to Beldon K's thirteen-year-old, nearly antique spread. "Who knows?" she finally answered Dick. "Probably until somebody who's smoking in bed—or who's needing the insurance money—burns it down. There's no long haul in this town, baby doll. Or anywhere else for that matter."

A new waiter, a clean-cut college boy, set down the coffee she'd just signaled for. Lest it get splashed, Sophie carefully set aside the proof of Friday night's New Year's Eve program, which had been delivered by the Opera House manager a few minutes before. Noticing her precaution, Kallman joked: "You know, I'm guessing they'd give Miss Sophie Tucker another copy of that should there happen to be a spill."

"This one is for the scrapbook," Sophie told him, with a stern look. She'd been assembling her albums, dozens and dozens of enormous volumes, since before Naughty Marietta was being played by somebody other than Zara Whitman. "You should save things. Like I say, there's no long haul, period." She knew this must sound funny coming from someone who'd been in the business forever, but she also understood the truth of what she was saying. "*Do* you save stuff like this?" She pointed to the program, now safely distanced from coffee splashes and grains of sugar.

"Well, I throw things into a drawer back home," Kallman assured her.

"Put them into a scrapbook. A good one—leather or silk." The New York Public Library had already put out feelers to acquire all of hers.

Kallman tried giving her a grateful yes-ma'am look but was distracted, aroused, by the close-up sight of the busboy, a much rougher kid than the Joe College waiter, clearing away the cream-puff plate.

"Deep down, you don't really go for the nice ones, do you?" Sophie asked, once the boy was gone.

She observed Dick's startled, found-out look, and laughed. And she wondered about the little woman in the woolen suit: *What had that dame done to this kid?*

CHAPTER 6

MARCH 4, 1980

Walking up First Avenue, I noticed a thin older woman on the northeast corner of Fifty-Fourth Street. She was waiting for the light to change, her eyes cast down at the pavement, shyly. She didn't lift them even when a gentle tug from the man whose hand she held told her it was now all right to cross. Coming toward me, she continued looking down, as if searching for a ring or some other object of happiness that had disappeared long ago. The two figures passed me just as I was turning east. The man, whose eye I caught, gave me a polite nod and an almost courtly smile. It was Mr. and Mrs. Richard Nixon, I suddenly realized. They were out for a morning stroll a few weeks after their move from California to the East Sixties of Manhattan. He appeared to believe that they'd at last attained a safe, anonymous afterlife; she remained skittish and uncertain.

The Nixons' relocation to New York had been covered in the papers, but I doubt the sight of them would have struck me the way it did if I hadn't been on my way to the reading of a will—a ghostly business that up to now I'd seen only in movies: the dead man speaking, in the first person, from the beyond; the executor transmitting his words sounding more like a medium than a lawyer.

But this old-fashioned, formal procedure was what Mr. Arnold Weissberger, a big-deal, very respected theatrical attorney, chose to use in the case of Dick Kallman—maybe because of how badly things had gone between Dolores and Mrs. K four days earlier, during the five minutes they spent together outside Dick's apartment. I was guessing Mr. Weissberger wanted to take charge of the situation and keep it from getting out of control. He had been in Acapulco on vacation at the time of the murder and was playing catch-up. Arranging for the will to be read at his home instead of his office seemed a peacemaking tactic, the recommendation of a dignified, personal solidarity for the survivors of this tragedy.

Mr. Weissberger's building on Sutton Place South overhung the FDR Drive, whose traffic ran like a rapids beneath the co-op's protruding eastern portion. When I got up to his apartment, I found Dolores already there, in the foyer with our host, both of them looking at a framed, signed photo of Ethel Merman and Mary Martin. Three years ago, thanks to Weissberger, they had teamed up to do a benefit. "It was for the Theater and Music Collection at the Museum of the City of New York," he explained at some volume. That benefit had been such a to-do I couldn't imagine Dolores needed reminding, but I soon saw that Mr. Weissberger's explanation was intended for tiny, hard-of-hearing Zara Kallman, who'd momentarily been hidden from view on the lawyer's other side.

Dolores, who had asked Weissberger if I might be included among those here today, introduced me to him.

"I remember that night," I told the attorney, pointing to the photo of Merman and Martin. "It was so hard to get tickets that Dixie Carter told me she volunteered to be an usher!"

Mr. Weissberger laughed a polished Harvard laugh. Here in the city he was part of not only the gay establishment but *the* establishment.

Dolores looked uncomfortable. In addition to her proximity to Mrs. Kallman, she seemed bothered by any prolongation of the Merman-Martin discussion. Their world was hers, too, of course, but she had lived in it several rungs below the two of them, and I knew by now that she regarded others' triumphs only as reminders of her setbacks. I think part of Dick's appeal for her was that he'd eventually failed his way out of show business.

"Shall we go inside?" said Mr. Weissberger, gesturing toward the enormous living room. Its decor was an expensive mix of traditional and modern, a vast blend of the sedate and the loud—sort of like his career, that combination of the Ivy League and William Morris.

Dick's very tall brother, Charles—who'd been with his mother when we encountered her outside the scene of the crime—had also accompanied her here today. He was a friendly, polite man, an Army intelligence officer who'd acquired an attractive, German second wife. On Friday he had tried to keep the peace between Dolores and his mother once he noticed the instant dislike each took to the other. It was visceral—and financial. Zara Kallman declared, on the stairs outside Dick's showroom abode, that she was a poor widow, "on her uppers"; I had to research this British version of "down at the heels" and I wondered where she got it. She made plain to Dolores, even before seeing the inside of Dick's place, that she intended to take everything she was entitled to; she even mentioned a meeting she'd had that morning with a man from a new city agency that offered compensation to crime victims and their families. Those apparently included terrier-like widows who lived in apartments in Beverly Hills. "There's Beverly Hills and there's Beverly Hills," she told Dolores, who'd challenged her assertion of straitened circumstances by mentioning the city where she resided.

As Mr. Weissberger opened the string clasp on a portfolio, Dolores drew my attention to a man in a club chair at the far end of the huge room. It was Detective Volker, obscured by a brass-and-glass wall unit and nearly out of earshot. He had a notepad on his lap, and Dolores's grimace indicated disapproval of that. Mr. Weissberger, behind a beautiful Louis XV desk and ever ready to soothe a star's irritation, gave her a commiserating look; he didn't like it, either, but there wasn't much he could do. He was, in any case, ready to get to the business at hand.

But then Zara interrupted: "The apartment—Dickie's—is now *locked*." This was her way of informing Miss Gray that even her son's business partner would no longer be getting inside the premises. Charles Kallman hurried to offer a diplomatic explanation of how and where the apartment's contents would be stored, an arrangement he'd made with Weissberger, the police, and Richard Ravenal, the landlord (and art dealer) who lived upstairs in the townhouse and had rented its bottom two floors to Dick. It was Ravenal's wife who'd heard noises at 2:30 a.m. on February 22, and Ravenal himself, always an early riser, who'd discovered the bodies not long after the sun came up.

Bodies. Plural. Everyone usually forgot about Steven. And there was no sign of anyone connected to him here this morning.

Charles kept talking in the matter-of-fact manner he seemed to believe might dilute the poison between his mother and Dolores, and maybe even the violence of the murders themselves. Without anticipating Dolores's annoyance, he somewhat nervously volunteered information he'd gleaned from Dick's desktop during his own visits to the apartment. "Those Chippendale dining-room chairs, the ones just bought from Paul Siegel Antiques? It's unclear whether they're fully paid for. And there's definitely money owed on the Reynolds oil sketch—eighty-five hundred due early in April." I would soon learn that Mr. Weissberger was already getting calls from consigners demanding to know whether their stuff had gone missing in the robbery, and if it hadn't, when they could expect it back.

The lawyer thanked Charles for the particulars he'd provided but urged people to focus on the task in front of them. Zara's smile conveyed a sense that her surviving son had somehow just underlined the family claim to all of Dick's things, even if bills for them were outstanding. She folded her hands and nodded to the attorney: she was ready to proceed.

Alas, Charles had "opened the door," as Mr. Weissberger's colleagues like to say, to a discussion of the merchandise, and Dolores was eager to show that she remained more interested in missing items than in any that were safely stored (albeit unpaid for). "If they want to find who killed Dick, they should look for the jade jewelry—the pieces he and I bought in Hong

Kong last fall. The stuff that was too big to steal—those Chippendale chairs and the 'Reynolds'—aren't going to lead you anywhere." I was startled by the way—in front of everyone, including a police detective—she crinkled her fingers to put air quotes around "Reynolds," as if she were not just owning up to its inauthenticity, but was proud of the ruse to boot.

But the gesture was a nervous slip and, realizing it, Dolores became rattled by what it may have revealed. As if to rectify things, to show that all was really on the up-and-up, she passed out Xerox copies—to everyone, including Detective Volker—of what she said was the official agreement that had established Possessions of Prominence on February 4, 1978: a two-paragraph handwritten note on lined paper, initialed by DK and DG, stipulating that "any + all pieces bought together by DK & DG will be jointly owned." I recognized the handwriting as Dick's, but there wasn't a witness to the document—if you could call it that—let alone a notary's seal.

Mr. Weissberger's patience was wearing thin, but he graciously accepted the piece of paper Dolores offered and seemed relieved when she retook her seat—only, it turned out, to interrupt him yet again with an exclamation. "I just remembered! The Renoir statuette—the bronze! *It's* missing from the apartment, too! It's worth twenty-two thousand dollars. On Friday I never noticed it was gone." No air quotes around the creator of this item—only an agitation that ran counter to her whole in-charge theatrical persona and betrayed—what? I wondered. Grief? Fear?

She'd succeeded in making everyone jumpy, except maybe Volker, who made quick, steady notes.

"Ladies and gentlemen," Mr. Weissberger at last intoned, sounding like an offstage announcer. "As the executor and trustee of the trust created under the last will and testament of Richard Kallman, I am now going to read that document to you. 'I, Richard Michael Kallman, also known as Dick Kallman, do make, publish, and declare . . .'"

Grammatically, Mr. Weissberger now turned into Dick, and after a few paragraphs of boilerplate the attorney got to the script's very thin meat: bequests of five thousand dollars to

Zara and to an Albert J. duBois. Following that, everything else got bundled into a trust whose interest income was to be paid out annually to Mrs. Kallman. Nothing for Steven, but another paragraph of standard legalese seemed, weirdly, to drag his corpse into the room:

> "'No person shall be deemed to have survived me who shall have died at the same time as I, or in a common disaster with me, or under circumstances which make it difficult or impossible to determine who died first, and I direct that all the provisions of this Will shall be construed in accordance with that assumption and upon that basis.'"

When Mr. Weissberger got to the end, there was a moment of respectful silence, broken by Dolores: "Who's this duBois?"

Zara answered: "An Episcopal priest—my spiritual advisor, and Dickie's."

Dolores shot her an are-you-kidding? look that did nothing to shrink Mrs. Kallman's satisfaction over this further evidence that Dick had had a life well before Possessions of Prominence and Dolores Gray entered it.

"He conducted the funeral mass at St. John's," Zara proudly informed us. This was the first that Dolores and I heard there'd even *been* a funeral—yesterday. Poor Charles Kallman looked at both of us apologetically. "My mother wanted it to be private. Only family." He then brought things back to the business of the will. "That's it?" he softly asked Mr. Weissberger. "Nothing even for Travis?" He laughed with a slight embarrassment. Travis, I later learned, was his five-year-old son by his second wife.

"The will was drawn up on April 25th, 1972," Mr. Weissberger explained.

Zara, wishing to emphasize that the document was not just pre-Travis but pre-Dolores, too, turned to her rival and said, "Of course you only met Dick three years ago."

"Actually, I met him *thirteen* years ago. A little Sunday brunch at Kaye Ballard's."

This was news to me, and I made a mental note to ask Dolores about it. All these outta-my-way women that Dick had been around! The night before, I'd been contemplating the Sophie Tucker souvenirs in his scrapbook, and now, looking toward the picture in the hall, I found myself imagining how he would have gotten on with Merman. "Sing out, Louise!" The thought of all this female brass soon had me longing for my own mother, who'd always, literally and otherwise, been so quiet and far-away; who'd all her life had trouble drawing breath, let alone belting.

We seemed to be done here, and I felt a little cheated by the brevity of the proceedings. I wanted to hear about keep-sakes and trinkets being parceled out with sentimental thanks to each legatee. I wasn't expecting anything for myself; the truth is, I'd never known Dick very well. I just liked any tribute to times gone by, even if it had to be uttered in dead Dick's carnival-barker voice. All my life I've loved the past as a place that can keep you safe from the present, an inert world, sleeping and finished, that can't push you around; a place that your imagination can make as pretty as the two-dimensional flats of the *Seventeen* sets.

Dick and I had always been throwbacks. All those summer-time tap dancers at The Balsams had given him the illusion that show-business past was still show-business present, whereas I liked things now resting in peace as a matter of temperament. Which I suppose is why I'd been leafing through Dick's alligator scrapbook night after night, attracted to the archaic typefaces in the playbills and advertisements, and thinking hard about his sudden obliteration, about how the past had offered *him* no protection against a loud, last, fatal knock on the door. Knowing just what had happened after the dinner party might explain something about Dick, who had always bemused me; and beyond that I think I wanted to know more because I feared the moment when my own fatal, unexpected knock might arrive—not that I even *had* a will.

Charles Kallman rose from his chair and explained that he'd be taking his mother back to California later today—a mannerly reassurance to Dolores that Mrs. Kallman would soon be out of her hair. Picking up on it, seizing what seemed a new advantage, Dolores addressed Dick's brother as if he were her new junior business partner: "One thing that should be sorted out soon is the Imari porcelain. It was owned by *three* of us: Dick, Mr. Ravenal, and myself."

Detective Volker made another note, and Mr. Weissberger got up from his desk to escort everyone out. Zara bid a good-bye to Dolores that was positively hostile: "I remember another old show-business lady who tried to convince Dickie that she had all the right answers." (Sophie Tucker? I wondered. In the scrapbook there was a snapshot of the three of them—Dick and Zara and Soph—in New Year's party hats.) Dolores pretended not even to hear. She shook hands with Charles, a sort of tall, benign, fairy-tale opposite of Dick when it came to height, coloring, the works.

Dolores clearly expected me to escort her home, two blocks up and a couple over. She wanted a postmortem of the postmortem. But Detective Volker thwarted her by saying "Mrs. Crevolin"—he had multiple ways of mispronouncing her married name—"I'd like to borrow Mr. Liannetto for a while." Dolores looked peeved, and I guess I looked alarmed. As it was, I had a piano lesson to give in ninety minutes.

Mr. Weissberger tried applying the same sort of finesse that had no doubt brought Merman and Martin together: he told Dolores he'd be happy to walk her home himself.

Would Detective Volker be taking *me* to a station house? What did he want, anyway? He wouldn't ask to go all the way over to Manhattan Plaza, would he? Had I left the scrapbook, which I probably wasn't supposed to have, out on my bed?

It turned out that a First Avenue coffee shop was fine for the detective's purposes. Once we were in a booth, he placed in front of me a "lease-termination agreement" made between Dick and Richard Ravenal on Valentine's Day, a week before the murders. This one-page document allowed Dick to vacate the premises on March 30th, earlier than what the original agreement had called for. Where would he have been intending to go? Had he decided to relocate the whole apartment's worth of merchandise with him?

At the bottom of the paper Steven made another ghostly

appearance: not as a cohabitant of the premises, just as a mere witness to the agreement.

I told Detective Volker that Dick had said nothing that night about a move; nor had Steven. He seemed to accept this and promptly put two other sheets of paper down on the Formica table. I got the feeling that these constituted the real business of this sit-down: sketches, one full-on and one in profile, done by a police artist. They showed a young man with a surfer's good looks and light hair. The detective awaited my response. "Nobody I ever saw," I told him truthfully.

"The doorman of the Hyde Park Hotel, two doors down from your friend Dick's place, managed to get a glimpse of this guy on the night of the murders. He was hopping over a fence and running toward a limousine. At about three a.m."

CHAPTER 7

MARCH 5, 1957

Dick Kallman squires Margaret O'Brien.

"Okay, give me the agendas," said Barbara Nichols. The actress and her date stood at the back of the Mocambo nightclub, looking toward the table down front where their four dining companions awaited them. "I'm not stupid, you know," Miss Nichols added, her defensive assurance that she could process and put to good use any information she was given.

"I know you're not, sweetheart," said Mike Connolly, *The Hollywood Reporter*'s rough gossip columnist. "Everybody does. Except for your audiences."

Miss Nichols hoped that would change when *Sweet Smell of Success*, which she'd filmed before Christmas, got released this summer. She played, as always, a dumb blonde—this time the loyal girlfriend of craven press flack Tony Curtis—but the movie showed her being on to him and, for that matter, to everyone else. Or *would* show all that if between now and June 27th they didn't cut the handful of shrewd glances and lines she'd been allowed.

Connolly could see her starting to brood, and there was no time for that. So he made haste to instruct his frequent beard, who was so busty and blond she probably looked like overcompensation. "Here are the agendas. First, Margaret O'Brien."

Miss Nichols, from a considerable distance, looked at the twenty-year-old former child star, whose career was fizzling.

"She's looking to get better TV stuff," said Connolly. "That's where she sees her future, assuming she's got any."

Miss Nichols nodded. "Who's she with?"

"Some young character named Kallman."

"What's *he* after?"

"Everything but her. He's out here from New York, where he's got nothing much going on, either on Broadway or in the clubs. He's just scored a bit part in some western—pure horse manure—that's shooting up in Simi Valley."

"So he wants attention from you. And from Henry." Further along the curve of the faraway table sat Henry Willson, the agent who'd made Roy Scherer Jr. into Rock Hudson, Arthur Gelien into Tab Hunter, and more lately Merle Johnson Jr. into Troy Donahue. "What does Henry want?" asked Miss Nichols. "Another client? Or to get into this Kallman guy's pants?"

"Unclear," said Connolly. "Maybe he's deciding that tonight."

"Have they even met before?"

"No. Henry's agreed to see him in order to return some little favor he owes Phyllis Rab at William Morris."

"She's repping Kallman?" Miss Nichols had heard of Miss Rab, an up-and-coming ballbreaker in the Morris Agency's New York office.

"Rab is married to Kallman's older brother. She considers her young in-law a pain in the ass and knows that agent-wise he needs somebody here on the coast. She's fobbing him off on Henry so she can tell the family she's done her bit." Connolly lit a cigarette and continued the tutorial. "She knows Henry won't be interested, because Kallman's been hungry for success in the business since he was in rompers. And you know Henry: if he'd 'discovered' the guy working in some gravel pit, he might be able to get it up for him, but since that's not the case here, I don't think we'll be seeing Dick Kallman turned into 'Biff Clark' anytime soon."

Miss Nichols, with a snort, recited Henry's well-known maxim: "'The acting can be added later.'"

Connolly laughed. "Aside from all else, I'm sure the kid is too Jewish for Henry."

"Is he too Jewish for *you*?"

The columnist looked genuinely offended, anti-Semitism being one of the few prejudices he didn't have.

"So *you* want to get in his pants," Miss Nichols now surmised.

"I guess we'll see," Connolly replied.

The columnist usually did his hunting elsewhere, apart from business, when he wasn't in the mood to go home to his boyfriend, a former hairdresser who was butcher than anybody in this semi-crowded room.

But you never knew.

The band struck up "Tangerine." Connolly knew that this old pseudo-Latin spot was on its last legs. Charlie Morrison, who'd founded the Mocambo and made it a sensation around the time of Pearl Harbor, was on his last legs too. The columnist gave Miss Nichols a gentle push and they at last began threading their way to Willson's table. As they went, the twenty-eight-year-old starlet remarked upon the fourth person seated there: "I don't see why Henry had to bring *her*. Like she's not getting enough attention already." Natalie Wood, still shy of her nineteenth birthday, commanded plenty of notice from just her newly adult beauty—tonight set off by a tight green dress and lots of ruby-colored costume jewelry—as well as the kind of attention Barbara Nichols craved for herself, what was coming from the recent big box office of *Rebel Without a Cause* and Miss Wood's involvement with the slightly less young but equally pretty Robert Wagner.

Connolly scolded his companion. "*Relax*, baby. She's Henry's client."

Willson's agency catalog so resembled a male physique magazine that it was hard to remember he also represented a handful of young actresses, most of them less successful than Natalie Wood, whose presence on his roster served the same camouflaging function that Barbara Nichols did in walking through the Mocambo on Connolly's arm. "She's also an old friend of Miss

O'Brien's," the columnist told his date as they got close to the table and flashed sorry-we're-late smiles. "Back when they were both nauseating little child stars," he whispered as they sat down. "So make nice."

Connolly nodded hello to everybody, one by one. Willson had ordered two bottles of champagne, as if it were prom night. Indeed, Wood and O'Brien did look young enough to be wearing wrist corsages, and Nichols, with ten years on them, clearly didn't enjoy feeling like some peroxided English teacher here to chaperone them.

"I'll have a double Jameson's," Connolly told the waiter. Pitching his voice lower, as he did when going about his business in public, he looked at Miss O'Brien and Kallman and asked, "So how did you kids meet?" Right now the problem with his vocalization wasn't the register; it was the tone, which betrayed a laughable indifference to whatever these two might answer.

Miss O'Brien looked over at the agent, needing to be reminded of how she'd first encountered the young man she was now supposedly dating.

"It happened last year," said Willson, "when Margaret was on a promotional tour in New York."

"That's right," said Miss O'Brien, a bit grandly. Connolly pondered the weird superannuation she was suffering at the age of twenty: here she was, the Norma Desmond of kiddie stars.

"I was doing publicity for *Glory*," she elaborated.

Yes, she'd been in her own horse-manure offering last year, some cowboy picture with Walter Brennan that had come and gone. He could see her exchanging smiles with Natalie: the two had no doubt done this whole drill with Henry before. The girls' sexual irrelevance amused and maybe even titillated them.

"Dick is such fun," said Margaret, warming to her role. "He took me out to play miniature golf the other day."

Kallman looked at Connolly with an expression that seemed to say "Shouldn't you be writing this down?" "When she got the mumps a couple of months ago," he declared with a big grin, "I bought her a doll almost as big as she is! You should see her collection!" He took Margaret's hand but kept his eyes on Connolly, not caring if what he'd just imparted was a non sequitur. The conversation didn't matter; only the column did. Connolly could sort and arrange the information however he liked, so long as it wound up in print.

The writer was momentarily entertained by the thought that this child actress was still, at twenty, getting childhood diseases. He already knew about Margaret O'Brien's doll collection; it was one of ten thousand bits of stale star trivia growing rancid in his brain as the years of practicing his profession accumulated. More crucially, he knew that wholesome young Margaret's "aunt," a dancer, was probably her real mother, and that her birth had occurred after the father got knocked off by a fellow gambler down in Mexico City. The rest was Tinseltown-tyke history: the little girl had delighted Vincente Minnelli, then as now the homeliest fag in town, who put her in *Meet Me in St. Louis* with *his* beard, Garland, when Margaret was all of seven.

"Are you completely over it?" asked Barbara Nichols, meaning the mumps. Exposing herself to that was above and beyond anything she owed Mike Connolly.

"Oh, yes," Margaret assured her. "I hear you just made a picture with Burt Lancaster. I've got such a crush on him!"

"Hey!" cried Kallman, comically jealous, his expression designed to look as if he'd just dropped his straw into a chocolate malted that he and Margaret were sharing. But he soon had Connolly back in the full bore of his gaze, and he unleashed a stream of what he hoped was item-worthy chatter: how he'd also written the title song for *Hell Canyon Outlaws*, that western he'd done; how he'd caught Nat Cole's show at the Tropicana while visiting his folks in Havana.

"Dick's been telling me he's gotten terribly good at polo down there in Cuba," Miss O'Brien offered, supportively, before undermining this contribution with another mirthful glance toward Natalie and a suppression of giggles over all the crap she was shoveling.

Kallman was the only one here tonight with much at stake—a possible item and a possible agent—so his nauseating push was at least appropriate. But the columnist didn't like how O'Brien, this little cunt on her way down, thought all of this was a game. If that's all it was, then that's all Mike Connolly's life was, too.

"I heard Debbie Reynolds was their first choice for what you got opposite Brennan," he now told Miss O'Brien, flicking some ash into his unused champagne flute and surprising even Barbara Nichols with the nastiness of his remark.

"Oh, Mr. Connolly," said Natalie Wood, coming to the defense of her friend. "That's just *gossip*." Nervous laughter followed from everybody except the columnist, whose *occupation* had now more or less been called a game.

"You know," said Miss O'Brien, affecting regal detachment, "when I visited the White House, I remember Mrs. Roosevelt saying, 'Great minds discuss ideas; small minds discuss people.'"

"I'm surprised you can remember that far back," Connolly replied.

Natalie, a little drunk on the champagne and responding to a pleading look from Henry Willson, tried to defuse things with some humor. "Maggie tells me that on the set of *Glory* Walter Brennan kept taking out his false *teeth*! Maybe *that's* something for the column, Mr. Connolly."

The writer did not join in the relieved chuckling that greeted this tidbit. It only, after all, underlined the frivolous nature of his craft.

Willson, who had so far added three dinner rolls to his increasing girth, announced that he was ready for a steak. Connolly noticed how troubled he looked; the agent's biggest current woe involved the breakup of Rock Bottom's marriage to Phyllis Gates, up to now the best casting Henry had ever been involved in.

"*You* know what *real* gossip is, don't you, Natalie?" the columnist asked.

This was a definite escalation of unpleasantness. The ensuing silence indicated that *everyone* knew the "real gossip" he referred to: how Natalie, in order to get the part in *Rebel*, had slept with Nicholas Ray, the director, when she was still sixteen. Right now her steely gaze told Connolly that Miss Wood was a lot stronger and smarter than Margaret O'Brien.

"Jesus, look at that cockatoo," said Willson, trying to smother the fire of Connolly's temper. He directed everyone's attention to one of the club's rusty tropical birdcages. "Poor slob looks as close to croaking as Charlie Morrison."

Miss O'Brien now did her part to change the conversation. "Dick, tell us about the show you're going to be in—that musical in New York."

Kallman, who Connolly suspected didn't embarrass easily, got red in the face.

"Is it the Gwen Verdon thing?" asked Willson. *New Girl in Town*, the dancer's big follow-up to *Damn Yankees*, was set to open soon.

Kallman, flustered, said, "Uh, yeah, it's Gwen's show."

Connolly had to hand it to him. Here he was lying his way out of whatever blunder O'Brien had made, laying it on thicker than necessary with that first-naming of "Gwen."

"Excuse me," said the columnist, getting up. "I need to visit the men's room."

"I think I need to go, too," said Kallman.

"Oh, brother," said Miss Nichols.

Kallman walked behind the columnist, instead of side by side, as each made his way to the Mocambo's "Caballeros." Connolly gave an impatient hello to the exiting Gordon MacRae and made no effort to introduce the supposedly rising young Kallman to the successful older singer. The writer lit another cigarette and went to a urinal. Kallman just combed his slight pompadour and regarded Connolly's back in the mirror.

Staring at the tiled wall, the columnist tried as a mere exercise to see if, without looking at him, he could work up any lust for Kallman. The effort, he guessed, would be unsuccessful. An hour from now, with relief, he'd be saying goodbye to young Dickie and Nichols and the rest of the table and heading over to see what might be available at the gym on Wilshire.

"Maggie's a great girl, don't you think?" Kallman asked.

"Not especially," answered Connolly. "And why don't you cut the bullshit?" he added, shaking off and zipping up. "You don't have any musical in New York." The bathroom's acoustics magnified his Chicago accent: "have" sounded like "halve."

"Yeah," said Kallman, "I do." But his face altered; the brazenness was routed by an abashed okay-you-got-me look. "It's an industrial, one of those Milliken Breakfast Shows"—at which, with a lot of otherwise unemployed actors, he'd be extolling the company's fabrics in clever patter songs to hundreds of out-of-town buyers on their semiannual trip to the big city.

"You know," he added, dropping the sheepishness as quickly as he'd exhibited it, "I read your column sometimes."

Connolly dragged on his L&M and laughed.

"I liked the stuff you were writing on Monroe and Arthur Miller a while back."

"Miss Monroe needs to remember who and what made her, instead of thinking she can trade up by heading off to the Actors Studio—and into the arms of that pink punk Miller. Sometimes people need to be put back in their place."

Connolly would swear that Kallman was getting hard from hearing him talk about doling out punishments to the mighty. The columnist stepped over and grabbed him, forcefully, by the crotch. He felt Kallman flinch, but flinch *forward*, pushing himself, literally, into the palm of Connolly's hand.

The writer laughed again. No, this kid wasn't his type: he might not be flaming, but he wasn't rugged, either. He might also have a lot of nerve, but Connolly liked being the one with nerve enough for two. He released his hand and backed away before the towel attendant could wake up and notice something.

"Look," said Kallman. "I know the best way to get into your column, or anybody's, is to give you something about someone *else*."

"Yeah, thanks for the big tip on Margaret O'Brien's kewpie dolls."

Connolly stared into the guy's good-looking, angry face and could see Kallman making something up, could see his mind working with discernible speed, the kind of velocity his career wasn't attaining. This evening's attempt at self-promotion having failed, he was shifting to Plan B.

"I know this guy in New York," Kallman said. He hesitated for no more than half a second. "I think he tends toward pink in more ways than one."

"Who is he?"

"His name's Nelson. He had the lead in *Seventeen* a few years back."

"*Who?*"

"He also played Henry Aldrich on TV."

"So did a half dozen other kids."

"He's about to do a revue in New York."

Connolly laughed. "Dickie boy, the first requirement for a revelation is that it reveal something new about *someone people have already heard of.*"

Six years after being rebuffed by him, Kenny still loomed so large in Dick's mind that he forgot how Kenneth Nelson didn't occupy space in everyone else's. In Dick's head Kenny *was* famous. There were still nights when he recalled what Kenny's face had looked like as he spurned the gift of the pin; which only made him remember his first sight of Kenny, at the auditions for *Seventeen*, gently kissing his sheet music for luck and then laughing at himself. It's what had excited Dick Kallman into imagining what it would be like to be kissed by such a guileless boy.

His feelings for Kenny were kept alive by his desire for revenge. The anger that should have extinguished love ended up feeding it. Dick understood that the only way he could permanently want something, even something as wonderful as Kenny, was to be denied it. Which made him realize, however dimly, that his happiness could only lie in misery, his success in failure.

"Here," said Connolly, "take my card and better luck next time."

"Are you going to write about this evening?" the actor called out to the older man's exiting form.

"No," said the columnist, turning around. "But after Miss Nichols and I scram—as soon as Henry's consumed another four thousand calories—I'll send this poor slob from *Screen Star*, who's been hanging around at the back of the club, over to you and your one-and-only, Miss O'Brien. Maybe some paper in Oshkosh will pick up something *he* writes."

Connolly could see Kallman's disappointment over the miscalculated fabrication. He could also see that the actor wasn't blaming himself or the columnist. He was blaming Nelson, who hadn't been big enough to inhabit the on-the-spot political lie that Kallman had created about him. It was *his* fault. The twistedness of this told Connolly that something might yet come of being acquainted with Kallman. "Hang on to that card," he told the actor, after tipping the towel man.

CHAPTER 8

APRIL 19, 1980

They're Playing Our Song is a good little show, a sort of musical two-hander with a small chorus. I'd gotten the call asking if I could do the two o'clock matinee while I was sitting down to lunch. I hesitated, then remembered the item in today's paper about Con Edison seeking a 15 percent rate hike. I thought: I'd better. And I wolfed down my sandwich.

Well, when it rains it pours. Minutes later, while I was rushing to get ready, Detective Volker called: "There's somebody I'd like you to get reacquainted with." I was wanted up at the 19th Precinct, but yeah, it could wait until five o'clock if it had to.

The score for this show (Marvin Hamlisch) is tinkly and easy, and I'd already subbed for the pianist before Christmas, but when you play something for only the second time after such a long interval, you're essentially sight-reading. Between the stress of that and my worry over Volker's summons, I'd sweated through my shirt by the time the curtain fell.

> *Oh ho they're playing my song*
> *Oh yeah they're playing my song*
> *And when they're playing my song. . . .*

The tiny cast was taking its bows, and I was banging out the title number—as choppy as "Chopsticks" and just as much of an earworm. I took a fast look at my watch, 4:30 p.m., and congratulated myself on getting through the last two and a half hours.

A full two months had passed since the killings (that somehow sounds worse than "murders," no?), and several weeks since I'd seen or heard from Dolores. I'd had a couple of calls from Jack O'Rourke, the braying guy from Gramercy Park who'd been at Dick's dinner party: "Have you heard anything, cookie?" No, I hadn't, and he hadn't, either. I'd even stopped reading Dick's scrapbook, though every so often I would wonder if I might have walked past the killers on the street that day.

There had been, I suppose, another three or four hundred murders since Dick and Steven's back in February. Along with the usual lower-level mayhem. During the intermission I learned the reason I'd gotten the call to fill in: the guy I was subbing for, who only did the matinees, had been mugged this morning—badly enough that they might need me again on Wednesday.

As the audience left for home, the conductor came over to offer me compliments and a little clap on the back. "Can you stick around for a few minutes? To go over one or two tiny things?" "Sure," I said, looking at my watch. But then the stage manager leaned over into the pit. "Miss Arnaz would like to thank you."

He led me to the star's dressing room, and for a moment I thought I saw Lucille Ball, her mother, sitting next to Lucie Arnaz. I was looking at a redhead, full of life, whose beautiful face also possessed a comic's rubbery mobility, like Lucy's.

"Lifesaver!" cried Lucie Arnaz, as she jumped up from her chair to give me a hug. I'd heard she was nice, but this was *really* nice, far beyond what I was used to in this sort of circumstance. "Tony"—her costar, Tony Roberts—"had to scoot, but he says thanks too. This is Carole!" She put her hand on the redhead's shoulder. "The great Carole Cook! *Her* show finishes up at three fifty, and she *finally* found the time to run those three blocks from the Barrymore and say hi."

"I needed *every* minute of the forty," said Carole, with a deep, Tallulah-like groan, exaggerating the ravages of age. (She looked about fifty, if that.) I was on the verge of placing her when Lucie explained things: how her mother, in 1959, after *I Love Lucy* had finished, put together the Desilu Workshop, a troupe of comedians and singers, Carole among them. With Lucy mentoring them, they performed some live shows at a Hollywood theater and did a big TV special.

Carole now expressed eternal gratitude for the break. "Oh, God," she told me, in the still-thick Texas accent of a girl long out of Abilene, "you should have *heard* me when I got the call from her mother. I was on a pay phone backstage at some little summer theatre in Ohio. 'Oh, *yes*, Miss Ball! I'm *thrilled*, Miss Ball! Of *course* I'll come out there, Miss Ball!' God, I sounded like fuckin' June Allyson."

I laughed hard and naturally. I'm still usually nervous around show-business people, and have certainly never had a relaxed moment in Dolores's company, but I felt instantly at ease with Carole Cook. And then it hit me: "Oh, my God!" I exclaimed, with what bordered on a nelly shriek. "How could I forget? Dick Kallman was in that workshop. You must have known him!"

"Oh, honey, *all too well*, God rest his soul."

"Did he *have* a soul?" asked Lucie. "I hate to speak ill of the dead—let alone the murdered—but Mother used to say that if Dick told you it was sunny, it was only because he wanted you to go out the door without an umbrella and get drenched."

"Yeah," said Carole, "but she was crazy about him for a while."

She then turned her gaze in my direction, as if worried she and Lucie might inadvertently have hurt me with what they'd said. "Did you know him well, dear?"

"No, but I did know him for a long time. I actually saw him the night he was killed. I was over at his place for dinner with a group of guys, before . . ."

Carole mimed a shudder. "I ran into him down at the Ballroom late last year, when I came to town to do this play. We talked about getting together and catching up, but you know how that goes. God, I'm glad I didn't get the invitation *you* did!"

It was Lucie's turn to shudder.

"It's funny being back in New York," said Carole. "Haven't

been here for a long time. God, every step I take reminds me of the years I was scrounging around for any job I could get. Throughout the whole not-at-all-fabulous fifties. But then Mama, Lady Bountiful, came along." She squeezed Lucie's hand, while Lucie assured me: "She's being ridiculously modest. She was Mrs. Peachum in *Threepenny Opera*!"

"I was still Mildred Cook then. Before her mother rechristened me."

"After Carole Lombard," Lucie explained.

"'Carole' with a piss-elegant *e*."

"I hate to go," I said, and they could both see I meant it. "But I need to go see . . ." I trailed off. Being more than a little afraid of Detective Volker, I thought it best to keep mum about my appointment at the 19th Precinct.

"Well, I'm sure to see you again," said Lucie. "That poor guy is in terrible shape"—i.e., the regular pianist wouldn't be back by Wednesday.

"Come see *me* sometime at the Barrymore," Carole insisted. "Come feel all the tropical heat generated by Mia Farrow and Tony Perkins! Have you got a card, Matty?"

I did, and I gave her one, and she wrote her number on a sturdy Kleenex from Lucie's vanity table. "Just call and tell me when I should leave a pair of tickets at the will call."

On my way out of the Imperial, I stopped at the orchestra pit. Everyone, including the conductor, was gone; I decided I could call him tomorrow to see what needed going over. I put the score in my shoulder bag and raced to catch a cab.

When it dropped me in front of the station house on East Sixty-Seventh, I thought, as I had the first time I was there, that I was back at PS 70 in Astoria: all the red brick and stone trim. I soon found myself sitting alone in a row of flimsy chairs outside a squad room shabbier than the one on *Barney Miller*. A thin boy, maybe mid-twenties, wearing a skinny tie, asked me if I'd like "a cup of the coffee that's been sitting here since this morning." His nametag identified him as Devin Arroyo—half Latino, I assumed from the name; with big green eyes. While I was growing up in New York, everyone was white or black or "Puerto Rican" (called such even if they were Mexican), with a sprinkling of Chinese. These days, at least from the sight of them, you don't know what biology and geography brought people here. If we don't all kill one another first, the mixing will probably do us good. It's certainly made people better-*looking*, or maybe just interesting to look *at*. I said yes to Devin Arroyo's offer of coffee because he was super-cute and saying yes would require him to make a second trip out to the corridor.

"I guess they want you to have a look at Jimmy," he said, handing me the coffee.

Jimmy? He existed in my memory of February 21st only as a voice: "Mr. Kallman, this here's Dante."

"They caught him?" I asked, with more surprise than relief.

"He came in voluntarily, sort of, this morning."

I felt sure Devin shouldn't be telling me this, and wondered why he was.

"I typed up the report," he explained. "How do you know Jimmy?"

"I don't," I replied, almost indignantly.

"*I* do," Devin informed me. "I only got a peek at him today, but I'm pretty sure I've talked to him a couple of times, at the corner."

"The corner?"

"Second and Fifty-Third," Devin explained.

Where the boy hustlers operate. Had Jimmy been a trick of Dick's? And had Devin, before going to work for the cops, once been a colleague of Jimmy's? I looked at him apologetically, as if it were rude of me to be accepting this uninvited candor.

"It's okay. I'm cleaning up my act. I can type fifty words a minute, and I spell a lot better than *they* do." A tilt of his head toward the squad room indicated the cops. A few seconds later, at the sudden approach of Detective Volker, Devin nodded, very young-professionally, to the older man. As he went back to his desk, I stood up and shook the detective's hand.

"How've you been?" asked Volker. "Ready to help us out?"

"If I can."

"I want to see if you can ID Jimmy."

Not wanting to get green-eyed Devin into trouble, I feigned

surprise at the mention of Jimmy's name. "The guy who showed up that night? I never actually *saw* him."

"Right. That's consistent with what you told me back in February. But you *heard* him."

"Yes, one sentence, loud. But that was it."

Volker nodded. "I'm going to try something a little unusual. A sort of vocal lineup. I'm going to put you on one side of a partition. You'll be able to hear through it. There'll be three guys on the other side—two of them cops and one of them young Mr. Ingrassia."

How did they even learn his last name, let alone get him to surrender? "Is this legal?" was all I asked.

"It's just for internal purposes," the detective explained. "To help make sure his story isn't total bullshit."

He invited me to follow him to a room in the basement. There I could make out three blurry forms on the other side of a dark, frosted-glass divider, one maybe skinnier than the others. There was no telling the color of anyone's skin or hair.

Volker slipped behind the partition. Loudly enough for everyone, including me, to hear, he said, "Gentlemen, I'm going to ask you, one at a time, to say five words. I want you to say them in a strong, audible voice: 'Mr. Kallman, this here's Dante.' Ready?"

I sat with my back to the glass.

"Mr. Kallman, this here's Dante."

It was him; the first one. I could almost feel the ghost of Steven—who'd heard those words with me—flinching somewhere nearby. The other two guys, once they spoke, weren't even close. Their voices were older and huskier, and one of them betrayed a touch of sarcasm, as if this exercise, or Jimmy's life, were a waste of time.

I saw no sign of handcuffs, let alone a lawyer, through the frosted glass.

"Okay," said Volker. "Let me take our guest upstairs."

It turned out that meant me, not Jimmy. Back on the main floor, shaking my hand, the detective said nothing more than "Helpful. We'll be in touch." He then instructed Devin: "Stick around. I'm going to give you something to type up in a few minutes." He started back downstairs, to rejoin his two buddies and, I assumed, to take Jimmy, that frosted shadow, to some kind of holding cell.

"I kept an eye on your bag," said Devin, once again seated at his desk.

"Oh, thanks,"

"So what'd did you think of Jimmy?"

I didn't think I should tell him anything, though presumably he'd know all of what little had gone on downstairs as soon as he typed up the results of the audio test. "I've *still* never seen him. They—"

"Well, here's your chance." Devin indicated that I should turn around. And once I did, I saw a scrawny guy with greasy blond hair who looked barely out of high school—but who also looked like the sketch Detective Volker had shown me at the beginning of March. He was wearing a green army-surplus jacket and wiping his nose with one of the cuffs as he walked out the front door of the station house, *by himself.*

I wheeled around toward Devin. "They're letting him *go*?"

"He's not under arrest. At least not yet."

"I thought you said he turned himself in."

"He did—at the direction of his much older boyfriend. Jimmy has been down in Florida for two months with his two pals— 'pals' being short for 'accomplices.' The boyfriend went down there to fetch him."

"How do you know all this?"

Devin hesitated a moment—and then simulated a light glissando over the keys of his Underwood manual, indicating that he'd learned everything he just told me typing up Detective Volker's reports.

"Why would he agree to turn himself in? And how could they let him walk out?"

For the first time Devin hesitated, only for a moment, before talking. "They're gonna flip him. To get whoever actually pulled the trigger. He's *used* to being flipped. The boyfriend's been flipping him, so to speak, since he was about fifteen."

I had more than twenty years on Devin Arroyo, but it somehow felt the other way around. "So where are Jimmy's 'pals'?" I asked.

"I don't think they know." He pointed toward the cops downstairs. "The other two have either taken off for parts unknown or are still hiding under 'the Florida sunshine tree.'" He sang the last phrase the way Anita Bryant used to in the commercials.

"And where's Jimmy going now?"

"I'll bet you anything it's to the corner. Second and Fifty-Third," he added, in case I'd forgotten. "The boyfriend is supposed to collect him somewhere later, but he's probably got time to let somebody *else* pick him up between now and then."

"He's free to go *hustling*?"

"I wouldn't say he's 'free' to do anything. I checked out his arms when he had the jacket off. I'd put his habit at three hundred dollars a day. And he's got to go feed it. Though he *could* be going down to the corner just to refresh his memory. That's where all this began. The murder of your friends."

I was seized by an enormous desire to get out of there, and not just because Detective Volker might be coming up the stairs any second.

But Devin, as if *he* were seeking a plea deal, seemed to want to keep me there by offering up more of the story. "There's a lot here," he said, riffling the typed pages on his desktop.

I shifted my bag from one shoulder to the other, trying to convince him, and myself, that I was at last about to take off.

"Take my number," said Devin, writing it down. "I don't bite. And my fucked-up percentage is dropping all the time." He paused and watched me hesitate. "You seem like a sweet guy," he added, coming forward with the card. "And I do have daddy issues."

I took the number.

CHAPTER 9

OCTOBER 3, 1959

"Lucy said the cutest thing to us the other day."

"Us," as was made clear by the pointings of Dick Kallman's index finger, meant himself and Robert Osborne, who sat next to him, along with Carole Cook and Howie Storm, in a horseshoe booth at Los Angeles's House of Murphy restaurant.

Storm rolled his eyes. The comic was already feeling underused in the much-publicized "workshop" Lucille Ball had recently set up for the grooming of young television talent. Of the sixteen performers in the company Kallman had managed to make himself the most central, to the annoyance of Storm and nearly all the others. Carole Cook, the nicest and most talented of the bunch—a singer-comedienne and a redhead like Lucy herself—patted Howie's arm and counseled patience. They were still in rehearsals for the month-long run of a live show that would start next week at a playhouse on the old RKO lot—with a TV special to follow. A clipping from Hedda Hopper's column, reporting on a rehearsal she'd seen, lay on the table. It predicted a bright future for them all: "I can tell you now it's a smash hit and better by far than many shows I've seen on Broadway!"

"What Lucy said," continued Kallman, starting an imitation of her smoker's growl, "is 'Kid, you need more of what *he's* got, and he needs more of what *you've* got.'" Those around the table needed no further explanation: that gentlemanly Bob Osborne could use more of Kallman's drive and that Dick ought to acquire a bit of his current roommate's college-boy polish and considerateness toward others. The glint of Kallman's pinky ring, as he pointed to Bob, demonstrated the contrast as well as anything could.

Osborne noticed how the ring—let alone the story, with its intimations of closeness to Lucy—was disgusting Howie Storm. Actually, it disgusted Osborne, too. Diamonds on a man? Flashy gems, he'd learned, were one of Dick's compulsions. The two of them couldn't drive past a jewelry store or pawnshop without Dick parking the car and dragging him in. The sex between the two of them, extremely discreet, worked insofar as it did because of the same disparity Lucy hoped to reduce. In bed, Dick enjoyed being worshipful of Bob's Anglo leading-man looks; his two years in the Air Force added to his otherness, and allowed Dick to be almost passive, to stop the obsessive rototilling through every imagined impediment in his career path. And as Dick calmed down, Bob gained confidence, or at least shed shame. Come morning Dick would return to his mad competitiveness while Bob continued discovering, for all his own enchantment with show business, a preference for being behind the scenes instead of in front of an audience. He was the only one in the workshop wishing for fewer occasions to shine.

Now, while the four performers waited for their Saturday-night steaks, Howie made a request of Carole: "Refresh my memory. I forget how *you* got mixed up in all this."

Dick answered for her: "I told Lucy she had to recruit Carole. If *you'd* seen her in the *Shoestring Revue* or *Threepenny Opera*—and if you'd known Lucy—you'd have done the same thing."

"And he never lets me forget it," added Carole, who at thirty-five was older than the rest of the workshop players. Her jab at Kallman was half friendly, half annoyed. For all her warmth, Howie wondered if he could trust her fully: if she was obligated to Dick, that was enough reason for Howie to keep his distance. He detested Kallman, and with the exception of Bob Osborne and Carole, so did every other member of the workshop.

Osborne had been noticing how Dick made use of Lucy's vulnerabilities, found opportunity in the upsets and moodiness caused by her husband's boozing and girl-chasing. Last month Desi had been arrested for being drunk and disorderly in the company of a woman who was probably a prostitute.

"Well," said Bob, pacifically, "I think we're all getting a lot out of it," meaning the workshop.

"I've told you what I think," said Howie. "I think Lucille Ball is going through second childhood a little early." The old theater they were rehearsing in was on the same RKO lot where she'd once gone to the acting/charm school run by Ginger Rogers's mother.

"I won't have a word said against her," Dick replied, with a gleaming don't-fuck-with-me smile. He was ecstatic to find himself where he was. For six months he'd had nothing except bits in a movie and two TV shows, one of them *Whirlybirds*, a western with helicopters instead of horses.

"Good," said Howie. "I *won't* say a word against her. That way you won't have to tattle it back to her." He turned to Carole. "Have you noticed how whenever Dick hears one of us criticize a sketch or a number, five minutes later Lucy shows up angry and says, 'What do you mean the number isn't working?'"

"Relax, Howie," said Kallman, more to warn than to soothe him. "This is going to be big, big, big, big!" He pointed to the Hopper column on the table.

"Maybe for you," Storm responded. "Right now my own future feels as bright as that copy of *Born to Be Loved* you made us all watch." The film, which had bombed in theaters over the summer, looked more like a cheap kinescope than a studio print. Still, Kallman had pressed it on them, if only to show that his bit in it was more than they were getting.

"Dick was badly cast in that," said Osborne, who quickly realized he was being supportive in a way that his roommate would only loathe: for Dick Kallman, failure was to be denied, not explained.

"You mean he played a nice guy?" asked Storm.

"Boys, boys, come on," said Carole.

Storm persisted. "I don't think Lucy even knows what she's doing."

"How can you say that?" asked Kallman. This was the First Lady of Television they were talking about.

"She knows nothing about music," said Storm, not inaccurately. "That's how you've gotten her to rely on *you*. And that's why this revue is overstuffed with songs and starving for laughs. I've got to hand it to you—making Lucille Ball doubt the worth of *comedy*." He wasn't finished. "You're all so thick with her—letting her take you to Palm Springs next weekend. Carole's even living with her!"

"Howie, you're making too much of everything," said Carole, though she had in fact turned into a kind of daughter during these last two months at Lucy's house on Roxbury Drive. Lucie Jr. was still too young to be her mother's confidante, so Carole got to hear Lucy's anxieties while they did each other's hair. Everyone in the workshop knew that Lucy had even renamed her, after pronouncing "Mildred" a worse name—for everyday life, let alone show business—than "Bertha" or "Gertrude." So Mildred became Carole, since Lucy thought she could discern in her new protégée the same screwball talents she'd venerated long ago in effervescent Carole Lombard. ("See?" Howie had said. "Second childhood.") Lately, since Desi's arrest, the new Carole had heard Lucy crying to Dr. Norman Vincent Peale, over the phone, about her marriage, and seen Bessie the maid shaking her head like Max the butler in *Sunset Boulevard*.

Kallman joshed as if Howie weren't even there: "Carole and I are going to steal this show out from under everyone!"

The exclamations, the big gestures, the loud voice: Carole, like Bob Osborne, understood how Dick's fake confidence managed to give back to Lucy some of what she'd been losing herself. But she could also see little signs that Lucy was growing tired of Dick—something he couldn't notice through his own bombast.

"Hey!" he cried. "Mom! Pop!"

Alvan and Zara Kallman approached from the House of Murphy's maître d' stand, and the elder Mr. Kallman now resumed explaining to the kids that he was managing this restaurant here at Fourth and La Cienega because he'd been kicked out of Havana seven months ago, his hotel appropriated by that stogie-chomping shit Castro.

"It's only a matter of time before he gets it all back—bigger than ever!" cried Dick. "Move over, Tropicana! In the meantime he's doing great here. Just look at this crowd!"

"He's a human pep squad," Carole said to Zara, hoping her assessment of Dick sounded more affectionate than sarcastic.

Mrs. Kallman, who had insisted to her husband on their joining Dick in California, still wore her dowager outfit and manner. She kissed Carole on both cheeks, with lips that felt as hard as the diamond on Dick's little finger—if one assumed, as Carole didn't, that the diamond on Dick's little finger was real. Carole liked "Torchy," Mr. Kallman, better than she did his wife. He, too, had been a martinet for most of his life, but his energy and his red hair, the source of his nickname, had both started to fade. And diminishment somehow became him; he was nicer, Carole thought, since his latest losses.

"Do you know how these two met?" Torchy asked Osborne and Storm, as if "Dickie and Mildred," as he called them, were having a romance.

"At a party," Carole explained for him. "At some chorus boy's apartment in New York. I started singing the 'Volga Boatman's Song' after somebody broke open a bottle of vodka, and Dick joined right in. We started going to plays together every once in a while." She didn't want anyone thinking they were close.

"Dick's *always* getting Mildred jobs. Not just this one," Zara asserted, with a smile, to Bob and Howie.

"Always?" asked Carole.

"Don't you remember the one at One Fifth?" Zara explained to Osborne and Storm that this was an elegant apartment house near Washington Square in New York. The Kallmans had until recently lived there, managing the Havana hotel from afar.

Carole recalled how Dick and Zara always *said* they lived at One Fifth, but she'd never actually been invited upstairs.

"The ground floor contained a very swank nightclub," Zara went on. "With two pianos. They had a talent contest every Monday night. The winner got a job performing at the club for the rest of that week. What was it you won with, Mildred?"

"A medley from *Oklahoma!*" Which was to say that she'd earned the job herself. But Zara and Dick needed to take the credit just for having invited her to the restaurant.

Mrs. Kallman laid the dinner check down on the table, far away from Dick. He was the only one being comped tonight; the others took out their wallets.

Alvan Kallman, perhaps by way of apology for the bill, said, "We bought some Desilu stock last year." After the initial excitement of the public offering, the share price had gone down, along with the ratings for some of the company's shows.

"But *The Untouchables* is shaping up to be a smash!" said Dick, reassuring his father and trying to inject some company spirit into his workshop colleagues.

Except for Bob Osborne, the actors would all be fighting for airtime when the Christmas special started filming next month. Beyond that, once the workshop ended, lay the matter of who would be getting roles in other Desilu productions, or even participating in the rumored revival of the Lucy character—with or without Desi—in a new half-hour series.

Late Monday morning, on the RKO lot, Howie Storm asked Carole: "How *did* you get involved with this? Don't tell me to believe what Kallman said last night—that he recommended you for it. He wouldn't buy a pencil from a bum."

"Actually, he did. I could hear him in the background the whole time Lucy talked to me on the phone. They tracked me down to some little theater in Warren, Ohio. I was doing *Kismet* in stock. The call came to a pay phone backstage, and I was so flustered that at one point, when I tried calling her Mrs. Arnaz, it came out as 'Mrs. Arzballs.' But a week later I was here in LA, carrying my crummy luggage."

"How did *he* get this job?" asked Storm, wanting hard information, not anecdote.

Carole pulled on the little bow at the neckline of her blouse, the demure one she'd be wearing in the revue number that had her step out of a frame as Whistler's Mother and turn into a bomb-shell "Red Hot Mama." "Dick had a slew of people write to Lucy," she explained. "People he'd made aware of himself, plus names his sister-in-law, who's an agent, gave him. He went at it like a sound-truck version of Dale Carnegie. And he got his audition."

Storm looked skeptical. "You actually believe that?"

Their conversation ceased, suddenly, as Lucy entered the rehearsal room. As usual, everybody's eyes went to their star-patroness, who had come in with Janice Carroll, another member of the workshop. Dick had told Carole to watch out for Janice: "She's a dyke, honey. Steer clear."

The room suddenly exploded in sound, as if an air-raid siren had gone off.

"'I love Lucy, and she loves me! We're as happy as two can be!'" It was Dick, running toward the boss, blaring out the first two lines of the old series's theme song before giving Janice a smooch. He knew enough not to kiss Lucy herself, who had a star's aversion to being touched, but he couldn't stand anyone else having her solo attention.

"I've had the best brainstorm I've had since you touched me with your magic wand! About a number we can add that'll let everybody shine! May I borrow Mrs. Arnaz?" he asked Janice. "It's called 'Summertime Is Summertime,' and it'll warm up a Christmas broadcast like nobody's business!" Lucy, with a tentative smile, allowed him to walk her off to a corner and make the rest of the pitch in private.

"Oh, my God," Carole whispered to Howie Storm. "That number is from a period show he did ten years ago with my friend Kenny Nelson. It's all boater hats and parasols and Gay Nineties waltzing. It'll be deadly. And the only one who'll shine in it will be Dick. She can't say yes to this."

"You watch," said Storm. "Little Rasputin will convince the czarina."

Two hours later, with sheet music for "Summertime" on a plane from New York, Kallman was energetically assembling a boy-girl-boy-girl chain between himself and Lucy to illustrate how the number would open. As all the participants grabbed hands at his direction, Kallman felt his mind flashing on the chain of persuasion that had actually resulted in his linkage to Lucy and an invitation to join the workshop: Mike Connolly made his column helpful to Henry Willson's clients; Connolly then asked Willson to be helpful to Kallman, because Kallman had become helpful to Connolly, feeding him items on various Pepsodent-bright young performers around town, information he'd learned to pick up in the right bars and from the right studio secretaries. Which made Willson, one night over dinner at Panza's Lazy Susan, plug Kallman to Lucy.

So here he was. Tight with the boss and well aware that he'd better come up with an item on *her*, something to pass along to Connolly, if he didn't want the chain to break.

CHAPTER 10

JUNE 13, 1980

I figured out from a couple of biographical dictionaries that Dolores had been knocking five years off her age. And so, since she'd actually been born in 1924, not 1929, it hardly seemed a big deal that we should be celebrating her June 7th birthday a week late. It was Friday the thirteenth, and she wanted to have a late supper after seeing *Urban Cowboy* down in Kips Bay. She claimed to have a professional interest in John Travolta's dance moves, though I knew even before we saw the film that she would be relishing the chance to make remarks like "*This* is a leading lady?" (Debra Winger) and "You call this a *musical*? It sounds like some jukebox in Fort Worth."

The movie ended at nine thirty, and she decided I should walk her home. We'd get there in time for her dog's last scheduled outing of the day—which I could help with—if we shook a leg. Use of that last phrase prompted her to pat one of her thighs and say, "Besides, I've got to keep the gams in shape," as if she had a morning call at MGM.

I hadn't seen Dolores for many weeks, because I'd been busy with a lot of lessons plus my new permanent part-time status at *They're Playing Our Song*: both regular pianists were now gone, and I was splitting the eight shows a week with a nice girl from Jersey. As Dolores and I walked up Second Avenue, I wondered if I'd finally tell her about the semiarrest of Jimmy Ingrassia. I'd never passed on that news, mostly from fear that Detective Volker would be mad if he found out, but also because of Dolores's disinclination to talk much about "Richard" since discovering his sex tools three and a half months back. She acted as if he'd been a distant acquaintance, his murder something from another decade. In fact, since Dick was the only thing linking us, I thought tonight might be the last time I saw her. I was sure she could find other sounding boards for her litany of show-business grievance.

She disapproved of my drinking a Coke while we walked north through Murray Hill; I'd offered her a sip through a second straw, and she made a face to remind me this wasn't something a star would be caught doing in public.

"These two boys—kids, really—are writing me a show," she announced, without saying more on the subject, as if it were too hush-hush to be further divulged. We walked on in silence, reaching the edge of Tudor City. I looked east, past the river, and could see the new skeletons of two buildings rising hopefully over the flat warehouses of Long Island City. I wondered out loud if New York might at last be starting on its way back, even though the whole country was now in a recession.

The subject of money stimulated Dolores, whose thoughts on the topic took an immediate personal turn. "I got my deposit back—five thousand—on the Reynolds oil sketch. Which was better than having to pay the eighty-five hundred still due on it." Colnaghi, the old London firm of dealers from whom the sketch had been acquired, more or less had to accept its return; to do otherwise would seem to align them with the auction houses who doubted its authenticity and refused to put it up for sale here in New York. I noticed it was "my" five thousand dollars Dolores spoke of, as if Dick had never existed.

She went on to tell me about other problems with the stuff in the apartment. Mr. Weissberger, the executor, wanted everything sold at auction, a more likely way of keeping things on the up-and-up than the unregulated private sales Dolores preferred. Either way, Possessions of Prominence would go out of business once everything was disposed of. In the meantime, the insurance policy had turned up, and Dolores and Zara had set aside just enough of their antipathy to file suit against the insurance company for not paying out on some of the things that had been stolen.

As we passed through the UN's neighborhood, where all the apartments have names like "The Delegate" or "The Envoy," Dolores was anything but diplomatic. She finally mentioned Dick's name only to attach blame to it, as if the disappearance of so much merchandise—some of the jade, some of the Imari porcelain, the bronze Louis XVI clock—were his fault. How could he have let the killers take it? "Who knows what kind of people were going in and out of there?" she asked. "You saw how he was living." Actually, except for the sex stuff in the closet—and Steven's wholesome, incongruent presence—I hadn't seen much. And I didn't want us to pursue the subject of Dick's acquaintances, which would probably lead to discussion of Jimmy Ingrassia.

"Oh, Jesus!" she suddenly crowed. "Home of the Funny Girl!" We were passing Mimi's, an Italian place that has been on the corner of Second and Fifty-Second for as long as anyone can remember. It was one of the spots where Streisand got her start. "Merman called her 'the new belter,'" said Dolores. "Baloney! You can't belt through your nose." She did a nasal send-up of a few bars from "Happy Days Are Here Again."

Which brought us to Second and Fifty-Third, where the boy hustlers, maybe a half dozen at the four corners of the intersection, stood with their summer shirts open to the navel. Dolores actually pulled her skirts close, as if preparing to ford a mud puddle. That was when I heard a youthful, Spanish-accented voice say: "Hey, Daddy, you never called." I looked to my right and saw Devin Arroyo.

For the past two months I'd looked at the paper with his phone number at least two dozen times but could never get past my certainty that using it would provoke trouble from both Detective Volker and my own psychology. I was now doubly relieved I'd done nothing; Devin had evidently returned to his previous job.

Reflexively polite, I stopped and said, "I'm sorry."

Dolores stopped, too. She looked at me and exploded: "Are you *kidding*?"

"It's not what you think," I said. Or not exactly.

In high dudgeon and with a grand display of dignity, she hailed a cab. And before closing its door, she called out: "Ring me sometime when you can come up with a better line than that!"

Devin exhibited no interest in who she might be. "Buy me supper, Matthew. My shift is just about over."

Well, I thought, *that* dispels all doubt about his current occupation.

But since I hadn't eaten . . .

The two of us went over to the Mayfair, on First, a kind of uptown, sit-down Julius' where a quiet older gay clientele drink old-fashioneds in dark wooden booths. I ordered a glass of red wine, and realized I was less shaken than I might have been: the retro glamour of Dolores had begun to fade for me. I was craving the warmth of someone more like Carole Cook.

Devin ordered a cheeseburger and a glass of orange juice, and I laughed at the combination: "That's disgusting."

"You mean it's charming."

We clinked glasses.

"I haven't told Dolores, the woman I was with, anything about Jimmy. So would you trust me with some more information?" I wanted to know, for example, if Jimmy was under arrest. But I was asking mostly to find out whether Devin still had his day job at the 19th Precinct.

"There's nothing new. They still can't find them."

"Who's 'them'?"

" 'Them' is Jimmy's buddies. Your two friends were killed by three men."

"And one of them is Dante?" *Mr. Kallman, this here's Dante.*

Devin ate his cheeseburger with a combination of natural delicacy and childish enthusiasm. As he munched, his green eyes looked like two pretty moons above the toasted brown roll.

"Yes, *papi*. Dante is one of them. You know, *papi* sounds like 'daddy,' but it doesn't really mean that. Can I call you 'daddy'?"

"No." I almost said "Not yet."

He just laughed.

"Did they ever lock Jimmy up? And how exactly did they find him?"

"They found Jimmy thanks to me. Little Miss Nancy Drew. I didn't exactly give you the whole story last time. Back in March they were turning up info that your friend Dick used to go to a lot of trade bars and maybe even to the boys on the corner, the kind who just freaked out your old-lady friend. So Detective V got the idea of putting an undercover cop out there to see what he could find out. The one they chose for the job was a little old and beefy, and Detective V saw me rolling my eyes. 'You got another idea?' he asked. 'Yeah,' I told him. 'Me.'"

"And he agreed to that?"

"He likes unusual methods."

I thought back to the audio lineup.

And then I pressed a little: "You must have told him you were, uh, acquainted with the area."

"I told him I looked the part. And I sort of *suggested* some past experience on the corner. He got the drift. I knew I would find out *something*, Daddy. The boys on the corner have nothing to do but yak while they're waiting around. So I kept listening. And I kept hearing 'Jimmy this' and 'Jimmy that' and 'Anybody hear anything from Jimmy?' There was mention of some serious shit that had gone down with a rich guy in a big town house. So I soon knew that a Jimmy was involved in your friend's murder. I even thought I might know the Jimmy they were talking about—a guy I'd met on the corner or over at the Ice Palace."

I'd never been in it, but I knew the dance club, a place in the West Fifties, that he was talking about.

"One night one of the boys says to another"—he began doing a Dominican accent—'You think maybe Andy knows where he is?' So I go back to Volker and ask: 'Ever interview anyone named Andy?' And bingo—turns out that your pal Dickie did lots of business—the antiques stuff—with an Andy Vitale up in Westchester. Andy had been one of the first people Volker talked to."

"So they went to see Andy to ask him about Jimmy?"

"No, first they went to the Westchester DA's office and the PD up where Andy lives. Detective V is smart: he asks both if they've got any investigations going into this local resident named Andy Vitale. I don't want to disillusion you about your pal Dickie, but if Andy did business with him, it's a good bet Dickie was crooked, too."

"Just go on with the story."

"Turns out that Andy sells drugs, lots of them. They're running a probe up there but don't yet have enough to move in. Detective V tells them he may have bigger fish to fry with Andy—like a murder. So he asks if they'll back off while he tries to get further with what he's looking into."

"'Unusual,'" I said, referencing Volker's methods once more.

"Time-honored. He goes to Andy and says, 'You're going to tell me everything you know about Jimmy or else I'm going to be up your ass every day for the rest of your life.'" Devin finished his cheeseburger and got to the crux of the story. "Detective V is not un-hot, but Andy decided to avoid that particular offer and tell him everything about this 'roommate'—Jimmy— that he's been fucking since the kid was fifteen. He gave the cops Jimmy like he might have given them a Christmas turkey or an envelope back in the day. The next thing you know, Andy was on his way down to Florida to fetch him."

"At which point Dante and the other one bolted."

"You're good at this, *papi*-daddy!"

All those cop shows I watch. "Tell me, Devin, what would Detective Volker do if he knew you were telling me all this?"

"Beat me with a nightstick."

"Is that what you're hoping for?"

"Would I be here if it was? You're like a little professor. That's the type I like. I like *sweet*."

"So you're the one who cracked the case, Devin." I tried to make this sound grandiose, a joke, but I was kind of marveling, really.

"I wouldn't say that."

With my heart in my mouth, I asked: "But what were you on the corner for *tonight*? Moonlighting at your old job?"

"Continuing with my new one. Going the extra mile for the NYPD." He made a snappy salute. "I'm out there trying to hear something about Dante and Paul—that's the name of the third guy, which they got from Jimmy. Maybe I can pick up something even Jimmy and Andy don't know, like where the fuck Paul and Dante have gone."

Relief flooded me! He was on the corner picking up intel, not tricks.

"Jimmy, by the way, is still not locked up. But they don't let him anywhere near the corner."

I was so happy that I playfully asked: "What would Detective Volker do to *me*, if I told all this to my friend Dolores and he found out about it?"

"Beat you with a nightstick. That what *you're* looking for?"

"Would I be sitting here watching you eat a cheeseburger if it were?"

He licked his fingertip and made an imaginary chalk mark on the air. It was unclear which one of us had won the point.

"I may be in trouble with Volker in any case," I told him.

"How so?"

"I'd have to show you something at my place in order to explain."

"I thought you'd never ask. Where is it?"

"Manhattan Plaza. Forty-Third and Ninth."

He groaned. "Does the Eastern Shuttle fly there?"

"We can take a taxi."

With a big smile he took a last, loud suck on his straw.

He sat too close to me in the back of the cab. He didn't care, and neither did the driver, whose past fares originating from the Mayfair had no doubt included odder couples than me and Devin. Or so I made myself think, to encourage myself.

Inside the apartment he looked at my framed celebrity

photos—not as impressive as Arnold Weissberger's, true, but Devin seemed enchanted by one of me and Carol Burnett from her long-ago *Once Upon a Mattress* days. When he asked about the picture on my night table, and I told him it was my daughter, he said, with a pleasure that was gentle and unaffected, "Pretty girl."

I decided to plunge in. "I'm probably not supposed to have this," I told him, as I pulled out Dick's huge scrapbook from under the bed. I hoisted it onto the comforter and opened to the Lucy section, which I'd lately been poring over. Devin studied pictures of Dick with Carole Cook, Dick with Bob Osborne, and especially, of course, Dick with Lucy.

"How'd you get hold of this? You got some 'splainin' to do, Daddy."

"Please call me Matt," I said.

"Whatever," he responded, before throwing me onto the vacant portion of the comforter and kissing me.

CHAPTER 11

DECEMBER 25, 1959

TELEVISION

Channel 4 ...WNBC-TV | Channel 7 ...WABC-TV
Channel 2 ...WCBS-TV | Channel 9 ....WOR-TV
Channel 5 ...WNEW-TV | Channel 11 ......WPIX
Channel 13..........WNTA-TV

FRIDAY, DECEMBER 25, 1959

7-9 A. M.—Today: Christmas program including pickups of celebration in Boston—(4).

10-11—Festival of Lessons and Carols, from the Protestant Episcopal National Cathedral, Washington—(4).

10-11:30—Christmas Cartoon Party: With Sonny Fox—(5).

10 A. M.-1 P. M.—Christmas Party: With Officer Joe, Bozo, Capt. Allen Swift and Jack McCarthy—(11).

12:30-2:30—Christmas Cartoon Party: With Fred Scott and Tim Gregory—(5).

12:30-1—Film Play: "The Great Gift," about an orphaned little girl—(13).

2:30-3:30—Cartoon: "The Amazing Gift," about a young boy who saves a kingdom—(9).

4-6—Teen-Age Christmas Party: With Richard Hayes—(5).

7:30-8:30—Walt Disney Presents: Repeat of feature cartoon, "Alice in Wonderland"—(7).

8-10—Play of the Week: Jean Anouilh's farce, "Thieves' Carnival," plots and counterplots at carnival time in Vichy. With Frances Sternhagen, Larry Blyden, Tom Bosley, Kurt Kasznar, Cathleen Nesbitt, Robert Morse and Pat Stanley (Repeated at 10:30 P. M. tomorrow and 3 P. M. Sunday)—(13).

8:30-9:30—Night of Christmas: Musical and comedy variety with Eddie Albert, host, and Katharyn Grayson, Jonathan Winters, Jeannie Carson, Dena Jones, vocalist, and the Norman Luboff Choir (Color)—(4).

9-10—Desilu Playhouse: Variety, with Lucille Ball, Desi Arnaz, William Frawley, Vivian Vance, Danny Thomas, Spring Byington, Hedda Hopper, Lassie, and others—(2).

9-10—77 Sunset Strip: "The Juke Box Caper," with Roger Smith—(7).

9:30-10—M Squad: "The Ivy League Bank Robbers," with Lee Marvin—(4).

10-10:30—Twilight Zone: Ernest Truex, Steve Cochran in "What You Need," fantasy about a kind old man who can give people exactly what they will need—(2).

10-10:30—Sports Highlights of 1959—(4).

10:30-11—Person to Person: In Paris, Charles Collingwood interviews Jean Pierre Aumont, actor, and his wife, Marisa Pavan, actress; Claude Terrail, French restaurateur—(2).

10:30-11—Mormon Tabernacle Choir, from Salt Lake City (Tape)—(4).

10:30-11—Jack Paar Show: (Repeat of Nov. 11 show, second of the telecasts from Nassau, the Bahamas. With Peggy Cass, Hermione Gingold, Phyllis Diller, Jonathan Winters and others—(4).

11:20-11:35—Cardinal Spellman's Christmas message—(11).

Feature Films

Noon-1:30—Movie Time: "The Emperor's Nightingale" (1951), cartoon version of the Hans Christian Andersen fairy tale—(9).

3-3:30—Quality Theatre: "The Browning Version" (1951), adaptation of the Terence Rattigan play, with Michael Redgrave as an embittered schoolmaster (Repeated at midnight)—(13).

2:30-4—Film: "A Christmas Carol," British version of the Dickens classic, with Alastair Sim, Jack Warner. (5).

5-7—Early Show: "Going My Way" (1944), with Bing Crosby as a young priest, Barry Fitzgerald and Rise Stevens—(2).

5-6:30—Movie Four: "Come Next Spring" (1955), story of a reformed alcoholic, with Ann Sheridan, Steve Cochran (Color)—(4).

6:30-7—Movie of the Week: About the social ostracism of a "Boy With Green Hair" (1948), with Pat O'Brien, Dean Stockwell (Repeated through Monday)—(9).

7:30-9—Million Dollar Movie: "The Halfbreed" (1951), Western, with Robert Young (Repeated at 10:30 and through Sunday)—(9).

11-12:30—Five Star Movie: "Adam Had Four Sons" (1941), about the devotion of a governess to her wards and employer. Ingrid Bergman, Warner Baxter—(5).

11:15-1:15—Late Show: "The Texas Rangers" (1936), with Fred MacMurray, Jack Oakie and Jean Parker—(2).

11:35—All Star Movie: "Western Union" (1941), period adventure, with Robert Young, Randolph Scott—(11).

12-1:30—Mystery Film: "A Strange Affair," with Allan Joslyn, Evelyn Keyes—(9).

12-1:30—Quality Theatre: "The Browning Version" (See 2 P. M. highlight)—(13).

12:15—Night Show: "Princess Cinderella," about what happens after Cinderella marries the prince—(11).

12:30—Five Star Finale: "Female" (1933), about a lady executive. Ruth Chatterton, George Brent—(5).

1:15-3—Late, Late Show: "Mad About Music" (1938), with Deanna Durbin, Herbert Marshall, Gail Patrick. An actress conceals the fact that she has a daughter—(2).

"It's *modern* colonial," said Lucille Ball, sounding more detached than house-proud as she characterized 1000 Roxbury Drive, her Beverly Hills home, for her three young guests. This was the first time they'd all been here together, and Lucy was talking as if she were one of the tour-bus operators who passed by several times each day. The guides had Christmas off, and she seemed to be subconsciously filling in for them.

Dick Kallman's questions showed him to be less interested in the house's architecture than in the neighboring residents: Jack Benny next door, Rosemary Clooney and Ira Gershwin down the street. It was almost nine p.m., but was there still a chance any of them might drop in? A little Christmas hello?

Lucy told him and Carole Cook and Bob Osborne to eat up the tiny sandwiches she'd arranged atop a glass table here on "the lanai"—a term Carole had certainly never heard in Abilene or Waco. The spread of food sent Lucy's mind back to the early 1930s: "All this little finger food reminds me of what Hattie Carnegie used to set out for the ladies coming into her showroom." Way back then she'd picked up work in New York as a leggy model and would stuff as many of the minuscule sandwiches as she could into her pockets and purse. As if realizing all over again how far she'd come in life, Lucy now looked out into the backyard and said, to no one in particular, "Whatever happens, I'm not going to leave here."

The remark surprised her young guests, who took it as an admission that things with Desi might really be over.

"I saw this house five years ago, thought it was perfect and just knocked on the door to ask the owner if she'd be interested in selling. Her name, if you can believe it, was Mrs. Bang."

Having imparted this cherished family anecdote, Lucy seemed to become embarrassed by her own wistfulness. "It's been quite a week," she said, getting up to clear a few things from the table; her tone indicated there would be no discussion of what had made it so. While she was in the kitchen, the "kids" didn't dare whisper about the past several days' events.

On Tuesday Mike Connolly had run an item in his *Hollywood Reporter* column: "Lucille Ball's black-and-bruised eye, cheek, and elbow did NOT come from anything as unexciting as bumping into a glass doorknob imported from Venice by Desi. . . ." The Venice reference derived from a quick, well-publicized trip to Italy that the Arnaz family had made a couple of weeks back. The implication of a beating had thrown Lucy and Desi into a brief, renewed solidarity, and just yesterday they'd gotten a retraction out of Connolly. Even so, Desi was spending Christmas Day by himself in Palm Springs and Lucy was still wearing heavy makeup around the eye. Tomorrow morning, along with Lucie and Desi Jr., she'd head off to Sun Valley. There was no holiday bustle in the house: Bessie had the day off, and the children were out with their friends.

At 8:55, Lucy moved her guests into the enormous living room. She noticed Bob Osborne sitting down next to Carole instead of Dick; so maybe *that* was already over, she thought.

"God, I'm excited!" cried Kallman, who began singing the first lines of "'S Wonderful." Lucy cracked a sentimental smile that didn't hold. Her nerves were taking over. But Dick persisted in trying to keep things aloft: "I had a Christmas telegram from Soph—Sophie Tucker." He looked straight at Lucy. "She said I'm in the hands of the very best."

Even for Dick, this was laying it on pretty thick. Carole whispered to Bob: "Is it hot in here, or is it me?" Both of them could nonetheless see the weakened Lucy trying to take Dick's fib to heart. "Really?" she asked. "You bet," Dick answered.

"Lucy," asked Bob, "why so jumpy?" After all, she'd been there for the editing of the special they were about to watch. She'd already seen the finished product.

"It was the same with *Lucy*," the star explained. "I never knew if an episode was any good until I watched it air. *Then* I could tell. The invisible fifty million people watching always felt realer to me than the executives who'd been in the screening room." Now that she was the executive, with no one, not even Desi, to tell her anything, she was more dependent than ever on those mass vibrations from the unseen audience.

She turned on the television. CBS was airing the last few minutes of a western, *Hotel de Paree*—fortunately not from Desilu—that was headed down the ratings tubes.

Kallman, appraising the tail end of the show, remarked admiringly: "God, how would the TV business even exist if Desi hadn't invented the three-camera technique?"

"Desi didn't invent it," Lucy replied evenly. "He improved it a little." It was unclear whether her response represented further hardening toward her husband or a new resistance to Dick's compulsive brownnosing. The first time he met Desi he'd denounced Castro to him as if they were both Cuban refugees.

Desi's image now shouted, from the television: "Merry Christmas, everybody! *Feliz Navidad*!" The special had begun, showing what was supposed to be the workshop's holiday party. Carole was at the punchbowl in her Whistler's Mother blouse, and Lucy was asking Janice Carroll to put up some Christmas lights. "She's butch enough for the job," Dick whispered to himself.

The scene moved from the party to the troupe's opening night at the playhouse, where their mentor, acting more like Lucy Ricardo than Lucille Ball, caused one comical crisis after another between the sketches and musical numbers. A bunch of established Desilu stars pitched in with cameos, from Ann Sothern taking tickets to Danny Thomas working a searchlight outside the theater. "Oh, Lucy!" cried Vivian Vance. "These kids are amazing!"

The opening number had the young ensemble ingratiating themselves with future employers and audiences: "'If you're the local gentry or the hoi polloi,'" sang out Kallman, "'we wanna be by you!'" His prediction last month—that he and Carole would steal the show—quickly came true. In "Hip to the Blues," the two of them, done up as beatniks, sang a duet celebrating the miseries of a misbegotten romance. A strangely sadistic undercurrent was played for laughs, with Dick crushing Carole's hand and Carole twisting his ear. These touches had been Kallman's idea, and the laugh track indicated that the audience was meant to appreciate them as being more klutzy than mean. Either way, they arrested the attention, and there was no doubting Dick's or Carole's skill.

But the rest of the hour felt listless and nostalgic, like some old show at The Balsams twenty years ago: a singing cowboy; tap dancing; ballad after ballad. Even "Summertime Is Summertime" had survived the weeks of editing and the gripes of every cast member except Dick. The production, which ended with the cast singing a Christmas song for their booster Hedda Hopper, could almost have been an hour of *Lawrence Welk*.

When it ended at last, a grim Lucy rose from the couch and declared: "I'm afraid Hedda's going to eat all of her hats."

"It was *great*!" Kallman protested. "It's going to murder *Sunset Strip* in the ratings. Wait and see."

Carole and Bob remained silent. And from this point on so did Lucy, lost in thought while staring at the now-turned-off TV.

"*Loo*-sie!" said Dick cajolingly, in Desi's voice.

He realized instantly that this attempt to cheer her up had been stupid and presumptuous. He saw a look of doubt cross her face, as if she were on the verge of realizing she'd been conned by him this whole time, had failed to see that his supposed musical expertise was weirdly passé. Kallman's own expression turned worried, almost panicky.

"I'm going to bed," said Lucy. "Take the rest of the food home with you."

The three protégés bade her timid good nights and waited until she was out of earshot to start talking about what lay ahead for them. Carole thought she might be getting a bit part in *Dobie Gillis*, and Bob had a walk-on in *Psycho*, which would finish filming after New Year's. He told the others, with a laugh, that his character's name was "Man" and that he didn't expect a credit. All that Dick had booked was a minute or two as the bellboy in a planned *Lucy-Desi Comedy Hour* episode with Ernie Kovacs, and given how things now were with Desi, who knew if it would even be shot? "I still think it could lead to a series for me," he insisted.

Nobody was in a mood to keep talking about all this. Even Kallman, chastened by his mistake with Lucy, started to sound like a 45 running at 33⅓. Carole, hoping to lighten things, finally said: "I can tell you a piece of truly good news. My pal Kenny Nelson has a shot at a little thing called *The Fantasticks* that's going to open Off Broadway this spring. He tells me the songs are incredible. And they are. He sang one of them to me over the phone." Kenny had auditioned for the show in some little apartment in the West Seventies and could be making forty-five dollars a week. "I'm thrilled for him. If it runs for three months, he says he'll be happy. He hasn't had anything for ages except bits in revues. He's about to turn thirty, but he still looks young enough to play the boy in this show."

"I hate to tell you," said Dick, with a mean edge to his voice, "but you were all wrong about the 'Volga Boatman's Song.'"

"What?" It took Carole a moment to understand he was talking about a story she'd told months ago at the House of Murphy.

"You and I did *not* first meet at that party," Kallman corrected her. "We met when you came backstage during a *Seven-*

teen rehearsal to meet your precious friend Kenny. What's so great about him? I have a better voice than he does."

"You probably do," said Carole, cautiously, startled by the vehemence, though she knew that Dick Kallman still carried an angry torch for Kenny.

Osborne said what he wouldn't have even a few weeks ago: "But Ken may stay in the business longer than you will. You know, Janet Leigh isn't the most talented actress in town, but she's good enough, and she's nice to people, so they'll want to keep working with her."

"Tell that to Laurence Olivier!" shouted Dick. "Tell it to Judy Garland!"

Even Kallman knew the remark sounded ridiculous, with its suggestion that he might rise to a stratum none of the others was even dreaming about. He stormed out of the house, hopped into his '54 Bel Air, and headed for home—which was now his parents' apartment instead of the one he'd been sharing with Osborne.

Once there, he got on the phone: "Why did you retract it?" he asked Mike Connolly. He had *seen* Lucy's shiner on Monday morning when he dropped over with holiday presents for Lucie and Desi Jr. And she'd *seen* him see it.

"Merry Christmas to you, too," said Connolly.

"It was *true*! You can *still* see the bruise beneath the makeup."

"Relax. I *had* to retract it. They told me that Desi himself, or some goon he'd dispatched, was on his way over to break down my office door."

"You caved!"

"Retraction doesn't mean a damned thing. Don't you know that? People never unbelieve something bad. When Lucy and Desi split up for good, I'll remind everybody that I was right all along."

"I was terrified the whole time I was over there tonight! She *knows* I was your source. She was looking at me funny, I swear."

"You can relax about that, too. I told Desi, when I apologized, that I got the story from some script girl at the studio. So you're in the clear. The script girl's already been fired, and Desi's told that to Lucy. Where are you calling from, Kallman?"

"My parents' apartment."

"I hope they've given you a long-term lease. I watched the show. You're not going to be moving anywhere plush anytime soon. Hopper isn't the greatest predictor of things." Connolly laughed at his rival. The two columnists had forever been lobbing insults, and on one occasion drinks, in each other's direction.

"I've got a couple of things on the horizon," Kallman insisted.

"You've got nothing on the horizon."

Kallman audibly hemmed and hawed.

"And why do you care that I retracted that item? We were square once you gave it to me. You know why you're bothered? Because you were proud of getting it. You *like* fucking people over, even the Queen of Comedy. And you like putting yourself in danger."

"Why would I like doing that?"

"Think about it," said Connolly, before hanging up.

CHAPTER 12

JULY 2, 1980

"Going undercover" became our joke term for having sex. Devin was no longer doing much spying at the corner of Second and Fifty-Third, since it now appeared that nothing further was likely to be gleaned there as to the whereabouts of Dante Forti and Paul Boccara—the full names of Jimmy's accomplices, according to Jimmy himself. Besides, the hot weather disinclined Devin to keep volunteering his services for Detective Volker's rule-bending operation. So he was back to his clerical duties at the 19th Precinct's headquarters, which at least had some balky window air conditioners. Two days a week he was allowed to leave early for some late-afternoon classes at a branch of CUNY, and on those nights he stayed with me instead of his three roommates up in Washington Heights.

He looked beautiful this morning, with only a portion of his slender, naked torso covered by section A of *The New York Times*. The paper had a story about Carter signing a bill for the construction of a memorial to the Vietnam veterans. The item prompted a few seconds of bitter murmuring from Devin about a nasty older half-brother who'd been killed in a helicopter in Da Nang. His spirits lifted when he changed his newsprint fig leaf to the arts section. "You're going to take me to this, right?" He showed me Janet Maslin's review of *Airplane!*, which did sound pretty hilarious.

"I guess I am," I replied.

He kissed my neck, got up from the bed, and threw on his clothes as fast as he'd thrown them off last night. A minute later he was off to another day at the 19th, leaving me to miss his silly jokes, his smarts, and the sweet smell of his skin.

I couldn't tell you which one of us was taking care of the other. I certainly wasn't his daddy in any financial sense; he had a clear independent streak and a sort of—I don't know—quiet self-respect. It was hard for me to believe that his early "experience" on the corner, what supposedly qualified him for Detective Volker's assignment, had ever involved more than a little thrill-seeking experimentation. Maybe I just felt better thinking that. He did, however, for certain, like "sweet," as he'd described his type to me at the Mayfair. And he'd made plain, the first night he was here, that *he* was to be the one gently, and always, on top.

Things had already lasted longer than I expected them to, which is to say longer than they usually did. Anxiety about the odds kept me jittery all morning. I had the day off, but I briskly ran a laundry and straightened up the apartment until it was time to head off to an early lunch with Carole Cook, at Café Un Deux Trois, before finally seeing her show.

The restaurant was crowded with busfuls of suburban matinee ladies and a sprinkling of desk-weary drones from *The New York Times* and McGraw-Hill. Carole's big eyes struck me the second she came in the door, but once at our table she made wry jokes about never being recognized. "On the plus side, however, I *am* at last playing Blanche." She took a beat. "Even if it's Blanche *Dailey*"—her role in *Romantic Comedy.* "It may not be the female lead, but then again I don't have to kiss Woody Allen when the curtain falls." Mia Farrow, who *was* the lead, had taken up with the director several months before, and the two of them now apparently lived, in unlikely bliss, on opposite sides of Central Park.

I wanted to tell Carole about Devin, knowing she wouldn't

react like Dolores, but along with my pride and excitement over him, there was also some guilt (perpetual with me) and embarrassment (the age gap alone). So I avoided the subject, realizing there wasn't much difference between my current silence and the way I would have acted thirty years ago. And this thought of "thirty years ago" made me think of *Seventeen*, particularly the "Summertime Is Summertime" number, which had resurfaced unexpectedly in the Lucy portion of Dick's scrapbook.

"Oh, God, what corn!" said Carole, when I brought it up. "He actually did tell Lucy that would be a good idea." After a kind of faraway, reflective pause, she added, "You know, that's when I met both of them."

"Both?" I asked, knowing she hadn't met Dick and Lucy at the same time.

"Dick and Kenny. During *Seventeen*. I don't remember meeting Dick backstage, though he later told me I did, and I guess I should take his word for it, even if taking his word for anything was always a ludicrous thing to do. Anyway, it would have been for just a minute or two."

"By 'Kenny,' you mean Kenneth Nelson?"

"Yes, a dear friend, never far from my mind, although he's packed up and gone to live in England, where there's more work, or at least more of the kind he likes to do. I went to Baylor, and so did Kenny, *much* after I did," she explained, her voice swooping down into that Tallulah-like rumble of self-mockery I remembered from Lucie Arnaz's dressing room. "He lasted one year. This was maybe 1948. And while he was there some old theater professor of mine invited me back to talk to a class. As if I were an old pro. As if I'd gotten *anywhere* by that point! But that's how Kenny and I met and became lifelong pals."

"Maybe you also met *me* backstage, too. At *Seventeen*. I was the show's pianist."

"You're kidding!" she cried, as loudly as she might have in a *Lucy* episode.

Even if everybody in this business eventually works with everybody else, it did honestly feel spooky that I was now wrapped in this double coincidence: Carole and Dick; Carole and Ken Nelson.

She seemed to feel the same little frisson, the oddness of all these mutual connections to an eventual murder. "Let me tell you what Janice Carroll said to Bob Osborne when he called her up a couple of months ago and asked, 'Can you believe it about Dick?' Janice replied, 'Of course I can. Karmic payback.'"

I must have winced a little, but Carole added: "I keep up with pretty much everybody who was in that workshop. You know what Howie Storm said when *he* found out about Dick?"

"No."

"One word. 'Good.'"

"Does Ken Nelson know about the murder?" I asked.

"I wrote to him, but the next little aerogram he sent from England said nothing. Which didn't surprise me. Kenny boxes things away."

It was unclear whether that meant the murder or Dick himself. As we ate, Carole, the opposite of Dolores, talked mostly of the delights her career had brought: playing Dolly Levi in Australia; sliding down a firepole in a *Lucy Show* skit. I was the one who suggested a single disappointing might-have-been, saying that I could so imagine a role for her in *Sugar Babies*, which it looked as if Mickey Rooney and Ann Miller would keep running forever.

"Oh, Matty, there wouldn't be room for me and Annie's hair. That's not a wig; that's topiary."

We headed to the theater through a light, humid shower. "Back in April," I reminded her, "you said that Dick had recommended you for the Lucy troupe. Why did he do that? I mean, aside from your talent. It isn't exactly the kind of thing he normally did."

"Oh, darling, I think he did it to stay connected—if only by a thread—to Kenny."

CHAPTER 13

APRIL 23, 1961

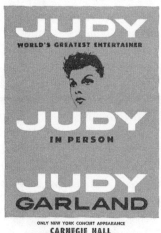

"Does Kate know what she's missing?" Betty Bacall asked Spencer Tracy.

"Not her cup of tea," Tracy replied, his smile both apologetic and proud.

"She's out of her mind—this is *fabulous*!"

"She doesn't like 'spillage,'" countered Tracy, knowing Bacall would recognize Katharine Hepburn's term for any excessive display of feelings.

Everyone stood, wrung out, during this brief intermission at Carnegie Hall, either marveling over what they'd been witnessing or, in a few cases, trying to find some conversational subject that was less oxygenated, less overwrought. It was almost too much. Several seats from Tracy and Bacall, Myrna Loy complained to

Henry Fonda, an equally ardent Democrat, that it now looked as if Jack Kennedy "was counting on *Ike* to save him!" The former president had visited the still-brand-new one at Camp David yesterday, less than a week after an invasion of Cuba by a group of US-sponsored exiles had blown up in everyone's face. Fonda grimaced, nobly.

But everyone within his and Loy's vicinity was speaking of triumph—Judy Garland's, which was unfolding on a scale past anyone's imagining, beyond even the Lazarus-like astonishments Judy had previously provided. Two young agents had just now brought her back, mostly sober and fifty pounds lighter, from the lowest point she'd ever been at. The scalpers on Fifty-Seventh Street who'd gotten five hundred dollars before the show were now offering a thousand to the handful of patrons willing to pass up the spectacle's last half hour by selling their ticket stubs. Everybody inside felt somehow not just lucky but *important* to be here, even those who could only pretend that they'd also been invited to the after-party down at Lüchow's.

Dick Kallman had managed to get a ticket from Phyllis Rab, now his ex-sister-in-law—in lieu, it seemed, of any tips about casting directors to see on his latest round of auditions in New York. Five days from now he'd be back with his parents in LA, lacking even the subterranean professional support of Mike Connolly, who seemed to have gotten leery of him ever since he volunteered that item about Lucy and Desi without asking for anything in return. As if that made him any odder than Mike!—a Catholic with a boner for Nixon who these days used up half his column inches going after Peter Lawford, Kennedy's brother-in-law.

The first half of this convulsive concert had left Dick unmoved, except when Garland sang "The Man That Got Away" and he'd thought—so ludicrously it made him angry—of *him*, as if Kenny would ever grow from boy to "man" in his memory. At least he didn't have to worry about running into Nelson here: *The Fantasticks*, his little show with unexpected legs down in the Village, had Sunday-night performances, and Kenny would never fake a sore throat for even a deal this big.

Garland would probably sing "Come Rain or Come Shine," which Dick used to do in his own club act, and he now experienced a sudden sick apprehension that after it she would segue into "Soon It's Gonna Rain," one of the *Fantasticks* songs that everyone was now doing on TV. For all he knew Kenny himself was singing it at this moment on the little Sullivan Street Playhouse stage. But soon enough he relaxed in the knowledge that Judy wasn't going to do anything new tonight, because that was the last thing anyone wanted.

He really needed to stand. To be the only one sitting, and by himself, made him appear alone and loserish. So he rose and looked around and immediately saw Comden and Green, whom he waved at as if they knew one another. Beyond them, in the front row, he could see Henry Willson and his money horse, Rock Hudson, a pal of Judy's. The dream idol was next to the singer's younger children, Joey and Lorna. According to a couple of know-it-all fans Kallman had overheard in his own row, Rock had been deputized to hoist the kids up onstage as soon as their mother finished her last sensational encore tonight.

There was no chance to get anywhere close to all of them. Turning in frustration, he could see, a half dozen rows back, the waving, stooped form of Matt Liannetto, who had spotted *him* and was threading his way through the nearest choked aisle. Liannetto was still so skinny that he quickly accomplished the maneuver and arrived at Kallman's row, where he excitedly explained how he'd gotten his ticket from the conductor, with whom he'd once worked. Kallman pretended to listen. The two of them had not seen each other in two years, and if Liannetto asked what the Lucy workshop had been like, Kallman was prepared to change the subject.

Matt was reaching for his wallet, planning to extract a snapshot of his brand-new baby daughter, Laurie, the smash-hit feature of his otherwise inadvisable marriage, but he halted himself before his hand even got to his pocket. He didn't want to trigger a mockingly raised eyebrow from Dick—assuming the news would excite any interest at all.

"I'm so sorry about Cuba," he offered instead. "I know that all must feel personal to you, given your dad's history there." Castro had just declared that the captured Bay-of-Pigs rebels would be dispatched without mercy.

Dick responded with a subdued thanks-for-asking smile. "It's another setback, sure, but no more than that," he said, the smile broadening, as if now to proclaim that in another month or two Alvan Kallman would be back in Havana and Castro thrown in jail.

"Come with me," he said, pushing Matt back into the aisle, turning him into a kind of scrawny tugboat that might get him toward that front row. After a minute of heavy jostling they had made it as far as they could: not exactly all the way but, if one spoke at the top of one's lungs, within earshot of Henry Willson and Rock Hudson.

"It's not a long scene, but it's *absolutely* pivotal to the movie!" Kallman heard himself saying at the top of his lungs. The volume turned a few heads, including Willson's, so he maintained the decibel level for several sentences of exposition about the film he'd done (one afternoon's shooting) in California last September—a remake of *Back Street* with Susan Hayward. "It'll blow you away!" The movie was a low-IQ confection of Jean Louis gowns and groaningly high-minded dialogue, but it wouldn't be released for another six months, and nobody listening to his Klaxon voice had to know the truth of its awfulness now.

He got no more than a nod from Willson; certainly no introduction to Rock. And the snatches of the two men's own normally voiced conversation that he was able to pick up didn't lift his spirits. He gathered that Garland had just filmed some great bit in *Judgment at Nuremberg*, all part of her young agents' comeback plan. Willson assured Rock that Judy could expect a Supporting Actress nod.

"I thought I'd split my gloves applauding!" cawed Hedda Hopper, suddenly coming through like some great flapping ostrich. Enjoying her own appraisal of the evening so far, she declared: "I think I'll use that in my column! And that Mr. Kenneth wig she's wearing? Better than any hat I've got at home!"

"I can't stand that cunt," Kallman told Matt, only a trifle less audibly. It wasn't just the phony optimism Hopper had created about the workshop; it was also the way she'd maneuvered John Gavin, over Gregory Peck, into the male lead for *Back Street*, making the picture even worse.

Three loud chimes and a flash of the house lights signaled people to take their seats, and in the scramble that followed Kallman managed to avoid telling Matt where he could be reached while he was in New York. As the orchestra vamped toward Garland's re-entry, he sat in the dark thinking of the show he wanted for himself more than any other, the crazily named *How to Succeed in Business Without Really Trying*, which would start rehearsals in a couple of months. But Abe Burrows wouldn't hear of anyone for it but Bobby Morse, that rubber-faced dwarf to whom Kallman had lost *Take Me Along* a couple of years ago.

He was twenty-seven years old, aware that he hadn't really started yet, but feeling shamefully in need of his *own* comeback, as if those supporting roles in *Seventeen* and *The Fifth Season* were glory days to which he sought to return. He'd heard that a musical about Sophie Tucker was in the works; at the rate he was going, he'd count himself lucky to get cast as a waiter in a nightclub scene.

As Garland got going, he paid scant attention to the supposed miracle that was still unfolding in front of everyone. He continued his gloomy calculations even during "Over the Rainbow," his pessimism now as strident as the confidence he'd projected for so long. Only when Judy was getting toward the end, steamrolling into "Swanee"—without a top hat or cane tonight—did he snap out of his depressed reverie; still not to focus on Garland, but on a terrified memory of his first summer at The Balsams, when his mother had forced him into somebody's act. Zara had plunked a tiny top hat onto his head after slapping his face. She made it clear that reluctance wasn't a choice he had; this was for the good of the hotel. He was to go out there and sing, and the louder he did, she hastily assured him, the more the audience would pretend to love him.

Garland's voice was stronger than a siren, and for just a second he now permitted himself to find some encouraging career message in her delivery. There *was* still an audience for the old Jolson razzmatazz, whatever people said! But then he turned to look over his shoulder—one old queen was even holding up a framed painting of Judy, as if this were Lourdes or Fatima—and he realized that the material was irrelevant to what was going on. The song was nothing and the singer was everything. Garland's aching, plangent need still came through the blare; you thought she'd never make the high, solitary final note—"shore!"—unless you *helped* her make it, let her feel that you were there for her.

Every other seat seemed filled by the kind of old homo he'd seen sneaking into every Third Avenue bar since before the El came down. Two of them here had tears running down their faces, and he bet if he looked farther back he'd see Liannetto's face glistening, too. As everybody and his uncle knew, whatever was broken in these guys was reaching toward and sparking whatever was broken in her. *He* would never connect like that with an audience; he had sensed it all along, and come to know it in some hard, real way during the last few stalled years. But at this minute he was finally sensing the exact, disabling reason why. It was because there was *nothing* broken in him, no ragged edge that could make the electrical connection. Or, more exactly: there had *been* something broken, but whatever it was had been soldered over, annealed in a way that left it unreaching and unreachable.

CHAPTER 14

SEPTEMBER 9, 1980

"So, *papi*, you ready for our little adventure?"

Devin and I were still in bed, and I was nervous about what he'd explained to me the night before—the task that Detective Volker wanted us to help him with.

I rubbed my eyes and said, "Okay, let me see if I've got it straight." We had shared a bottle and a half of wine in front of the TV before going to sleep.

"There is *nothing* straight about you or me or this whole situation. We may have had *Monday Night Football* on—on *mute*—but that didn't butch things up much."

Last night he'd given me an update on all he knew about the investigation, one that mixed what Volker had told him directly, what he'd picked up by typing reports, and what he'd just managed to overhear. He went through the case's dramatis personae for me one more time. Its mysterious star was the third guy, probably the actual killer, whom we'd begun calling This-Here's-Dante, like a character out of Damon Runyon, from the words he'd been asked to repeat at the audio lineup; the one sentence—"Mr. Kallman, this here's Dante"—that I'd heard from upstairs on the night of the killings.

"Jimmy met Paul Boccara on Fifty-Third Street," Devin's summary had gone. "He told him he had an idea to rob Kallman, and then they got This-Here's-Dante to go in on it with them. The theory is that This-Here's-Dante shot Dick and his sweetie while Douchebag Jimmy and Douchebag Paulie watched the little burglary they'd cooked up go off the fucking rails. Andy—that's Jimmy's daddy man—had nothing to do with it. In fact, the whole thing might have happened because of a fight Jimmy and Andy had a few days before, when they saw your buddy about some antiques business at the town house. Anyway, our three boys, the morning after the killings—just before they got their asses to Florida—went and fenced a bunch of the stuff they'd swiped from the apartment. Left the bodies behind, but not the merchandise!"

Our "adventure" today was supposed to take us to a place called Delectable Collectibles, at Fifth and Twenty-Seventh. It's a sort of pawnshop or consignment store or wholesaler for antiques and art and jewelry—I still don't really grasp how the business is supposed to run. Two guys at the place, an owner named Vestros and his assistant, named Colzer, had been arrested a couple of months back. The case was dismissed because of some screwup by the New York Housing Authority cops who, for one reason or another, made the arrests. Mug shots of the two guys had recently come Detective Volker's way, and he showed them to Jimmy Ingrassia, who responded that he couldn't recall the guys or that specific store or its location: he and Boccara and This-Here's-Dante had tried a number of different places with the stolen stuff the day after the murders.

"Is Jimmy playing dumb?" I now asked Devin.

"He *is* dumb. He thinks he *may* remember a lady who works at Delectable saying 'What beautiful plates' when they dumped some on the counter. And that she might have given him a cup of coffee. *That* seems to stick in his mind, which ain't exactly made of Velcro."

"But how did they know to go there, or to any other place, to fence the stuff?"

"He told Detective V that he and Boccara just ripped a page

out of Andy's address book, a list of the places Andy goes to sell stuff he's come by in ways that aren't legit—antiques without any—what's the word?"

"Provenance?"

"Such a smart *papi*! See why the 19th Precinct needs you?"

Detective Volker wanted to take Jimmy to Delectable Collectibles to see if, when put on the premises, he could ID anybody or anything. And Volker, applying one of his "unusual methods," wanted *me* to go in there, thinking I might spot some object I could recall seeing at the dinner party before the killings. Devin explained: "He told me, 'Get hold of the guy who ID'd Jimmy's voice. You've still got his number in the files?' I told him I thought I could find it." He now laughed and pinched my ass.

What's more, Volker wanted Dolores to be part of today's outing; maybe *she* could notice something that would further incriminate Jimmy and Paulie and Dante. In any case, everyone was supposed to meet outside the place at eleven o'clock.

"We should get moving," I told Devin. "I've got to vote first." It was primary day.

The two of us walked to the nearby ancient Holy Cross School, with its wine-red bricks and Roman arches and separate Girls and Boys entrances. The polling-place sign instructed voters to head through the old Girls door, but Devin pushed me toward the Boys, imitating Anita in *West Side Story:* " 'Stick to your own kind!' " I managed to find my way to the voting line.

The big contest was for the Democrats' Senate nomination. Voting for a former Miss America, Bess Myerson, could have been the gayest thing ever, but I had a soft spot for beautiful John Lindsay, who'd loved all things Broadway and was now trying for a political comeback. Not the greatest mayor, true, but as an old gay violinist argued to me when we both did *Mame* and Lindsay was running for re-election: "You'd rather look at Mario Procaccino for the next four years?"

Devin agreed. When I tried imparting some municipal history to him, he just tapped Lindsay's handsome photograph in my copy of *The New York Times* and said: "Keep it simple." So I did.

We were five minutes late reaching Delectable Collectibles. But once at the corner of Fifth and Twenty-Seventh I could see a third-floor window lettered with a sign for the business. I could also feel Dolores's starlike impatience as she drank coffee from a Greek-diner cup. "I could have gone to Altman's," she said, nodding to the department store several blocks up.

"I stopped to vote," I explained, while nervously eyeing Jimmy Ingrassia, who was wearing a baseball cap and who'd had his hair cut since I saw him at the station house.

Devin, whose presence further annoyed Dolores, pretended that he and I had come here independently: "I ran into him getting out of the subway," he lied to the detective.

"So what's *your* excuse for being late?" Volker wanted to know.

"My watch is running slow."

"Did you vote for Bess?" Dolores asked me.

"No."

"Good. She's as crazy as a shithouse rat." The proof of this that Dolores provided was some bizarre behavior she'd witnessed when the two of them were panelists on a quiz show in the 1950s.

"Okay," said Volker. "Let's get started."

Jimmy and I buzzed the metal front door and took the stairs to the third floor after somebody looked us over through a black-and-white security camera. A tall guy with a combover introduced himself as Mr. Vestros. "What can I do for you?" He didn't look at Jimmy with any particular recognition.

Jimmy himself stared at a woman tapping on an IBM Selectric—the lady who'd given him coffee in February? She looked up and offered a casual hello, but she, too, gave no indication of having seen him before.

Mr. Vestros put us in the hands of his younger colleague, Terry Colzer. I asked if I could see their selection of jade.

"Knock yourself out," Colzer replied, after leading me to a large metal cabinet that he opened with a tiny key. I tried to appear knowledgeable and discerning, but I was really just trying to give Jimmy time to look around and decide if he could remember being in this place before. I certainly hadn't been at

Dick's long enough on February 21st to recognize any of the green trinkets and figurines in this cabinet.

"Okay, thank you," I said to Colzer after a few minutes. "I'll think about it and maybe get back to you." It was at this point that I saw him start to look uneasily at Jimmy. A penny had dropped. I could tell he was now hoping we would leave, and for all I know he was trying not to scream.

On the stairs, going back down, Jimmy told me: "I remember the younger guy."

"Are you sure?"

"Yeah. He argued about the price for something in one of the bags. He gave us a hard time."

"How so?"

"He complained there was blood on one of the necklaces. But he bought it."

I considered how the person telling me this was someone I routinely referred to as "Jimmy," as if he were an ordinary good guy or even a pal. Ten minutes ago, on the sidewalk, I'd even shaken his hand—and found him kind of cute. I was disgusted with myself.

Outside, while Dolores cooled her three-inch heels, Jimmy conveyed his identification of Colzer to Devin and Volker. The detective just nodded and took out his pad, before telling Dolores it was her turn to check out the merchandise, with Devin. She was distinctly unthrilled by both the choice of partner and Volker's lack of deference.

While they were up there, I moved down to the next store and read the paper while leaning against its window. I could see Volker talking to Jimmy, regarding him as a mildly amusing asshole. Jimmy looked bored, as if hoping the cop would buy him something for having behaved well.

Dolores and Devin were back on the sidewalk in less than ten minutes. She took Volker aside and spoke to him in what looked like a businesslike whisper. Meanwhile, Devin came to my spot and filled me in: "We get in the elevator and she tells me, like I don't already know, 'You're supposed to be my nephew.' Then she's kind of thinking out loud and says, 'I suppose my sister could have married a—.' I swear she was gonna say 'spic' before she caught herself. So we get up there and get in, and the head guy looks ready to wet his pants. He's probably just talked to the younger one who got so freaked out by Jimmy a minute before. I guarantee you: back in February they saw the *Post* hours after they bought that bloody necklace, and they realized they'd been drawn into some serious shit. And up until this morning they hoped they'd never see Jimmy again. Well, that little bubble's burst."

I could picture the scene: Vestros and Colzer were probably relieved to have Dolores and Devin walk in instead of a cop—without knowing that Volker stood out on the sidewalk and Devin was a sort of understudy with New York's Finest. Dolores, I know, would have been having a slight fit of pique over their not recognizing her.

"Your old lady looked around kind of disappointed," Devin continued, "like she thought her stolen stuff should have wound up in a higher-class place than this. The two guys were getting more and more edgy—they sensed we were connected to the visit they'd already had from you and Douchebag Jimmy. 'Anything you have in mind?' the older one asks. And your old lady answers him, very actressy, 'Do you have any small bronze statuettes?'"

He imitated what I already knew would have been Dolores's pretentious attempt to Frenchify the way she said "statuette." Legend had it that she'd once pronounced Bonwit Teller as "Bone-wee Tay-yay."

"Bitch is a trip!" Devin continued. "The younger guy, Colzer, said no, we don't got nothing like that here."

But Dolores had a surprise for everybody. Detective Volker called us over and passed on what she'd just told him: namely, that she'd spotted a carved, rock-crystal ram's head that she and Dick had purchased in Hong Kong last fall. When asked if he remembered it, too, Jimmy just shrugged.

"Okay," said Volker, very pleased with what he'd learned. He said he had enough to make an arrest, so he radioed a cop who had been stationed on the other side of the building in case Vestros and Colzer got so spooked they decided to flee out the back.

Dolores didn't move. She seemed to believe the cops would soon deliver the ram's head to her here on the sidewalk. As I looked at her, I realized she was more annoyed at not recovering the little bronze Renoir than elated over how our work here this morning might help to catch Dick and Steven's murderers.

While we waited for the cops to come down with Vestros and Colzer, I asked Devin to *remind* me of exactly how this was all supposed to help.

"To nail down the timeline. And to get these guys they're arresting to ID Boccara and Forti—if they're ever found."

Like autograph seekers at a stage door, we kept eyeing the entrance to the building. Our vigil was interrupted only when Dolores suddenly turned to Jimmy and asked: "Did you kill Richard?"

"Who's Richard?"

"*Coño*," Devin muttered. "*Qué tarado.*"

"Oh, you mean Dick," said Jimmy. "No, lady, I didn't. And none of this woulda happened if he only—"

Estúpido as he might be, Jimmy was smart enough to shut up and not finish saying something he clearly hadn't told anybody, not even Volker.

CHAPTER 15

MAY 24, 1961

Kenneth Nelson and Rita Gardner are starring in "The Fantasticks."

Lucy, fake red tresses running down her back, had just started singing "Hey, Look Me Over," supposedly *Wildcat*'s showstopper. But her lifeless, hoarse rendition only feebly echoed the razzmatazz versions, by other singers, that everyone in the audience had been hearing for months on the nation's TV variety shows. The girl driving the prop Model T in this number looked vaguely familiar to Kallman, but she too was a source of disappointment to the woman sitting next to him at this matinee in the Alvin Theatre: "I do wish that were Vivian Vance."

Wildcat would close in a couple of weeks, after a run of six months that should have lasted sixteen. Lucy had been out sick a lot; she'd collapsed onstage the night before the Garland concert, and Kallman could hear her suppressing a cough right now. The papers had lately said she was planning to take a few weeks' leave soon; then word came that the musicians' union wouldn't accept cuts in pay during any hiatus, and a decision was made to shut the show for good.

So here Kallman was, with two days left in New York, seeing *Wildcat* while there was still time. It wasn't as if he had much else to do. He'd reached the end of an extended stay on different friends' couches. His trip east had been a bust, resulting in a handful of failed callbacks and a growing, generalized rage toward everyone in the business.

Lucy had agreed to see him after the matinee. She'd called his service when he left a note at the theatre the other day; more than a year had passed since they'd last spoken. He was nervous—something he rarely used to be—as he made his way to her, but he still swanned through the stage door and past the autograph seekers who lacked his invitation.

"Mr. Kallman, she'll be with you in a sec," said the dresser, before the "sec" turned into twenty minutes standing outside Lucy's closed door. Once admitted, he saw her face in the mirror. Stage makeup had been replaced by the ordinary, if overapplied, street variety. The long wig rested on a faceless head mannequin. She didn't turn around, but the mirror made apparent her misery and exhaustion. She was dating Gary Morton but still worn out by last year's divorce. *Wildcat* had been undertaken as a last-ditch diversion from her protracted marital woes, and in keeping with the couple's long, ambivalent goodbye, Desi had money in the show.

Kallman came up to her from behind and, even though he knew better, put his hands on her shoulders and kissed her cheek. She still didn't turn around, and she didn't return the kiss.

"You were amazing out there," he said.

"Yeah, that's me," she said with self-disgust. Not so much as a smile in the mirror.

"When's the TV special?"

Something called *Lucy Goes to Broadway* was said to be in the works—a zany, scripted behind-the-scenes look at *Wildcat* that sounded very similar to the Christmas special they'd done about the workshop.

"It's scheduled for never," answered Lucy. "Don't want to do it, period."

"I'm really sorry about the musicians' union. Those bastards always make things hard."

"Those bastards did me a favor. I want out of this, and they gave me an excuse. And"—she at last turned around—"if you tell that to your friend Mike Connolly, I will kill you. I mean that literally."

"Connolly?" asked Kallman.

"Don't bullshit me. I know what you did."

He couldn't bring himself to deny it, or to admit that Connolly no longer wanted anything to do with him.

"What have you been up to?" Lucy asked. "I gather not much."

He told her of two scheduled supper-club dates; one actual, the other made up.

"Still living with your folks in LA?"

"I've got a line on my own place as soon as I go back."

"And you're hoping I've got some Desilu work for you. Maybe an episode or two of *Guestward, Ho!*" With the divorce now final, she was the studio's CEO.

"There's been some good stuff on that show!" he declared. He'd seen the dude-ranch comedy a couple of times.

"We're cancelling it. Of course *The Untouchables* is still going strong."

"It gets better and better, Lucy. The other night—"

"But I wouldn't expect anything there, either."

"Oh, I didn't mean—"

"Yes, you did." After a pause, she added, "Funny, there's no one here but us." She gestured with her hand to the otherwise empty dressing room.

Not even trying to mask his confusion, he said, "I don't get it."

"I mean, where's Janice Carroll? Shouldn't she be here? In a nice little love nest like this?"

He tried to laugh. "I still don't get it," he said, though now he did.

"Don't think I didn't hear the filthy nonsense you started spreading within two months of the end of the workshop. You didn't get what you wanted out of it, so you blamed me. And you made up five different lies, the worst of which was that Janice came on to me and I was delighted."

"I never—"

"Yeah, just like you never talked to Connolly. The only reason I said you could come back here today was to have the pleasure of throwing you out. Scram."

She turned back to the mirror.

Exiting his way through the backstage clutter, he made himself slow down, so he didn't appear to be fleeing. He came upon the woman who played Lucy's younger sister in the show, even though Lucy was old enough to be her mother.

"How'd things go in there?" she asked, pointing to the star's dressing room.

"Great! It was like seeing Mom after a long time apart."

"Not as long as it's been since you saw *me*."

"Pardon?"

"I'm Paula Stewart. I was Ann Crowley's understudy in *Seventeen*. You made dinner for me one night—for a bunch of us—in Brooklyn. Ten years ago."

"Of course!" he said, as if it were a clear, happy memory. He could recall the evening only because it had occurred two nights before the catastrophe with Kenny.

"I even dated your brother Charlie a couple of times!"

"How about that! You were super this afternoon, Paula."

"Thanks. Fat lot of good it does. She's in terrible shape." She nodded toward Lucy's closed door.

"Is she?"

Paula made a face to indicate she couldn't bear going into the whole sad subject of *Wildcat*. "Do you ever see any of the old *Seventeen* gang?" she asked instead, as if that long-ago cast had really been a close-knit bunch of smalltown Hoosiers.

Kallman, losing interest in the conversation and afraid that Lucy might come out, replied, "Just Matt Liannetto. The pansy pianist? I run into him every once in a while."

"He's a sweetheart. He played on a record that my husband, Burt Bacharach, did a couple of years ago."

"Oh," said Kallman, regaining interest.

"Or *ex*-husband, I should say." Her lip curled upward, and Kallman's level of engagement redescended. "You don't still see Kenny, do you?" she asked.

"No, never."

"Not even his show? Really, it's as good as they say. The book's ridiculous, but the songs are to die for."

"I'm based on the coast."

"I can't imagine it won't be out there soon, too."

"I'll check it out." He made a move to go.

"Did you ever get to go on for him? For Kenny, I mean, in *Seventeen*. You were great in your own part, but I did all one hundred and eighty-two performances in the chorus. Ann never missed a show."

Kallman spent a second trying to decide which answer, yes or no, would make for a better story. He settled on the truth: "No, I never did."

Paula laughed. "We all knew you were sweet on him," she said, before seeing the cloud that passed over his face. "Oh, not in any serious way. You know, just kid stuff." *I certainly wasn't implying . . .*

His expression turned unreadable. "Yeah, kid stuff," he said, before turning the lights of his face back on. "Nice seeing you, Paula!"

A moment later he was out on Fifty-Second Street, pounding the pavement due east, willing it to be five o'clock so that the Blue Parrot, between Third and Lex, would be open. Maybe he'd spend the evening doing the whole "bird circuit" of fag bars in the neighborhood, though he prided himself on not soaking up booze the way so many queens did. "Jews *eat*," as guests at The Balsams used to say of their own sobriety. He also never liked choking on the smoke in the various birdcages. Charlie had knocked a cigarette out of his mouth when he was twelve, and he'd never picked up another. But he badly wanted a drink.

As he walked, he shook with the anger and failure this New York trip had brought. It would finally come to an end on Friday—not that he had anything going on back in Los Angeles, either. He had started lying about his age to casting directors, knocking three years off his twenty-seven, though anyone doing the arithmetic could see that would have made him only fourteen when *Seventeen* opened.

How long could he keep this up? That might be the big new question, but it was the past, *Kenny Kenny Kenny*, that was on his mind as his feet struck the sidewalk. The passing transistor radios played "Travelin' Man" and "Mama Said," all at the same tinny volume, audible from the little single headphones stuck in everyone's waxy New York ears.

Then real music at last: Jo Stafford singing "The Nearness of You" on the Blue Parrot's jukebox as he came in the door. When he heard it he knew he would now get drunk enough to go down to Sullivan Street and get a ticket for *The Fantasticks*. So that he could watch Kenny in the dark.

The playhouse was smaller than most nightclubs. Kallman took his seat at the very back, but the rows were hardly banked and he couldn't be more than thirty feet from the stage. He only hoped the spotlights would be turned up high enough to blind Kenny to the farther reaches of his audience.

He knew that for most of the late fifties Kenny had done the kind of flailing *he* had. He would hear about him doing one industrial or another, and there was supposed to have been a chorus part in some Miami production. It had been comforting to think of him making a similar downward slide through the business; but then Kenny's slide had stopped, a year ago, with this show. He was even now probably getting no more than $1.40 an hour, and one of the write-ups had mentioned that the cast all shared a single dressing room, but there had been *dozens* of write-ups, and one of them was bound to lead to something. The show was becoming a cult; every few days one of the columns reported the delight of another celebrity who'd just seen it. In fact, he'd just spotted Jennifer Jones down in the front row.

Kallman had listened to the cast album and tried to spot holes in the score, to dislike it, but he couldn't. Now, minutes into the show, he was at least relieved to discover that Paula Stewart had been right: the book *was* ridiculous, a little fairy tale. But it didn't matter to the audience, who'd already heard the LP; they listened raptly to "Try to Remember" and couldn't care less that two of the three original leads had already left the show—the girl for a movie and the guy who'd first sung this number for a bigger musical. Either of which, Kallman now supposed, with a sick feeling, might also happen to Kenny.

He'd just made his entrance. You couldn't tell he'd reached thirty-one; he still looked like the boy next door, which was literally what he played in this. The pasteboard character's name was Matt, which made Kallman give a quick thought to Matt Liannetto, who now, he'd lately heard, had a wife and a little girl. Matt was *living* a lie when it came to sex, whereas he and Kenny were only telling one; speaking it with their silence, same as nearly every actor, singer, and dancer he knew. All the nighttime risks, the misjudgments, the occasional black eye and sunglassed trip to the VD clinic—none of it was spoken of, not by him and not, he was sure, by Kenny. Not even Kenny's precious Carole, his pal and confidante, ever heard about it, you could be certain.

Kenny and the new Luisa had begun their duet, "Soon It's Gonna Rain," and soon she was struggling with a sudden mishap: the fringe of her costume had gotten caught on the lid of the trunk she sat on. One could tell, as the music swelled, that she was supposed to rise and walk toward Kenny, but she was trapped. So Kenny came to her instead, kneeling down beside the trunk and effortlessly freeing the fringe. It seemed a generous, protective gesture, though he was really just saving himself.

This impossible book—a "rape ballet"?—now had Kenny fighting with a wooden sword, as if he were still Willie Baxter. The lights weren't as bright as Kallman had hoped, so he sank lower in his seat, wishing he'd worn dark glasses or the close-cropped man's blond wig he'd swiped from Desilu. If he tried to slip away, getting up from his seat would only make him more conspicuous, so he decided to sit through, bearing the fear of detection and the pain of just looking at Kenny.

As the set's cardboard sun was replaced by a cardboard moon, all his mind's eye could see was the pin, the little ruby and the constellation of tiny diamonds embedded in platinum that he'd given Kenny on the opening night of *Seventeen*, what he'd put into his hand backstage the moment the curtain fell on the action and the cast rushed to assemble for their bows. The pin had shone in the semidarkness, resting on Kenny's palm as if it were Dick Kallman's own heart, before Dick gently took Kenny's fingers and closed them over the gift. "Now *we're* pinned," he'd told him. When the curtain rerose, there was only time enough, between the chorus's bow and Kallman's own, for Kenny to shove the pin back at him and say, "I will never feel that way about you."

He had known at once what the words meant: not "I'm flattered, but I'm not that kind." No, they meant "I could never feel that way about you," about steamrolling Dick Kallman.

That was the message, the verdict, from the beautiful young man he'd loved during those weeks of rehearsal; the boy so close in his real life to the character he played; the darling of the company recreating Tarkington's turn-of-the-century town inside the Broadhurst. Kenny had plenty of ambition—if anyone could recognize that, it was Dick Kallman—but one never saw it in his performance, whereas on Dick Kallman ambition stuck out like a cowlick or a horn, fatal to an audience's complete belief in almost any character he was playing.

That night in the wings—for an instant—the usual Kenny had disappeared, turned momentarily fierce and raced away to save himself from something awful. Seconds later, by the time he went back onstage to bend at the waist for the audience's cheers, he'd returned to being both beloved Willie and beloved Kenny. During the bows, the orchestra reprised "If We Only Could Stop the Old Town Clock," and Dick could feel his own heart stop for good, could imagine the giant minute hand of the prop behind them turning into a sword, a real one, not wooden but steely and sharp, something with which he might cut Kenny in two.

Now, as this performance of *The Fantasticks* drew toward its own curtain, Kenny's character reunited with the girl, and he sang to her of all the things he'd seen during their separation:

> . . . *When the stage was hung*
> *For my holiday*
> *I saw shining lights*
> *But I never knew*
> *They were you*
> *They were you*
> *They were you . . .*

Before the final line was sung he knew that Kenny had at last seen and recognized him, and he knew that the sight had affected him not at all. Kenny was still the boy onstage, in character, unaltered, because he had never felt anything for Dick Kallman but that quickly forgotten moment of backstage horror.

Ten years later the sharp pain remained in Kallman's heart; the sharp sword was still in his hand, undroppable. He looked for an exit sign and slipped out the back of the theater. Out on Sullivan Street, he found a pay phone and called United Airlines, getting himself rebooked on the first flight to LA tomorrow morning, hastening his escape from New York City and the only thing he'd never gotten over.

CHAPTER 16

DECEMBER 17, 1980

"You have a high voice for a lesbian!"

The club erupted in laughter at this riposte to a heckler, who might have been a plant, but I laughed as hard as everyone else.

"I stole that line from the play Harvey's working on," said Charles Pierce, who was in drag as Bette Davis and soon singing a filthy version of "They're Either Too Young or Too Old," Bette's long-ago *Hollywood Canteen* number. "That's a song I did during the war—the *Civil* War, dear. You know, I was with Grant when he took Richmond. Richmond *loved* it!"

I'd never seen Pierce's act before, but had heard about it for years from West Coast friends. Here at Grand Finale on West Seventieth I sat close to the back beside Devin and Carole Cook, who'd known Charles for years in California and suggested we catch his late show tonight after she finished up at *42nd Street*. The musical had become a smash and I hoped it would keep her here in New York for years.

Offstage changing costumes while the piano player (a woman in a tuxedo) vamped, Charles launched a couple of purely audio impressions from the wings. A loonlike Eleanor

Roosevelt: "I've just returned from Manila, where I congratulated the people on their lovely envelopes!"

Unlike Dolores, Carole had instantly taken to Devin, who'd seen the occasional drag queen on the corner of Fifty-Third and Second, but never a performance like this. I had to explain to him who Mrs. Roosevelt was, but he was having such a good time that he leaned over and said, "I think I'm going to piss myself."

A few seconds later I thought he actually had. His leg shot out and hit mine under the table—the result, it turned out, of his being startled by the buzz from a pager attached to his belt. "'Scuse me, *papi*. 'Scuse me, Ms. Cook. I'll be right back."

"Of course, sweetheart," said Carole.

I couldn't bring myself to say anything. I was completely dashed. A pager? Didn't hustlers use them? And drug dealers? All my suppressed worries—my Dolores-like suspicions—came bubbling back up, warning me that Devin might not, after all, be what I wanted to believe he was. Really, I now thought, how could one expect anything but grubbiness in this city of mayhem and murder? A minute's walk from here would take you to the Dakota, where John Lennon had been gunned down the week before.

Carole, sensing my anxiety but uncertain of its cause, reassuringly patted my right knee. But Devin still hadn't come back by the time Charles returned to the stage, this time as Katharine Hepburn in her *Lion in Winter* wimple. Shaking with what she always insisted was "familial tremor," not Parkinson's, she delivered commentary on the sex lives of the current British royal family. "Princess Anne! *Plain?* Every time she finishes sex with Captain Phillips she gets a cube of sugar." Worried though I might be, laughter over this tilted my frame leftwards—knocking it against Devin as he slid back into his place at our table. He sported a big smile and he squeezed my left thigh with much more pressure than Carole had applied to my right knee.

Had he made a big coke score? Arranged a date for tomorrow night with some rich decorator? I pondered which it might be as Katharine Hepburn offered an explanation for Princess Margaret's nymphomania. During the roars and applause, Devin leaned in to me and said "*Papi.*" I expected him to ask me who Princess Margaret was, but his next whisper into my ear was a statement: "They got them."

I put down my drink, somehow knowing I should be serious and sober as he delivered the rest of his message: "Douchebag Paulie and This-Here's-Dante. They're locked up out in California."

I started babbling. "You're kidding! How did they—?"

He squeezed my thigh again. Hiding his triumph inside the overdone Googie Gomez accent he sometimes put on for me, he concluded: "More later. For now, watch dee cho."

Before long Charles was exchanging Hepburn's wimple for Mae West's diamond choker, and having Mae tell us about the handsome croupier she'd met in a Las Vegas casino. " 'Miss West,' he told me. 'I'd love to lay you ten-to-one.' 'Mmm,' I replied. 'It's an odd time, but I'll be there.' " Glissando from the tuxedoed piano girl; rim shot from the drummer; a narcotic wave of relief within yours truly. Devin's pager, now resting on the table, with a stamped "25-MILE RANGE" promise near its Motorola logo, belonged to the 19th Precinct of the NYPD, to the forces of truth and justice and the American way, as did my darling Devin himself. When Charles ended his act with a touching version of an old Dietrich song, "(Want to Buy Some) Illusions," I thought: thank God, I don't need to buy them after all!

"Can we tell Carole?" I whispered during the standing ovation. Devin knew, from the scrapbook and some things I'd told him, about her connections to both Dick and Kenny Nelson.

"Not yet. We need to wait until those two sorry asses get hauled back to New York."

So I settled for turning to Carole and saying "Everything's okay." We made our goodbyes out on the sidewalk, with Carole telling Devin, whom she'd met ninety minutes ago, "You know, I've always liked you better than Matt." I was drunk and giddy and I loved the shtick. I gave her a huge smooch before we put her in one taxi and then got another for ourselves to Manhattan Plaza.

"So, tell me everything!" I said to Devin, as soon as it pulled away from the curb.

"Wait till we're home," he whispered, nodding toward our cabbie, one who this time didn't seem thrilled by the double-fag fare he'd just picked up. In fact, he looked dangerous enough to have killed Dick and Steven himself. No matter. Devin's use of the word "home" delighted me. Once we were there I made my young hero a nightcap and said, *"Now*. PLEASE."

"Okay. Terry Volker and another cop went out to California yesterday to follow up on something I picked up involving your late boy, Dick. Before they left, a sergeant in the 19th gave me the pager. He buzzed me tonight and told me to call Volker, collect, at a number in California. So I found a pay phone and missed half of Katharine Hepburn."

"Yes, you did," I said, doing my own quavery Hepburn imitation.

"Papi, you're so fucking dippy tonight. I love it! But let me back up a second. Volker and his partner went out west because of something I heard two weeks ago at Rounds, the last time I was doing my undercover number. At least it was indoors! With me getting my drinks bought by old guys wearing too much Clinique and too many rings."

Rounds: the hustler bar where Jack O'Rourke and Jeff Mathis, two of the dinner-party guests, had gone after being at Dick's.

"So I'm trying to fish. And as soon as somebody makes crime in the city the subject or starts talking about an apartment they're redecorating, I say, 'Wow, remember the murder of those antiques guys back in February?' Well, one of the times I do that, this real oldster—could be *your* father—says he heard from a friend of a friend of a friend that the guys who did it are out in Anaheim. The friend at the end of the friend chain, by the way, is some hairdresser in Jackson Heights. So I'm thinking: who knows? I'm also thinking: *Anaheim?* Like, Disneyland? Are they hiding in those big Snow White and Mickey costumes?"

I was glad that this tantalizing new information didn't involve some sickening twist—like, say, its turning out to have come from O'Rourke and Mathis.

"Next morning Detective V tells me I've done good, and he gets some guys from the great big fraternal order of police—

some grunt cops in Anaheim—to comb through arrest records out there. And sure enough, Douchebag Paulie's name turns up on a local summons from last summer—for throwing beer cans into the pool of some shitbox apartment complex. So Volker and his partner fly out yesterday and find Paulie, and he's so dumb they convince him they're local cops, that they're there in connection with the beer cans—because he didn't show up for whatever California calls a desk appearance. You've heard Volker's Bronx accent? His partner's is even thicker."

"I'm guessing Paulie wasn't the brains of the operation in New York."

"Paulie makes Jimmy look like Dr. Carl Fucking Sagan. And once Volker lets him know why they're really there, he pukes up the whole Kallman story and leads them to This-Here's-Dante, who denies everything. 'Never knew your friend Dick; never at his apartment.' Says he's been detoxing from a little drug problem and hasn't worked since he had a job a year ago in New York at the Fulton Fish Market. Talk about fishy, huh? Tells them he's been out in California for about seven months. Says he's never been to Florida."

"Are they on their way back here?"

"Not yet. Dante's managed to get a lawyer who's resisting extradition. So Detective V and his partner are flying home by themselves."

My disappointment showed. I'd somehow been imagining me and Carole and Dolores and the dinner-party guys being there when the plane landed, like the good people of Holcomb, Kansas, lined up outside the courthouse after the guys who killed the Clutters were brought back from Las Vegas or wherever it was they'd been caught.

"Patience, *papi*. Things are good. They'll get them here. And the bright side's already shining. Just think: only you get to cop a feel of my ass from now on. No more for those guys at Rounds."

CHAPTER 17

OCTOBER 12–26, 1962

"I can't take the tsuris! It's constant!" cried Zara Kallman.

She was speaking about her younger son, her darling, to her elder one, solid and reliable Charles, who had unexpectedly dropped by his parents' LA apartment on a Friday night.

"It's gone on too long," she continued. "*This* is the Dickie we used to know? He's in that room twenty-two hours a day. Better he should die than go on like this!"

Charlie shifted uncomfortably on the plastic-covered couch, making a loud squeak. He was hearing his mother speak in the way she permitted herself only in the company of family, with whom she would drop her own plastic shield, the assumed polish of her Episcopal conversion.

"It can't be that bad, Mom. I'll talk to him."

"Ach," she said, waving her hand in disgust. "What good will it do?"

Charles's wife, Phyllis, had once said, "Dick would fuck a snake if it got him a step ahead." As a theatrical agent, she'd said it admiringly, offering the observation as the kind of accolade her colleagues at William Morris wished they might include on a client's résumé. But these days snakes were safe from Dick Kallman. As the old saying had it, his get-up-and-go had got up and went. Over the past year his always-constant blaze of ingratiating talk had been scuppered by defeatism and bitterness.

Despite what he'd just said to his mother, Charles realized that things were serious, that this was now about psychological paralysis, not just a stalled career.

"What does Dad say?" he asked.

"Your father says nothing. He just works himself to death at the House of Murphy, like he's doing tonight."

Torchy's fiery personality was guttering just like his son's. The young man who'd courted Zara with spins in his barnstorming biplane; the middle-aged one who'd singed employees at The Balsams with his demands and wrath: gone. At sixty, continuing to oversee the restaurant at Fourth and La Cienega, Alvan Kallman was an old man beset with heart problems.

"Has he said anything about Cuba?" asked Charlie. New York's Senator Keating had the other day disclosed intelligence suggesting that Soviet missiles had been installed on the island. A sense was in the air that Kennedy would soon have to do something.

Zara allowed herself another "ach." "We'll all be blown up and dead before they ever get rid of Castro. It's too late for your father, Charles. But it shouldn't be too late for Dickie!"

That Charles Kallman, an engineer, was doing well—even ahead of where he should be at thirty-five—seemed unworthy of his mother's notice.

"Is Dick dating anyone?" he asked her.

"Never," she said, pulling down both sides of her cardigan

sweater. Her tone conveyed both proud possessiveness and a certain embarrassment.

"Is he—?" Charlie couldn't bring himself to complete the question, couldn't ask his mother if she thought Dick might be fooling around with men. But even so, she read his thoughts. "You think that teacher at Tilton ruined him forever! He didn't! It was an *incident*. You know what an incident is? It's like a traffic accident."

"No, Mom, but . . ." His voice trailed off again. Tilton had only reprimanded the history teacher during Dick's last year there, and the elder Kallmans had said they were satisfied with the outcome. If Torchy had made too much of a stink, drawn more attention to the offense, things would have been worse for Dick. But at the time Charlie had wondered, without asking: had his brother maybe been the instigator?

Dick was in his bedroom, listlessly composing a letter to Richard Whorf, who'd directed the nonmusical parts of *Seventeen* and later played the father of Dick's character in *The Fifth Season*. Whorf was now out here directing episodes of *The Beverly Hillbillies*, the new cornball blockbuster on CBS. Dick's heart wasn't in this job-begging letter, and he couldn't concentrate with Zara's decibel level rising outside his door. "Stop with the Tilton *umzin*, Charlie! It was a dozen years ago—*more* than that!" The yelling compelled Dick to emerge from his room.

"Dickie! Finally! Come join us." Zara cut him a piece of cake.

"I don't want cake," he said wanly. "I just want quiet." He went back to his room.

"Go after him! Go in and talk to him!" Zara ordered Charles. "I can't take any more!"

Charlie entered his brother's bedroom and closed the door. He sat down in a chair beside his brother's not-fully-paid-for hi-fi. "Dick, you've got to snap out of this."

"I love how you all think I got damaged by that fruitcake teacher at Tilton—how you make it like I lost a leg in the war!"

"Well, didn't it—?"

"You know what I would never tell Mom? And what I've never told you? The real way I—sort of—lost my virginity. Remember the summer of '48, with everybody at the hotel listening to the political conventions on the radio? You remember a left-wing actress named Roberta Green and her husband, Gerald? Guests for a couple of weeks?"

"No."

"Mom was crazy about them both. Thought Roberta was the new Helen Gahagan. She *was* just as pink, but she was stuck in little hole-in-the-wall plays in New York. Mom fussed around the Greens for the whole two weeks and got Roberta to take an interest in me, 'such a talented young performer, don't you think?' A couple of months later, during a class trip to New York, I broke away from the group and looked up Roberta. She was doing a benefit performance, for Henry Wallace, of some experimental play. Just her and a few other lefties in some microscopic theater on Broome Street. I was actually *impressed*—I was fifteen—and she introduced me to the other actors who were passing the hat for their commie candidate. She told them that from what she'd seen at The Balsams I'd no doubt be performing in New York in a couple of years' time."

As he wondered where Dick's story might be going, Charlie lit a cigarette, no longer worried about his kid brother's picking up the habit.

"She even took me back to her slob apartment on Grove Street—she and Gerald must have blown all their dough on those two weeks at The Balsams. She said she would give me a late-night supper. It turned out Gerald was out of town, and two minutes after we got inside she was undoing my belt." He laughed with what sounded almost like admiration for her nerve.

"What did you do?" Charlie asked.

"I flinched. And then I let her rub me for half a minute, before I pulled away. And then she told me I was a lousy snotnose, that Dad was a shyster, and that Mom was a pretentious bitch. I left there hating her and hating all left-wingers. And I've hated every bit of avant-garde theatrical crap I've seen ever since."

"Why are you telling me this now?" Charlie asked. He took a long, frustration-filled drag on the cigarette. "Is it because you heard us head-shrinking you out there?"

After a considerable silence, Dick absently asked, "Telling you what?" He seemed entirely to have forgotten the story he'd just told.

"What the *hell*, Dick!"

Zara, who'd been listening at the door, burst in as Charlie realized his brother was seriously disoriented. "That's it!" she cried. "No more! I'm sending you to New York!"

"You can't just get *rid* of him, Mom!" yelled Charlie.

"I'm sending him to Father Albert!"

Albert J. duBois Jr. was Mrs. Kallman's High Church canon, the man who a dozen years ago had converted her to the Episcopal faith she liked to pretend she'd been born into.

"Oh, no, Mom," said Charlie. "That—"

"Yes! Doobie can straighten him out!"

Dick, the subject of this debate, who had three hundred dollars to his name, looked at his mother with an expression Charlie had never seen, a slack facial passivity accompanied by a shrug of the shoulders that signified "Okay, I'll go."

Within two weeks the Cuban Missile Crisis had come and gone, leaving the world unobliterated and Castro still in place. Alvan Kallman would, as his wife had prophesied, remain in Los Angeles. But by Friday evening, October 26, his son Dick had been living for eleven days in Father duBois's comfortable quarters on the grounds of Long Island's Cathedral of the Incarnation.

The elder Kallmans had met the priest in 1950 at a large business banquet held inside the Garden City Hotel, across the street from the church. The then forty-four-year-old canon, newly installed in the diocese after several years in Washington and a few before that as a chaplain to General Patton's troops, had been invited to give the banquet's invocation and benediction. Before heads were bowed, and after they were raised, he'd made jolly remarks about being an anomalous Anglican in this crowd of mostly Low-Churched or heathenish hoteliers.

For all his merriment, the bald prelate, whose star was on the rise, remained serious in his reactionary longings, which extended all the way to reunification with Rome and left no room for any weldings with Methodists and Presbyterians and other Protestant denominations he regarded as barely distinguishable from Ozark snake handlers. He preferred the rustle of fancy vestments, the smell of incense, and the castratolike sound of choirboys.

But that night in the Garden City Hotel, when he joined Zara and Alvan Kallman at the head table, his conversation was jokey and charming and "regular," his frame of reference surprisingly popular. He told the Kallmans that he and the other priests had acquired a television for their comfortable parsonage right near the Cherry Valley Golf Club, and that they'd become, like everyone else, devoted watchers of Milton Berle.

Quickly enchanted with him, Zara decided that Father duBois could offer her an easy ascension in status from all the Jews who sought only their own brethren during summers at The Balsams. Soon she was inviting "Doobie" (he insisted on the nickname) to suppers in Brooklyn, and taking the Long Island Rail Road out to Garden City for "religious instruction." Within a year, while Dickie was in *Seventeen*, she was received into the church. If not eternal salvation, she had achieved a position among the socially elect.

For years thereafter, on trips into New York, Father duBois had been presented with free theater tickets and the occasional, vivacious company of bright-eyed Dick Kallman, a very different soul from the frail one before him on this autumn night in 1962. For the past eleven days, in this spare room of the parsonage, the priest had each evening counseled, sermonized, and encouraged the still-young man, and then, by day, made sure that Dick followed through on an almost impossibly strenuous undertaking for someone in his reduced condition: auditions for the lead in the national road company of *How to Succeed in Business Without Really Trying*, still the hottest ticket on Broadway a full year into its run. The odds against landing the role were enormous, but Doobie insisted that Dick not squander the sudden "in" from his sister-in-law, Phyllis, which had got him through the stage door and into the first round.

And which, through his own talents, he had parlayed into a third callback! Anyone looking at Dick right now, so battered and bedraggled, would have trouble believing it. Dick scarcely believed it himself as he sat in the priest's recliner, his bare feet encircled by Doobie's gentle massaging hands.

The cleric wanted to hear every detail about the latest tryout, but a remnant of the old, ambitious Dick refused to jinx things by speaking of this afternoon's effort. He preferred to continue telling the story of the socialist actress who'd attempted his seduction in Greenwich Village fourteen years ago. It had been on his mind ever since he'd imparted the first portion of it to Charlie, two weeks earlier, and to Doobie the other night. Eager to complete the tale and explore its meaning, as if the recliner were a psychiatrist's couch, he now launched into a monologue, which itself sounded like a prepared audition piece, though he'd never spoken it to anyone before.

"A month after I bolted from her apartment, I was back at school in New Hampshire, and at the crack of dawn on Election Day I got a ride up from Tilton to Dixville Notch. Charlie was at the hotel, doing off-season maintenance and helping our old man think through his plans for adding a winter ski season to the usual summer-only operation. I just wanted to skip school and see my brother, but when I got there Dad was listening to the radio report on Hart's Location's first-in-the-nation vote, and saying that if The Balsams had a winter season he could steal the idea from that little town and do it better. He'd only lately realized that the handful of winter workers, the carpenters and so forth, had to travel fifty miles if they wanted to vote. And now he figured that if he could get permission from the state board, he could, next election, set up a polling place right inside the hotel. He'd have Charlie make a 'Ballot Room' sign and get whoever in town wanted to vote to come do it at midnight—with lots of photographers present—in exchange for a big free breakfast."

"A combination of canniness and generosity," remarked Father duBois. "Very typical of your father." His massaging hands went to work on Dick's calves.

"Dixville Notch was almost all for Dewey, of course. But one of the carpenters, an eccentric guy whose father was an old socialist, actually intended to vote for Wallace. So my dad gets the idea of calling the newspaper in Lancaster, fifty miles away, to say that his young son, Dickie Kallman, who only has a learner's permit, will drive this man fifty miles to the polls. It'll make a great civic-minded story and photo for the paper, doesn't the editor agree? Not to mention how it'll also create some nice publicity for the first-in-the-nation voting scheme my father intends to try in '52. So I drove the guy the whole fifty miles to Lancaster."

"Then what happened, Dick?" asked Father duBois, whose hands began attending to the area behind his guest's knees.

Kallman laughed, and suddenly looked very different from the wreck who'd been living here in the parsonage these past eleven days. "As a reward for my good citizenship, the election official in Lancaster gave me the honor of putting the guy's vote into the box. But during the fuss of setting up the cameraman's shot for the local paper, I managed to drop in a blank ballot instead."

DuBois hesitated for a moment but asked no questions. It was important for the young man, who'd been so depressed, to tell his story in his own way, without interruption or judgment. The priest went on with his physical ministrations.

"And I pocketed the actual ballot the guy had filled out for Henry Wallace. That afternoon I ripped it in two and mailed the pieces to that cunt of an actress in New York. I never felt better in my life!"

It had been a surge of strength he experienced back then, a kind of superheated annealing; not just an undoing of what had happened on Grove Street, but a repair that bordered on rebirth. Ever since that triumphant Election Day, when he had to supply a little bio for a playbill or program, he'd listed New Hampshire as his birthplace, no matter that he'd actually been born in New York ten years before his old man acquired The Balsams. Alas, before Torchy could implement his early-voting scheme for the '52 election, he was already losing his financial grip on the resort; it would be left to the new owner to follow through, several years later, for a bonanza of national publicity.

"That day in '48," he said, looking into Doobie's eyes, "I decided I would never be taken advantage of again. I'd be in charge and successful no matter the cost. Bulletproof."

Right now, before he lost the rush of excitement brought on by the memory, he unzipped his pants and thrust himself forward toward the priest, who didn't know that Dick had remained bullet-proof for only three years, before he faltered with a horrible, sudden slip into vulnerability—the rejection and anger that had come from putting his heart in Kenny's hand. As Doobie leaned forward, Dick closed his eyes and let the priest do his work, trying not to think of the feelings he'd spent the last ten years strangling and smothering: any early buddings of emotion for anyone, but especially the never-disappearing pangs for Kenny, the remembered ardor he despised himself for cherishing. The repair work of 1948, he'd come to realize, was always fragile; the efforts it took to keep it in place were a lifelong and sometimes failing enterprise.

"Well *done*," said Doobie, applauding the young man's strong, sudden physical release. The priest wiped his own mouth with a spare corporal cloth that had found its way here from the altar, and made a joke about who was the real "cannon" in this room. "Dick, tomorrow you will go back to that theater for, yes, the *third* callback, and you just wait and see. You're going to be chosen!"

The seven astronauts had come to see it. Kennedy himself had been in the audience one night. It *was* still the biggest show going, the one out-of-towners wanted to see, and soon it would be coming to them. There was already a big advance sale for Cleveland. Dallas, LA and Chicago would follow.

Abe Burrows had decided to hold the touring-company auditions at the 46th Street Theatre, using the show's actual sets, on days without a matinee. And he'd insisted on being here for them himself. A year ago they'd held *no* auditions for the starring role, Bobby Morse having been in the producer's head from the start; the show was more or less written for him. But Bobby couldn't be in two places at once, and everybody from both coasts was asking to be considered for the road-company lead: Frankie Avalon had taken his shot the other day, without getting a callback.

Dick sat quietly in the front row, so solemn he might have been here trying out for *Saint Joan*. His was the first name that

Burrows, as bald as Doobie, called out this morning. "Kallman! 'I Believe in You.'"

"Glad to hear it," joked Dick, turning on the charm, the mischief, as he jumped up from his seat.

At the second callback he'd been asked to sing "Been a Long Day," the hero's duet with the girl. But today Abe was back to wanting Bobby's big solo, so he bounded up to the executive-washroom set and positioned himself before the giant mirror, electric razor in hand.

Everyone knew how it had taken a little stroke of Burrows's genius to bring this number to life in the show. Frank Loesser had written "I Believe in You" as a hymn of encouragement that loyal Rosemary would sing to Finch—Bobby's character—after he despaired of being able to climb the ladder at the World Wide Wicket Company. But then Abe got the idea that Bobby, with his gap-toothed charm, his devilment, should sing the song *himself*, to his own face in the mirror. Loesser had a what-the-fuck fit, but Abe had insisted and Abe was right.

So now, looking at himself, his back to the audience, Dick Kallman began singing to Dick Kallman. For once there was no distance between himself and the character. In this song about ambition, none of the actor's own showed through; there was only one man, the man in the mirror, for the audience to behold. His reflection at last made him real.

> *I hear the sound of good*
> *Solid judgment whenever you talk.*
> *Yet there's the bold, brave spring*
> *Of the tiger that quickens your walk.*
> *Oh, I believe in you!*

By the time he reached the last verse, the cellular unity of himself and Finch, achieved against the brutal failures of the past year or two, was making his eyes glisten, making him understand that his defeats and sufferings had had a purpose, that they had at last reconnected him to his old unstoppable self, the one born on that long-ago morning in northern New Hampshire. Was this "extasis"? The body/spirit exchange that Doobie had yammered on about the other night? Whatever it was, it was sublime.

But then, as he hit and held and let go of the last note—"you!"—he heard the horrible, cackling sound of over-the-top laughter. It came from behind him, from the row midway back containing Abe and two choreographers and several investors. He froze, and in his confusion over what was happening, became aware that his eyes had brimmed over and that two tears, made Niagaran by the magnifying mirror, were actually running down his cheeks. Had he made a fool of himself?

No, he hadn't. The half dozen men in the audience, his judge and jury, thought he'd turned on the tears with bravura artificiality, accomplished an acting tour de force, coaxing the tears out of himself while behaving *comically*. They saw a genuine feat of mental disconnection; a demonstration of skill they hadn't seen from anyone else who'd auditioned. This was beyond what even Bobby had accomplished with this number.

Kallman turned around to see and hear all of them, including Abe, applauding. He nodded a modest acknowledgment of their praise, then immediately left the theater for Penn Station and a train back to the parsonage on Long Island.

———

Several hours later, after dinner, Doobie was back at work on Dick's calves, listening to what little the young man could bring himself to say about his several minutes onstage this morning. It was at this point that the phone rang and the actor reached for the receiver. Dick's saying "Hello" visibly increased the priest's own pleasure: there was an illicit thrill to be had from continuing the massage while whoever was calling Dick remained unaware of what was happening on this end of the conversation.

It was no ordinary call. The person on the line was Abe Burrows, and he was telling Dick Kallman that he'd gotten the part.

Even before Dick could say "Yes!"—and then "When? . . . Where? . . . Of course!"—the actor was realizing what this could, would mean: how this was the real beginning of everything; how he would make a smash success of the tour; how there would be scouts in the audience in every city where he scored; how this show would lead him back to Hollywood, where this time it wouldn't be just for little scenes in episodes of somebody else's show, but rather for a show of his own; and not for just a few dozen frames of some Susan Hayward movie, but for a movie he would carry on his own—if, that is, he had the time to film it between seasons of his TV series, or before his own Broadway show—not just its national touring company—reached opening night. It was this sort of scheduling dilemma he would be discussing with the profile writer who came to interview him at his large house, with his perfect career displayed in high relief against his perfect private life.

He put the phone down and looked at Father duBois: "I got it."

"Oh, saints be praised!" cried the priest, who let out a big, bellowing laugh. He reached for Dick's belt buckle by way of congratulation and reward—both to Dick and to himself, whose pastoral care over the past two weeks had brought Dick to this moment of fulfillment.

But before Doobie could release the belt's prong from its notch, Dick pushed the priest's hand away, none too gently, and said, with the klieg-light smile he hadn't displayed in ages: "Sorry, I don't do that anymore."

CHAPTER 18

JANUARY 26, 1981

If you want to grasp the essential difference between the *Daily News* and the *New York Post*, you only have to compare two clippings I have, from two weeks ago, when each of the papers ran a brief item on the extradition and arraignments of Dante Forti and Paul Boccara. Needing to refresh readers' memories of the previous year's murders, the *News* reminded them that Dick's body had been discovered "nude from the waist up," whereas the *Post* recalled the corpse as being "nude from the waist down," a condition that, true or not, was in keeping with its bolder slant on things. A similarly brief item on the suspects' capture and return to New York had appeared in the *Times*, with no reference to nudity north or south of the waistline.

I put all these clippings into an envelope, even though several empty pages at the end of Dick's scrapbook seemed to have kept themselves creepily available for items pertaining to the surprise finish of his life. The only other blank page, in the middle of the album, commemorated Dick's leanest year, just before his biggest break. It had been marked "1962" by Dick himself and left otherwise bare, sort of like the chapter called "My Marriage to Ernest Borgnine" in Ethel Merman's memoirs.

Devin joined Detective Volker and his partner at the arraignment late on the evening of January thirteenth, immediately after a plane carrying the cops and the suspects from California touched down at LaGuardia. When he got to my apartment at two in the morning, Devin said: "The brothers-in-law are not getting along."

"Brothers-in-law?" I asked.

"Turns out This-Here's-Dante is married to Douchebag Paulie's older sister." Forti was twenty-seven, Boccara just twenty-one.

Early this morning, before he went off to the 19th Precinct, Devin reminded me to watch for signs of bad blood between the two partners in crime when they appeared in open court at eleven a.m. I had made plans the other day to attend the plea hearing, and had since been commandeered by Dolores to be her escort. I decided to wear the trinket Dick had given me the night of the murders—the cheap little *Seventeen* prop that was supposed to be a fraternity pin. I put it on as a tie clip, in what I guess was a gesture of solidarity with my not-always-very-nice friend.

When Dolores and I got out of our taxi on Centre Street—you didn't think she was going to take the subway, did you?—we saw a lot of policemen around, a couple of them carrying machine guns. Nothing to do with Boccara and Forti; just extra security in light of yesterday's attempt by some gang to spring their drug lord from the Metropolitan Correctional Center—by landing a helicopter on its roof! All of that had happened just a stone's throw from where Dolores and I now stood in that little jigsaw puzzle of courthouse streets next to Chinatown. We could see and hear, amidst the cops, people with boom-box radios listening to live reports of the Iranian hostages landing at a military airport upstate—six days after Reagan had replaced poor old Carter.

Dolores seemed stimulated by this double dose of commotion. I could see her wishing that all the bustle were somehow connected to her; the longing showed in her carriage and facial expression, which were on the order of Norma Desmond coming down the staircase toward the newsreel photographers.

Once inside the small courtroom we took seats at the back, and she calmed down, replacing her excitement with a sort of low-level disgust, as if we'd shown up for a stinkeroo opening. We were the only spectators in the three available rows of benches—there was no sign of even family members awaiting the appearance of Boccara and Dante Forti.

Judge Harold Rothwax came into the courtroom and signed some papers at his elevated desk. He was thin, taut, and—one could tell without his even saying a word—no-nonsense. Dolores sized him up approvingly before he went back to his chambers, after maybe half a minute. The bailiff hadn't even given us an "All rise" command, and there was still no sign of the lawyers and the defendants.

As we waited, Carole Cook, who'd just arrived, slipped quietly onto the bench beside me. Dolores took an instant dislike to her, heightened no doubt by my introductory mention of how Carole was "currently being fantastic in *42nd Street*." "Oh, yes, of course," Dolores replied, adding with wistful grandeur: "I wish *I* could take supporting roles"—as if MGM were stopping her from doing that, lest she get overexposed.

And then it was Devin's turn to join us. He'd come down, after putting in a couple of hours at the 19th, to function as Volker's eyes and ears, since it apparently would be prejudicial to have the detective himself present at a plea hearing. Needless to say, there was no sign of Jimmy Ingrassia, whose reluctant confession had led to the arrest of the two other "alleged perpetrators" (my cop-show lingo) soon to enter the courtroom.

"This Rothwax is no pussy," Devin whispered to me. "Last year he threw a lawyer into the can for ten days—on the spot."

"What for?"

"Just some bullshit defense-lawyer delays."

"Are you sure you didn't vote for Reagan?" I asked.

"I'm still not registered, but maybe next time."

He remained full of surprises. I had comps that evening for *Bring Back Birdie*, a doomed sequel with Donald O'Connor and Chita Rivera. I thought Devin would be excited to go, but when I told him he rolled his eyes and said, "Okay, but only if you take me to the auto show this weekend."

The work tables, only feet away, were suddenly filling up. The assistant district attorney walked in; a big, tough-looking young guy with a mustache. Then it was the defense lawyers; one dapper, the other schlubby. Seeing two of them instead of one, Devin surmised: "Our boys aren't on the same team anymore."

And then came the boys themselves, escorted by armed corrections officers. Dante Forti was much the taller of the two, wearing blue jeans and somebody's suit jacket. Long, dark hair, olive skin, and, as Devin had said, late twenties. My first thought, God forgive me, was: *He's kind of hot.*

Paulie was an altogether different story. He couldn't have been more than five feet four, with a round little nose and a facial expression that bordered on the idiotic. He giggled almost continuously, except when he caught Forti's eye, at which point he looked terrified. He wore gray pants, a tan shirt, and a pair of sneakers. "Same stuff he had on at the arraignment," Devin whispered. "*Thirteen days ago.*" He pinched his nose and quietly hummed the music to "Funkytown."

Dolores regarded the accused with scorn and hauteur. I half-expected her to demand that the two of them be ordered to empty their pockets, so that everyone could see whether they were hiding a little jade bracelet or her bronze Renoir statuette.

The hearing lasted less than five minutes. Paulie said four words—"Not guilty," twice—in response to charges of robbery in the first degree and murder in the second. His indictment, read out by Rothwax, proclaimed that "another participant" in the crime had done the shooting. That would be Dante Forti, whose spoken-words total came to ten: five "Not guilty"s denying charges that included criminal possession of a weapon and his murderous use of it. In both indictments Dick got top-victim billing, maybe for alphabetical reasons. But both he and Steven, along with the violence itself, got lost in a stream of judicial verbiage and criminal-code numbers.

Forti and Boccara were led out the back of the courtroom by the armed guards. The defendants had no apparent idea of who any of the spectators, including Devin, might be. But This-Here's-Dante stopped in his tracks when he caught sight of, believe it or not, me. He was looking, with intense focus, at my tie clasp, the frat-pin prop from *Seventeen*, and with a sharp snap of his head he directed his fellow defendant's attention toward it.

Then one of the guards nudged them forward. Dante's expression of contempt was complemented by Paulie's flickers of fear and confusion. And with that they were gone.

CHAPTER 19

JANUARY 16–17, 1964

Following the long, sold-out runs in Cleveland and San Francisco and Los Angeles, plus some shorter ones in between, *How to Succeed* had arrived here at the Shubert in Chicago in mid-November. Nothing could dent the box office—not even the assassination, a week or so after they started.

Six foreign companies were now performing the show, but the US touring franchise belonged to Dick Kallman, and he was the production's only star. His sole problem involved the girl, Miss Dyan Cannon, who played Finch's loyal girlfriend, Rosemary. She'd been upstaging him since Christmas, with a lot of winsome mugging that stepped on laughs designed to come his way, not hers. So tonight, with a mixture of calculation and spontaneity, he had blown his cool at the end of the elevator-bank scene, where Finch and Rosemary wait for a going-down car, singing "Been a

Long Day" to each other while a motherly colleague encourages them to get over their hemming and hawing and *flirt*, for God's sake.

It was a charming number, but by the time it came to a close tonight, he'd had a bellyful of Miss Cannon's adorableness, so when they at last stepped into the elevator car he closed its plywood doors a little faster and a little harder than usual—a lot harder, actually—and smashed her ring finger. The audience thought her howl was part of the show, as if it were the old S&M beatnik number he'd done in the Lucy workshop with Carole Cook. As he and Cannon made their exits, out of sight through the false back of the car, she'd been too shocked to say any actual words beyond her yelp of pain. But during intermission she came and pounded with her good hand on his dressing-room door. He believed her exact statement was "You fucking animal! You goddamned fucking animal!"

He didn't let her in. "Sorry!" he'd called out, in an almost lilting voice. "Accident!" She kept pounding until she had to go off and change her costume, leaving him in peace to contemplate the walls of his dressing room, which he'd festooned with treasures of affirmation, including a now-framed *Chicago Tribune* review:

> A cherubic barracuda . . . He has an avid choir boy's face, the mouth of a killer shark, and gleaming blue eyes . . . he could have been Pal Joey's roommate in college.

Tacked to the same wall were congratulatory telegrams from Abe Burrows, Henry Willson, and Sophie Tucker—probably all sent by their secretaries, but still. The more personal wires came from his parents, his brother, Carole Cook, and—the grapevine extending as far as it does—even sad-sack Matt Liannetto.

Not everything had gone as he wished, at least not yet. He'd written Abe Burrows a couple of times during the summer and fall, wheedling him (charmingly, he hoped) like a son, asking if he could play Finch in New York when Bobby Morse finally gave up the part. Abe never exactly said no, but by now Bobby was gone and Abe had replaced him with Darryl Hickman. Burrows had moved on mentally from the big success he'd had with the show; all his attention was now on a musical version of *What Makes Sammy Run?*, headed to New York with nice-guy Steve Lawrence in the lead—practically a publicity stunt of against-type casting. The one time Abe responded to his letters from the road, he'd joked that "Dick Kallman would be *too* perfect for Sammy Glick." Which only showed how quickly Dick Kallman had snapped back from the morose 1962 self Abe had seen walk into the auditions for *How to Succeed*. Abe now understood that confidence was Dick Kallman's normal, essential element. By excluding him from consideration for Sammy, Abe was saving him from a too-much version of himself.

All the mail he was receiving! Even letters from high-school girls with crushes. They were stacked beside the heaps of pictures and embossed-stationery thank-you notes to be sent out. At the top of that last pile, awaiting an envelope, sat a *How to Succeed* program with its now-famous swivel-chair illustration; he'd boldly inscribed it to Bob Osborne, who these days, having failed *at* show business, was now writing *about* it—some history of the Academy Awards, Kallman had heard. "Dear Bob, I hope with all my heart that you too someday experience this kind of success. Warm regards, Dick."

He picked up another program, this one set to go to Carole Cook. He'd learned that she would be doing *Stop the World—I Want to Get Off* with her beloved Kenny this summer in Sacramento. Not exactly Chicago! And for that matter Dick Kallman had never had to understudy Bobby Morse, the way Kenny had to do for Tony Newley in New York. He now wondered: should he wait until summer to send the program—mail it to Carole at the theater in Sacramento, where Kenny was likely to see it as well? Yes, he'd wait, because with luck finally running his way, there would by then, no doubt, be more and even bigger news to send.

———

The day after the finger smashing, Kallman took his place on a luncheon dais at the Ambassador West. He was there to emcee the annual gathering of Chicago's Sarah Siddons Society. Since arriving in town with *How to Succeed* he had become a top choice for events like this, whether it was the Chicago Drama League party or the West End Suburban Hospital benefit. His calendar for the next few months was full of such bookings.

The society's president introduced him. Mrs. Loyal Davis, an old-time actress, was now a mink-stoled society matron married to a rich surgeon. "Mr. Kallman is currently delighting us in *How to Succeed in Business Without Even Trying*," she told the diners as they finished dessert. Her slight mangling of the title impelled a loud correction from some ancient walker at a nearby table: "It's '*Without Really Trying*.'" Mrs. Davis recovered quickly. "You're right. That's not a fluff my son-in-law would have let himself make!" Everyone here knew that her daughter had married General Electric's smooth-tongued TV pitchman, Ronald Reagan.

Kallman took the podium with the same big grin that reached the back of the Shubert every night. "I confess that I thought the Sarah Siddons Society only existed in *All About Eve*," he told the mostly female audience. As he'd recently learned, it *had* existed only in the movie, until Edie Davis and some local thespian pals decided to boost Chicago theater by setting up a namesake club to honor the best actress in any local production from the previous year. "So I guess," said Kallman, "this is life imitating art that imitated life!" He assured the guests that this year's winner, Julia Meade, was much nicer than the Eve Harrington character in the film that had started things off. "I can also assure you that she's just as beautiful as the two lovely ladies I get to play with every night. Hey, wait, that sounds wrong!" He paused for the laugh. "I mean, get to perform opposite in *How to Succeed*." He asked both of them to stand up at their tables. Maureen Arthur, who played the boss's knockout secretary, rose and waved, her bouffant hair redder than Lucy's; and then came the girl Kallman now described as "my own nightly theatrical love interest—eat your heart out, Cary Grant!— the lovely Miss Dyan Cannon."

Miss Cannon, whose apt nickname was "Frosty," stood up in her little black dress, a Jewish-princess version of Holly Golightly, thought Kallman. She smiled thinly, while the attendees laughingly acknowledged their awareness of what every gossip columnist in the country had lately been telling them—that out in

Hollywood Dyan Cannon was hot-and-heavily involved with Cary Grant, thirty-three years her senior.

Kallman thought about making an age joke, something on the order of how, if you reversed the sexes involved, he could now make a play for Tallulah Bankhead, but he decided against it, since Miss Cannon seemed to have learned her lesson last night. He registered the icy stare she was giving him, and could see that the ring finger of her left hand was in a small beige-colored splint—a bit of theatricality more subtle than anything she managed most nights at the Shubert.

She was a horrible person; always, if not today, putting out too much sparkle and too much drive. Her eyes were as green as his were blue. Grant had spotted her on the tube, like some piece of televised candy being offered for his delectation, when she did an episode of *Malibu Run*. The English film legend had soon made it known that he would like Miss Cannon delivered to him on a Hollywood platter.

"There's so much pulchritude in this audience that a guy doesn't know where to look first!" said Kallman, who acknowledged several female presences, including Margaret O'Brien, who'd come to town with *A Thousand Clowns*. "Margaret and I once went on what I hoped would be a first date. She was too smart for a second one!" The self-deprecation got a laugh.

After the main course, he presented the presenter of Meade's award, and after that, as coffee was served, he made himself part of the mingling, getting photographed with his date, a Chicago Rockefeller named Abra Prentice. He'd mostly been making himself seen with Joanne Field, a more directly lineal heiress (the department store), but she hadn't been available today.

Leaving Abra in order to work the rest of the room, he planted a big kiss on amiable Maureen Arthur, and then a more restrained but nonetheless photographed one on the left cheek of Dyan Cannon. They whispered to each other through tight, faked smiles. "What's with the splint? Looking for an Equity settlement?" "Oh, I'm after more than that." To a reporter who asked about the hand, Cannon just made a dumb-blonde remark about being klutzy.

Kallman looked around for Irv Kupcinet, the city's most important social columnist, but saw no sign of him—maybe he was still mourning his daughter, murdered out in LA a few days after Kennedy got killed. So he settled for saying hello to Margaret O'Brien. "Hey, angel!" (Really, besides the very short-term gig she had at the moment, what had she done lately? A guest shot on *Perry Mason*—maybe a year ago? At this point she should be dating *him* for publicity.) "If I ever get a free night, I'll come and catch you in *A Thousand Clowns*."

"That's okay," O'Brien replied, with a laugh. "You'd only make it a thousand and one." It was hard to figure her mood. Genial? Edgy?

"Still going on dates with Henry's clients?" It was all he could think to ask; at least he hadn't phrased it "Still being a beard?"

"I'm Mrs. Harold Allen Jr.," she said. "And have been for about five years."

"Harold Arlen? Sounds like you're still Judy Garland's little protégée!"

She gave him a bored, unflummoxed smile and a suggestion: "Why don't you go catch up with your other old friend?" She pointed to a man seated nearby and none-too-steadily holding a cup of coffee. It took Kallman a minute to realize that he was looking at a shrunken Mike Connolly. The columnist laughed when he noticed the actor staring at him, but he didn't get up; just wheezed and lit another cigarette. What was he, Kallman wondered, fifty? He looked seventy.

Connolly waved him over, and he sat down, solicitously, as if visiting a shut-in.

"How did that little accident happen?" the columnist asked.

"Running into O'Brien?"

"Smashing Cannon's finger. I heard she went to the emergency room."

"You heard wrong, because I'm sure you heard it from her. She thinks that'll get her an item in the column?"

Connolly let go a phlegmy laugh. "Cary Grant is telling everyone out on the coast that he's going to have you killed."

Kallman just smiled. "He'd better hurry up. I hear production starts soon on *Father Goose*." His tone mocked Grant's project as a has-been's venture.

Connolly didn't make a note; in fact he didn't even have his pad out. And when Kallman remarked that he didn't appear to be working, the columnist admitted that was true, that he was back in Chicago just to see some old friends.

"Mike, you don't look so great. Take care of yourself."

He walked away thinking that this Cary Grant story was bullshit; Connolly was just breaking his balls. Even so, it wouldn't be the worst thing to have that rumor get around. Its circulation would provide a measure of protection if the threat was true, and a measure of publicity if it wasn't.

He found his way back to Abra Prentice and gave her a squeeze.

"Are you going to be in *The Hollywood Reporter*?" she asked, pointing to Connolly.

"Yeah! How about that?"

Abra was sophisticated and rich, but not right for anything long-term. He needed a girl who was rich and *potentially* sophisticated, but even younger than Abra's twenty-one years. He required a girl whose awe of him would activate in him a feeling of command, something to compensate for the obvious, unspoken stumbling block. Maybe one of those starstruck high-school girls writing him fan letters, as soon as she was legal.

A women's-page writer from the *Trib* came over for a quick interview, and he said what he'd said in Cleveland and San Francisco and Los Angeles and the places in between—that he felt "terribly lucky" and "very blessed."

Affecting envy, the reporter asked Abra, "Is he as perfect as he seems?"

"Oh, he's got one or two little vices," his date conceded, though she scarcely knew him well enough to have detected any qualities at all, positive *or* negative.

Still, hearing this suggestion of flaws, Kallman surreptitiously used his thumb to turn around the big ring on his right hand, so that its giant gold mound, studded with an emerald chip, would be hidden from the interviewer's gaze. In one recent Q and A he'd admitted to being a spendthrift, explaining the weakness as a reaction to his dad's devastating losses in Cuba. Right now he tried to draw the most selfless picture possible: "I'm so glad to be here, because the *greatest* gift God gives any of us is the chance to *share* whatever *other* gifts we've got."

Unlike Connolly, the *Trib* girl was taking assiduous notes. While he gave her time to get it all down, it occurred to Kallman that he'd never really repaid Doobie for those life-changing weeks in the fall of '62, which had included bromides like the one he just uttered. He had, however, sent him a printed copy of some remarks he'd recently made, very much in this gifts-from-God vein, at a Christmas-toy charity luncheon. "You know," he now told the reporter, "it's tremendous to be young and have things go your way." And as he once more waited for her to take down the quote, two men, both appearing to be in their late forties, approached. He'd earlier noticed them paying a bit of court to an indifferent Mike Connolly.

"Dick—if I may," said one of them, extending his hand.

"Hey, nice to see you!"

"We've never met," the man corrected him.

"Oh," said Kallman, executing a quick recovery, "I thought maybe we chatted a week or so ago—during the intermission at Burton's *Hamlet*?"

"Must have been someone else. I'm Hugh Benson. And this is Bill Orr, head of TV production at Warner Bros."

"Oh, my gosh!" said Kallman, who knew from his sister-in-law that Orr was married to Jack Warner's stepdaughter. "*Maverick*! *Cheyenne*! *77 Sunset Strip*!"

Both men laughed. "Finch couldn't have done that any better," said Benson.

Kallman's heart pounded at this reference to his eager-beaver *How to Succeed* character. But he played things as cool as he could. "I suppose you're here to talk to Julia Meade—talk about a hot commodity!"

"No," said Benson, "we're here to see *you*. We came all the way from LA to do it."

"Of course," added Orr, "we've both *already* seen you—last night."

"You were terrific, Dick."

"We both thought so."

Someone from the Junior Women's Advertising Club cut into the conversation. "Mr. Kallman, you're so *approachable* that I can't resist—*approaching*!" She handed him her card. "We are so thrilled that you've agreed to be one of the special guests at our luncheon at the Drake in March! I've just gotten word from someone else who'll be joining us. You'll never guess who! But want to try?"

His smile was so forced, so angry, that one could notice the gums above his bared teeth: "Can't you see . . . ?" he whispered seethingly, with a cock of his head to indicate she was interrupting his conversation with these two men. Then he checked himself, remembered his party manners, relaxed his lips, and pretended to be excited and fully attentive. "Okay, let me close my eyes and think who it might be!" He turned to Benson and Orr. "Have you got any ideas, fellas?"

His eyes stayed closed for two seconds, until the woman's loud, beside-herself voice made them pop open again. "Miss America!" she cried.

"Oh, wow!" exclaimed Kallman. "Am I lucky or what, huh, guys? Maybe I'll get even luckier and convince Miss America to become a Mrs.!" He gave the advertising woman a hug and pivoted back into a tight circle with Orr and Benson that she could not penetrate.

"How old are you, Dick?" asked Orr.

"Twenty-five." He hoped that the leaves of the huge nearby rubber plant were shading him from the ceiling lights, and that Margaret O'Brien hadn't told either of these men that their date had been a full seven years ago.

Benson looked reassuringly at his associate, as if to say, "Yeah, twenty-five could still work."

"Dick, we'd like to change your life," said Orr. "How soon can you get out to the coast?"

CHAPTER 20

MARCH 10, 1981

"I love having you here, Freckles."

My daughter, Laurie, inherited the sprinkling of dots across her nose and cheekbones from Lois, her mother, dead six years now. Laurie had just begun her spring break from Georgetown and was spending its first two days with me.

"Thanks, Dad," she replied, "but I hate depriving you of your honey."

"Stop!" My face reddened, even as I laughed. Last night, with a mixture of embarrassment and pride, I'd told her a bit about Devin, and on her own she'd figured out the rest. The three of us had plans to meet for lunch today.

"It's ridiculous that you guys think you can't stay in the bedroom while I sleep on the couch out here," she protested. I put my fingers in my ears, and when I unplugged them, she asked: "Would you like to know the actual arrangements of my dorm suite?"

"No."

She got up to get more juice before coming back to the just-refolded living-room sleep sofa, where we were both sitting in our pajamas. Dick's scrapbook sat on the glass coffee table. A crucial hearing in the case would take place later this morning, and its imminence had prompted a long talk about him last night. Laurie now reopened the giant album to the pages on *Hank*, his TV show. It was the scrapbook's biggest section by far: dozens of interviews, profiles, and promotional pix from the Sunday papers' TV supplements.

"I thought it was amazing, when we used to watch him, that you actually knew someone on TV." She was recalling our regular Friday-night visits during 1965–66, the single season the show had lasted. Lois and I had split the year before.

"It's a good thing you were only five years old. Any viewer six or over was saying 'Oy vey.'" The show's premise was preposterously goofy: Dick played a college "drop-in," Hank Dearborn, a knowledge-hungry orphan unable to afford an education who, in order to hear lectures, disguised himself as students he knew would be absent from class. The rest of the time he worked like a Trojan: selling sundries from a van, delivering dry cleaning, whatever. He was also raising a kid sister only a little older than Laurie was then. Oh, and—inevitably—he was in love with the daughter of the registrar he had to stay one step ahead of.

"I *loved* the show," said Laurie.

"I know," I responded, rolling my eyes. In one early episode Dick dressed up as the only Indian student at the college, looking sort of hot in a fringed buckskin jacket, a feathered headband, and a full face of bronzer. As "Sam Lightfoot" he resisted the blandishments of the track coach, who hoped to turn him into the next Jim Thorpe. His reply to the coach's pleadings—"Not want talk!"—became Laurie's catchphrase, for years, whenever she misbehaved and I demanded some explanation from her.

The show's single distinguished feature was its theme song, which had lyrics by Johnny Mercer, no less. I now took my coffee to the little piano across the room and played it for Laurie:

> *He's up with the sun,*
> *And he's got the college winging,*
> *As he goes off*

UP WITH THE SUN

On another swinging day.
There's jobs to be done
Or errands to run.
He's A—number one—OK!

Once I was through, Laurie assured me: "Rex Harrison couldn't have talked that song better."

"It's called parlando, my dear." That my ability to play anything had come with a complete incapacity to carry a tune had been a lifelong joke between my daughter and me.

She dashed off to the shower. Before she met Devin at lunch Laurie had planned a morning of downtown shopping for semi-punk beachwear (don't ask) that she could bring to Fort Lauderdale. She would fly to Florida tomorrow with two girlfriends. For all I knew they'd be taking the same New York–Miami flight that Jimmy and Paulie and Dante took after the murders—with blood on their clothes, according to Devin; just as there'd been blood on that necklace they fenced at Delectable Collectibles.

It was the same courtroom on Centre Street—Part 50—where the pleas had been entered. But this morning, and for all future proceedings, Devin and I decided to sit far apart. We feared a suspicious look from a judge or attorney who might wonder what connection the two of us had to the case and to each other.

We ourselves hardly looked at Judge Rothwax today, fixated as we were on Douchebag Paulie, the only defendant here this time, with his lawyer. How different he looked from six or seven weeks ago! He was puffy with indolence and starchy jail food and probably sedatives that were not quite taking care of his fear of This-Here's-Dante: every few minutes he began to shake a little, and a look of terror would dilute the stupidity of his expression.

The same tough-looking assistant district attorney from

January, the one with the mustache, was here again, impassively informing the court that Mr. Boccara intended to plead guilty—that is, to *change* his plea—to a Class B felony, robbery in the first degree, in exchange for his testimony in the people's separate case against Dante Forti. "We ask Your Honor that, some months from now, before imposing sentence, the court agree to be informed regarding the nature, extent, and quality of Mr. Boccara's cooperation during the homicide trial to which it will have been relevant."

The legal diction and that *"Mr.* Boccara" made Paulie sound like a consequential, respectable figure, almost an officer of the court. But his decision to testify against his brother-in-law explained the terrified look on his face.

Rothwax asked Mr. Vincent, the defense lawyer, to stipulate his approval of the deal, and the attorney offered it, along with a petition for protective custody. He pointed out that Paulie had recently spent several days in the Bellevue Hospital prison ward.

"And why was that?" asked the judge.

"For a nervous breakdown," explained Mr. Vincent, who walked a sheaf of medical records up to the bench. "Threats have been reaching Mr. Boccara through the Rikers Island grapevine ever since he concluded his arrangement with the district attorney's office."

"Has any physical harm come to him?" Rothwax wanted to know.

"No, but—"

"Good," the judge said crisply, turning his head toward the assistant DA. "And I trust you'll do what you can to make sure it stays that way?"

"Yes, sir."

"Fine," Rothwax replied. "That's done." He ordered Paulie sent back to the prison's general population.

Paulie was just intelligent enough to realize that his lawyer hadn't gotten what he wanted, and that he himself was in renewed danger. A new look of doughy fright crossed his face, but his brain seemed mercifully unable to sustain the emotion.

As they led him out, he waved hello to me, apparently thinking I had some official function here, since I always seemed to be present. And again he reacted to my prop-pin tie clasp—with a sort of idiotic grin, like a kid recognizing an old toy. It creeped me out.

The proceedings continued for a few more minutes, with Judge Rothwax signing a warrant for the arrest of Jimmy Ingrassia up in Westchester.

"Poor Andy," I said, with a laugh, once Devin and I reconnected out on the sidewalk.

"Don't worry," Devin replied. "Andy'll get him back in a few nights."

"Really?"

"They'll let him go on bail. Detective V explained it all to me."

"Then why does Paulie have to stay on Rikers?"

"Because there's a pecking order. Paulie is like backup, icing on the cake. Jimmy's the one who delivered the story and the shooter. What is it, tenderhearted *papi*? You feeling sorry for Douchebag Paulie?"

"No," I replied, though you'd have to have a heart of stone not to feel *something* for the quivering mess we'd just seen. "In fact, here's what I really don't get: they make him plead guilty to robbery—but not even to manslaughter?"

"Pretty sweet, isn't it? But that's what it takes if you want to put away the worst guy, which in this instance, believe me, is This-Here's-Dante. He pulled the trigger on both your friends."

I remembered the January indictment that described Forti, unnamed, as "another participant."

"It's the opposite of Ronnie Reagan, *papi*. If you want justice, it's got to trickle *up*."

I'd arranged for Laurie to meet us for lunch on Franklin Street at Peggy Doyle's restaurant, an atrocious place out of another legal era, when every cop and process server was Irish. I'd wandered into it sort of by accident when I had jury duty a few years ago, and it was the only restaurant I could think of near both the court and Laurie's punk shopping venues.

She was already there, jumping up to greet us as soon as we entered. "Hola! It's Devin, right?" She gave him a big hug, and the two of them immediately began chattering away in Spanish.

"Show-offs," I said.

"Five years, New York City public schools!" Laurie declared proudly.

"From birth, Dominican Republic, baby!" Devin offered as a topper. The two of them high-fived each other, and I felt a strange moment of dissociation, being here with a daughter I wasn't really "supposed" to have as well as a lover who wasn't supposed to be this young.

They ordered hamburgers, and I got a plate of roast beef and mashed potatoes. Laurie showed us her purchases, including a black bikini with deliberate rips in it, and we told her all about the hearing. I'd already let her know how the case had been cracked, and she now declared, "If *I'd* been a gay guy on that corner or in that bar"—*Jesus, my daughter knows about Rounds!*—"I'd have spilled every bean to Devin. Dad, your taste in men, the little of it you ever let me see, was *never* this good." She looked genuinely delighted for me. As she saw things, there was no "inappropriateness" to me and Devin; it was appropriate for me to be happy, and that was that.

"So, what were the others like?" Devin asked her.

"Scared little accountants with dandruff" was her answer.

He looked at me. "I love this place. I love her."

Some talk about Georgetown followed, including mention of how Laurie's plans might include law school. (Where would I get the money to help with *that*?) Her interest in the bargaining and leverage that had led to this morning's plea deal made me realize this was a serious postgraduate possibility. Devin interrupted his explanation of some legal particulars only long enough to say to me, "Careful you don't get gravy on your tiepin." We told Laurie about the weird fascination this object seemed to exert on the defendants. "Are you sure this is a prop?" she asked, leaning in and tugging my tie to get a better look. "It doesn't seem cheap."

When Devin told us that the trial would probably start in June, Laurie seemed pleased: her exams would be over and she planned to come up for it. The waitress then came around with a little étagère on a cart. The piece of cake that Devin chose looked as if it had been there since *Seventeen* was playing at the Broadhurst. "So gross it's almost good" was his verdict.

Laurie had to scoot, to go meet another Georgetown classmate. She kissed us both and said to Devin: "See you in court, if not before!" I wondered if I really wanted her to attend the trial, which would put who-knows-what features of the gay world on display. "Well, it'll be your chance to meet Dolores Gray" was all I said.

"Who the hell is that?" she asked, lingering for a moment.

"Exactly," said Devin. "Or more like who the hell does she *think* she is?"

I laughed and decided to relax. I took a large swallow of my second glass of wine and sang of the cruelties of show business, knowing one line would be all Laurie could stand of my voice: "'First you're another sloe-eyed vamp . . .'" I felt pleasantly lit. Here I was, happy, with my little family. So much for that earlier dissociation.

"Do you cook?" was Laurie's parting question for Devin.

"A little bit."

"Then fatten him up. He's way too skinny." She pointed to all the mashed potatoes I'd left on my plate, as if that were my fault and not Peggy Doyle's. True, I had less of an appetite these days. But I put it down to being in love. Which by this point—oh, my God—I guess I was.

When Laurie was gone, Devin said, "Don't tell your old lady, Mrs. Gray, because I'm sure she wouldn't trust me, but—"

"But what?"

He gently removed my tie clasp. "I think maybe we should have this appraised."

"Really?" I wondered if this might not create more potential problems with Detective Volker, who could wind up thinking I'd helped myself to it, whereas in fact, unlike the scrapbook, it had been foisted upon me. "Suit yourself," I told Devin.

"Your girl's fantastic, *papi*. I'm glad she's coming to the trial. It'll give you support."

"Support?"

He gave me one of those looks, like "Really?" And it then occurred to me, for the first time, that I'd have to testify.

CHAPTER 21

SEPTEMBER 9–17, 1965

"I be-*lieve* in *you*!"

The Applause sign—a cooperative presence never available in nightclubs or on film sets—prodded the studio audience into prompt, enthusiastic clapping, during which Skitch Henderson, the *Tonight Show* conductor, nodded a signal to Kallman and they segued into the theme song from *Hank*.

Amping up his smile, the new sitcom star sang of himself in the third person:

He'll drive, clean your clothes,
Be your butler or a porter,
If it means another quarter
In the bank.
He'll get his degree,
His Phi Beta key,
And get 'em both for free!
That's Hank.

Everyone watching understood the lyrics, because a few minutes earlier Johnny Carson had explained the premise of the series premiering eight nights from now, when he introduced "a very talented newcomer, Mr. Dick Kallman." And now, having delivered Mercer's catchy lines, Kallman acknowledged a second round of applause by flashing the audience a smile as he walked over to the chair between Carson's desk and Ed McMahon's couch.

"I called you a newcomer," said Johnny, beginning the interview, "but you've actually had some top-notch TV tutoring that prepared you for *Hank*, didn't you?"

"Well," said Kallman, with the feigned reluctance he'd rehearsed an hour ago with Johnny's producer, "I had the chance to work with a certain redhead who appears 'on another network,' as they say."

The Applause sign instructed the NBC live audience that it was okay to clap for the empress of CBS, and Kallman then elaborated on his participation, "a couple of years ago," in Lucy's workshop. "It was a comedy education that money can't buy."

"And the fellow you're playing in *Hank*: he doesn't *have* the money to buy a college education. Is that right?"

Kallman elaborated on the show's gimmick, mentioning that it had cost fifteen thousand dollars to transform a 1934 model ambulance into Hank's jack-of-all-trades service-and-vending vehicle.

Carson did a slow, pensive take. "Fifteen thousand on a prop, huh? And I'm guessing that a Johnny Mercer theme song doesn't come cheap." Another silent pause, before picking up the ashtray from his desk and showing the Made in Japan label on its bottom. "You always know where you stand with NBC," he concluded, to a roar from the audience.

Kallman was the evening's last guest. Tonight's program had become a stag party after a bronchial condition forced Selma Diamond to cancel at the last minute. Perched on the couch, to Kallman's right, were Henry Morgan, who'd done the curmudgeonly bit he'd been doing on radio and TV since the forties, and Myron Cohen, who'd told the Catskills jokes he'd been telling since the thirties. Kallman himself, only eight years younger than Johnny, felt that he was out here in costume. Bill Orr had insisted he do tonight's show with his dyed-blond varsity *Hank* hair, which looked so unnatural it might have been a wig.

Seeing the director give Carson the one-minute signal, Kallman sped up his explanation of how Hank's situation was actually similar to that of Hugh Benson, the show's creator, who way back when had struggled—and scammed a little—to get an education at USC.

Johnny expressed the scripted hope that Hank's adventures as a "drop-in" might inspire some young viewers not to drop *out*, and prophesied that his guest would have a big hit on his hands once the show aired next week on NBC. At this close range—in person, though not to the camera—Johnny looked bored, and resentful about having to shill for the network. Over the last several days he'd already had on John Forsythe and Ben Gazzara to plug their new NBC series, and now, after saying good night to Kallman, he was telling the audience that tomorrow night's guests would include "Roger Smith, TV's new Mister Roberts"—Bill Orr's other upcoming show on NBC.

As the credits rolled, Johnny, now inaudible, affected the kind of animated private conversation that made people at home wish they could lip-read. "You fit right in here," he said to Kallman, with a bigger smile than the remark required. His guest felt momentarily flattered, imagining that the host referred to the realm of network television. But then he realized, from the tilt of Carson's head, that Johnny meant he'd perceived something in Kallman that seemed to belong to the antique world of Henry Morgan and Myron Cohen. After buttoning his jacket and coming out from behind the desk, Carson shook hands with the older men and left.

Kallman was out on Forty-Eighth Street by 7:10 p.m. *Tonight* taped here in New York several hours before it aired in the East, and another three before it was broadcast in California, to which Kallman had to return on a 10:45 p.m. reverse-redeye. The flight would get him back to LA around two in the morning, allowing him to show up for the seven a.m. call on *Hank*'s brutal production schedule.

He had more than enough time to get to the airport. He could have booked a nine p.m. departure but had chosen the later flight because he allowed himself to imagine that Johnny, or maybe Skitch, might ask if he wanted to grab dinner at Sardi's once the taping was through. Either way, the coast-to-coast logistics were ridiculous. Johnny was known to be unhappy in New York, to be thinking of moving his show permanently to LA, not just for the two weeks each year that the network allowed him to do it there. But in the meantime, all the stars of those NBC series—Forsythe and Gazzara included, in the midst of their own heavy shooting schedules—had to be dragged across the country to Rockefeller Center for a single night.

And yet, just sharing in this predicament made Kallman feel like show-business royalty. Sitting in first class on the plane, he permitted himself a cocktail, though he was already experiencing the difficulties of maintaining Hank's college-boy figure. A minute after takeoff, instead of fuming about it, he decided to revel in the time-zone tyranny: the show he'd just taped would come on in the East when the plane was over western Pennsylvania. A few hours later the program would begin airing in whatever western state Hank's "Western State University" was supposed to be in. Within six hours' time, tens of millions of people would know his face and name, this time not as a player in some one-shot ensemble production, but as a star. He imagined the gate agent who'd be greeting this flight at LAX: "Oh, my God, you were on TV an hour ago!" By that time he'd have been seen by Mike Connolly; maybe by Lucy herself. And maybe even by Kenny.

In his trailer, at seven thirty the next morning, he was running lines with a script girl who told him how great he'd been on

Carson. She was reading the part of the track coach, telling Hank, who'd be dressed up as Cherokee Sam Lightfoot, that he should go talk to the captain of the team. "'Not want to see captain,'" Kallman responded. "'*Captain* sound to me like United States cavalry.'"

He wasn't yet dressed as the Indian. He was outfitted in Hank's any-and-all-chores uniform, with its cap like a milkman's, for a different scene that he had to shoot first.

"Let's take a break, honey," he told the script girl.

"Sure," she said, setting down the pages beside a copy of Robert Osborne's new book, *Academy Awards Illustrated*, which had just been messengered over with Bob's good wishes for *Hank* and some nice words about the *Tonight Show* appearance. The inscription was Bob-nice and Bob-gentlemanly, but the accompanying note contained no suggestion of their getting together.

Once the girl left the trailer, Kallman rang his service to find out whatever Carson-related accolades had started coming in this morning. Sure enough, there'd been a call from Abe Burrows, which he ought to answer before the day was out, no matter that the long-delayed *How to Succeed* movie had finally gone to Bobby.

He looked down a list of print interviews scheduled for the run-up to the premiere—three today and four tomorrow. It was hard to believe the frantic crescendo things were reaching, given how long it had taken to get *Hank* off the ground. Warners hadn't signed him until August of last year, seven full months after he'd met Benson and Orr in Chicago. That period had then been followed by a lengthy, stomach-churning stretch spent waiting to see if the pilot got picked up. During that time he'd wound up doing *Come Blow Your Horn* in some playhouse forty miles from where he'd scored with Finch at the Chicago Shubert—a circumstance that had gotten him wondering if his downward slide was going to start all over again.

The script girl was back. "They want you now. To shoot the scene at the truck with Linda."

"On it."

He was at the soundstage a minute later, making an exaggerated bow to acknowledge the crew's applause for his having scored on Johnny. But he didn't fail to notice a pair of grips with their backs turned to him. Maybe his perfectionism was starting to bother some people? Well, let *them* travel to New York and back in less than twenty-four hours for the sake of this show. He could use his mother here right now; she'd be bawling out these guys as if they were two sullen clerks behind the check-in desk at The Balsams.

Hugh Benson, the ever-present producer, hovered ten feet away. In those impending print interviews Kallman would be mentioning how Hugh had become a "father figure" to him, though Benson was mostly a pain in the ass, always trying to rein him in, make him take it down a notch and not overdo what Benson himself had liked so much in Chicago. Whenever he laid on Hank's ingratiating shtick a little too thickly, the producer would shout the name of his over-the-top *How to Succeed* character, scolding him, supposedly with good humor.

Like everyone here, Benson worried about the show's going up against *The Wild Wild West*, with its big CBS budget and great advance word of mouth. *Hank* might prove too good-hearted and silly to survive beyond twenty-six weeks, or even thirteen. But the present moment's pressure involved getting this fourth episode into the can. The director was speeding things along, trying to wrap up this truck scene before Kallman had to be slathered in Indian makeup.

The lead hit his mark and said a fast hello to Linda Foster, who played the registrar's daughter, his love interest, and who unlike Dyan Cannon wasn't a problem, at least so far. The cameras rolled, and she threw herself into warning him against the Sam Lightfoot scheme and disguise.

DORIS

Honey, it's too risky!

HANK

C'mon, Doris, you know how I feel. I want all the learning I can get. I may have had to quit high school and get a job, but I refuse to let that get in the way of my education.

"Cut!" called the director, apparently pleased.

"Finch! Finch!" cried Benson, apparently not.

Sniggers from the two guys who'd turned their backs.

"It's really a triplex!" Kallman insisted. "C'mon and see!" He urged Erskine Johnson, the Hearst reporter getting a tour of his new apartment on Doheny Drive, to come up the last flight of stairs.

After a quick look at the partial third floor, the two men returned to the spacious living room on the first. "I really wanted this to feel like something out of *Carefree* or *Swing Time*," the actor explained, gesturing toward the white and mirrored walls. The reporter made note of this somewhat arcane reference to those penthouses Fred and Ginger once cavorted through, but was puzzled by the heavy antiques filling the airy space; hardly the sort of art deco stuff you'd find in the old Astaire movies.

Kallman sat across from an ornately carved armoire. He had thought of having Linda Foster here with him for a couple of these interviews: a suggestion of offscreen romance would be good publicity for each of them as well as the show. But he couldn't bring himself to share the ink, and besides, she was dating the star of the by-now-sputtering *Ben Casey*.

He proceeded to give Johnson more information than necessary about the vases and paintings, all of them acquired since May, when he leased the apartment with the beginnings of his *Hank* salary. A couple of drawers contained the results of accelerated jewelry buying, but he decided it wouldn't be in good taste to display such items to a reporter.

"I'm really a businessman at heart, like my dad was. I've furnished the place with these expensive pieces because I know that three years from now I can sell everything for three times what I paid. I've already been offered twice what I shelled out for that carved cabinet!" As he went on talking and the reporter said nothing, he thought of how he actually *could* go about selling these things on a rolling basis—sort of be living with them and not living with them all at once; it would be a way of turning a continual profit on his own home. But he didn't share the musing with Erskine Johnson. He didn't want to divert attention from *Hank* or to sound as if he had some sort of fallback business plan. Because he didn't. The show was going to succeed, and then lead to a better one, until that led to the movies or he became a top-tier TV staple like Lucy herself.

So instead he talked about how his new success represented the redemption of his father's unjust, late-in-life failures. The theme for this afternoon would be dutiful son, not swinging bachelor or unlikely aesthete. Johnson recorded everything with no objection or skepticism. He seemed glad to be handed his angle by the subject himself.

Kallman felt thoroughly relaxed, devoid of the nervousness he'd always felt in the presence of that other show-business chronicler, Mike Connolly. But even Connolly seemed to be bending in his direction. Since yesterday the actor had been carrying in his pocket a wire that the columnist had sent after the Carson show: YOU'RE IN THE PICTURE—certification that Dick Kallman had entered the pantheon of prime time.

———————

At six p.m. on Thursday, after eleven hours on the set, he ducked into his trailer to pick up the latest rubber-banded stack of mail, which he brought out to the car that would take him to a recording studio in west LA. NBC trumped Warner Bros., so the album they had him making, *Dick Kallman Drops In as Hank*, would be coming out from RCA, the network's parent company. This was certainly not *his* idea of a first album—the cover would have him sporting Hank's blond hair and letter sweater—but they wanted it in stores within weeks of tomorrow night's premiere.

He still had two tracks to lay down this evening. One was "Come Rain or Come Shine," which he'd fought for against Orr, who didn't want "too much of this old stuff" and would have preferred that he cover a couple of Beatles songs. The second number to be recorded tonight, Les Baxter's "Lookin' Around," gave him a chance to belt in an almost angry way, the song's lyrics being a hipster's plea for relief from his own hurt and cynicism. As the industry cliché went, it had a good beat and you could dance to it. The song's mood didn't fit Hank's image, and it wasn't kid stuff, but at least it was *new*, and that was enough for Orr:

> *My only road's a lonely road*
> *And love's a one-way track,*
> *Bein' true to people who*
> *Don't ever love me back!*

They had everything finished by eight fifteen. While being driven home to the place on Doheny Drive, he leafed through the packet of mail still on the back seat: lots of letters from girls who'd seen him on Carson, and from a couple of guys, too, whose praise for his singing and sophisticated conversation was easily decodable as interest in something else. The strictly-business letters, which tried to do an end run around Ted Witzer, his new agent at William Morris, included one that asked whether he'd be available to open a supermarket in San Diego in November. There was even an aerogram all the way from New Zealand, which he slit open with an index fingernail that could use a trim.

Its author turned out to be Carole Cook. The main page and little back flap were entirely covered in her big, friendly handwriting. She'd composed the letter in her dressing room in a theater in Auckland on Monday afternoon; its arrival seemed a miracle of speed, as if it had been conveyed by Telstar. Carole wrote that she had done *Hello, Dolly!* for six months in Australia and was now taking it to three different cities in New Zealand. She'd been having the time of her life; had gotten married last year, at forty, to an actor, a lovely guy named Tom Troupe—with Bob Osborne as the best man!

Kallman nearly stopped reading. With the exception of himself, almost everyone from the Lucy days had seemed to remain pals, either with Lucy herself or with one another. But a letter to him from Carole, who'd shown up in a dozen episodes of Lucy's current sitcom, felt like an act of charity, proceeding from her exceptional good nature. She'd been moved to write, she said, by the arrival of a houseguest that morning: Kenny Nelson, who'd just finished doing *Stop the World* at some summer playhouse in Connecticut and was giving himself a three-week adventure below the Equator, seeing her and Tom in New Zealand and then a couple of friends in Brazil. She'd read about Dick's upcoming series, but hadn't known about Carson until Kenny reported that he'd seen the show Thursday night, hours before getting on his plane out of New York. Carole passed on his appraisal: "'Dick was very good,' he said in that shy, solemn way of his."

And with that she was out of space on the aerogram, having just room enough to squeeze in congratulations and some Xs and Os.

He was thunderstruck. Yes, this might be Carole being Carole—bubbly, generous, with no hidden meaning—but what was the meaning of what *Kenny* had said? This could *not* be a casual remark. It *had* to be a sort of message. And with everything going his way, he decided that it could only mean everything.

"For the woman in my life!" Kallman proclaimed, comically descending to one knee as he presented his mother with a pricey topaz ring, a thank-you-for-everything gift. So as not to outshine it, he'd tonight worn none of his own new jewelry from the drawer at home.

Charlie and Phyllis applauded. It was just the four of them for this early-evening family dinner in what was now solely Zara Kallman's apartment. Since Torchy's death last year, his widow had grown harder to please—even Dick, on occasion, could now do wrong. "I'm proud of you" was all she said in accepting the ring, as if bestowing a gift instead of receiving one.

The meal, just concluded, had been Chinese takeout, though Charlie and Phyllis, who were not getting along, had brought a good bottle of wine.

"Go sit," commanded Zara, shooing her sons and daughter-in-law to the living room. She wanted a free hand to get everything cleared away before they turned on the television at eight o'clock.

Once on the couch, Dick nervously fingered the only bit of jewelry, hidden beneath the lapel of his blazer, that he had on: the pin that Kenny had spurned during *Seventeen*. He wasn't sure why he was wearing it. Probably to remain defiant and "fixed" as he triumphed on this opening night infinitely bigger and more important than the long-ago, misery-making one for *Seventeen*. But maybe he had put it on as a secret true-love badge, a token of his faith in whatever signal Kenny had just sent him via Carole, and in whatever signs were bound to follow: A confession that years ago Kenny had just been too scared to accept what was being offered? A plea that he be forgiven for his cowardice and his mistake?

Dick had spent today shooting the episode that would air a week after "Cherokee Hank," but he'd thought of little except Carole's letter. When he left here tonight, he wouldn't be able to go have a drink at the Hub, because forty minutes from now his face would be known to additional tens of millions of Americans beyond those who'd seen Carson last week, including the patrons of West Hollywood bars. Besides, as he'd told Doobie three years ago, he didn't do that kind of thing anymore, or not so much that anyone had a chance of knowing. Maybe a few months from now he'd have the industry clout to do a specialized, super-discreet version of the "ordering in" that Cary Grant had done with Dyan Cannon.

The wall telephone in the kitchen rang, and the deferential voice with which Zara began chatting indicated to those in the living room that it was probably Father duBois on the line. "I'm honored that you'd call on this night," said Mrs. Kallman. "This wouldn't be happening without what you did for him." Back in '62, she meant.

"Dick!" she summoned.

"Tell him I'll call him tomorrow."

Charlie, who knew a lot but not all about '62, shook his head. His brother responded to the rebuke by saying, "*What?* I'll be more relaxed then."

Doobie had already seen the show a few hours ago on the East Coast. "He says that it's terrific and that so are you," reported Zara, after she'd hung up and gone back to putting away the dishes.

Charlie, still annoyed over the discourtesy to the priest, picked this moment to confront Dick about some recent interview quotes concerning their father. "'People were lucky to get out of Cuba with one suitcase each'? Really? And you were going to be the 'heir to twelve million dollars'?"

"What's your point?"

Phyllis, who knew show business and knew her brother-in-law, laughed.

To change the subject, Dick showed her Mike Connolly's wire: YOU'RE IN THE PICTURE. "I've got to say, it's pretty sweet when even *he* affirms it," the new star told Charlie's wife.

Phyllis laughed again, this time over what, she told Dick, the telegram actually meant. "You don't remember that quiz show Jackie Gleason had about five years back? That was its name: *You're in the Picture.* It lasted one episode—and flopped so badly that Gleason apologized for it a week later—on the air."

Dick put the wire back in his pocket, with a smile that pretended he'd gotten Connolly's joke all along. Phyllis's chortling reminded him, at three minutes to eight, how he dreaded hearing the laugh track that would accompany *Hank*'s premiere episode. Orr and Benson had promised that the show would never need or have one, but the network had insisted otherwise.

CHAPTER 22

JUNE 9–10, 1981

I was walking through the theater district in my good tuxedo, just before eight o'clock—but I wasn't bound for a theater. *They're Playing Our Song* had a few months left to run, but I'd bowed out and was just giving lessons for a while. So I was free to be heading toward a party, in the Algonquin's Oak Room, for what would have been Cole Porter's ninetieth birthday.

Dolores, set to perform a number at it, had asked me to go as her guest: a reward for helping her to rehearse it last week at the baby grand inside her apartment. But she wanted me to meet her at the hotel, not to escort her there. "This is business," she'd explained, which might sound insulting, but I get it. She would be showing up for *work*, no matter that she'd be lavishly dining and drinking along with everyone else. If arriving solo helped her to compartmentalize things and keep control of her nerves, I understood.

Devin, who still couldn't stand her, was happy to have me go. "If it was Carole," he'd told me, "I'd be jealous of you both. But that one? Good luck having a good time." In any case, Devin was taking another night course, in English composition, at a community college in Queens. He'd be at the apartment (he'd had a key for months) when I got home.

A little west of Sixth Avenue I got momentarily engulfed by about fifty demonstrators. Half of them were in the street and half were on the sidewalk. They were marching to the UN to protest Israel's surprise bombing of a nuclear reactor in Iraq. The US had made a point of deploring the attack, but everybody knew we were happy to have the Israelis do our dirty work. The long-term meaning of all this was over my head, but it made me nervous. I missed Jimmy Carter.

And the first people I recognized after stepping into the Oak Room were straight out of Ronnie Reagan's new era: Pat Buckley (Mrs. William F.), fantastically tall and large-eyed, talking to Jerry Zipkin, the walker whose most famous walkee, Nancy Reagan, was the subject of their conversation. "So what's it going to take to relax her enough to come to something like this?" Mrs. Buckley asked, annoyed by the First Lady's reluctance to leave her husband's side more than two months after the Hinckley shooting. Zipkin answered, about his supposed best friend: "I doubt she'll emerge for ages. She wants to be accorded that one-year period of mourning Jackie observed, even if Ron didn't actually *die*."

Unknown from Adam, I was happy to gawk and mingle as I looked around for Dolores. While I gazed at the flowers atop the piano—Porter's beloved carnations—Mary Lindsay glided by without her beautiful husband; I still felt bad about the failure of his comeback. Judith Jamison, gorgeous in a white pantsuit and almost as tall as Mrs. Buckley, stood a few feet away. And I saw Anne Slater, another of what Ed Koch would call the "richies," as she pushed into a little circle containing Al Hirschfeld. "Why don't you caricature *me*?" she asked, ten seconds after introducing herself. "I'm off the clock," Hirschfeld answered, with a smile, though I got the feeling he would have liked to reply, "What have you ever done except wear those ridiculous blue sunglasses indoors?"

Bacall, who'd won a Tony two nights ago for *Woman of the Year*, was being mobbed. The awards had taken place at the

Mark Hellinger, where in April I'd finally seen *Sugar Babies*. Was there any chance that Ann Miller—who'd been in Hollywood's *Kiss Me, Kate*, after all—had the night off to be here? I asked an older, evidently gay guy if she might be on the program, and he answered "Too darn *not*, I'm afraid."

When I found my table, I noticed there were little rows of carnations even between the place settings. Dolores, already seated, extended a hand but not a cheek. She mentioned that she'd been with her husband—Crevolin, the millionaire horse owner—at some big party in Washington the other night, and that he'd since gone back to California. I'd never met him, and I didn't really get what the two of them had going on—but who would get what *I* had going on? Of one thing I was sure: she wouldn't ask me about Devin.

This was actually a *party*, though it looked like a benefit and its organizers had designed the event to promote the kind of cabaret that was now being produced regularly here in the Oak Room. As everyone awaited the first course, Steve Ross did a round of quiet songs at the piano, before having Celeste Holm sing an abbreviated version of "Miss Otis Regrets."

Dolores, who wouldn't come on until after the food, mostly stayed quiet. Across from us somebody's wife asked everyone within earshot whom we felt more sorry for: Billie Jean King, having to admit to a lesbian affair at a recent press conference, or her spouse, having to sit loyally beside her and act as if this had been just a teeny, uncharacteristic lapse on Billie Jean's part. The husband of the woman who'd just asked the question wanted to change the subject; he said he thought that Liz Taylor's performance in *The Little Foxes*, up for a Tony the other night, was overrated. Dolores and I had to tell him that neither of us had seen it. I was just glad that *42nd Street* had won Best Musical, because that might ensure a longer run for Carole Cook.

When we made it all the way to the poached-pears dessert, Ross returned to the piano to accompany Miss Mabel Mercer herself, who sang "I Get a Kick Out of You." As we got closer to Dolores's number, a last pause in the program allowed for a quiet, tense conversation between the two of us.

"So have you met Mr. Ehren?" she asked. By now I knew that this was the name of the tough-looking assistant district attorney.

"I'm supposed to see him tomorrow morning," I replied. As Devin predicted, I'd been asked to come in and go over the testimony I would be giving at the trial, which was finally set to begin next week.

"I didn't like him," Dolores said, with predictable finality.

I now worried about what might be in store for me. "What did he do?"

"He took me through the questions he'll be asking me—mostly about the business, it seems. He'll want me to explain what was missing from the apartment after the murder and so forth. Which is fine. But he also suggested that I 'dress down a little'—as if I need to be told about professional attire! And he told me I should be prepared for questions from the defense lawyer about my 'friendship' with Richard."

I said nothing. Despite my curiosity, I had never pressed Dolores for much enlightenment on this score, not after her "My beautiful Richard!" outburst at our first lunch, and certainly not following her icy reaction to the implements she discovered on Dick's closet floor. Everything about her tonight was as tightly controlled as her makeup and chignon, but her agitation stayed evident. She clearly had something to get off her *poitrine*, as she might have put it.

"Mr. Ehren says that the defense lawyer may suggest I was *in thrall* to Richard, that I *allowed* myself to be used as some kind of prestigious cover for his sharp business practices."

I tried, cautiously, drawing her out on this. "I'm guessing the lawyer would do that to blame the victim? To make it seem not so terrible that someone shady got killed?"

"To make us both look louche. To make the jury think I was emotionally . . . dependent on Richard."

She seemed to be tiptoeing toward what she regarded as the crux of the matter, something more awful than anything else she'd endured since the murder. "Mr. Ehren," she gravely concluded, "believes that the defense attorney may suggest to the jury that I was *older* than Richard."

At which point—thanks to Devin's impact on me?—I actually managed to say, "Oh, for Christ's sake, Dolores."

———————

It was past two when I got home. Devin was up watching a Mary Tyler Moore rerun.

"No Joe Franklin?" I asked. One recent night at this hour I'd shown him how, when I have insomnia, I'll sometimes watch Franklin's gentle, eccentric talk show, always full of old vaude-villians and girls from the *Ziegfeld Follies*. "*Papi*," he'd said, "I don't know if you're an old soul or just *old*."

He turned off Mary and told me how he'd watched Carson after arriving at the apartment. Charles Nelson Reilly had been one of the guests.

"You know," I pointed out, "Reilly was in *How to Succeed*—not on the tour with Dick but in the original Broadway produc-tion. He didn't talk about that tonight, did he?"

Devin looked at me like I'd gone 'round the bend. "You know, in two weeks," he said, therapeutically, "you'll be able to forget about Dick Kallman."

According to Detective Volker, the trial, starting on the sev-enteenth, would last maybe five or six days. Laurie had arranged to take time off from the summer internship she had in a Wash-ington law office; she would stay with a friend up here and meet us at court each day.

"You're right," I conceded, in the face of Devin's concern. "But just now he's almost *always* on my mind." I lifted the left lapel of my tux and showed him the prop pin. What fraternal impulse had made me put it on again tonight? Maybe knowing that a party for Cole Porter was the sort of occasion Dick would have loved, even as he felt envious of anyone who'd been asked to perform instead of *him*?

"*Ay ay vey*," said Devin, using his Latin version of the Jew-ish phrase once he saw the pin. "You shouldn't have worn that."

"I know. It's just—"

"It's just that you ought to get it insured before you take it outside."

I looked puzzled.

"I got it appraised."

This startled me. We'd had the idea to do that and then kept putting it off, Devin seeming to decide that any focus on the pin would only increase my preoccupation with the murders. But now he told me that he'd gotten it done because Laurie was coming next week and, after all, he'd promised her back in March that he would.

"Where did you bring it?" I asked.

"Delectable Collectibles."

"*What?*"

"Relax, *papi*. Nobody remembered me from our little drop-by last fall. And I wore a baseball cap. It was the only place I could think of—what do I know from jewelry? It's not like I'm Liberace."

"How much did they say it's worth?"

"About three thousand. It's real platinum and those itty-bitty chips are actual diamonds, not some rhinestone-cowboy shit. And that little ruby may be little, but it's a ruby."

Well, I was speechless.

"So three thousand was maybe like *one* thousand back then?" Devin figured. "Not a fortune, but just like your smart little girl guessed—this was no prop."

"It makes no sense. Did it belong to his father?" I had started thinking out loud. "From what I know, I doubt Mr. Kallman would have let Dick be careless with it. Dick did always like jewelry—maybe he bought it before *Seventeen* got under way? But how would he have paid for it? No matter how much money his family had, we were *kids*. And why would he offer an expensive pin to the prop master?"

Devin didn't want me to go down this rabbit hole. He started removing the studs from my tuxedo shirt. "Ooh," he said. "Studs. My man likes them?"

I laughed.

"So what did your old lady Dolores sing tonight?"

"'My Heart Belongs to Daddy.'"

"Fucking *hot*, *papi*!"

Five hours later I woke up having sweated through a pillow I held against my chest and stomach.

"Mattito," said Devin, as he made a start at some big-spooning. "You're soaked."

"It's nerves."

While Devin dried my back with a T-shirt he'd picked up from the floor, I told him, "I'm worried about this guy Ehren. I'm worried about *everything*—even about walking off with the scrapbook a week after the murders."

"The scrapbook is nothing. Maybe you should tell him about the pin instead? How Dickie made you take it on the big night?"

I groaned. "Now I'm afraid he'll think I stole it. If it's worth as much as you say. Maybe I should split the difference—tell him about the scrapbook but not the pin. I can be like Jimmy and Paulie, confessing to one thing to get off the hook for another!"

"*Papi*," said Devin, comfortingly, "let me tell you a little about Jimmy—courtesy of Detective V. You never heard this from me, but Jimmy's been having the same cram sessions with Ehren that you're gonna have today. And when he went in for one of those last week, he asked, very casual-like—how do you say it?—*hypothetically:* 'Mr. Ehren, if Andy had two hundred and fifty thousand dollars, would it help with his troubles up in Westchester?'"

"A bribe?"

"What else? The balls on this Andy! He told Jimmy, I'm sure, to word it exactly that way. So they could technically deny they were *offering* the money."

"What did Ehren do?"

"He stood up and gave Jimmy a look that almost made him piss his pants. 'Okay! Okay! Sorry!' Jimmy said, holding his hands up in front of his face like 'Please don't hit me!'"

"Is Ehren going to charge him with bribery?"

"No, because if he does, Jimmy's credibility goes farther south than Argentina, and Dante gets away with murder."

"Jesus," I said, with a sigh. "Jimmy must be as terrified of Andy as he is of Forti."

"Oh *yeah*," said Devin, getting loud with sarcasm. "I feel *so* fucking sorry for Jimmy. I feel sorry there's no more death penalty in New York, because if there was, he could help get *that* for Forti in exchange for a life sentence for himself—instead of whatever dinky little stretch he's going to get as a reward."

I covered my ears, wanting to shut it all out.

"Come on, *papi*, you need a hot shower. Which means any shower with *me*."

Robert Ehren was very courteous. Maybe he found me to be respectable relief from Jimmy and Paulie. Still, he was so butch I felt I had "GAY" written in huge letters across the front of my jacket. And here I was, required to reconstruct an "all-male dinner party" that had included talk about Eric Heiden's thighs and going to Rounds.

"Ingrassia pled guilty on April 13 to a Class D felony," Mr. Ehren informed me when I was through. "So we'll have his testimony and Boccara's against Forti."

He went over how the trial was likely to proceed. I would be called to the stand twice. The first time I'd be asked to describe the evening of the murders, and then, after Jimmy testified, I'd be called back and asked if the voice I just heard was the same one that had said, on that night, "Mr. Kallman, this here's Dante."

I indicated that I understood.

"So what's that?" asked Mr. Ehren, pointing to a Bloomingdale's bag.

I took out the scrapbook and put it on his desk. I explained how I'd acquired it and how, in my own agitated state, I'd failed to mention it. In truth, I'd immediately become aware of not wanting to part with it, of wanting to hide it in an alligator case that contained the past, even if it was a past that belonged almost entirely to Dick.

"Keep it," said Mr. Ehren. "It doesn't add anything."

He seemed almost pleased, as if my nervous scruples were proof of my honesty. But he knew nothing about the pin, which I really *had* just forgotten to mention to Volker. And of course he knew nothing about Devin! (No, I probably *shouldn't* be having the most intense, loving, and monogamous sex of my life with a police clerk who'd been involved in the undercover investigation of the murder I was soon to testify about—don't you think?)

"Are you okay?" Mr. Ehren asked me. "You won't get rattled on the stand?"

"I'll be okay. It's just that I sometimes can't believe the strangeness of it all. Can't believe how totally out of hand things got. I mean, those guys were only intending to rob the apartment, right?"

I was remembering Devin's explanation of the crime's origin: "Jimmy met Paul Boccara on Fifty-Third Street. He told him he had an idea to rob Kallman, and then they got This-Here's-Dante to go in on it with them."

"I wouldn't regard what happened as a matter of great wonder, Mr. Liannetto. Once they all showed up, your friend Mr. Kallman's murder had to happen."

My face expressed skepticism. Surely things didn't *have* to degenerate into what I saw two days later in that crime-scene photo.

"Keep in mind," Mr. Ehren continued, "that Mr. Kallman *knew* Ingrassia. Which means that Ingrassia knew Kallman could identify him. There was no way they were going to leave him alive. And they knew that when they pressed the doorbell."

I thought about this while I put the scrapbook back into the shopping bag. Mr. Ehren had never even flipped through it, and he now must have detected a question in my eyes: "Aren't you even interested in the victim?"

"We're doing our best with this, Mr. Liannetto. Your friend and his boyfriend were actually lucky."

"Really?"

"Yes, they were lucky to have been white and to have gotten killed in the East Seventies. Gay, schmay, if that's what you're thinking. Race trumps sex and money trumps everything. If your friends had been black and poor and over in Bushwick, do you think anybody would have stuck with this case long enough to crack it?"

CHAPTER 23

OCTOBER 25, 1965–FEBRUARY 22, 1966

They'd dressed the girls in white sweaters, white skirts, and go-go boots, and had them jumping and flailing and shaking their teased heads. The boys made the same moves, looking as if they'd come down with Saint Vitus' dance or maybe just cooties. But Peter Matz, the musical director of *Hullabaloo*, kept signaling *faster, faster, faster*.

Kallman had, yet again, been given one whole goddamned day off to fly to New York and shoot this program in Studio 8H, two floors above Carson. His appearance was part of a desperate ongoing salvage operation for *Hank*, which had started off at number 92 in the Nielsen ratings and had scarcely risen since.

Hullabaloo was NBC's knockoff of *Shindig!*, a rock 'n' roll dance party designed to appeal to the under-twenty-five demographic.

Kallman's fellow guests for this episode, set to air in two weeks, were Lola Falana, Lesley Gore, and The Lovin' Spoonful, all of whom had been introduced in the opening segment by just their names, whereas *he* was "NBC's Hank, Dick Kallman," like a ward of the state. This week's host, the lead Herman's Hermits kid, was supposed to introduce Kallman's segment by showing a wall of pictures with Hank in several different disguises—yet another of the network's attempts to acquaint an audience with the show's far-fetched premise.

And here was the head Hermit now: "Hi, I'm Peter Noone. How's it Hankin'?" he asked, laughing at his own joke.

Surprised by the goofball approach, Kallman snapped into friendliness. "Oh, that's a *lengthy* story."

The toothy kid smiled his enormous and apparently genuine English-schoolboy smile. He was cuter than Kallman had expected, enough to make him wonder: despite all these squealing girls in the audience, could he be had? Was he even legal? Before he could reach a conclusion, they cued Kallman to the Hullabaloo Au-Go-Go set, the show's "discothèque." The ten dancers, who'd barely had time to wipe themselves down after their opening-number exertions, were summoned as well.

Kallman had been assigned this booby-prize showcase by a process of elimination. Lola Falana would have been perfect for it, but she didn't want all the jiggling, quaking kids to divert audience attention away from her, so she'd insisted on singing a hip version of "Chicago" against a bare background. More precisely, Sammy Davis Jr., with whom she was appearing on Broadway in *Golden Boy*, and whom she was fucking, had insisted on it for her. That left, as other possibilities for the Au-Go-Go segment, The Lovin' Spoonful, too gentle and soft-voiced, and Lesley Gore, who, alas, moved like a bread truck and was already, at nineteen, something of a throwback. She'd managed to stay above water during the first wave of the British Invasion, but pretty soon it would be Lesley's turn to cry.

So Kallman was it, though he wanted this Au-Go-Go crap no more than Falana did. If he had to do it, he'd at least do it his way—with less blond tint in his hair and clad in a beautiful London-made three-piece suit that he'd been measured for in LA. Bill Orr would be pissed off at the look, and so would Kallman's agent, as if either one of those had a better idea. Things in the business were now moving so fast that nobody knew what "worked," let alone what would work three months from now. Hip *Hullabaloo* was clinging to a spot in the ratings not far above *Hank*'s, and the show had recently been cut from a full hour to thirty minutes. Besides, who said the old couldn't be new? Hadn't Herman's Hermits just gone number one with "I'm Henry VIII, I Am," a fifty-year-old music-hall song?

So right now Kallman mounted the riser behind Hullabaloo Au-Go-Go looking as well-tailored as he had for nightclub engagements a decade in the past. From his album (lower down the *Billboard* charts than *Hank* was in the Nielsens) he'd picked "Lookin' Around" to sing here, since its slashing beat would at least *seem* to jibe with the gyrations of the dancers. Carrying a long-cord hand mike, he now strode through their idiotic, jumping-bean moves, as he tried to make himself look menacing and longing by turns, the alternations appropriate to lyrics that were both dark and yearning. But it was no use: to maintain *Hullabaloo*'s unfailingly wholesome feel, Peter Matz had some of the dancers shouting "Go, Dick, go!" as if he were performing in a talent competition, or at a field day, back in junior high school.

Halfway through the number he turned his mind off to his surroundings and let himself hear only what his own voice was loudly singing—"and love's a one-way track"—so that he could think, of course, of Kenny, whose next signal had by now been so long in coming that he'd decided the greeting from New Zealand had been some piece of teasing cruelty.

"That was great, Dick," said Matz, not looking up from his clipboard.

During a break before taping the next segment, the crew wheeled out a birthday cake with eighteen candles for the show's guest host. "Even though your big day doesn't arrive until November fifth," the musical director explained, "we couldn't let it go unnoticed!" Well, that answered that: Peter Noone was still *seventeen*, that number and name and state of mind that had imprisoned Dick Kallman since the spring of 1951.

He denied himself a slice of cake and any proximity to Master Noone, staying well in the wings after the little party broke up and this dog's breakfast of a show continued with young Peter doing a peppy version—complete with finger snaps!—of Dylan's "Positively 4th Street." Once that was done, all that stood between him and getting out of here was the performance of a quick duet, "Everybody Loves a Clown," with Lesley. Christ, they were being made to cover a song by Jerry Lewis's kid! While they sang, he leaned his head into Lesley's short, perky hairdo, hoping their own evident this-is-enough-to-make-you-puke feeling might somehow serve as a substitute for their absolute lack of sexual chemistry. The age gap looked creepy enough. He was the older one by thirteen years, even if people thought it was only eight from the fib he'd been supplying this year to interviewers.

Lesley was a nice Jewish girl from New Jersey via Brooklyn. She went off with him for a cigarette while the dancers sped into another number and the two of them awaited word on whether a retake of the duet would be required. As they smoked, he trained his gaze on a swiveling Bobby Rydell look-alike in pencil-thin trousers. His mother wanted him to see Doobie before he left New York, but he wasn't going to waste a one-night suite at the Waldorf, not when there was a chance he might click with the Rydell double, whom he now pointed out to Lesley: "There's a cute kid. And just your age, I'll bet. Perfect for you, no?"

Lesley shook her head and pointed to another one of the dancers, a girl whose leaps and spasms indicated the absence of any bra underneath her cheerleader sweater. "If I can't have Lola," Lesley declared, "I'd love to have *that*."

Kallman almost did a spit-take with his cigarette, before some fast calculation had him realizing that his duet partner here, an ambitious Brooklyn sister, would make for an even better public romance than some hero-worshipping fan-letter girl. What a great press story they could make together, and what a great cover they could provide for each other!

For a moment, despite the ratings, despite his *Hullabaloo* billing below Herman and Lesley, and despite the vest he was wearing that felt too tight, he thought it might still all come together for him. It was all he could do to keep from saying "Marry me!" to Lesley Gore.

———————

"I know what you're thinking," said Abe Burrows, the last of Billy Rose's eulogists, to the roughly seven hundred mourners. "All twelve hundred and thirty-two seats of this theater could have been filled if Abe Lastfogel hadn't chartered those train cars to Hartford today."

Laughter ascended from the crowded orchestra to the half-full mezzanine. Up to now Rose's funeral had been an almost stately affair, what with Rabbi Perilman and Senator Javits paying sonorous tribute to his philanthropies, his mentorings, his devotion to this and that. There had been a little color and salt from Jimmy Cannon, the sports columnist, but not much showbiz tattling or anything too raucous inside this theater once called the National and in recent years renamed the Billy Rose. The coffin holding the impresario and onetime songwriter lay at the foot of the stage, covered with a thousand roses.

Burrows kept on about those who would be here if, thanks to the largesse of the Morris Agency's Abe Lastfogel, they weren't up in New England attending Sophie Tucker's burial. He then paused, and sighed, over Billy and Sophie's simultaneous departure for the beyond: "These *alte kakers* are tipping over like dominoes."

Kallman looked at the date on his program, February 13, 1966, and pondered the strangeness of Sophie's having died only a day before Billy, as if running a race with him, the same way her own failing lungs and kidneys had been in a contest to be what put an end to her after sixty years of onstage schmaltz and shtick. Her big sendoff had actually taken place up at Riverside Chapel on Friday, with Jessel, of course, as toastmaster. But today she and Billy were in direct competition, with Sophie being lowered into the cold Connecticut ground while Rose was extolled in his well-heated Midtown theater.

When he told Bill Orr he needed four days off to go to New York for this double-header of death, the producer had complained, as if the star of *Hank* were once more jumping into his three-piece suit for some time travel back to the Jolson era. He reminded Orr that he had personal history with both Sophie and Rose, and told him, moreover, that he could go fuck himself. He pointed out that he'd just spent an excruciating weekend with a *TV Guide* profile writer. Besides, as the star, he was just as unfireable from their floundering series as he would have been from a hit.

Burrows was on a roll, making jokes about Rose's height (five foot three); his money (twenty-five million, including more shares of AT&T than Ma Bell had herself); and his claustrophobia: "Look at all those roses he's under. You can't tell if he died from pneumonia or just won the Preakness. But I know he's having a panic attack." And of course there were all the marriages. Yes, Abe was willing to go there, even with the widow and two of the exes in the audience. Of those two, Joyce Mathews had come out the winner, if anyone could consider being married to Billy a victory. He eventually married her twice, but before she'd displaced Eleanor Holm she was just the mistress and down on points, so close to being cashiered that she made a gesture at suicide in the bathtub. She'd famously denied it to the press—yes, Abe was even going *there!*—by telling them, "Oh, please, I was just shaving my wrists."

All of that Winchell-worthy drama had occurred during the run of *Seventeen*, and Kallman's mind now traveled back to the months he'd spent just before that as a kid in Rose's office.

"If Sophie were here," mused Burrows, "I know that she would be crying—tears of joy at the mention of her name. But Billy is outdoing her over in Israel. She planted trees there; Billy donated his sculpture collection. There are no leaves falling off those marble statues, and they don't have to worry about Dutch elm disease—or whatever it is palm trees come down with in greater Galilee."

Joey Adams, sitting next to Dagmar, was two rows behind Kallman, who thanks to *Hank*—hey, it was a flop, but it was still on in prime time—had been placed on the fourth-row aisle. Dick's connection to Billy Rose, as to Sophie Tucker, had been brief but in its way formative. After doing Rose's 1950 Christmas show, he'd been sprung from Tilton by Torchy, a semester early but with his diploma. (The school was hardly going to say no after that dustup two years before with the history teacher.) Foisted upon Rose by his father, the showman's distant pal, Dick Kallman had then lived his glorious spring of '51: trying out for the show; experiencing the thunderclap of meeting Kenny on the day of the auditions; losing the lead to him but still getting a part; then waiting for rehearsals to begin, when he could *once more see Kenny*, up in Boston.

But before that could happen came all those days in the Rose office with its boxes of money. "It's *all* 'petty' cash when you've got as much of it as Billy," someone had explained to him.

He'd seen the pin on a Thursday lunch hour, in a window on West Forty-Seventh Street. "How much?" he asked the diamond dealer in the rabbi's homburg. "Eighteen hundred dollars," he was informed.

He'd stolen the money for it over the course of two weeks, in six after-hours grabs from three different boxes. No one noticed anything missing, let alone suspected him. He kept the pin under his pillow in Brooklyn until the rehearsals in Boston started, ten weeks before he gave it to Kenny, or tried to, on opening night in New York.

He wore it now—it was holding his tie—as the mourners applauded Burrows and heard the recessional music, a sentimental choice: Sophie's recording of "Me and My Shadow," some of whose lyrics had been written by Billy Rose. People sniffled, thinking about Billy and Sophie shadowing each other into the hereafter.

He shut his eyes and thought of Kenny, his own ungraspable shadow. And he thought about this whole antique, dying show-business world he'd glimpsed each summer at The Balsams, and to which, for all his remorseless drive, he knew he belonged more than he did to today's current, frugging, living-color world of TV. With his eyes still closed, he listened to Sophie, and the only ambition he felt was a momentary and consoling one to be dead. He could hear, but not see, the coffin, as it came up the aisle with the eulogists behind it. His eyes opened only when Abe Burrows touched his arm in greeting, and whispered: "Hey, kid, how are the numbers? Not too good, I hear."

———

A week later, on Monday, February 21st, Kallman was filming *Hank*'s twenty-third episode, set to air in mid-March with an even-more-than-usually ridiculous plot: Hank has shelled out a lot of money on flowers and food to cater a wedding, but the prospective bride and groom have quarreled, and he stands to lose all he's spent unless he can find another couple willing to get married in the next forty-eight hours. Hey, how about the assistant football coach and his girlfriend?

Line for line, the script was irredeemably awful.

He'd had a few days of fun last month when Maureen Arthur, his *How to Succeed* pal from Chicago, had a guest role as a Soviet exchange student, a Ninotchka type who went from shot-putter to bombshell in twenty minutes. But everything since had been misery. After ten months, the blond hair rinse had begun giving his scalp a rash, and sexual continence was bringing on migraines. He'd at last gotten a response from Lesley Gore to the surprisingly direct how-about-it? note he'd written her: "Are you kidding?" she'd replied, amidst some Xs and Os and hearts. He had given up hearing from Kenny, though in a bold moment he aroused a bit of suspicion on the set by proposing him to Benson for a guest role to which he wasn't remotely suited. On top of everything, right now he had a scene coming up with his eight-year-old "kid sister," the child actress from Kentucky who made his flesh crawl worse than the hair rinse was doing.

A production assistant reprieved him momentarily with news that an urgent call had come in to his trailer. His mother—whose idea of an emergency was any passing irritation?

No, it was Ted Witzer: "Congratulations," said his agent, as soon as he picked up.

A movie role? Something to look forward to this summer? "For what?" he asked, with as much energy as he could muster.

"You're the first person in history to be the subject of a take-down profile in *TV Guide*. I just saw it, and the supermarkets will have it on sale tomorrow morning."

"Did they give us the cover? The writer hinted they might."

"No. Of course, *Time* did once put Hitler on its cover as Man of the Year, but *TV Guide* isn't quite that edgy."

"How bad is it?" he asked, impatience raising his voice.

"It's four pages of awful. What did you *do* to this guy?"

"The writer? I just *talked* to him."

"Yeah, that's most of the problem. The rest of the problem is that he talked to people who *know* you."

"Who?"

"Pretty much the whole Desilu Workshop: Janice Carroll, Roger Perry—"

"They're just fucking jealous. Not to mention lazy."

"Roger has one of the nicer quotes about you: 'You're trying to swim but feel yourself sinking and he's the one with his hand on your head.' I guess he wasn't susceptible to what the writer calls 'the aggressively ingratiating Kallman manner.'"

"What's so terrible about that? And what evidence do they even give of it?"

"The cloying notes you write to entertainment reporters and network management. The name-dropping. Who the hell is Lord Harrison Hughes, by the way? And it's not just names. Quote: 'It's difficult for Kallman to mention a moneyed friend without indicating his bank balance.'"

"Cut me a break! Do you know how much money my old man lost? Do you know how insecure that makes you feel?"

"Answer to your first question: no, but not as much as you claim. Answer to your second: no, I don't, and neither do readers of *TV Guide*. 'Dick's need for constant reassurance sometimes gets oppressive.' That's from your associate producer. But let's go back to what you say about yourself: 'I want to be the *best*. I want to walk down the street and have people say, "There goes Dick Kallman," not just because they recognize me but because they feel about me as a comedian the way I feel when I see Laurence Olivier.' Oh, by the way, that's the title of the piece: 'Move Over, Laurence Olivier.'"

"That's not so bad," Kallman replied, affecting cool. "Readers will think that's how the *magazine* sees it."

"Yeah, so long as they don't read anything further. Like the first sentence: 'A lot of people don't like Dick Kallman.' Oh, and while I've got you, who's this priest? Father duBois?"

Kallman asked, in disbelief, "Doobie's in the article?"

"Your mother makes it sound like she asked him to perform an exorcism. Says she sent you to him when you were 'moping' a few years ago."

"I *told* her not to talk to this writer."

"Well, she didn't listen."

He hung up on his agent, a move that before today would have made him feel important, and that now seemed maybe just foolish.

God, had Doobie *said* something—given the reporter a vibe? Was this an anti-fag piece? And those voices from the workshop: did Lucy refuse to give a quote herself but then arrange to get the reporter those *other* quotes, so long as he didn't mention he'd talked to her? Was Mike Connolly's hand in this? Cary Grant's?

He called his mother. "I *asked* you! And why would you mention Doobie, of all people?"

"Because I'm proud of my Episcopal faith—and I'm proud I did the right thing. You wouldn't be where you are right now if I hadn't gotten Father Albert to step in."

"Do you *know* just *where I am* right now?"

"Don't raise your voice to me."

Before he said goodbye, he said he was sorry. But she was the only one to whom he apologized that day. Not to Hugh Benson, who burst into tears that afternoon when he got word from the network that *Hank* had gotten the axe. And not to Bill Orr, who took him aside, out of everyone's earshot on the now-funereal soundstage: "Don't let anyone tell you the timing of this cancellation was a coincidence. I don't care what the numbers are—it was the article. If you were less of a prick, we might have been able to keep promoting *you*, which might have given us a shot at a second season in a different time slot."

"Don't lay this on—"

"Keep singing 'I Believe in You,' Dick. Because nobody else does. Not anymore."

The following day the network determined that in the final episode of *Hank*—the twenty-sixth, airing on April fifteenth—the hero would marry the registrar's daughter and be admitted to Western State, with a scholarship, no less. The annoying little child actress from Kentucky would be the flower girl in the final shot.

Eight hours after NBC disclosed its plan to the cast and crew, Dick Kallman washed the blond rinse from his hair and went, at one a.m., to the Hub, where he was not recognized by any of the six patrons still there and where ninety minutes later he did the first line of cocaine he'd ever done in his life. Three minutes after that he was, once again, feeling very much like a star.

CHAPTER 24

JULY 21–22, 1981

On the second day of the trial, which had gotten started only after numerous short postponements, I continued to sit on a bench outside the courtroom, formally "sequestered" from all the action preceding my own testimony—yesterday's jury selection, this morning's opening statements, some others' testimony now in progress—lest viewing any of it undermine my ability to tell the truth. So there I was at 12:10 p.m., fanning myself with a copy of *Backstage*, when Devin and Laurie emerged from *People of New York State vs. Dante Forti*.

"Lickety-split, *papi*. They're moving along, and everybody's got to be back by one thirty—when you'll be on."

We hurried over to Peggy Doyle's, as in March, and asked the waitress to expedite our orders of the awful, plentiful food. As we waited, Devin told me about Mr. Ehren's opening statement. "Basically, just everything *I* already told you, but in a lot more syllables." The jurors had been informed by the prosecutor that James Ingrassia had during the week of February 18, 1980, formulated a plan to rob Mr. Richard Kallman, a well-off Upper East Side antiques dealer with whom Ingrassia's "roommate and employer" frequently did business. The plan, Ingrassia decided, would work if he and the young acquaintance to whom he confided it, Paul Boccara, could acquire some "muscle," which was soon provided by Mr. Boccara's brother-in-law, the defendant, Dante Forti. It was Mr. Forti who wound up shooting Mr. Kallman and Steven Szladek (yet another "roommate" in Ehren's description) in the early-morning hours of February 22, 1980.

My daughter opened for the defense (as it were) by taking over the narrative from Devin and summarizing what Mr. David Foleo, Forti's new attorney, had argued to the jury. She had even made notes—"You've got some organized little girl here," said Devin—about how the lawyer had characterized Dante Forti as "an innocent family man" who'd never so much as met Mr. Kallman, let alone been in his apartment, let alone shot him in the head. The robbery and murders had been entirely the work of Mr. Ingrassia and Mr. Boccara, who together invented Mr. Forti's presence at the scene in order to frame him for crimes that they alone had committed.

After these wildly divergent theories of the case were presented, the first witnesses, guests at Dick's dinner party, conveyed the murders' mise-en-scène—a phrase I would never use with Detective Volker, having learned my lesson a year and a half ago in describing one of the guests as "decorative." As it turns out, neither Jeff Mathis nor Fred Johnston, the rich old heir to the nickel fortune, was called to the stand, which left the bulk of the description to Jack O'Rourke, the brassy Bill Blass look-alike. In Devin's judgment, "he didn't end up doing such a good job for our boy Ehren."

"How so?" I asked.

"Well," Laurie volunteered, "I think Ehren wanted him to look like this responsible, established guy who'd done business with Dick—"

"Which seemed to be working okay for a while," Devin added. "But then, during the cross-exam, Roly-Poly Foleo made the evening sound a little creepy. 'Did you ever discuss the skater Eric Heiden?' 'Oh, yes, those *thighs*!'"

"And this actress Janet Gaynor," Laurie said, scanning her notes. "O'Rourke: 'Steven had never even *heard* of her!'"

"Yeah," said Devin, "by the time he was done, Foleo had O'Rourke looking like one overmoisturized, chichi man. He also got him to bring up Rosalynn—your boy Jimmy Carter's wife—and when O'Rourke rolled his eyes, you could see it bugged the blacks on the jury. And, oh yeah, he got him to talk about all the jewelry Dickie was wearing—to the point where it looked like he was *asking* to be robbed."

"But the worst came last," said Laurie. "Foleo asked O'Rourke if he'd bought a Calder 'gouache'—is that how you say it?—from Kallman. And he answered: 'Did I ever! It turned out to be a fake!' "

"This was a big bad surprise to Mr. E," Devin added. "He looked like he wanted to slug both O'Rourke and Roly-Poleo."

"Next up was Kyle Waterman," Laurie continued. Our food had arrived and she was trying not to get hamburger grease on her notes.

"The well-mannered Southerner," I recalled. "A designer."

"You make a pass at him, *papi*?"

"He talked about the rushed meal that Kallman served," my daughter continued, after swatting Devin on the wrist. "But he was polite, said the food was excellent. He also commented on 'Mr. Kallman's general agitation.' "

"The DA," said Devin, "asked him what he thought of Stevie boy. Waterman found him to be very respectable—Columbia Law School and all that—so much so I thought Ehren was going to high-five him."

"Waterman," added Laurie, "also talked about how Kallman had described Possessions of Prominence. His version made it sound more legitimate than O'Rourke had."

I now quoted, from the *New York* magazine article, Dick's most grandiose flight of fancy and bullshit, which after so many months with the scrapbook I knew by heart. " 'It's a terribly, terribly exciting thing to be able to live with this kind of beauty.' "

"Yeah," said Devin. "It gets *really* exciting when you're stupid enough to let in lowlifes who'll kill you for it."

My turn to take the stand came as soon as we hustled back from the restaurant to 60 Centre Street. Finally permitted into the courtroom, I saw how Judge Rothwax had given way to a Judge McGinley, a pacific and pleasant presider who seemed intent on putting everyone at ease.

As with his other witnesses, Ehren clearly wanted to emphasize my respectability, a small piece of some very basic groundwork meant to establish that Dick and Steven had not been exotics, but rather a little household not much different from the jurors' own—and that therefore those jurors had better do them justice. I later learned that a man in the front spectators' row, taking even more notes than Laurie, was keeping an eye on things for some kind of gay civil-rights organization.

Ehren made me recite the long string of shows I'd worked in; he had me mention my private pupils and my college-going daughter. At one point I wondered if he might even be trying to create the impression that I was straight, in order to anoint Dick with some waters from life's mainstream. The jurors also got to hear how my acquaintance with Dick went back thirty years, all the way to *Seventeen*. Ehren got me to work in a few credits from Dick's own show-business career—risking his attempts to normalize him by dusting him with a trace of celebrity, something that could appeal to the bit of starfucker in all of us, and maybe make a few of the citizens in the jury box feel they had a chance to earn a dead TV star's personal esteem by sending his killer to prison.

The prosecutor then moved me as quickly as he could to the end of the evening. He got me to describe the commotion; to mention how Dick had said "We're going to be rich!" after the soon-to-be killers called; and most importantly, to reveal what I had heard from down below when I was with Steven in that loft-style library: "Mr. Kallman, this here's Dante." I concluded with a description of how frantic Dick seemed after the killers' initial departure, while he awaited their return.

I made no mention of the pin, because the prosecutor didn't know to ask about it. And truthfully, at this moment I couldn't see what difference it made.

Ehren turned me over to Foleo, who was loud and confi-dent, almost a fat-lawyer version of Dick. He had only one piece of business with me, to undercut my assertion that I'd heard his client's name. "Mr. Liannetto, are you saying that this person—who the prosecution wants us to believe killed Mr. Kallman and Mr. Szladek—allowed one of his accomplices to introduce him by using his *actual first name*? Is that your testimony?... It is? Well, did you ever hear *his* voice—that is, Mr. Forti's?"

"I heard voices, plural, after that. But I did hear one distinct voice say, 'Mr. Kallman, this here's Dante.'"

Mr. Foleo finished with a contemptuous flourish: "And *this here's* all I have. Nothing further."

Now that I'd testified, I was permitted to remain among the spectators, and as I took a seat far from Devin and Laurie, I won-dered whether I had helped or hurt the DA's case. There wasn't much time to consider the question before the next sentence spoken by the prosecutor filled the courtroom: "The People call Mrs. Andrew Crevolin."

Plainly furious at the use of her married instead of marquee name, Dolores, attracting less attention than she otherwise might have, marched down the center aisle in her cobalt-blue suit.

Mr. Ehren's perfunctory direct examination, mostly about Possessions of Prominence with an emphasis on its legitimacy, further displeased her, as if Dolores Gray's participation in the drama were being reduced to an uncredited role.

The script, however, got a little meatier once Mr. Foleo began his cross.

"What's the most that the business ever made in a year?" he asked.

"I don't know."

"More than fifty thousand dollars?"

"I haven't the slightest idea," Dolores answered, even more dismissively, as if she couldn't be bothered with these trifling matters that she left to an accountant. For his part, Foleo seemed to be trying to create an impression that Richard Kall-man's apartment wasn't even worth robbing.

"Did you know that an item purchased by Mr. John O'Rourke, who believed it to be a Calder gouache"—the lawyer made it sound like "goulash"—"was actually a fake?"

"Of course not. And I *still* don't know that it was."

"Did you and Mr. Kallman ever quarrel over business?"

"Quarrel? No. We had the normal disagreements that business partners have from time to time." She seemed to be doing a kind of late Barbara Stanwyck imitation.

"Did your partnership with Mr. Kallman ever extend into a more personal realm?"

"We were *friends*, even before we started the business."

"You were never involved romantically?"

"Certainly not!"

Was he trying to make the "all-male dinner party" into Dolores's competition? To suggest she'd gotten Dick bumped off? Whatever his intent, he didn't go deeply into this area or any other. I concluded that, given the weakness of his case, his basic strategy was to make the jurors walk through muddy waters with dust in their eyes, to keep flinging as many sordid suggestions as he could, to imply that the last years of Dick's life had involved arrangements that his upstanding family man of a client, Mr. Forti, would never have gotten near, even by accident.

———————

The next day, after lots of procedural business and sidebars and delays, we got to hear from Jimmy Ingrassia, the prosecution's star witness. (Dolores, also now eligible to sit among the spectators, having already testified, couldn't be bothered coming. She told me to call her when there was a verdict.) Devin had warned me not to expect any sign of Andy Vitale, Jimmy's keeper, and there was none. From the way I saw Jimmy look at Ehren, it was clear to me that he understood who was Daddy for the rest of the trial.

Jimmy had cleaned up; his hair was washed and shorter. But he didn't wear a suit or tie, maybe so as not to overdo it; just a sport coat and a solid-colored shirt, open at the neck. I again, as I had last September, hated myself for finding him sort of cute. With Forti it was even worse: sitting there at the defense table, he struck me as a sort of sullen, sexy New Wave film star. He understood how to gaze off at nothing, and he got away with occasionally chewing gum.

Ehren prompted Jimmy, now twenty-two, through a discreet account of his long relationship with the absent Andy. It had begun when he was fifteen and Andy thirty-five, a fact that made Jimmy, I thought a bit softheartedly, also the *victim* of a crime, one that for expedient legal reasons would never be prosecuted. At the time of the murders—and even now—he was an employee of A&J Antiques, living and working with Andy up in Dobbs Ferry.

"So you were mentored by him?" Mr. Ehren asked.

"What's that mean?" Jimmy responded, giving rise to a couple of sniggers. He must have forgotten the word since his rehearsal sessions.

On Monday, February 18, he had gone to Dick's apartment with Andy. They'd often been there before, "doing business," and on this occasion Dick showed them the very expensive Patek Philippe watch for which he was seeking a buyer.

"Was anything out of the ordinary that afternoon?" Ehren asked.

Jimmy paused, trying to remember, or maybe to suppress, something. Then he said no.

"Were you aware of the *New York* magazine article that had just appeared describing Mr. Kallman's business?"

"Yes."

"And did it help you to form the intention of robbing him later that week?"

Confused, as if Mr. Ehren were forcing him to get ahead of his story, Jimmy finally replied: "No, I already knew about his place and all the stuff in it." Ehren said okay and after that kept Jimmy attached to a strict timeline that began on Tuesday evening, February 19, when Jimmy and Andy drove into New York "to pick up some prostitutes." It was Ehren's phrase, and he spoke it with as much casualness as possible, as if describing a night out with the kids, no doubt to avoid having the jurors think too much about the witness's (or Dick's?) "lifestyle." As it was, they seemed unfazed.

On this trip to New York, the joint proprietors of A&J Antiques made the acquaintance of Paul Boccara at the corner of Second Avenue and Fifty-Third Street. All three men were soon on the way back to Dobbs Ferry for a night of "partying," with cocaine and Quaaludes, that stretched well into the next day. Ehren spared everyone the sexual particulars.

The following evening, Wednesday, after an argument between Jimmy and his mentor, who'd apparently had enough of Paulie, the two younger men went back to New York, where they made brief stops at the Ice Palace disco and the Ninth Circle bar. Devin later explained: "Trust me, they'd run out of drugs. And were looking for trade. A boy's got to work for his dope." I made an effort not to think of the days when Devin had done a little of the same, and was encouraged to believe that that era had been short when I saw no sign that Jimmy recognized his erstwhile Ice Palace colleague, whom he'd also never recognized at the 19th Precinct.

Late Wednesday night, February 20th, once Jimmy and Paulie were through mixing business and pleasure in New York, they headed back to Westchester and checked into the Tarrytown Hilton, deciding not to risk Andy's wrath over in Dobbs Ferry. And then on Thursday, Jimmy awoke in the hotel with the idea to rob the town house on East Seventy-Seventh Street.

"Did you confide this idea to Mr. Boccara?" asked Ehren.

"Yes."

"What was his response?"

"He said he knew someone who could help us pull it off. His brother-in-law in Queens."

And so Jimmy and Paulie, probably still high, went and got fifteen hundred dollars—presumably for post-robbery flight—from a safe-deposit box at Andy's bank, after which they traveled down to New York to begin a murderous twenty-four-hour zig-zag between Manhattan and Queens. After meeting Dante Forti under the Triborough Bridge, where they all did some drugs, they headed to a coffee shop in Astoria. There, on a napkin,

Jimmy sketched the layout of Dick's apartment. That evening they rode into Manhattan in a limousine that Dante occasionally drove for some chauffeur service. Jimmy was going to surprise Dick with the news that he'd found—and had with him—a buyer for the watch. There was, at this point, according to Jimmy, no gun in the car.

Did they really need Dante Forti, unarmed, for muscle? After months in prison he still appeared taut, but he bordered on the slight. When did they acquire the pistol, and when would we learn about that? In the meantime, was Jimmy's credibility supposed to be somehow enhanced by the druggy illogic of this whole haphazard "plan"?

Jimmy walked up the steps of Dick's brownstone at about eight thirty, intending to ring the bell, before he noticed, through the window, all of us around the dining-room table. Oops! He then decided to go to a pay phone around the corner to call Dick with the news that he had a buyer for the watch. Dick, through the Chinese houseman, said just what he hoped he would: come by later, when he would be through with his guests. So Jimmy went back to the car and, along with his two colleagues, waited until they saw what they thought was everybody, including the cook, clear out. They didn't know that Steven and I remained upstairs.

Once they got inside, Jimmy introduced Forti to Dick—"Mr. Kallman, this here's Dante"—telling him that this young man was a model, very successful, and interested in the Patek Philippe. (Jimmy pronounced it "Philip.") Dick showed Forti the watch and discussed a price while Paulie, silent and irrelevant, stood nearby. Forti attempted to be smooth. According to Jimmy, he said, while pointing to the watch with a smile, "I hope you have that insured."

"You should see the place I keep my really *good* stuff!" Dick replied—and I don't even feel the need to say "supposedly" here, because I can so imagine him saying it. Jimmy testified that he pointed to a painting on one of the walls and made a little dialing motion with his fingers, to indicate a safe behind it.

"Then we left and said we'd be back," Jimmy now explained,

getting to something else I'd always wondered about: why had they made *two* visits to the apartment? Mr. Ehren now asked that question for me.

"We told Mr. Kallman it was to go home and get money, that Dante didn't want to be carrying around twelve thousand dollars until he'd seen the watch."

"Was that true?" Ehren asked.

"No."

"What was the real reason that you left and came back?"

"To go get a gun."

"Whose idea was that?"

"Dante's. He told the lie about the money, and when we got back out to the limo he told me, 'If we're gonna do this, let's do it big and let's do it right.'"

"So he was saying you needed a gun?"

"Yes."

"And you agreed?"

"Yes. But, you know, just to make threats with."

So it was back to Queens and then back to Manhattan, this time with a gun from Dante's apartment.

"Once in Manhattan," Ehren asked, "did you go directly to Mr. Kallman's residence?"

"Not exactly. We stopped inside the hotel a couple of doors down to take a leak. Excuse me," Jimmy said, as if this were the most indelicate thing we were going to hear about that night. "We'd been drinking in the car."

Jimmy said that once they got back inside the town house, he left Dante to transact the watch sale with Dick in the living room. He asked if he and Paulie could have a glass of water, and Dick told them to help themselves in the kitchen.

"And did you get anything else from the kitchen besides water?"

"Yes. Both of us took knives out of a kind of wooden rack."

At this point about half the jurors leaned forward.

"Why did you get a knife?"

"I don't know. I guess I was scared. Paulie took one when he saw me take one."

"Of whom were you scared?"

"Of Dante."

"Then what happened?"

"We stayed in the kitchen for a little bit while Dante talked to Dick. Then we went out to the living room, 'cause we was worried that Dante might be thinking 'What's taking them'—me and Paulie—'so long?' And when we got there I saw that Dante had pulled the gun out of his pocket. He was standing over Dick, who was sitting in a chair."

"What did you do?"

"I ran upstairs and locked myself in a bathroom."

A court officer, a guy in a white shirt with handcuffs dangling from his belt, turned away so that we couldn't see him starting to laugh.

Ehren asked Jimmy why he was frightened when he knew that Forti would be using the gun "just to make threats with."

"He looked like he meant business."

"In the bathroom, were you still holding the knife?"

"No, I put it down somewhere."

"Then what happened?"

"I heard two shots and then a minute or two went by and I came out of the bathroom and went back downstairs. I saw Dick, still in the chair. There was blood dripping onto the rug. From his head."

"What did Mr. Forti do when he saw you?"

"He yelled at me to go back upstairs and see if anyone else was in the house."

"Was there?"

"Yes."

Mr. Ehren held up a picture of Steven.

"Yeah," said Jimmy. "He was in bed, sitting up, with no clothes on. He looked scared. I guess he heard the shots."

In the row in front of me, a young man put his arm around an older woman: Steven's brother and mother, surely. Devin stole a glance at me from across the courtroom, as if to say, "Don't *you* cry, *papi*. It's almost over."

Jimmy went downstairs and delivered Steven to his death by telling Forti he was in the apartment. With his gun, This-Here's-Dante bounded up the stairs and forced Steven back down into the living room, where he made him look at his dead but still-bleeding boyfriend. And then he shot Steven in the head.

"What did you do?" Mr. Ehren asked.

"I think I looked at the floor," Jimmy answered; a first indication of any shame he might have felt. "I said, 'He's still alive.' He was sort of twitching. Dante said it was nerves."

"'Sort of twitching?'" Mr. Ehren asked. "Did Mr. Forti find a way of putting a stop to that?"

"Yes. He kicked his head."

I flinched. Half the people in the courtroom gasped.

"Was this action effective?" asked Mr. Ehren.

"I'm not sure. I know the twitching stopped after Dante shot him again." Groans, even from a couple of the jurors. Ehren had succeeded in creating disgust toward Forti, but the testimony was also making Jimmy Ingrassia repulsive.

The three thieves spent about fifteen minutes shoving everything they could steal into two Hefty bags they found in a kitchen cabinet. And in the rush to finish up and get out, Jimmy forgot to take his own jacket with him. Hearing things like this left me unsurprised that these master criminals hadn't even remembered to bring with them any bags into which they could stuff the valuables they were after.

Only back in the car did Jimmy realize he'd left the jacket inside the now-locked house. It contained his passport; apparently Jimmy entertained dreams of escape beyond Florida. Retrieval of this telltale garment necessitated yet another trip to Queens—for a pair of wire cutters, with which, once he went into the yard behind Dick's brownstone, he could slice through the chicken wire against the glass of the back door.

"Did you succeed in recovering the coat?"

"Yes."

"Did you come out with anything else?"

"Yeah. This little bronze or copper knickknack of a girl. It was on a table in the living room." So there was Dolores's bronze Renoir statuette. A good thing she hadn't come today; she would have interrupted the testimony to demand its return.

In order to keep the focus on Dante's depravity instead of the witness's, Mr. Ehren asked no questions about the state of the bodies that Jimmy must have walked past during his third visit to the town house that night.

A last trip across the bridge took the three young men back to Queens, where they unloaded the Hefty bags and briefly admired their takings.

And so to bed.

As I listened to the rest of the testimony, mostly about Jimmy's time on the lam in Florida, I waited to be recalled to the stand. This would come as a surprise to the defense, and I could feel an asthma attack coming on. I also realized I was without my Primatene inhaler. I looked over at Devin and managed to keep breathing.

Mr. Foleo's questions for Jimmy tried to cultivate a sense of what a lowlife Andy Vitale must be, and to plant in the jurors' minds the evidence-free idea that Andy might have put Jimmy up to the whole thing.

"Did you ever sell drugs to Mr. Kallman?"

"No," Jimmy answered, not altogether convincingly.

"What happened on the night of February 21st wasn't a drug deal that went bad?"

"No," said Jimmy, with a touch of annoyed pride. This particular night, at least, had been about something else, something he'd set in motion.

"Did Mr. Kallman ever proposition you for sex?"

"*No,*" Jimmy replied, emphatically—but without, I thought, conviction. Whose reputation was his denial meant to protect? Dick's? His own?

"Mr. Ingrassia, didn't the gun involved in this crime in fact come not from Mr. Forti but from your own and Mr. Vitale's safe-deposit box?" I had to remind myself that, incredibly, the defense's case was that Dante Forti had never even been in Dick's apartment.

"No," said Jimmy, denying this additional handful of dust that had just been thrown in everyone's eyes.

The next thing I knew, Foleo had sat down and Ehren was on his feet, recalling me to the stand. That brought Foleo back to *his* feet with an objection that sent both lawyers to the bench for a whispered conversation with Judge McGinley. Ehren, though told to "be quick about it," got his way. A second later I was on my way to the witness chair, hoping that no one besides me could hear the wheezing in my left lung.

"I have only one question, Mr. Liannetto," said Mr. Ehren. "Does the voice you heard saying 'Mr. Kallman, this here's Dante' on the night of February 21st, 1980, match the voice of Mr. Ingrassia, whose testimony you just heard in this courtroom?"

"Yes, it does."

"Nothing further."

Mr. Foleo, taking his turn, spoke with a molasses-thick drip of sarcasm. "Mr. Liannetto, are you able to distinguish all eight million voices in the Naked City, one from the other?"

I made sure I held his stare. "I know what I heard."

"Nothing more," he said with a smirk.

My daughter was smiling delightedly, and Mr. Ehren, knowing that I could have just answered "No, of course not," gave me a nod that I took to indicate surprise and respect: "Good job, you little fruitcake."

I just wanted to breathe and get out of there with Devin.

CHAPTER 25

JULY 9, 1966–JULY 7, 1967

Kallman had walked across town for the Saturday matinee, all the way from the San Carlos Hotel, and he was schvitzing. Another day in the nineties; the heat wave seemed likely to last the whole two-week run. The first marquee to catch his eye on West Forty-Fourth was the St. James's: *Hello, Dolly!*, with Ginger Rogers's name, huge, above the title. But just a little farther on, at the Broadhurst of all places, the name atop the title was *his*.

Like Ginger, he was replacement casting. Now that Tommy Steele had finally left *Half a Sixpence*, he'd be doing it here on Broadway for the next couple of weeks. Even so, and even with the billing, this amounted to a comedown, the two weeks here being a glorified dress rehearsal for a national tour that would keep him on the road with the show for almost a whole year: San Francisco, LA, Chicago, Detroit, Cleveland, Cincinnati, Washington—all the way to next June in Montreal at Expo 67, where the mouths in the audience would be dripping cotton candy and the crumbs of Belgian waffles. This tour would feel even more never-ending than the one for *How to Succeed*. He'd been kicked back three years and could only hope that another, better Benson-and-Orr team would some night show up backstage with a better sitcom than *Hank*, or an honest-to-God movie.

In the three months since production of the series ended, he'd shot what now seemed likely to be his big post-*Hank* film role. And what was it? A part way down the supporting cast of *This Way Out, Please*, a sexless sex farce with Sandra Dee and George Hamilton that wouldn't be released until next spring, by which time Hamilton's romance with LBJ's elder daughter would likely have ended, depriving this bomb of its only chance for a little publicity. *Hank* was already so forgotten that the director of the movie hadn't been bothered by the fact that a character in the film, played by somebody besides Dick Kallman, was named Hank. The possibility that this would confuse anyone in the audience was deemed remote. His evaporating TV stardom had this past week been unable to fill more than half the house with summertime tourists who'd been seeing him on their hometown tube as recently as April.

Half a Sixpence had had a solid year at the Broadhurst, five-hundred-plus performances, and if it was now running out of gas in New York, it would probably, thanks to good management, do very well touring. In fact, a second, smaller-scale road company, still being cast, would make its own, simultaneous tour to mostly second-string venues like Reading and St. Petersburg. He even had a tiny, token slice of the first company's receipts; Steele, of course, had gotten the movie version, just as Bobby Morse had gotten *How to Succeed*.

Kallman never went into the theater through the stage door. He always crossed the lobby, hoping to startle some early bird, a rare diehard *Hank* fan who'd be thrilled to get a picture with him. But none was to be found today, and the only person awaiting him backstage was a reporter from some little Jersey paper. He'd forgotten that the show's publicist had made the appointment. Weary though he was, once inside his dressing room he took out the old Dick Kallman, turned on the juice, and told the reporter that *yes!* he was perfect for the role of Arthur Kipps, the hero of this musical adaptation of H. G. Wells's novel *Kipps*. In speaking about the poor Cockney boy transformed by, and then swindled out of, a surprise inheritance—a fellow who finds happiness only when he opens a small shop with the right girl—he unspooled the story of his own father's lost fortune. Truthfully, he was all wrong for the part: he had a surfeit of Kipps's oomph but none of his sweetness, and certainly no contented acceptance of his own comeuppance.

He told the interviewer that he'd spent a thousand dollars on a Cockney voice teacher, whereas he'd actually prepared for the part by listening to recordings of the coachman in Disney's *Pinocchio*. Really, they should have gotten the Herman's Hermits boy to replace Steele; every seat in the house would have been filled.

"Got to get made up!" he told the reporter, who rushed to finish his notes. "If you need anything more," Kallman assured him with a big smile, "come see me after the curtain calls."

Two shows today, and after that he was committed to dine with the still-smitten Doobie, who was smart enough to know that the above-the-title Broadway billing, their supposed reason for a celebratory supper, couldn't mask the actual career facts and wouldn't alter the depressed mood of his companion. Kallman knew that, sitting face-to-face with the priest, he would wind up on the receiving end of a pep talk and, if both flesh and spirit proved weak, the receiving end of a blow job back at the San Carlos.

He plunged into the matinee. He had a slew of songs to do and a lot of honest-to-God dancing, vigorous old music-hall stuff, more intense than anything in *How to Succeed*. Like the title of one of its numbers, the show was all "Flash Bang Wallop." Within minutes after the overture, he was jumping around and banging on a banjo, struggling to keep his straw hat from falling off. During just about the only breather, a soft duet called "Long Ago," he sat and listened to his costar sing—"I was longing to say I loved you so, so long ago, but what could I say?"—while he pretended to look at her. He was actually staring into the wings, toward the exact spot where fifteen years ago he'd tried to give Kenny the pin. But then he cranked himself back up and kept the energy high all the way through to "The Party's On the House" and the show's manic little finale, after which he more or less collapsed in the dressing room that had once belonged to *Seventeen*'s Miss Pratt.

He heard someone opening the door. The Jersey reporter? He didn't think he could bring himself to turn it on yet again.

"Hey, Joe, it's Willie," spoke a sudden, beautiful presence. "I'm shaving now."

It *had* to be an apparition, but it wasn't. It was so clearly and really Kenny, using their *Seventeen* names, that his hand almost reached into the makeup table's drawer, where the pin, his lifelong fetish, was spending the two-week run. He could give it to Kenny, this time get him to accept it, and thereby repair everything. His heart was hammering as if he'd done three fast bumps of coke.

No, this was not his imagination. In fact, evidence of an all-too-earthbound reality now appeared. Gene Saks, *Sixpence*'s director and the overseer of its new road companies, entered the dressing room, grinning, as if he'd just played a successful practical joke. "Dick, I believe you know this fellow. In fact, I believe you may have worked with him in this very theater."

Kallman noticed that Kenny—albeit smiling, albeit politely charming—looked very reluctant. It had not been his idea to come back here.

"I knew this would be a nice surprise," said Saks, who went on to explain how he'd wanted Ken to see Dick Kallman's performance before Ken embarked on the same lead role himself, with that second touring company. Saks had just finished casting it. "Kipps, meet Kipps! Give him a few pointers, Dick. I've got to scoot up to the Winter Garden and grab dinner with Bea between shows."

Kallman started to sweat. The excitement of standing next to

Kenny had been crushed by the realization that he was here following orders. The joy had been extinguished so abruptly that the change was actually nauseating him. Kenny appeared perplexed by his evident discomfort; embarrassed, too, at having come to see the show only as part of his job. Searching for something to say, he could only come up with "Have you seen Bea's show? She really made me laugh." Gene Saks's wife, Beatrice Arthur, was the second banana in *Mame*.

"I haven't had a chance," Kallman replied. "I only got to New York a week before starting this." It sounded like a boast—he was so successful, so busy—but it was the simple truth, and he was too undone by what was now happening to say anything else.

"I still don't like moving around," Kenny sympathized. "I'll never get used to it." With a modest laugh, he added, "I just hope there's a Holiday Inn in West Lafayette, Indiana." That was one of the stops on his tour.

Inside himself, Kallman could feel the machinery of lying start to whir, reflexively, pointlessly. The words were forming to tell Kenny that he himself would be at the Mark next week in San Francisco; but he stopped himself, rendered speechless by the realization that he felt no competitiveness, no desire to draw attention to how they were here again at the Broadhurst, with Dick Kallman's name above the title, all those years after he'd lost the lead in *Seventeen* to Kenneth Nelson.

"I start rehearsals in Dallas on August tenth," said Kenny. "They've saved the biggest city for first," he added, with a laugh. "I really haven't given the show any thought since my audition, but while I was watching out there I decided I'm going to steal that banjo move from you." He mimed it, playfully.

"Have you read the novel?" Kallman asked. "The H. G. Wells thing?"

"No."

"Me neither." It was a plain, nonmendacious fact, and as soon as he added his admission to Kenny's, the two of them laughed: a pure moment, a sip of ice water on this humid summer day.

Kallman looked at Kenny, now thirty-six. They were *both* a little too old to be playing Kipps, but as Kenny stood there before him—still so slim, needing a haircut, with the faintest sheen of sweat on his neck—he looked heartbreakingly close to the way he had in 1951.

"Anyway," said Nelson, breaking another awkward silence, "I made some notes at intermission." He took out a tiny spiral pad, the kind students use to write down homework assignments, and flipped it open to a couple of diagrams and a stretch of neat printing.

Kallman took the pad from him, looked at it, and thought: he was writing this about *me*, even if it was only because someone told him he had to. He continued staring at the pad, fascinated, making Nelson uncomfortable all over again.

"I'm sorry your series was cancelled," said Kenny. "I saw it a couple of times. Thought you were great."

"It was junk," Kallman replied. The liberation he felt saying this! And saying it to *him*!

Nelson waved his hand to dismiss the remark. "Well, Dick, I don't want to hold you up. You must be beat. I don't know where I'm going to get the stamina for this show!"

"How about dinner tomorrow? You could catch me up on what Carole's doing!"

"I wish I could, but my sister's in town with all kinds of plans for me before I head to Texas." He looked at his watch. "In fact, I've got to skedaddle."

"Skedaddle": Oh, God, he *was* Willie! Kallman looked at him, all but pleading "You can't leave!" He struggled to keep his fingers off the drawer handle. Was Kenny really not going to say a word about what had happened between them, just feet from here, so long ago? *I will never feel that way about you.*

"You're sure? I mean, about dinner?"

"Afraid so. I wish it were otherwise!"

But he clearly didn't. He was starting to leave.

Would he have to do it himself? Have to say "About the other night . . . ," as if June 21, 1951, were only last week?

Kenny was already out the door, trotting backwards and waving. "Well, I guess we're both back in boater hats! Have a great run!"

———

He had an injury to his Achilles tendon, along with some damaged cartilage and a torn rotator cuff. He was a couple of days into the Chicago run, and he'd been at it for four months and five cities. He had stayed off all drugs other than prescribed painkillers but was beginning to feel himself coming apart, separating from himself. And now this: fucking William Leonard in the *Trib*. He'd seen the review first thing this morning and been carrying it around all day, like a bad splinter in his toe. The critic acknowledged the actor's "indisputable talent" but complained that he couldn't resist overplaying every scene he stole. "Mr. Kallman probably puts sugar in his saccharine."

He could hear Benson shouting "Finch!"

So far no new Benson and no new Orr had come backstage with any offers. His career and his life were running in reverse: Charlie and his mother had been in the LA audience for *Sixpence*, just as they'd been for *How to Succeed*. And at a dinner that he prepared for cast members in his San Francisco rental (the Mark having become too expensive after three nights), he felt as if he were again cooking for the kids in *Seventeen*. Indeed, Matt Liannetto had been there, in town for something like the funeral of his ex-wife's mother.

Now, sitting and aching in his dressing room after the second Saturday show, he spotted a telegram beside the makeup table. Who still sent wires, except maybe on opening night? He tore the envelope and saw that its contents were signed CONNOLLY—whom he'd last heard from, also by wire, with that stupid YOU'RE IN THE PICTURE prank.

LEONARD AN ASSHOLE STOP COME BY FOR DRINK STOP HERE AT AMBASSADOR PRIOR TO MAYO CLINIC STOP DON'T EXPECT TO BE AROUND MUCH LONGER

Didn't expect to be around at the Ambassador? Didn't expect to be around *period*? Mike was only in his early fifties. Kallman had heard that the columnist was making a fool of himself over some college basketball player and trying to write a screenplay for a movie version of *Ulysses*, since nobody was too interested in his *Reporter* stuff anymore, not even Mike himself. But the telegram made it sound as if he were dying.

Kallman's instincts flinched. His body could recall the terrors Connolly had once engendered in it. Despite the wire's apparent friendliness, and possible desperation, was there some piece of news he needed to know, maybe even fear?

He jumped into a cab and rode the two miles from the McVickers Theater to the Ambassador. He rang Connolly's room on the house phone and was told to "come on up": three words choked out between two hard coughs. A minute later he heard Mike struggling with the doorknob. Obviously sloshed, the columnist greeted him with weird, big-grinned delight.

"You'll cry tomorrow," said Kallman, playing with the title of Lillian Roth's alcoholism memoir, half of it ghostwritten by Connolly a dozen years before.

The drunken grin got even bigger. "Not many people remember that! Not many people remember *anything* anymore!" He made his guest a Scotch with water from the bathroom faucet, then lurched across the rug to deliver it to him on the couch. He started rambling about the midterm elections three days away, emphasizing how Nixon, "a leader, a *genius*," now out campaigning for everyone, was collecting IOUs that might finally propel him to the White House in two years' time, fulfilling one of Connolly's most fervent wishes.

"What's taking you to the Mayo Clinic?" asked Kallman.

"My heart."

"Didn't know you had one! Joke."

Connolly roared. "That's what they're trying to find out—it's exploratory surgery!" His smile was sweet and sloppy. Gone, it seemed, was the bullhorn omniscience, the thumb in the eye, the trolling for dirt and advantage. But the self-deprecation soon curdled into sentimental anger, a belligerent nostalgia that had him extolling the old studio system and railing against today's crude films and disrespectful kids, especially the boys dressing in paisley shirts and *wanting* to look like fairies.

"I saw your show the other night," Connolly said, almost confidentially, without the bellow. "You were good. The songs rhymed. The book was clean. You stand for the right things, Dick. You know, you're old-fashioned, like me." He poured himself another drink and left the club chair for a place on the couch beside his guest.

Each slurred sentence, by itself, managed to contain sense and grammar. But their aggregate incoherence came from the way nothing aligned inside the speaker. The impending surgery had somehow removed his outer layer, exposing the rat's nest of contradictions held together by the fears of a lifetime and now, it appeared, the fear of death. Sitting beside him, Kallman regarded the columnist not as some coarse avatar of the passing show-business era, but more like his own harrowing Ghost of Christmas Yet to Come.

Connolly grabbed his crotch, not to establish the animal dominance he'd sought in the Mocambo men's room a decade before; just with the desperate, sloppy reach of a drowning man. The actor sat there while Mike planted a kiss on his lips and said, "Kallman, you need to find a nice girl and settle down. No, really, I mean it."

She couldn't be more than five foot one, this Mary he was talking to, a pert little blonde who'd joined the New Year's Eve party that the Detroit cast was throwing itself onstage.

"You smell great!" Kallman told the girl. "In fact, I think I've been up against that perfume before," he added, with a rakish, 'nuff-said smile.

"It's English Leather!" cried Mary. "It was a fad at school last spring—all the girls were wearing men's colognes."

"Oh!" the actor responded, hoping she wouldn't think too hard about how he might have experienced proximity to this particular fragrance. "What school was that, Mary?"

She explained that it was the Kingswood girls' school at Cranbrook. She'd graduated only six months before and since then had spent a single semester at the University of Michigan, where she'd liked absolutely nothing. Having just dropped out, here she was, trying to come up with a plan for the future.

Kallman lit the Newport cigarette she took from her purse. He noticed that she held one of her arms across her waist, the gesture of a girl who's convinced that she's a little heavier than she should be. She moved the arm only when he handed her a cocktail, which she proceeded to drink not with the mannerisms of someone try-ing to look grown up, but with the natural movements of some-body who'd already learned that she likes liquor.

"I saw you here years ago," she told him. "In *How to Succeed in Business Without Really Trying*."

"*Years* ago?" he protested. "Maybe three? Three and a half?"

"And I've watched you here during the rehearsals for this one. My parents throw a lot of money around, and I get to hang out in theaters and museums pretty much when I want."

"So what about that 'plan' for your future, Mary? What are your ambitions?" He could see that she loved the way he kept say-ing her name.

"It's hard to know. I would love to act—not that I'm any good at it. And I like to weave. I'm *very* good at that. Maybe I could make costumes."

"I'll bet you could do anything you want." He maneuvered her under the mistletoe for a goodbye kiss, then moved stage left for a noblesse-oblige greeting to the girl who ran the box office. On his way to her, he got stopped by the actor playing Coote, the char-acter in the show who oversees Kipps's self-improvement. "Boy, you're *really* getting into your role," said this fellow performer, who began whisper-singing "She's Too Far Above Me," a number from the first act.

"What do you mean?" asked Kallman.

"That girl you were talking to. Her old man, Fisher, is one of the biggest big businessmen in this state, a regular Ford or Rom-ney. He made huge money in oil, and if you were from around here you'd remember all the old Aurora Gasoline stations. The guy's now a kind of Jewish Carnegie, giving it all away. That little girl you were talking to is *loaded*."

"Little girl? How—"

"Eighteen. Go get her, tiger."

Kallman responded with his Lothario laugh.

"Look how she's looking at you," said his castmate. "Maybe she'll follow us to Cleveland."

Kallman directed a glance toward the staring Mary. Was she attracted to *him* or to the world he represented? With any luck, he thought, working his way back toward her, it would be mostly the latter.

———————

An "excruciating, tasteless little comedy" was *The New York Times*'s judgment of *Doctor, You've Got to Be Kidding!*, the desperately retitled *This Way Out, Please*. The review made no mention of Dick Kallman, fortunately, except to list him with the rest of the cast in almost unreadably small type. There was also no mention of Lynda Bird Johnson, who sure enough had split from George Hamilton, just as the country had soured on her father. LBJ remained stuck in the White House a few blocks from Washington's National Theatre, where Kallman sat alone in his dressing room after a *Sixpence* performance, catching up on the papers, making a couple of phone calls, and dispatching a few postcards, including one to his girl. The front of that one showed Lincoln's box at Ford's Theatre draped in red-white-and-blue bunting.

May 11, 1967

Mare-Mare,
Every actor playing D.C. still feels he carries a little bit of
the stain of John Wilkes Booth, who also played the National
(where I am) before his last "show," with Abe, over at Ford's.
Can't wait for my next rendezvous with vous. Cleveland and
Milwaukee still glow in my mind. LOVED the snaps you sent!
And can't wait for the real you in July.

With kisses from your swain,
*   Dick*

She'd made trips from Franklin, Michigan—first to Ohio, then to Wisconsin—just to see him. He'd been a perfect gentleman, gotten her her own hotel rooms and wouldn't let them be paid for by dad's bazillions. He'd taken her to dinner with the actors and encouraged her to spend as much time backstage as she liked. There'd been lots of hand holding and kisses before, just once, a drink-assisted and aborted run toward second base, followed by an apology for his loss of control. What he'd really reached, of course, was the limit of his ardor.

But he would keep at it, because if the next Benson and Orr ever did show up, Mary would be the right adoring companion for the big success that followed.

Washington wasn't a town that would bring any producers backstage. This evening's crowd had consisted of tired suburbanites whose males would trudge off to work tomorrow morning at the Department of Whatever. The little nightlife that remained in the city was dying. The old Blue Room at the Shoreham would soon be gone, and the Willard was on its way to closing altogether.

His mind now went back to his own long-ago booking at the Shoreham, and to the handsome, try-anything State Department guy—Fuller?—who would tonight be past forty and probably posted halfway across the world in some locked, darkened room with some smitten caballero or adoring little Communist.

He placed his postcard to Mary next to another that was already written and stamped and addressed to Mr. Kenneth Nelson, one in a series he'd sent to every venue on Kenny's parallel and now-completed *Sixpence* tour. All of them had gone unanswered, and this final one—"How did it go?"—was marked "Please forward," in the hope it would be sent on from Kenny's last stop, the Shubert in New Haven.

He couldn't bear to ask Carole for his regular address.

———

The plastic numbers stuck into the frosting on the big restaurant cake said, like the program for *Girls Are the Funniest*, that he was twenty-six. Mary's own research had no doubt disproved this to her, but she'd remained silent about it, just as no one in the cast here, celebrating his birthday, had remarked on the obvious fact that the red-white-and-blue party hats were left over from a Fourth of July celebration three days ago.

Despite its title and the wall poster's promise of a "smash new comedy," the play, which would open next week, wasn't funny at all. William Leonard would no doubt murder it, as well as him, in the *Trib*, if Leonard even bothered to drive the forty miles from Chicago to St. Charles, home of the Pheasant Run Playhouse and this restaurant.

Kallman felt a surge of panic and unreality, as if he weren't in a prosperous suburban town but somewhere on the prairie, with the wind rushing toward him in the middle of the night. Worn out from the year of touring, he had exactly one booking for the next six months: a guest shot on *Batman*, two minutes of screen time as Little Louie Groovy, for which he would be so heavily costumed— as a bearded, robed, and amulet-wearing record promoter—that no one would even recognize him.

Once back in LA, he would no longer be able to afford the apartment on Doheny. So what was he supposed to do? Move in with his mother? And have her soon be shipping him off to Doobie for a second rehabilitation, five years after the first? He felt in his pocket for the little foil packet, the last of the coke he'd scored in Montreal a month ago. If he was to get through this party, he would need to go into the bathroom and use it. In the meantime he was drinking, and winking at the playhouse's summer intern, a boy he'd been with twice before Mary got to town. He was paying for her room at the Drake while he could scarcely pay for his own, let alone the limousine's runs between St. Charles and Chicago.

He put one arm around her, and with the one left free clinked a knife against a water glass. The little crowd now expected the leading man to make a generous toast to the whole company and its impending success. But he kept an arm around Mary, and when he raised his tumbler of vodka, it was to say: "The only engagement better than a booking at the Pheasant Run is being *actually engaged* to someone like *this*. Ladies and gentlemen, meet my fiancée, Mary Fisher!"

Mike Connolly, who had died a couple of weeks after his heart operation, wasn't here to record this item for syndication, but a local news photographer did capture the look of surprise on Mary Fisher's face.

CHAPTER 26

JULY 23–SEPTEMBER 18, 1981

By the fourth day of the trial Devin and Laurie and I had settled into a routine, become accustomed to the little bureaucratic mysteries of the courtroom, the stretches of tedium and occasional surprises that filled the hours before and after our lunches at Peggy Doyle's.

The morning of July twenty-third belonged to Paul Boccara, whose time on the stand couldn't help being anticlimactic after Jimmy Ingrassia's gruesome testimony, which the prosecution for the most part just wanted Paulie to confirm. As he spoke, he wouldn't meet his brother-in-law's gaze. The eyes of Dante Forti were no longer looking into the middle distance, but drilling his chief betrayer, a member of his own family. I wondered if Paulie had been sedated a little, because even in Dante's presence he managed to answer Mr. Ehren's questions and to corroborate Jimmy in all essentials.

But he also gave us a handful of new particulars about what had happened in the last minutes of Dick's life and Steven's. When Forti first fired the gun, it was a warning shot, underlining his demand for the combination of the safe whose existence Dick had proudly pointed out during the trio's earlier visit to the apartment. Only when Dick refused to disclose the sequence of numbers did Forti shoot him in the head. And when Forti hustled Steven down the stairs, he never asked if *he* might know the combination; he just went ahead and shot him, too. By this time the only point of the violence was to get rid of a witness.

Mr. Foleo's cross-examination tried to cast doubt upon all the back-and-forth movement between Queens and Manhattan, to suggest the impossibility of so many crossings of the East River and the likelihood that Jimmy and Paulie had made up Forti's participation altogether.

"No, really, the three of us made all those trips!" insisted Paulie, with a smile, as if the commutings were a distinguished accomplishment. I remembered Ehren telling me how, during their prep sessions, he would let Paulie have a beer with his sandwich and that that little pleasure would for a while wholly relieve him of his Rikers terrors. I realized that Paulie's idiotic credibility on the stand came from an inability to hold two stories in his head at once—a basic requirement for lying. When Foleo asked why he'd taken a knife from the kitchen, Paulie replied that it was a meat cleaver, something bigger, its acquisition thereby becoming a commendable feat, like all those trips over the Queensboro Bridge.

"*Why* did you take hold of the meat cleaver?"

"'Cause Jimmy grabbed a knife. And I was high."

"At what point in the evening had you *gotten* high?"

"The whole time."

His round goofball nose was running, adding to the courtroom's short supply of comic relief.

The witness procession on Monday the twenty-seventh passed very quickly. The doctor who did the autopsies suggested that some secondary wounds to Dick's face could have resulted from a brief pistol-whipping (between the two shots?), and that "most significantly" the entry hole for the bullet indicated a contact wound, what's produced when a gun is held directly against the person into whom it's being fired. Steven, moreover, had a "laceration of the ear"—the result, it would seem, of some other horrible little cruelty that Forti had performed and Jimmy left unmentioned. Unless, of course, it was caused by the kick to Steven's twitching head. I couldn't keep from looking at the ears of his brother in the row ahead of me.

The coroner was followed by the doorman of the Hyde Park, the hotel a couple of doors down from Dick's town house. He remembered, in a blow to Forti and Mr. Foleo, *three* white males coming in late that night and heading to a bathroom off the lobby. Yes, the defendant was one of them, and yes, the doorman would agree that the police sketches made from his information had a "high correlation" with the eventual photographic mug shots that were now placed in evidence.

A high-school boy named Jack Chang—Paulie's brainy opposite—was the next to take the stand. Literally pocket-protected, he looked more as if he were in *junior* high. I caught a smile from Devin a few rows away. He seemed to be saying "Pay close attention. This little guy has a surprise for you."

Master Chang's presence related to a rare piece of conflicting testimony between Jimmy and Paulie, each of whom had said the other threw Dick's wallet out the window of the limo when they drove over the bridge with Dante, yet again, to fence the stolen goods on the afternoon following the murders. But they were both wrong in believing that the wallet landed in the river. It had actually fallen onto the pedestrian level of the bridge, below the one that carries cars. Jack Chang found it a little later in the day, while walking home from school. He showed it to his mother and she called the police.

I—and most of the jurors, I imagine—concluded that the wallet's discovery, with Dick's driver's license and credit cards still inside, was being used by the prosecution just to further establish the frantic to-and-fro between Queens and Manhattan. But there was more to it. The next witness, a police forensics expert, told us that a fingerprint lifted off one of the credit cards matched the left thumbprint of Dante Forti.

The fast-paced witness parade began to remind me of

auditions. The guys we'd seen last summer at Delectable Collectibles admitted to buying the bloody necklace that Jimmy offered them. And after those two, Mr. Ehren offered someone better still, a witness with something to contribute that even Devin hadn't gotten wind of. An Asian woman took the stand and identified Dante as the man who'd come into her shop in Queens, some months after the murders, with three pieces of jade to sell. He signed his real first and last names in her sales book. She particularly remembered him because he had a nice tan. He told her he'd gotten it in Florida and soon hoped to refresh it in California.

We never got to hear from Forti, and even though we'd never expected to, the three of us, over at Peggy Doyle's the following evening, talked about what that might have been like. The jury had now been charged, their chief instruction being that, yes, Ingrassia and Boccara could be regarded as "interested witnesses" who'd cut a deal with the prosecution and might therefore be considered untrustworthy—but that this was something for the jurors to decide for themselves.

During closing arguments, Mr. Ehren had said, "It's a good thing Mr. Liannetto left when he did; otherwise he'd be dead, too." I couldn't count the number of times over the past year and a half that I'd stared into space thinking the same thing. Maybe my obsessiveness with Dick's murder had to do with a feeling that if I'd been killed that night, my not-very-big-to-begin-with life would have, like Steven's, shrunk to a page in Dick's evidence file. Some members of the jury threw me a sympathetic glance when Mr. Ehren suggested the might-have-been, but the DA's speculation was deemed to go beyond even the wide latitude given to lawyers during closings, and Judge McGinley struck it from the record.

The defense hadn't put on much of a case. Foleo mostly stuck to his generalized theory of a frame-up, tossing around some insinuations of police corruption and giant payouts by Andy Vitale.

"All of which is bullshit," said Devin, as we reviewed the afternoon. "Okay, it's probably a *little* corrupt for me to be fucking a witness—meaning you, *papi*—but Detective V and the other guys have been pretty much on the level about all this."

He was so certain the jurors would make short work of things that he suggested we order only coffee and slices of that gross cake he liked so much. He was carrying the pager I remembered from last December. A cop friend down at the courthouse had promised to buzz him once the verdict came in.

As it turned out, a lot of time began to pass, and our conversation drifted away from the case to tomorrow's royal wedding of the couple Laurie liked to call Mr. and Mrs. Chuck Windsor. Devin eventually conceded that we should at least order sandwiches.

A bailiff came into the restaurant to pick up some takeout. He recognized us from the courtroom and walked over to say that the jury had been "asking for several read-backs" of testimony. I groaned, fearing that Foleo's scattershot strategy might actually be working, but Laurie said, "No, no, Dad. This can be a good thing. They're being conscientious. If they don't screw up, there'll be less chance of anybody overturning a guilty verdict on appeal."

Just hearing the word "appeal" made me think of how this might go on for years. I actually began to sweat and excused myself to go to the bathroom, where I splashed cold water on my face and used my inhaler a couple of times. Walking back to the table, I saw Laurie showing Devin a newspaper clipping. Had one of the tabloids finally done a story on the trial? No, it was something, apparently unrelated, from the *Times*. Laurie put it back into her shoulder bag with an it's-nothing gesture. And Devin said we should order more cake.

When I sat down, he put his arm over my shoulder, unafraid of the malign stares coming from all the butch, unsmiling portraits of a long-dead Irish judiciary that darkened the restaurant's walls. And he gave my ear a kiss, the tenderest thing I'd ever felt. I realized that here, in front of my daughter, I was now not embarrassed but proud. I also understood, strangely, that this moment would never be occurring if Dante Forti hadn't killed Steven and Dick.

———

No verdict came until the following afternoon.

An hour after Judge McGinley thanked and dismissed the jurors, I called Dolores from Manhattan Plaza. In the background, once she picked up the phone, I could hear Channel 4's recap of the royal wedding.

"Let me turn that down," said Dolores. I imagined she wanted to be suitably grave when I imparted whatever news I had. Maybe she was even worried that Dante Forti had escaped justice. But when she got back on the line, all she said was "I never had *any* difficulty with the queen." It seems the TV coverage had included talk of Lady Di's difficult ongoing adjustment to her new family. "She was *always* lovely to me," Dolores added, summing up what I knew to be the two occasions, five seconds apiece, on which she'd met Elizabeth II in receiving lines at Royal Variety Performances. After a short pause, she concluded her regal observations: "Princess Margaret, of course, is a twat." I was surprised she didn't choose the more Frenchified *chatte*.

"The verdict?" I said, trying to change the subject.

"Honey, that was *everybody's* verdict."

This absurd act—designed to keep showing me that she'd once occupied a different world, and had the sangfroid to go on living in her current one—was not going to trip me up again. I would merely wait it out. Devin, now mixing drinks for me and Laurie and himself, had made me into a tougher customer than I used to be.

"Oh, you mean Richard," said Dolores, finally.

Yeah, him. "They convicted Forti of second-degree murder—the same for both Dick and Steven."

"How much will he get?"

"Maybe life. He'll do at least twenty-five years."

"I'm assuming that's for the killings. What about the robbery? How much will he get for that?"

I looked at Devin and Laurie and cupped my hand over the receiver. "Did I miss something?" I asked them. "Did they convict him of robbery, too?"

"No," Devin answered. "The trivial shit is on Jimmy and Paulie. They didn't even bother taking that to the jury with Forti."

"Oh, my God," Laurie groaned. "She's thinking about her *stuff*!"

I conveyed Devin's information to Dolores. "Ridiculous!" was her response. She felt affronted that her own injury hadn't been recognized by the court. "I'll have to ask Marty if this is going to affect the lawsuit," she told me, referring to the attorney overseeing the action that she and Zara Kallman, after achieving a financial entente, had brought against the insurance company used by Possessions of Prominence.

Trying to get back on track, to restore some sense of proportion, I let her know that "they'll sentence the other two, Ingrassia and Boccara, before they sentence Forti." And that was all the news I had. I could sense the end of my usefulness to Dolores, and didn't know what I ought to say further: "See you for lunch sometime"? But she preempted any awkward silence with a new command: "I'll need you at my deposition for the suit. That's still some months off."

My presence there could serve no legal or practical purpose. I wondered if she simply wasn't ready to let go of this—not just her little Renoir bronze and her jade jewelry, but whatever she still had bottled up inside about "my beautiful Richard!" Was there something she needed to resolve?

Devin, who wanted Dolores to make a final exit from our lives, called out, loud enough for her to hear: "These potato chips are getting cold."

"Well," I told her, weakly, "call me when the time comes." With that I said goodbye and joined my little family across the room.

We raised our glasses in what seemed to be a toast to the verdict or at least to the end of the trial. "Are we *celebrating*?" Laurie asked, a bit sheepishly.

"Not as much as Jimmy and Andy are," said Devin. "You can bet on that, *papi* girl."

What Devin said was borne out two weeks later, on August 11, when Jimmy Ingrassia was sentenced for third-degree robbery, something that would no doubt please Dolores, but which provoked a duel between Mr. Ehren and Judge McGinley. Jimmy's expensive-looking and articulate lawyer, no doubt paid for by the still-absent Andy Vitale, was Herbert Lyon. Devin and Laurie wouldn't remember that years before he'd defended Mrs. Alice Crimmins of Kew Gardens—"the shapely former cocktail waitress," as the tabloids always called her—against the charge that she'd killed her two small children, lest their existence inconvenience her new boyfriend.

Mr. Ingrassia, Lyon assured the court, had provided all the help required by his plea agreement and "brought Messrs. Forti and Boccara to justice." He made it sound as if Jimmy had personally apprehended them while wearing a Superman cape. Paulie had already received two to six years and been shipped off somewhere upstate, but Jimmy—still out on bail, we learned—had just gotten his GED. While it was true, Mr. Lyon told us, that his "proclivities" continued to bother his family, Jimmy hoped to move back in with them and attend community college. (I suspected that Andy Vitale had other ideas.) Jimmy's three-to-four-hundred-dollar-a-day coke habit was, Mr. Lyon further insisted, "in remission," as if it were my asthma at the end of winter. Sending him to prison would be "terribly dangerous"—to Jimmy, that is, since he was now a known snitch.

Was Mr. Lyon actually asking for *probation*?

Jimmy himself made a brief statement. "I'm working now. I

want to be back with my parents. I'm very sorry." He didn't say for what.

Mr. Ehren had for so long been so focused on putting Forti away that he seemed to have almost no appetite for punishing Jimmy. According to him, his star witness had "very little understanding" of right and wrong or of how the world works; Andy still pulled his mental strings. "It's hard to say what's a just punishment for Mr. Ingrassia," the prosecutor mused, though he supposed the two-year minimum required by conviction on the robbery charge was okay.

Without that requirement, I now wondered, would *he* be satisfied with probation?

Mr. Lyon, asked by Judge McGinley to respond to the assistant DA, joked that "Mr. Ehren seems to be trying to take over part of my job."

The judge was exasperated by this amiable display. "In my view, Mr. Ingrassia has literally gotten away with murder. If not for him, Mr. Forti would never have been in that apartment to kill Mr. Kallman and Mr. Szladek." The jury, he informed us, had been more than skeptical of Jimmy's deal with the prosecution, making it the subject of some written questions to him during their deliberations. But, "constrained by the plea agreement," he could hand down a sentence of only two and a third to seven years, so that's what he pronounced, with an order for "administrative segregation." Whether that was justified by Jimmy's being a snitch or a fag was unclear. Whatever the case, we were done here. Except for one thing I'd promised myself I would do.

I was seated in the first row of spectators behind the defense table, and as fast as I could I attached the pin in my pocket to my lapel. I'd not wanted to provoke a reaction to it during the proceedings, but now I did want to go through with a little test I'd planned and confided to Devin, something that would let me be sure I hadn't been imagining things when I saw Forti and Boccara get startled by their own sightings of the pin.

As Jimmy now stood up, the court officers turned him around so that he could—at last—be handcuffed. The rotation brought him face-to-face with me. And sure enough: it had *not* been my imagination. Upon noticing the shiny pin, he actually whispered "Fuck that thing"—as if this pin were the source of all his troubles.

I turned around to look at Devin in the row behind me, hoping somehow to understand the meaning of what I'd just seen.

"Forget it, Daddy," he whispered. "You'll never know why, and what good would it do if you did?"

CHAPTER 27

FEBRUARY 5, 1971

"Dick!" cried Robert Osborne from one of the bars edging the Beverly Hilton's International Ballroom. Encircled by press agents, producers, and writers, all of them cultivating the long-term approval of this now-established journalist, the unceasingly polite Osborne excused himself and walked over to his old roommate Dick Kallman.

Rather than mortify Dick with the "What are you doing here?" question, Robert modestly explained what he was doing there himself. "I'm working on something we're calling the *Academy Awards Oscar Annual*, and since the Globes are the yearly warm-up for the real show, here I am."

It was de rigueur for everyone attending the Golden Globes to make fun of the event even while they were at it, and Kallman now did his part. "Yeah, it's sort of like a vanity press compared to a real publisher," he said. "To make an analogy from your new game."

"Exactly," said Osborne, who was happy to have his *old* game, acting, well in the past and a solid publishing house behind his new venture. His grin was warm, genuine, displaying affection for the Globes as well as the Oscars, no matter the Globes' cheesy reputation. The Hollywood Foreign Press Association, which bestowed the prizes, was a sort of newsprint Potemkin village, hospitable to backscratching and even bribery when it came to picking the nominees and winners.

"You know," Osborne added, further highlighting the contrast between the Globes and the Academy Awards, "it's really the difference between *Love Story* and *Women in Love*. Ali MacGraw will win here tonight, but I guarantee you Glenda Jackson gets the Oscar two months from now." Dick could tell from his tone that Robert liked both actresses, the one who couldn't act and the one who could. And every performer liked Robert. Angela Lansbury, half a ballroom away, was blowing him a kiss.

Dick smiled, and dreaded having to tell Robert what he'd been up to lately, because the account would be so simple: almost nothing. As for why that might be, Dick had pretty much stopped wondering, since he pretty much had the answer: because nobody, at least nobody who knew him, liked him. Yes, he was talented, but plenty of others were equally so, and so why not hire them instead of putting up with Dick Kallman? It was a myth that nice guys finished last. If they didn't get hired first, they at least got hired again. He remembered once hearing Robert, already steeped in showbiz lore, going on about this over dinner at the House of Murphy—how it was only the truly outsized and unique, the Davises and Crawfords, who could afford to be monstrous, enhancing their legends with each new cruelty or outrage they perpetrated. Ninety-nine percent of actors who worked had no legend to enhance. They only had reputations.

And Dick Kallman's was lousy.

"Lucy's not here, is she?" he asked Robert. His expression made it plain he hoped she wasn't.

"I doubt it," Osborne answered, too gracious to add the obvious: while *Here's Lucy* might still be in production, the world of situation comedy now belonged to Mary Tyler Moore. "It's good to see you, Dick," was all he managed to add, before Ring Lardner Jr. swept him back toward the bar.

Kallman ventured into the ballroom to find his table, aware that he was a placeholder here tonight and trying to look casually confident in a red shirt and blazer with gray pants and patent-leather shoes. He'd been invited by an assistant producer of *Medical Center*, last-minute, to park his tuchis where Lois Nettleton's would be if she hadn't taken sick. He'd guested on the show back in November, a week or two after Nettleton did: his last TV job since *Batman* nearly three years ago. Yes, the *Medical Center* bit had been a *bright spot* in the nightmarish drought he was going through, an endless scrounge for short-term singing gigs and commercial voice-overs. His prospects were so flimsy that he couldn't even inflate them with the helium of his old bullshit. At thirty-seven (now claiming thirty-one), he'd become a fogy, talking about *Hank* to people who'd never heard of it, dropping Sophie Tucker's name to those who'd already forgotten it.

He took his seat next to Jayne Meadows, *Medical Center*'s Nurse Chambers, who introduced him to her husband, Steve Allen. She laughed her odd laugh, which seemed to achieve audibility through inhalation, while listening to a story being told from across the table by *Medical Center*'s star, Chad Everett, one of Henry Willson's last big beefcake successes. Unable to relax his butch act for even thirty seconds, Everett kept performing it while somebody went up to accept the Best Musical Score award for *Love Story* and the waiters came around with yet more booze for the already half-plastered audience.

Kallman looked around at all the stars and ersatz half-stars and thought: Mary Fisher would have loved this. He and Mary had never really broken off the engagement that they'd never really made; they just let it collapse, without discussion, from the weight of its own implausibility. Mary was on his mind only because in a couple of weeks he'd have to duck in and out of Chicago (or, more exactly, St. Charles, Illinois) hoping she didn't find out he was onstage once more at the good old Pheasant Run Playhouse. Some comedy about adoption needed him as a three-night substitute for the lead who'd pulled out. He had ten more days to learn the script, whose words were so awful they had so far defied memorization.

The second-most-dreaded moment of the evening now

arrived. Dyan Cannon, all tresses and beading and teeth, arrived at the Lucite lectern where—as one of last year's Best Supporting Actress nominees, for *Bob and Carol and Ted and Alice*—she would present this year's Best Supporting Actor award.

"Do you know her?" whispered Jayne Meadows.

Was Jayne fishing? Maybe she'd heard that he once smashed Cannon's finger and now wanted the whole story?

He shook his head and replied: "I'm hoping old Cary Grant is finding a way to keep himself occupied." The Grant-Cannon marriage had already come and gone, after producing a little girl.

"I imagine young Jennifer will someday be Miss Golden Globes," said Meadows, breathing in a low-decibel version of her whooping laugh. It was a Globes tradition to each year crown an envelope-carrying ingenue, the offspring of an established star. Jayne made the prediction with simple playfulness; she wasn't the wounding kind, Kallman decided. Whereas he, as Carole Cook once observed after he'd made dinner for the workshop kids, took less pleasure from eating the lobster than from dropping it into the pot.

John Mills thanked everyone for the little supporting-actor Globe he took from Cannon. Johnny Mercer and Henry Mancini then followed him to the stage for some song they'd written for *Darling Lili*, the Julie Andrews bomb.

Could Mercer, Kallman wondered, remember the lyrics to "Hank"? Could he remember that he'd *written* them?

Too many people from his life were in this room. It came as a relief when his eyes landed on ones he'd never met, whether it was George C. Scott or Rita Hayworth or Jack Nicholson getting drunk with Joan Crawford, who looked as if she were encouraging Nicholson to go ahead, commit lèse-majesté and come on to her.

There was a time when he would have been trying to figure out how to get to every one of these people before the program was over. But now? Where would he find the energy, or the point?

His gaze fell on the chief element of his past who was present here, three tables away. Jayne Meadows saw him staring. She followed his eyes and asked: "Did you see *Boys in the Band*?"

"Just recently," he replied, creating the impression that he didn't believe it was worth anyone's while. "I thought the real star of the film was the balcony of Tammy Grimes's apartment in New York! I've been to a couple of parties there." He wouldn't tell Jayne that he'd also been, often, to Julius', down in the Village, where they'd shot the gay-bar scene.

"Steve and I saw the play in New York. I thought it was pretty good. And *he* is *awfully* pretty." She was nodding toward Kenny, who'd done the play for two years and then gotten the film, while Dick ate his heart out. Love means *always* having to say you're sorry. "But," Jayne wondered, "isn't he a little old for the award he's up for?"

"Do you *think* so?" Dick answered, in mock astonishment. Jayne inhaled a laugh, while he admitted, "I actually know him. A little."

"Oh?"

Before he could supply details, Jayne was obligated to direct her attention to some new bit of bloviation, about the animals on his ranch, from Chad Everett.

Yes, Kallman thought, Kenny—forty this year—was ridiculously old to be up for New Star of the Year. And while he might even now still look like a boy, it was a boy who suddenly and unexpectedly *needed* this award. *Boys in the Band* had always been a mixed blessing. Recognition, yes; but what movie casting director would ever again want Kenny in a straight role? And his first post-*Boys* foray back into theater had been an unadulterated failure. *Lovely Ladies, Kind Gentlemen*, a musical version of *Teahouse of the August Moon*, had opened on Broadway just after Christmas and closed the week after New Year's. While the critics groaned over the lackluster material, a bunch of Asian actors and knee-jerk theater lefties had squawked over this white, onetime juvenile actor being allowed to play Japanese. As if passive, perplexed Kenny were Mickey Rooney doing Mr. Yunioshi in *Breakfast at Tiffany's*.

Would the Globes be a big redemptive moment for him? Katharine Houghton, Hepburn's niece, read off the names of Kenny's competition, the other male New Stars of the Year: Assaf Dayan, Frank Langella, James Earl Jones, and Joe Namath. The last one produced giggles throughout the ballroom, even though the jock's first film had made money. Kallman kept his eyes on Kenny as the envelope was ripped open and the award went, thank God, to Jones, who'd also been around too long to be in this category, though at least he was a Negro playing a Negro.

What was Kenny feeling at this moment? A southern white boy's resentment? And what was Dick Kallman hoping to see on his face? Pain and hurt? He was surprised to realize that he wasn't sure. In any case, he was seated too far away to see anything more subtle in Kenny's expression than a gentlemanly c'est-la-vie look, successfully assumed.

He wouldn't have gone over to Kenny's table if Kenny had won. But now that he'd lost, he thought he could. Everyone here milled about and table-hopped even while film clips played and acceptance speeches rambled on. He'd make it quick. He'd just go over and tell Kenny something like "You wuz robbed"—impart this bit of Brooklynese affection like a man offering sincere commiseration. And, actually, that's what he *would* be, because both of them, after running parallel to or around each other for twenty years, had been robbed. Neither was ever again likely to work as big as Dick had in *Hank* and Kenny had in *Boys*.

He whispered a quick excuse-me to Jayne Meadows, and was up out of his chair, on his way to see Kenny for the first time in five years. Dyan Cannon, he noticed, was heading in the opposite direction, more or less coming toward him, presumably to greet somebody else nearby. A couple of ushers deferentially pleaded with stars and semistars and nonstars to take their seats before the night's biggest awards got presented. The pleas went ignored, and the boozy shuffling around kept Kallman a couple of feet from the New Stars table, close enough only to hear Kenny joking to Frank Langella and Joe Namath, his now fellow losers: "Maybe playing gay in *Boys in the Band* wasn't such a great career-boosting idea after all. Well, that's the way the nookie crumbles."

Namath, sitting next to Kenny, found this hilarious—especially, no doubt, the business that Kenny had only been *playing* gay. The football star roared with laughter and gave a squeeze to Kenny's neck with his enormous, meaty hand. Kenny, for a split second, actually rested his head on Namath's big shoulder, accepting the tender condolence of this famously overexperienced heterosexual.

The sight filled Kallman with a potent mixture of erotic excitement and jealousy: this was the kind of protectiveness he'd occasionally received from his brother, Charlie, and what he had, from the first moment he'd seen him, wanted somehow to offer Kenny, that angelic, hesitant boy who a few weeks earlier had been demonstrating a potato peeler in Woolworth's. But being Dick Kallman, he had to overdo things, offer it with the hard sell of a too-expensive gift, and frighten him off. And once he'd blundered, his ardor could only increase, along with his fury over Kenny's rejection. The coup de foudre he'd experienced at the first sight of his opposite, his missing half, had ended up leaving him, even now and presumably forever, in this obsessive double bind.

Right now it was a momentary surge of sentiment that he felt, a desire to break through the row of people between himself and the table, to play against type, as Kenny had done with his brittle character in *Boys in the Band*, and to say, truthfully: "Remember who won the 1951 Theatre World Award for Most Promising Newcomer? It was me. And look where it got me."

But an usher was now actually pushing him, however gently, back toward his seat, even as Dyan Cannon, finished with her work at the podium, was permitted to advance straight toward him. He thought he could see her flipping him the bird. But as she got closer it became evident that her ring finger, not the middle one, was the digit pointing straight up. She rubbed the side of it with her thumb, indicating the still-unfaded scar from their ugly little incident at the Chicago Shubert.

Her whitened teeth, bared and flashing, fooled those around them into believing she was just getting ready to air-kiss an old friend, after showing him triumphantly that she was now shorn of Cary Grant's wedding ring.

"You *sick bastard*," she whispered. "How did you even get *in* here?"

He looked at the hand and realized, almost abstractly, that he could no longer smash anyone's finger in a door—not from ambition or competitiveness or even from anger. He did, however, understand, as he fake-smiled her back, that the idea of smashing, of pain, had not entirely lost its appeal. What he now thought he wanted, and maybe always had, was for someone to smash *him*.

CHAPTER 28

SEPTEMBER 18, 1981

"I know she won't recognize me," whispered Carole Cook, pointing to Dick's mother. "It's been twenty years. But I should go over to her at some point."

We were in the third row of spectators inside Judge McGinley's courtroom, there for the sentencing of Dante Forti. Zara Kallman was down front, close behind the prosecution table. Looking shrunk, she sat between Dick's brother and an older man I at first took to be Arnold Weissberger, the attorney at the reading of the will; then I remembered seeing Weissberger's obituary in the *Times* a few months before.

The dozen or so people who'd come to watch this morning sat in widely spaced clusters. All the way across the room, Forti's wife and young daughter talked softly to each other, waiting for him to be brought in. The Szladeks—mother, father, and two sons, the males all wearing jackets and ties—remained mute, as if at a second funeral. Two rows behind me and Carole, at the back, sat my own little family, Devin and Laurie—separated from me because we knew Detective Volker would also be in court today. I turned around and smiled at them as we waited, nervously, though the proceedings required nothing of us, and their outcome was a virtual certainty.

By last night I'd gotten halfway through *Terms of Endearment*, and I should probably have held on to the novel—nothing still calms me like reading—instead of sticking it in Laurie's tote bag when we went through the security check. But Carole, a year into her role as Maggie Jones in *42nd Street*, was good, warm company, quietly telling me backstage stories about what was itself a backstage musical.

Everyone suddenly seemed to come in at once: Ehren, the assistant DA; the defense attorney, Foleo; and This-Here's-Dante, who blew a kiss to his little daughter. Judge McGinley entered a minute later, calmer than he'd been at Jimmy Ingrassia's jackpot sentencing the month before. One realized that justice wasn't going to get miscarried through any loopholes *this* time.

Mr. Ehren nodded to Mrs. Kallman and the Szladeks before voicing his recommendation of two twenty-years-to-life sentences, "the maximum," he explained with emphasis. "It's that way, Your Honor," he said regretfully, "because we no longer have the death penalty in New York State." The prosecutor's whole manner and view of things seemed opposite to what he'd shown at Jimmy's sentencing. Did the change stem from a guilty conscience? Or was today's behavior just the last step in realistically doing what it took to put away an actual killer?

Unlike Jimmy's lawyer last month, Mr. Foleo had no sense that Ehren was doing his job for him. The best he could manage for his client was to delay the inevitable for a minute or two. He stalled by mentioning some academic conferences on sentencing that he himself had attended, "including one at the University of Miami." Finally, he launched into what he must have known was a nonstarter of an argument: if Mr. Ehren's two recommended terms were imposed, it was only fair and merciful that they run concurrently, not consecutively. He wanted the killings of Dick and Steven to feel like a single crime, even if that required believing the two men together amounted to only one person. He assured us, apropos of nothing, that Dante Forti's wife was "a person to whom a mean thought has never occurred." Several heads furtively turned toward her. The irrelevance of the comment, along with the composed look on her face, made it impossible to avoid thinking that the reverse might be the truth.

McGinley moved things to the point where the murderer was at last allowed to speak for himself. Before Forti rose to do that, the judge indicated that everyone in the courtroom should listen respectfully. He didn't say, but somehow conveyed, that we could afford to be patient, since the convicted man would soon be going away for a long time.

Forti talked in a strong, aggrieved voice, more polished than I expected, directing his words to the judge as if the two were in private conversation. This feeling was enhanced by the way he referenced and quoted from letters he'd sent the judge in the weeks since the guilty verdict. The killer's resentments extended to his own lawyer, who had kept him from taking the stand by insisting "the prosecutor would make a fool of me." The murders, according to Forti, were all the fault of Jimmy, who "killed a rich business associate over money and drugs. I was never in Manhattan, never in that apartment. There were two wallets in the bags of stuff that Paulie and Ingrassia brought to my house in Queens late that night. That's how my fingerprint got on one of them—"

Judge McGinley interrupted, telling him not to relitigate the case, to remember that we were in a different phase of things now.

Forti apologized and adopted a heart-tugging approach. The loneliness of jail, he said, was already killing him. He missed his three children and his wife of eight years. "The man with a family is the one who's going to jail—for life, let's face it, if you let the two terms run one after the other."

In keeping with Foleo's trial strategy, this new perspective— "the man with a family"—announced one more theory of the case, a final scenario for everyone to consider. "This crime was a homosexual one," Dante now explained. "They always stick together, and you've gotta ask yourself: why was Mr. Ehren so easy on Jimmy? Think about it."

Ehren—easily the butchest man in the courtroom, beyond

even Detective Volker—snorted with secure amusement. The judge, who seemed to be seeking an admission of guilt that might lead to an expression of remorse, pointed out to Forti, almost sorrowfully, that this wild swing, too, constituted relitigation rather than anything called for by the present moment. Frustrated, Forti ended his speech by declaring: "I'm an escape goat." I saw the court clerk in his white short-sleeved shirt barely trying to suppress a laugh, and I winced. Even if This-Here's-Dante had shot two people in the head, this didn't feel like the moment to make fun of him. Not when his own little girl was sobbing.

Judge McGinley asked him to remain standing while sentence was pronounced. Yes, the terms would be twenty years to life, and they would run consecutively. Despite everything, the judge wished the defendant, now a convict, good luck, and he expressed his sympathies to the Kallmans and Szladeks.

Forti had to turn around while his wrists were recuffed, which briefly had him facing all the spectators. As on every other day in court, I had the pin with me, but today it was inside the breast pocket of my jacket, invisible to This-Here's-Dante. Why the sight of it had so agitated him at his plea hearing—and had done the same to Jimmy at his sentencing—would have to remain a mystery, I'd decided: *Forget it, Daddy. You'll never know why, and what good would it do if you did?*

People avoided Forti's eyes, and with a different sort of courtesy avoided the Szladeks', as the family made a hasty exit. Once they were gone, everyone who remained began milling about, like an audience reluctant to depart the theater after a show that's left them shaken. Ehren went over and spoke to Mrs. Kallman, expressing the hope that she might take some small comfort from the severity of the sentence. The man from the gay-rights organization, pen and pad in hand, monitored their conversation. Carole and I stood close by, next in a kind of receiving line, waiting to condole with Zara.

"Mrs. Kallman, I'm so sorry," Carole said, once we were able to approach. "You won't remember me, but—"

"You're the girl who won the weekly contest at One Fifth."

"Well, yes. And I performed with Dick in the Desilu—"

"He *got* you that job."

Dick's brother shot us an apologetic glance while, with the help of the priest, he tried to draw his mother away. But Zara wasn't in a mood to go. She introduced me and Carole to the older man beside her—her new lawyer, it turned out. "We're suing the insurance company," she informed us. "Can you *believe* how much that guy stole from Dickie?" She pointed to the spot where Forti had so recently stood. Nonetheless, it took us a minute to realize whom she meant, and to comprehend how, like a hunched, diminutive Dolores—her partner in the lawsuit, absent today—she seemed to view a double murder and the heist of some jade as comparable crimes.

I said goodbye to Mrs. Kallman, who held on to Carole's hand, tightly, still wanting to know what she thought about the extent of Dante Forti's thievery.

I saw Carole, politely aghast, murmur a few words of reply, and when she freed herself, I asked her what she'd said.

"'Kids today, huh?' Idiotic, I know, but it just slipped out."

I started laughing, and got an odd look from Mr. Ehren and Detective Volker, who were talking to each other. The prosecutor handed the cop a souvenir, which I soon learned was a copy of the court's sentencing form, freshly filled out by the clerk. Volker came over to thank me for my help over the past year and a half and to show me the form, which indicated that Dante Forti would receive 254 days' credit, time already served, toward completion of his sentence. He'd have about fifteen thousand days to go before his first parole hearing in the year 2020.

I asked Volker why the bottom of the form instructed that another copy of it go to the Board of Elections.

"To make sure that Forti doesn't try to cast a ballot. You know the lengths that civic-minded fellows like himself will go to just to participate in our democratic process."

I began to understand why Volker and Devin got along so well. Pointing to the facility-assignment box on the form, I said, "Going to Sing Sing. Just like in the movies."

"Oh, that's only the first of many places that will have the honor of hosting him. He'll do a lot of shuffling around the franchise over the next forty years." With that, Detective V said goodbye and left, telling Devin he'd see him back at the pre-cinct.

I noticed that Volker avoided shaking hands with the court clerk, who had a sort of purple bruise on his left cheek and half the time appeared to be sweating. Did the detective have the feeling that this guy, who was wearing an earring, was sick? With the "gay cancer"?

Nobody at this point knew anything for certain about the medical rumors and stories that were creeping into the gay papers and even the *Times*. Was it some sort of virus? I had a friend who talked about the "homo Andromeda Strain." Or was it maybe a cumulative thing? Or maybe guys were getting sick because they had had such an overwhelming amount of sex and venereal disease in the last several years, along with so many routine penicillin shots, that their natural defenses were crumbling "like the walls of Jericho," as the same friend put it. Well, that wouldn't apply to me, but I did sometimes worry about Devin, and whether his past—though he still seemed too young to have one—had been more extensive and dangerous than I'd allowed myself to believe. Laurie worried about both of us, and the two of *them* seemed especially worried about me: I couldn't cough without getting a *look*. I now knew that the clip-ping I'd seen them whispering over at Peggy Doyle's had been one of the first press stories about whatever this thing was.

With Laurie now talking to Carole, and Volker having left the courtroom, Devin could at last come over to me. On the way he exchanged a few words with the court clerk at his desk. As they conversed, I saw the guy shaking his head in that New York Italian whaddya-gonna-do way.

"What was that about?" I asked Devin when they were through.

"He and I were just wondering whether This-Here's-Dante will do a whole forty years or even close to it."

"What's his guess?"

"He doesn't give a fuck. His exact words were 'Hell, I'm gonna be dead before the *other* one gets out.'"

He meant Jimmy, who'd end up being released in less than three years.

CHAPTER 29

OCTOBER 20, 1972

Alvan Kallman had been dead for eight years, and the living room of what remained Zara's apartment looked less fussy, the chairs denuded of their plastic coverings. Had she engaged in such protections only for him, and so now there wasn't any point to them? No, the coverings, Dick knew, had all along been the assertion of her own authority over the intrusive ass of every guest and relative who sat down in her domain. Fewer of them came around these days, and it was their absence, not Alvan's, that had liberated the upholstery.

Dick now lived with Zara, the place on Doheny having become too expensive. On this early Friday evening, while his mother grocery-shopped at Vons, he sat alone on the sofa, watching himself on TV: "Those cats were the thieves!" he shouted from the screen, as the hippie-robed, amulet-wearing record producer Little Louie Groovy. "The chick with the swinging outfit! The creep with the green hair!" His character was telling a courtroom that Catwoman and the Joker had been the ones who robbed his apartment.

Los Angeles's ABC affiliate had been rerunning *Batman*, tonight presenting the second of the two episodes Dick had shot five years ago. Watching it, he recalled how during the filming Eartha Kitt had been unable to stand the sight of him, as if she were not Catwoman but an actual cat, operating on snap-judgmental feline instinct.

The closing credits now rolled for several seconds over a still photo of Burt Ward, the show's Robin, and his large, snugly costumed bulge. "Terminally straight," he'd been cautioned by a queeny crew member about Burt. But even five years ago the warning was becoming less pertinent: the young, the clean-cut, and the straight-appearing had already started to lose their appeal. With the exception of his memory of Kenny, a tarnished and hidden holy relic, his taste had begun running to much rougher and more easily obtainable stuff, like the busboy at Dan Tana's restaurant he was supposed to meet in a little while.

He decided he'd get dressed and go there early, instead of awaiting his mother's return with purchases that she would pronounce, as she unloaded them one by one, either overpriced or substandard. He was soon starting up his Mustang convertible and heading toward the 9000 stretch of Santa Monica Boulevard. The radio poured out its coverage of the Nixon landslide that seemed to be shaping up, and it felt all wrong to him: Dick Nixon was supposed to be a loser, just as Dick Kallman was supposed to be a winner. That's what had been written into their characters, and it was a mystery why nature lately had been reversing their destinies.

But right now there was the busboy to consider. They'd met a week ago in a bar he'd gone into alone, only to discover an old acquaintance standing near the back with this young man, the two of them looking joined at the hip or, more exactly, at the wallet. "This is Dick. He used to be on television" was the old acquaintance's idea of an introduction. Luckily, the busboy's interest appeared to be stimulated rather than killed by the information. He did go off with the old acquaintance for the rest of their evening, but before that he managed to make a date, for tonight, with Dick Kallman. The basis of a transaction had been established, though the financial terms remained less explicit than the physical arrangements, whose outlines, if not details, had been plainly laid down. Kallman had sensed that his "fame" might actually be payment enough: television being television, those who'd never glowed inside the box regarded those who had, even if in the past, as a different, near-magical order of being, whether they'd hosted a local kids' program or were prime-time network stars.

The boy had an early shift tonight at Dan Tana's, and he'd said he would be free as soon as he finished the last setups of the dinner tables. Parking the Mustang, Kallman decided to go into the kitchen to let him know he'd arrived early and would be having a drink at the bar while he waited. He entered the restaurant to the sound of some loud Nixon supporters at the front, out-of-towners enthusing over their man and mocking the infatuation of liberal Hollywood, Shirley MacLaine in particular, with George McGovern. It all felt irrelevant on several levels.

Heading toward the kitchen, he suddenly noticed Carole Cook and her husband, Tom Troupe, also in the business, having predinner drinks at their table. She was surprised to see him—not exactly delighted, but as usual pleased with what the world chose to throw at her. "As I live and breathe," she said, motioning for him to join her and Tom.

"I'm here to meet someone," he responded, abruptly enough that it sounded rude, or maybe just a little guilty.

"Well, wait with us until whoever it is gets here. We're having old-fashioneds; not as good as the ones Tom makes at home, but good enough to get the job done."

He declined to sit down, but rested his hands on the back of a chair while he stood and chatted for a minute or two. He learned that Troupe had just done an episode of *The Rookies* set to air in about ten days.

"What are *you* up to?" he asked Carole, hoping not to get the same question from her.

"I just did a bit on *McMillan & Wife*." This was the Rock Hudson–Susan Saint James detective dramedy.

"How is Rock doing?" Kallman asked.

"He's doing everyone," Carole responded. A little nervously, he joined her laughter and Troupe's.

"I just finished another *Medical Center*," he volunteered, without adding how, aside from that, he'd done nothing, anywhere, since his previous appearance on the show two years before. "You can call me Dr. Styles."

"Oh, *I* played a naive widow who sees her husband's ghost at a séance." She turned to Troupe. "I think this means you're going before I do, sweetheart."

Carole was always working—steadily, happily—whether it meant singing "Poor Johnny One Note" on an episode of *That Girl* or sliding down a fire pole on Lucy's latest sitcom. She and Troupe now waited for Dick to say something—it was more or less his turn. They got only dead air, but Carole kept making an effort: "I heard you saw Robert at the Oscars in April."

"It was the Globes. Last year, not this year."

All at once he could see her thinking of Kenny, of how much it would have helped him to win the award that night. And *he* was now so obviously thinking of Kenny that Carole didn't even feel the need to use his name when she said: "He's doing *Show Boat*. Over in London."

"So I've heard," Kallman responded, trying to remain low-key. "Isn't the run about over?"

"Yes, but he says he's going to stay over there for good."

"Really?" Kallman's tone revealed that this was not a rhetorical question.

"He's getting married."

Kallman immediately brightened. Only a man, not a wife, could make him feel jealous.

"It's just so he's allowed to work," Carole explained, lowering her voice a little. "To get a green card, or whatever they call it over there."

Kallman liked this a lot less. If it was only a marriage of convenience, then a boy, an *extra* convenience, might be coming with it. But there wasn't room in his brain to consider this as he anticipated his evening with Kenny's opposite, the busboy.

"Well, I'd better get to the bar, so that my pal will be sure to find me. Great to see you both."

Walking away, he heard Tom say to Carole, "Isn't the bar in the other direction?"

He entered the kitchen and was told by one of the busboy's colleagues: "Mino's waiting for you out in the parking lot. Away from the boss's prying eyes."

He found him out back leaning against the Mustang.

"Hey, Mino!" he called out, with the full-on smile he could these days flash only rarely.

"Hey there," came the reply, along with a facial expression that was both slyer and more natural than Kallman's own. "Mino" made the guy sound delicate, Japanese, but it was a nickname derived from El Camino, the Chevrolet truck. He was half Mexican, half Russian; he had a service tattoo on his right forearm. Kallman pegged him for mid-twenties. Getting closer, he could see that Mino was still impressed with him, a man who'd been on TV, a visitor from another planet. Fortunately, as Kallman had learned from their mutual acquaintance, Mino had no ambitions of his own to be in the business.

As they drove off to the guy's apartment here in West Hollywood, Kallman pondered the absurdity of being himself unable to "host"—because he lived with his mother!

Mino had two roommates, one of them home—"not a problem," he assured Kallman.

At least he had his own room, where the TV was playing a special with Dinah Shore that had started at nine p.m. on good old NBC. Had the box been on the whole time Mino was working his shift?

"You're very well put together," the young man told his guest, after Kallman draped his sport coat over a chair. For a second he thought Mino was flattering his physique, which he had less and less reason to keep fit. But Mino was talking about the coat and the now-revealed bespoke shirt beneath it, something bought years ago, when he'd been in London to lay down a single track on an album.

"Thank you," he said, almost paternally. He had, what, fifteen years on this guy?

He was finding it difficult to say much of anything. At one time he'd been used to directing a show like this one, to being in charge sexually. Frustration entered this present moment because he was supposed to be *not* in charge sexually—their informative sex banter had made that much clear at the bar last week—yet he would now have to issue somewhat more specific instructions, which meant being in charge.

"So," asked Mino, with the sly, parking-lot smile, "what exactly do you want, Hank?"

He definitely did *not* want to be Hank. *All wrong*. Unless, maybe, it was suddenly just right? To have Hank roughed up a little? To have the Hank smacked out of him? Leaving something else entirely in its place? Something new? If that was the plan, yeah, they could keep the TV on in the background, like a sound-effect instrument of torture. Dinah would do, though it was too bad *Hank* itself had never run long enough to go into reruns, to earn him residuals and be available for this specialized use.

Mino took off his T-shirt, revealing two more tattoos, their multiplicity making Kallman curious about whether he'd ever been in prison. Which, if it were true, would make Mino a dream date, from what he'd heard, for Paul Lynde. Did this thought of prison, he now wondered, excite *him*? Scare him? Had excitement and fear become the same thing?

The rest of their clothes came off. Mino undressed himself with efficiency, and then undressed *him* with an element of tenderness, at least toward the bespoke shirt and creased wool trousers.

Instinct told him that this would be quick, that he'd be home before Tom Brokaw delivered the eleven o'clock local news.

When they got to the bed, Mino asked, "You sure, Hank?"

The question made him feel like a game-show contestant. Yes, he was ready to be dunked for charity if he came up with the wrong answer. The question also indicated, usefully, that Mino had not forgotten the broad outlines of what they'd come here for, even before the specificity of Hank was added.

"Yeah, I'm sure." He decided he could dispense with further instructions, at least for now.

A moment later he felt Mino bring a hand to his face, a hard slap, and he heard himself say "Yes!"

Twenty seconds after that, with the hand closed, Mino nearly clocked him, not from viciousness, but from his own exuberance and semiprofessional desire to please. But apprehending this—that someone was trying to *please* him—filled Kallman, momentarily, with anger and disgust. He was here to be degraded, not pleasured.

"Go over to my pants," he told Mino. "There's a pin in one of the pockets. A little piece of jewelry. Take it out."

Mino did as told. "Okay," he said, looking quizzically at the object. "Now what?"

"Stab me in the right side of the chest with it. Just enough to draw a little blood."

Mino looked for an instant as if this were too much, but then gave him a you're-the-boss look, which pleased what was left of Old Dick and revolted what was still maturing into New Dick. The two selves within him collaborated in a sharp cry of protest/approval when the pin pierced the flesh of his chest. Along with Mino he watched and waited for the trickle of blood that arrived seconds later.

Mino walked quickly to the bathroom and came back with a small round Band-Aid.

Kallman knew this was the end of the evening. Like the writer of a show going through out-of-town revisions, he was happy to have had this little brainstorm about the pin and now decided that that was enough for today. He left Mino some money on a chair, pretending it was a gift. The recipient smiled, before expressing further admiration for the clothes his guest was putting back on.

As Mino walked toward him, Kallman felt afraid that the younger man might propose to see him again or, even worse, request a kiss. Instead, abashed and not the least sly-looking now, Mino asked: "Could I have an autograph?"

Kallman obliged and two minutes later began the drive home to his mother's place. It was still warm enough to keep the top down, and the moderate headwind felt half like a caress and half like a buffeting. He wondered whether the resale value of the Mustang, if he decided to get rid of it and move away, would cover the payments on it that he still had to make. Everyone—Zara at the kitchen table, Father Doobie over the phone—was lately asking if he'd considered going back to New York.

He looked down to the spot beneath his shirt where the tiny wound would be. He could feel it throb but saw no sign of it bleeding through. The Band-Aid, well applied, was doing its work nicely; he decided that Mino was too fastidious to have any real future as a dom.

The downward glance gave him a quick, encompassing look at the shirt, the pants, and the shoes. He *was* well put together. It struck him more forcefully than ever that clothes were a form of acting, and as he considered the idea, he wondered if he shouldn't make *them* his business.

Maybe clothes could remake the man.

CHAPTER 30

OCTOBER 10, 1981

It was ten thirty on a Saturday night, and I was in the bedroom flipping through Dick's scrapbook. I'd long since gone through it a second and a third time and knew that its last quarter—the sputtering and the aftermath of his show-business career—moved very fast. In the years after *Hank*, Zara must have been the one to do some of the archiving. Traces of what looked like a woman's handwriting could be found in some of the annotations, which occasionally mentioned "Dickie" doing this or that.

There were also extraneous items, ephemera tossed in between the pages, that seemed to come from Dick himself. But the rationale for their inclusion was cryptic. A postcard of Dan Tana's restaurant? I mean, not a place up there with Chasen's or Ciro's. What's it doing there?

Among the unmounted insertions were several bits and pieces pertaining to Kenny Nelson: an article about the casting controversy over *Lovely Ladies* (I knew a couple of guys who'd imagined a two-year gig in that pit and who wound up with two weeks instead) and some trade-paper items mentioning Kenny's expatriation to London in the early seventies.

Kenny was back on my mind because lately, from time to time, I'd been subbing for the it'll-never-close *Fantasticks* down on Sullivan Street. In fact, I'd done the Saturday matinee several hours ago. Pictures of Kenny with Rita Gardner and Jerry Orbach, the other original cast members, still hung on the walls backstage.

I remember how Carole, early in our acquaintance, explained Dick's occasional efforts through the years to contact her: *Oh, darling, I think he did it to stay connected—if only by a thread— to Kenny.* From this and some things I myself had noticed nearly thirty years ago, I figured *something* must have passed between the two men—still really boys then—but in the midst of everything going on with the investigation and trial I'd never questioned Carole, who was protective of Kenny, about it. When just the other day I asked her for Kenny's address in England, she told me she was worried about him. He'd been over there for a decade now, working often but not living with the wife he'd married in order to ensure that. Instead he was overly devoted and generous to a boyfriend that nobody liked or entirely trusted.

I told her I was thinking of writing to him, of sending him a keepsake or two from Dick's scrapbook—not any of the self-lovingly pasted items from *Seventeen*, but some of the later, unfastened odds and ends about Kenny himself. Carole looked a little worried about *me* when I mentioned the idea, but she gave me Kenny's address in Surrey and then gently asked why I was still preoccupied with Dick, who was, as she put it, "not terribly likable as murder victims go."

I'd been wondering about this myself, and so had Devin, who had recently moved in with me full-time, and who now came into the bedroom. He plopped himself down beside me on the comforter.

"That thing *again*? What the fuck are you doing?" He took the scrapbook from my hands and closed it.

I tried laughing it off. "I'm just tired and bored."

"Didn't we watch that old crone on TV the other night? That's a big enough hit of the past for one week, no?" He was referring to our late-night viewing of *Mr. Skeffington*, where the very young Dolores had that one scene singing in the night-club. When I pointed her out to Devin, he got up and went to within inches of the screen, peered closely, and said, "That's a former nose, *papi*." He also declared Bette Davis, the movie's star, to be a less convincing version of herself than Charles Pierce.

I knew that after a long day at the precinct Devin—darling Devin!—would like us to be going out. "Daddy issues" were one thing; they enlivened our daytimes, and they disappeared (or raucously reversed themselves) in bed. But someone still *so* young was also entitled to—what can I call them?—"disco issues"? Even if disco was dying, for *his* sake I ought to be able to summon enough energy to go out on a Saturday night.

With the scrapbook firmly returned to a shelf, Devin nearly dragged me into the living room for a drink. There he began telling me what he'd been hearing from Detective V and a grapevine that wound through both Ehren's office and the 19th Precinct: updates on each of the new prisoners Devin called "the Three Fucked-up-teers." I got the feeling that he was telling me this because it was a less crazy way of being preoccupied with Dick than disappearing into the unrecoverable world of the scrapbook.

I learned that Jimmy Ingrassia, now at Green Haven prison, was having lots of visitors. They didn't include Andy, who chose instead to dispatch a rotation of deputized callers from Westchester and Manhattan, all of them bearing more gifts than regulations allowed. "It's not clear if Jimmy is still the number-one boy at home," Devin explained; maybe Andy was carrying a torch for his return or maybe he was just expressing gratitude for Jimmy's having saved the family drug business by copping to the Kallman murders he'd so foolishly set in motion.

Paulie, a simple soul, was actually doing quite well behind bars. Unable to hold any thought in his head for long, he apparently no longer felt scared. "He can't see why This-Here's-Dante might still be a little, let's say, annoyed. The way Paulie views it, he and his brother-in-law are both now in jail, so things are sort of even." Paulie, it seemed, couldn't quite grasp the difference between two years and forty.

Which left Dante, literally up the river, to be reported on. "They've spread out a whole menu of treats and opportunities for him," said my tough-on-crime Devin. "Does he want to get his GED? Step right up. Maybe a little therapy? Write stories in a 'workshop'? They're even starting some program that'll allow the guys to put on plays or musicals."

"You're kidding," I answered, as I started to imagine Dante Forti as a murderous Willie Baxter in a jailhouse version of *Seventeen*.

The phone rang. "Surprise!" It was Laurie, who'd taken the LSATs last week and had just made a spur-of-the-moment Columbus Day weekend trip to New York. The girl she was staying with was out tonight with a boyfriend.

"Give me your phone," Devin said, excitedly. "The whole thing."

I handed him both the receiver and the box, which via some quick work with the jack he attached to an old Ericsson speakerphone he'd brought home the other day, having acquired it during a squad-room sale of obsolete police property. "Hello, *papi* girl!" he shouted, once the connection took hold. "We're hearing you loud and clear!" He explained the device to Laurie.

"What are you guys doing at home on a Saturday night?" my daughter asked.

"Exactly *nothing*," Devin answered. "Your daddy's head has been stuck in Dickieland again. Don't you think it's a little— what's the word?"

"Morbid?"

"That's it. I bet you aced that law-school test."

"Results next week!"

I chimed in. "Brunch tomorrow, you two?"

"*Papi*, if you're gay enough to take your girl to brunch tomorrow, you can be gay enough to take us to a club tonight."

I looked at him wanly. All that smoke? All that pounding noise, against my general exhaustion? I suggested that the two of them go out tonight by themselves, together—a scenario straight out of the post-*Hank* era of American sitcoms.

"You know what I'd rather do than go to a club?" Laurie interrupted. "Go see *Mommie Dearest*. There's a midnight showing at the Loew's on Thirty-Fourth Street. *Please*? This would be gayer than a club crawl and brunch *combined*."

Devin asked: "Is this the one about the old lady who beats her kids?"

"Old lady?" I interrupted, with campy indignation. "You're talking about Miss Joan Crawford."

"I don't see the big deal here," Devin said to both of us. "She sometimes lost her shit, and so her daughter writes a book about it?"

"*Pleeeeze?*" Laurie asked again.

I realized I was too tired even to go to the movies, let alone a club. Why did it feel as if I'd done *both* shows of *The Fantasticks* today instead of just the matinee?

"Bring a wire hanger," Laurie instructed. "I'll bet you anything people are carrying them on the ticket line."

"Kinky bitch!" Devin cried with a delighted smile, before flashing me a sorry-*papi*-that-was-inappropriate look.

I laughed and insisted that the two of them go, even though I knew they'd spend part of the time talking about me—their concern over my lack of energy, my continuing absorption in yesteryear. Laurie said she'd come back here with Devin after the movie, sleep on the couch and thus avoid a round trip to Brooklyn between two a.m. and tomorrow's brunch.

Left alone, I went back to the bedroom and curled up under the covers with *Gorky Park*. But it couldn't hold my interest. It was the past, any part of it I'd lived through myself, that called to me these days. Today's paper, with its story of Nixon, Ford, and Carter going to visit Sadat's widow before his funeral, had had me reliving my own 1970s. It was the same thing with long-running shows and revivals: I'd now rather see or be part of them than have anything to do with new ones.

I got up and went over to the desk near the window. I began writing, in longhand, a letter to the address in Surrey that Carole had given me.

UP WITH THE SUN

Dear Kenny,

You won't remember me, I'm sure, but I was the pianist for Seventeen *all those years ago, as well as a friend of Dick Kallman's (not very close). I'm sure you've heard about his terrible death, maybe from Carole Cook, another mutual friend we have.*

I've come into possession of Dick's show-business scrapbook, which goes all the way back to Seventeen *and has all sorts of items relating to the show. The album also contains several more recent things pertaining to you, including a folded piece of sheet music for "Dance Away the Night," a Jerome Kern/Oscar Hammerstein song that was news to me—even though by now I think I've played just about everything.*

Anyway, the first page of the music is marked, in what I recognize as Dick's handwriting, "Kenny." I'm guessing that that's you, and I'm thinking that you might want to have it as a memento of Dick. I'm enclosing it in this envelope along with best wishes from

Matt Liannetto

Why was I sending the sheet music—or writing to Kenny at all? Was I imagining a sentimental pang Dick had felt for him, something somehow triggered by that song? I still didn't believe his feelings for Kenny could have run very deep. Was I trying to convince myself that Dick was nicer than he had been? No, I don't think so. Nor did I, even at this point, believe my continuing immersion in Dick and his premature death was part of my preference for the past over the present. The truth is that I'd never been happier than I was right now, waiting for my family to come home safe from the movies.

I decided I would wait up for them, and before I sealed the envelope I sight-read the sheet music and softly sang Hammerstein's lyrics:

Dance away the night
And we can all be happy till the morning.

Dance away the night
And we can stick together till the dawn.

I realized that I was now devoting myself to the past—hiding in the scrapbook as if it were a museum to lock myself in at night—because I was, for the first time in my life, too much in love with the *present*. And I was scared to let myself be too happy in the now, because my instincts told me there wasn't much now left.

CHAPTER 31

DECEMBER 7, 1972–OCTOBER 4, 1976

He'd had to leave LA at the crack of dawn, but flying into O'Hare he was struck by his own good mood. This really *was* one town that won't let you down; what was to say he shouldn't live *here*? He'd almost forgotten how all through *How to Succeed* and every turn at Pheasant Run, they'd always wanted him on the local talk shows or emceeing fundraisers for cystic fibrosis.

Ten days ago Irv Kupcinet's producer had called. Some titled Englishman named John Chichester-Constable had done Kup's show to make a pitch for the baronial spread in East Yorkshire that he was restoring: the one hundred and sixty-five rooms of Burton Constable Hall were falling apart, and all the Chippendale furniture hadn't been reupholstered since the middle of Queen Victoria's time. Rejuvenation would require boatloads of (American) money, since Chichester-Constable was determined to do it without the British Trust—something that ruggedly individualistic Yank tourists would surely admire, and chip in toward, once they saw the place. The triple-named lord ("Oh, call me JCC, Kup") would throw open the doors sometime next year.

Kup had suggested flying in Dick Kallman, "who's got lots of pizzazz," to serve as master of ceremonies for the fundraising affair being held tonight by Chicago's English-Speaking Union. So here he now was, checking into the Palmer House, changing into his best Gieves & Hawkes suit, and heading off to the Racquet Club. Cocktails were already under way when he arrived to find a sprinkling of British aristos and the local consul general, but mostly the sort of Americans that JCC hoped would soon be hopping across the Pond, checkbooks in hand.

Picking up a hand mike, he knew exactly how he would perform his bit before turning things over to His Lordship.

"You know, I used to open for Sophie Tucker, so coming here tonight I figured: if I can just maintain the level of decorum and formality we used to practice in Las Vegas, I should be able to function as the lead-in for a landed baron!" The assembled drinkers in their straight-backed chairs laughed over whatever bawdy memories they had of Sophie, and the smattering of English attendees got an extra chuckle out of the brash American's apparent failure to grasp the difference between a baron and a lord—though, in fact, Zara had long ago tutored Dick in such distinctions, which were as important to her, aspirationally, as those between an Episcopal priest and a Presbyterian minister.

He soon turned sonorous, "reminding" them of a "famous passage" he would now recite: "'At a place in Yorkshire, England, Burton Constable by name, a certain Sir Clifford Constable has in his possession the skeleton of a Sperm Whale . . . Sir Clifford's whale has been articulated throughout; so that, like a great chest of drawers, you can open and shut him, in all his bony cavities—spread out his ribs like a gigantic fan—and swing all day upon his lower jaw.' That, of course, is from *Moby-Dick*, chapter one hundred and two."

The audience applauded, more for the feat of memorization than for the great house's literary cameo.

"Our host this evening, John Chichester-Constable, played

with that whale skeleton when he was a boy in the 1940s, and once I'm through up here he's going to present *you* with a whale of an opportunity—can I get a groan? there you go!—to help with the restoration of Burton Constable Hall." He winked at a couple of old gals he remembered from the Sarah Siddons luncheons, then called for lights out, so that he could begin presenting a quick slide show that featured twenty of the mansion's hundred and sixty-five rooms. The patter propelling his talk was both archly funny and more informed than people expected. He'd done his homework. Before turning things over to a clearly pleased John Chichester-Constable, he promised he was looking forward to meeting everyone back by the sherry and the cucumber sandwiches.

"Marvelous job!" JCC told Kallman, once he'd finished his own spiel.

The actor greeted Chichester-Constable with his exact title: "The forty-sixth Lord Paramount! Hey, I've made a couple of pictures at your studio!" Chichester-Constable's wife, Gay, laughed as Kallman continued: "I hear they want to do a remake of *Moby-Dick*, but I think they're going to need a prop model with a little more meat on its bones than what you've got at Burton Constable Hall."

"And an Ahab who's a little edgier than Gregory Peck," suggested the wife, before being snagged away by one of the potential American donors.

Kallman was surprised to find that Chichester-Constable was only several years older than himself. This lord and lady were hip, sort of swinging in the Princess Margaret/Earl of Snowden way. He'd heard that they once managed a local rock band that did well enough to tour the States.

"You couldn't get the Hullaballoos to play here tonight?" he asked, once he remembered the group's name.

Chichester-Constable laughed. "The boys broke up several years ago, I'm afraid."

"We had a rock TV show with that name over here."

"Yes, we investigated to see if they'd stolen the name from us. No infringement, alas. Our boys were named for Hull, the city, which is quite near the estate."

"I did a guest shot on that program," said Kallman, while shooting his cuffs. "I insisted on wearing a Hardy Amies suit instead of denim bell-bottoms."

"Good man. We dressed our lads as if they were headed to a May Ball during the Regency. Even if we did bleach the hair they had hanging down to their shoulders."

Kallman gave a big wave to a miniskirted young woman several feet away. "Abs! Come meet our lord!" He hadn't seen Abra Prentice, the Rockefeller daughter, since his *How to Succeed* days, when he'd palled around with her and the Marshall Field heiress.

"Oh, God. Dick Kallman." Abra looked less pleased than amused. "I was his twenty-two-year-old guide to how to behave in haute Chicago," she explained to Chichester-Constable. Kallman could remember her telling him to "lose the Man Tan lotion and at least one of the rings." She now regarded him intently, seeming to register that in the last eight years he'd toned down the look if not the ingratiation, which—on rare nights like this, when he could still crank it up—bordered on the assaultive.

"Abra's married to a bigtime journalist now," Kallman explained to Chichester-Constable. "And she did some reporting herself—covered the Richard Speck trial for the *Sun-Times*. Hard to imagine someone so lovely and soignée writing about *that*, isn't it?"

"Crikey," said Chichester-Constable. "That was a huge story even where we are."

Abra let out her still-familiar laugh, almost as loud but a degree more sincere than Kallman's own. "I learned one imperishable life lesson from it. If all else fails, hide under the bed." Chichester-Constable remembered that was how one little Filipina nurse managed to survive while Speck slaughtered her eight flatmates.

"I always thought Abra's last name should be Cadabra," said Kallman.

"And I always thought Richard's should be Nixon."

"Glad you didn't say Speck!" Kallman countered.

Once Abra forsook them for a cluster of old friends, JCC said to Kallman: "Dick, you really can talk to anyone, can't you?"

He replied with a grin that he hoped would convey: "If the price is right, yes."

"You ought to come over to England in the spring. Help us kick off the tours and do some more fundraising. We've got ideas for things like a fashion show—both women's stuff and men's." He pointed approvingly to Kallman's suit.

"That'd be swell!" The double opportunity for cash and social climbing provided him with a mild sexual excitement, which increased with the sight of a white-jacketed waiter behind the Christmas-season punch bowl. He looked like an uninked version of Mino from a month or two back.

"We'll manage to round you up a valet while you're there," Constable promised.

"No need!" Kallman assured him. "I'll bring one along."

Not some presentable boy, either. He knew just the right Anglophilic and reactionary older man for the occasion.

———

"Never!" cried Father Albert duBois, with a genial, dramatic shudder. He was commenting on the possibility that the American Episcopal Church might soon ordain women. The fundraising party here at Burton Constable Hall was in full swing, and the cleric was drinking a second gin-and-tonic with the Catholic bishop of Norfolk. The two of them were enjoying some High Church high dudgeon; they would have been flouncing their vestments in agreement if they weren't wearing light-colored suits and boutonnieres on this lovely Saturday afternoon in May 1973.

As the party drifted through the great Elizabethan house and out into its eighteenth-century gardens designed by Capability Brown, Kallman reflected on what an excellent choice of companion Doobie was proving. The priest made him feel less like some tummler engaged to make the traipsing tourists write bigger checks, and more like a man of parts who actually belonged among the people he was jazzing up. For occasions when he and Doobie were by themselves, the priest, eager to maintain his connection with the younger man, had willingly made the switch from worshipfully servicing Dickie to the humiliation and light scourging the fellow seemed now to require. "Yes, of course," Doobie had said, even joking that it was just a matter of "backing up a few stations of the cross." The prelate had performed well in their shared cabin on the voyage over. After striking and insulting Dick (as soundlessly as possible) he had shifted to the sort of encouragement he offered back in '62, telling Dick that bright possibilities still lay ahead, no matter that he was soon to be forty. During next week's trip home, after a mild flogging and a pep talk, they'd go back up on deck, where Doobie would extract choice items from the little Fortnum & Mason hamper he'd already ordered, and the two of them would entertain some American old ladies with descriptions of the Capability Brown gardens they'd been privileged to have trodden.

"Ease up, young man!"

The voice of the squire himself brought Kallman back to the present moment. Here inside the great gallery of Burton Constable Hall, JCC was scolding a teenaged boy who'd gotten a little too friendly with the fragile bones of the articulated whale. A stylish elderly woman, observing the admonition, informed Kallman, in a whisper: "He can be quite cross with people. Nothing more touchy than an aristocrat without real money."

"Oh," he replied. "Are you one *with* real money?"

"Certainly not." She gave him her name, Raemonde Rahvis, and extended her hand. Born in South Africa at the turn of the century, she had for almost forty years run a small London fashion house with her sister. They'd both made frequent visits to Hollywood to create costumes for the movies. "Soon I am moving to the States for good. The unions are ruining this country."

"Retirement in sunny California?"

"Heavens, no. I will be going there to work. Couture may be dead, but fashion still allows for *novelty*. And the possibility to make a living off that."

"Any particular plan?" He didn't need to feign interest in this conversation, as he'd had to during the dozen weren't-you-once and didn't-you-used-to-be chats he'd had with American tourists this afternoon. He actually wanted to know what this lady had to say.

"Terry cloth."

"Oh, beachwear."

"No. Dresses. Terry-cloth beachwear would not be novelty. Novelty *startles*."

"I'll bet I know who you are! I'll bet you're the woman who created the 'look' for milord and milady's rock 'n' roll band."

"Yes," she replied with considerable gravity. "I designed the Hullaballoos. I am afraid they are not aging well." She pointed to a still-young but balding, overweight man out on the terrace. "That is a Hullaballoo. One of them."

A reporter came by, asking to know how Dick Kallman and Raemonde Rahvis spelled their names, and whether they were enjoying themselves. "What do you think of the house's prospects as an attraction for visitors?" he further inquired.

After opining that the sky was the limit, Kallman asked the young man what paper he wrote for.

"I'm over in Manchester."

"*The Guardian*?"

"No, another one. Much smaller."

Which meant, alas, that Kenny wouldn't see the story.

At this moment Chichester-Constable approached to tell Kallman and Miss Rahvis what a fine time he'd just had exchanging army tales with Father duBois—his own about his time in the Rifle Brigade, and Doobie's about his wartime chaplaincy. "The two of *you* seem to be getting along nicely as well."

"Oh, yes, even better than Raemonde realizes!" declared Kallman.

JCC laughed, and Miss Rahvis asked: "What do you mean?"

"You and I are going into business in the States."

"But you are an actor."

"Oh, no. Unlike you, I *am* retired, at least from all that."

———————

He was coming up Fifth Avenue from—where else these days?—the bank, and he was early enough, rounding the corner of Fifty-Seventh Street, to take a look at Tiffany's windows, always a little art gallery unto themselves. One of them today displayed nothing more than a diamond bracelet lying on a black cloth beside an egg. The arrangement was, Kallman supposed, meant to demonstrate the perfection of simplicity. No, he thought: less is . . .

less. He fingered his gold pinkie ring—forget what Abra Cadabra had once told him—and made sure it was facing full out. Boldness, punch, and *novelty* (La Rahvis habitually used the term): all of it was working. Three-point-eight million in sales in four months! Bigger than the advance gate for any show he'd ever been in.

It was Wednesday, March 26, 1975, and this evening's event (5:30 p.m.) at Bonwit Teller had gotten a mention in today's *Times*. From that and the copious invitations they'd sent out, there ought to be a good crowd, just as there had been at Martha in Palm Beach last week, and just as they would get at Neiman's in Dallas five days from now.

He peeked out from the makeshift greenroom on the department store's second floor. Every chair was filled. The standees along the sides and back were two deep. Down in front he spotted Virginia Graham, loud and blond and battle-hardened. Kallman turned to ask Joyce Bowen, who managed the whole shebang now called Burton Constable Fashions, whether Virginia still had one of her talk shows on the air. "See if you can get her to book us and the dresses."

Time for him to go out there and sell. Before stepping into the showroom, he pumped his forearms up and down, whispering "Fuck 'em, fuck 'em, fuck 'em!"

"What *ever* are you doing?" asked Raemonde Rahvis.

"What Judy Garland used to do." The "Fuck 'em"s weren't an expression of scorn for the audience; they were a revving-up of whatever it would take to overwhelm and satiate them.

He went out and got to it.

"I know what you're thinking, ladies: '*Towel* he convince us that terry cloth is no longer just for the beach?'" The groan; the laugh; even a smattering of applause. "Well, I'm going to do it in four easy steps. And away we go!"

The first model came out in a cabana-style wrap with a pattern they'd knocked off from Lilly Pulitzer. Nothing surprising there. But the next girl made her entrance terry-clothed in what appeared to be a gold cocktail dress. "Look at that material! You thought it was crushed velvet, didn't you?" As the audience registered surprise, Kallman explained how Raemonde Rahvis had scoured the Middle East for the exactly right type of cotton. A quick tease followed: a model walked out in just a terry-cloth towel, looking like Monroe in those stills from her last, doomed movie. "Terry cloth practically invented the strapless look, right? Now watch it create something you couldn't imagine!" Out came a bare-shouldered model in a ruby-red evening gown made of, yes, terry cloth. And the ladies clapped as if it were the wedding dress at the end of a Givenchy show.

This was fundamentally different from what he used to do: he didn't want this audience's love, only its money. It was a cleaner transaction, the way sex now typically functioned in his new apartment on East Fifty-Sixth Street. But one similarity did hold when it came to applause and money and sex: the more you had, the more you wanted. And the money was coming in hand over fist.

Two lines for orders now formed: a retail queue for the ladies who lunch and a shorter, surreptitious one for wholesalers. Bonwit's frowned upon but tolerated the latter, which Kallman spent his time attending to. And bingo, by next week the dresses would be finding their way to A&S in Brooklyn and Hempstead.

Raemonde Rahvis drew him aside. "There's someone here that JCC wants you to meet."

She presented Kallman with an unbelievably tall, grinning, somewhat pink-faced man in his mid-thirties. He wore a high-end three-piece English suit. "This is Charles Spencer-Churchill," Rahvis explained, "brother to the current Duke of Marlborough."

"Although while I'm over here," the man said, "I'm better known as the great-great-grandson of Commodore Vanderbilt, on the maternal side of things. Which relates me to your Gloria. Who I gather lives here in town."

Kallman switched on his own big grin and summoned up his old *Half a Sixpence* voice: "Well, if 'e was a commodore, we'll 'ave to call you guv'nor!"

"Oh, please, call me Nutty," said Churchill, offering what turned out to be the actual nickname of this six-foot-six colossus out of *Debrett's*.

Within twenty minutes they were all having drinks across the street at the Plaza—prearranged, it turned out, by Joyce Bowen. Jack Straussburg, a men's designer, along with another Manufacturers Hanover banker, rounded out a table with Kallman, Rahvis, Spencer-Churchill, and Joyce.

"So, Nutty, what brings you to the States?" asked Dick.

"I'm over here promoting Blenheim, raising money for the old palace, even if it does belong to my brother. It's a monster version of Burton Constable Hall, Dick—thrice the size and five times as hungry."

"Don't *any* of you titled fellows have money?" Kallman asked.

"Not for ages. Why do you think Granddad married a Vanderbilt?"

"This is where you come in, Dick," explained Joyce Bowen. "You can help everyone get a little richer—by putting the money from terry cloth into tweed. Menswear. Charles can be the face of a line of suits, and you can be the pitchman. Jack here can do the designs and Mr. Millman and his colleagues at Manny Hanny can advance the cash. You could be selling the suits in less than a year. That's the long and short of it."

"Actually, Dick," instructed Nutty, "you and *I* are the long and short of it." He pointed to their disparity in height; Spencer-Churchill remained a head taller even while they were sitting down.

Kallman laughed, as he rapidly decided that the next step was to make sure Miss Rahvis, no matter that she'd made the connection to Nutty, was cut out of the venture. He looked across at her; she might as well have been a terry-cloth towel discarded on a hotel-room floor.

———————

In the marble palace that was Robinson's department store, a company executive led Dick Kallman and Charles Spencer-Churchill to a top-floor conference room decorated with antique ledgers and cash registers from the emporium's earliest days. The room was being made available to the two men for an interview with the *LA Times*. Kallman and Nutty were in the middle of ten weeks' travel, crisscrossing the country as busily as the campaigning Ford and Carter, visiting retail outlets and local TV stations. They'd just finished a public showing of the line down on the third floor, and posed for the by-now-usual pictures, with Nutty looking like the Tower of London and Dick resembling a lawn jockey.

"Was that your mother out in the audience?" the reporter asked Kallman.

"Yes, my biggest fan for all my thirty-seven years!" He'd gotten her a new place on South Crescent here in Beverly Hills, as well as a gold-level charge account at Robinson's, now that "Augustus Man" had already pulled in fourteen million dollars.

"Can you tell me how the business got its name?"

"Well," answered Spencer-Churchill, "'Augustan' has some fine old classic associations. Very eighteenth-century, you know."

The reporter nodded and made a note as the remark sailed over his head.

"What's unique about the clothes?"

"Dick can tell you about the vests."

Kallman went over to the rack they'd set up for the interview. "Take a look," he said, extracting a waistcoat from one of the hangers. "See how much longer than usual it is?"

"It conceals the paunches on my older friends," said Nutty.

"And hides the too-long ties that too many American men wear," added Kallman. "Makes you wonder what *else* they wish were longer." He winked at the reporter, knowing there was no chance the remark would make it into a family newspaper.

"Is there anyone buying the clothes that our readers might have heard of?"

"My pal Lord Hertford has ordered four suits," said Nutty, "and we've had some interest from Constantine."

"The once and future King of Greece," Kallman explained. "Did Nutty tell you about being born at the Dorchester Hotel?" he asked the reporter, hoping to liven things up.

After a sip of coffee, Spencer-Churchill elaborated. "July 1940. The Blitz and all that. The Dorchester was thought to be less of a target than Blenheim. Turns out Hitler had no plans to disturb so much as a gargoyle on the old house. He wanted it for his British residence!"

Kallman had reached a point where he preferred to have

Nutty do the talking. He liked listening to the accented waterfall of words, those guineas and crowns striking the marble floor and pooling into an enormous fortune. The only interview angle he disliked was the one now, inevitably, being arrived at. Here came the questions about *Hank* and *How to Succeed* and *Half a Sixpence*.

"Yep, that was me! King of the Broadway road shows!" He wanted his menswear success to be seen as a step up, or at worst a lateral move, not an escape from failure. "Fashion is all theater anyway," he declared.

"You don't miss TV? Sitting on Johnny Carson's couch?"

"Johnny was once a colleague. Now he's a competitor. Johnny Carson Apparel?"

"Oh, of course," said the reporter, remembering Carson's own menswear line, but not stopping to think that Kallman's country-house tweeds were hardly competition for the loud colors and Sansabelted pants of Johnny's line.

"Carson has to please his overlords," Kallman pointed out. "Hart Schaffner & Marx own 51 percent of his brand. We're independent." He looked at his watch, a gesture he never would have permitted himself with an entertainment reporter. "Well, Lord Spencer-Churchill here has to see a man about a horse."

Nutty laughed. "He means it literally. I may be investing in a potential Kentucky Derby winner with some fellow over in Century City."

As Spencer-Churchill spoke, Kallman got up, went over to one of the ancient cash registers, pressed two keys, and cried "Ka-*ching!*"—as they made that very noise.

CHAPTER 32

DECEMBER 1, 1981

"Come on, *papi*. Deeper. Take it deeper."

With the third inhalation I showed some evidence of relief, enough to start laughing and to hear Devin laugh too. I was "surfacing"—that's how it always feels—from one of my worst asthma attacks in years. Devin was actually administering to me some super-squeezes of Primatene mist. My episodes had lately been frequent enough that he carried a small bottle of it in his own pocket, in case I forgot mine.

"This is *not* good," he declared, emphatically. "You need to see the pulmonary guy again."

I demurred. I was already seeing a doctor about the weight I'd lost, and going to my GP for general crumminess and occasional fevers, although most days I felt okay. We—Devin and Laurie and I—had actually stopped talking about "gay cancer," which had not yet been renamed GRID (Gay-Related Immune Deficiency), let alone AIDS. One kept hearing about more people getting sick, but it was happening amidst such near-total ignorance and wild guesswork that conversation about the disease, at least among us three, seemed pointless, likely to leave us more misinformed than keeping our mouths shut would.

Whatever this ailment might be, there was no test and no treatment for it; the whole thing felt more like a hallucination than a diagnosis. Even when the supposedly more precise "GRID" started finding its way into print, Devin said the term "sounded like fucking *Hollywood Squares*" instead of some respectable condition ending in "ia" or "itis."

On the morning of this asthma attack, we were already scared and getting more so.

But right now Devin just said "Breathe," urging me to hold in a last lungful of Primatene for as long as I could. "They should teach you asthmatics to *smoke*. If you knew how, you'd inhale better." When I finally relaxed and expelled some air, I kissed him and said, "You're the one who's taught me to breathe."

Devin's "issues" (as we say these days) don't always allow him to take compliments; he didn't hear many growing up. His way of deflecting them involves their comical, exaggerated embrace. "*Papi*, I am *spectacular*. You are the luckiest middle-aged daddy in New York City."

He proceeded to coat my chest with Vicks VapoRub. "Maybe this morning the smell of this will open up those pinched, nose-in-the-air nostrils of your old lady."

I was scheduled to join Dolores at ten thirty for her deposition in the lawsuit against the insurance company. Devin insisted on walking me over to 230 Park Avenue, where her lawyers were located. On our way out of Manhattan Plaza, we picked up the mail in the lobby: still nothing from Kenny, whom I was starting to give up on. Devin noticed my expression. "Let all this *go*," he commanded. "Let's make today the last day of the Dickie drama, okay? Curtain coming down."

When we got near Grand Central, I realized that 230 Park was the Helmsley Building.

"*Another* bitch," Devin remarked. "She's the one who runs her ancient daddy's hotels, right? Maybe she can give your has-been Dolores a job as a chambermaid." With no desire to run into my "old lady" upstairs, Devin said goodbye to me in one of the Helmsley Building's pedestrian arcades and reminded me to use my inhaler.

"It's supposed to take a couple of hours," I told him.

"If you buy her lunch, I'll kill you," he replied, before starting his twenty-block walk up to the 19th Precinct.

Inside the offices of Moore, Wohl & Newman, a legal secretary let me into a conference room once she found my name on an approved-access list. I was identified as "Miss Gray's personal assistant." A good thing Devin didn't see that.

I sat all alone until Dolores arrived in a dark-blue suit that Edith Head might have created for the occasion. She had on less makeup than usual, perhaps hoping, as a victim of theft seeking compensation, to look injured and wan. At the same time, she was still wearing plenty of good jewelry, maybe to suggest that her missing property would have been similarly expensive. After another couple of minutes, the other principals filed in, and Dolores introduced me to Bernard Gettlin, the man representing her.

A notary public swore her in and took down some basic information, like her birthday: she claimed June 7, 1929. I realized that if I could be given all the years that she and Dick at various times had knocked off their actual ages, I would live to be a hundred.

"I am always self-employed," she answered, with defiant pride, when the notary asked a simple W-2 kind of question. Dolores made it sound as if she'd never been let down or passed over by a producer.

The attorneys reviewed, conversationally, how after Dick's death the estate's executor had advised Dolores to liquidate at auction any inventory of Possessions of Prominence that hadn't been stolen. Because of the currently depressed art market, Dolores had argued for less-scrutinized "private sales." Now sick of the subject, she grudgingly stipulated that over the last year they had "worked it out" through a mixture of the selling modes. She expressed regret over the huge amount of time it had all involved, but I wondered: had she maybe strung it out deliberately? On some level, for all her pulverized illusions, had she remained reluctant to let go of "my beautiful Richard" in this final, material way?

Mr. Gettlin tried to depict the reasonableness of his client by highlighting some unusual aspects of the situation. Miss

Gray, on a number of occasions, had been "an adversary of the estate," but on others had been helpful in settling claims against it.

Dolores didn't care for the praise. "Christ, the way that Sprehe woman nagged me about the silver soup tureen she consigned to us! I had to tell her six times: 'It was stolen, honey.'"

Mr. Friedman, the insurance company's lawyer, soothingly announced that the parties could avoid a court trial by reaching a settlement over the items never recovered; Mr. Gettlin had agreed to stipulate that "certain fraudulent and illegal business dealings of the decedent" had been uncovered both at the murder trial (the phony Calder gouache) and in the course of itemizing the missing materials.

"With no imputation of such fraudulent practices to Miss Gray," Mr. Gettlin emphasized for the record.

"I should hope not," said Dolores.

Mr. Friedman proceeded stolen object by stolen object, making fast offers of what he thought Dolores and Zara Kallman—the other, absent party to the lawsuit—were entitled to. "By the way," he asked, "is Possessions of Prominence technically still in business?"

"That I wouldn't know," Dolores answered.

Really? Was Dick supposed to be running it from the afterlife? Gettlin and Friedman exchanged a glance that indicated they would let this eccentric, starlike utterance pass.

"Miss Gray," continued Friedman, showing her a piece of stationery, "you're listed on the firm's letterhead as 'Associate Director.'"

"Yes. It was fifty-fifty."

"And Mr. Kallman is 'Director of European Fine Arts and Furniture.'"

"I suppose he was."

"Did you yourself keep any of the business's records?"

"Richard had a stock book. That's all I know."

Whenever Mr. Friedman had questions about particular objects, Dolores's vagueness disappeared. As she talked of valuables that she and Dick had "joint-ventured," one got a sense of her hands-on involvement in the whole enterprise.

"I regularly asked Richard if *everything* was insured, and he always said yes," Dolores insisted, as if mere assertion of the point was enough to make the company meet its obligations.

"Were there burglar alarms at 17 East Seventy-Seventh Street?"

"Absolutely. Richard had them installed at my request."

"Could you describe the methods for displaying the merchandise in Mr. Kallman's apartment?"

The question made Dolores impatient: hadn't she long ago told all this to the police?

"There were glass shelves, similar to a department-store display, for things like porcelain plates. That made it easier for clients to look. But everything still appeared to be inside someone's home."

Dolores's effort to describe the trompe l'oeil premises was somewhat undermined when she twice referred to the apartment as "the gallery." When Mr. Friedman had her recount the inspection she'd made of the crime scene eight days after the murder, she mentioned objets that "Fortunato," rather than Forti, had made off with. Her carelessness in these instances made her precision in describing the stolen Renoir statuette almost weirdly jarring: "It was a nude bronze figure of a kneeling girl with water running between her hands. The green-and-white marble plinth supporting it was about eight inches high and fourteen inches long. It weighed between eight and ten pounds and had been consigned to us by a man named Zimmerman. We were offering it for twenty-two thousand dollars. And it is *still missing*." She seemed to be suggesting that Mr. Friedman go out and find it, immediately.

He picked up the pace when they arrived at the low-end stuff. From a large miscellaneous pile of receipts he extracted one of Dolores's Visa bills, which showed a charge for a gold bracelet bought at Alexander's, for five hundred and eighteen dollars, on July 21, 1978.

"Did you and Mr. Kallman subsequently 'joint-venture' this object?"

"Yes, I had hoped we could sell it for much more than I paid.

You'll remember that that week gold went from four hundred dollars an ounce to nine hundred."

Mr. Friedman, who thanked her for reminding him of that economic development (Dolores was impervious to sarcasm), returned for a moment to the big picture. "Could you define Possessions of Prominence?"

Dolores assumed a quizzical look. "That's difficult to do. Richard always thought the phrase sounded elegant. It's the name under which he did business." Her answer forced me to wonder if Dick also used the name for *other* kinds of business, ones that involved something besides the sale of often-fraudulent antiques? Like maybe drugs? I thought back to the trial, to all of Mr. Foleo's—and even Forti's—fusillade of random theories and insinuations.

Mr. Friedman eventually reached items in the fifty-dollar range but was interrupted by Dolores before he could start work on them.

"There's one article that's nowhere on any of your lists," she said. "There's a gold ring that's missing. Richard wore it all the time, and it was taken off his dead body."

I had never heard anything about this—not from Detective Volker or Mr. Ehren or even Devin.

"How do you know that?" Mr. Friedman asked Dolores.

"Because they showed me some of the crime-scene photos. To help me figure out what items had been stolen. The ring wasn't on his hand."

"Is it possible he sold it shortly before his death?"

"No. I saw him wearing the ring on Monday, three days before they killed him. I *gave* Richard that ring." She produced a receipt for eight hundred dollars from Martin Busch Jewelers, from 1979. "I bought the ring for Richard to celebrate the first anniversary of Possessions of Prominence."

"Why didn't you include this receipt with the ones you previously supplied?"

"I think I repressed the whole matter. It was too awful. I only remembered it last night." She gave Mr. Gettlin, her own lawyer, a damsel-in-distress look, and treated Mr. Friedman to a little shudder, which didn't keep him from asking: "So, even though Mr. Kallman wore this ring every day, and it was your gift to him, you consider it a loss to the business?"

"Richard always said that *everything* was for sale. It was still merchandise."

The session didn't end until twelve forty-five. Claiming to be worn out as we rose from our chairs, Dolores told me she ought to be getting home to her dog, but admitted that she was famished. So we dropped down to the Oyster Bar in Grand Central, where deep below any gleam of city sunlight she put on dark glasses. As her Bloody Mary arrived, she asked me: "How can someone be only 'slightly intoxicated' after 'seven or eight glasses of wine'?"

I knew what she was referring to: the story of Natalie Wood's autopsy, which even the *Times* had carried this morning. Dr. Noguchi, the LA coroner, had determined that the actress died trying to step into a rubber dinghy tethered to the yacht she and Robert Wagner were on, just off Santa Catalina Island.

"Socks and a nightgown," added Dolores, shaking her head disgustedly over another detail of the autopsy report, which seemed to reveal to her that Natalie had violated stardom's dress code.

I thought about the weirdly nautical picture of Natalie Wood in Dick's scrapbook, where she's holding up a shrimp cocktail at the Mocambo.

But I wanted to know more about this gold ring Dick was supposedly wearing when he got killed. I had no recollection of it from that night, though I did recall his talking about an *emerald* ring he'd sold to that guy who liked to fondle his fingers. I thought I'd now ease my way toward the subject with a little conversation about the Renoir statuette. "With such an exact description from you," I declared, "you'd think they could find it."

"I bought it in France ages ago," Dolores admitted. "As a present to myself." (So there was no consignor? No Mr. Zimmerman?) "I thought I'd just gotten the female lead in an Astaire film to be shot in Paris," she went on. "But then a script for *Funny Face* came along and they decided *that* would be Fred's

Paris film, not the one I'd been cast in. They then offered me the Kay Thompson part, but I threw it back in their faces."

This was either a lie or a piece of real career stupidity.

"So you eventually decided to 'joint-venture' the statuette with Dick?"

"Yes."

"I hadn't heard about the gold ring before," I told her, "but I can believe that anybody who'd kick the head of someone he's just shot would be capable of stealing a ring off a dead man's finger."

"That's not how it happened. Richard is wearing the ring in the crime-scene photos."

I didn't try to hide my surprise.

"Look, I got a guy in the Medical Examiner's Office—just in time, before the autopsy—to set it aside for me." Her expression turned from mere self-satisfaction to pure cruelty. "I realized that that ring, my *gift*, had been on Richard's hand for the whole past year, whenever he was playing with those disgusting things you and I found in his closet."

She didn't want him to be buried, or even cremated, with the ring. I'd been wrong the last few months; there was nothing left that she had to "resolve" about her self-deluding infatuation with her "beautiful Richard."

"So," I dared to ask, "you still have the ring?"

"That's right."

"Then why did you tell Mr. Friedman otherwise?"

"To add eight hundred dollars to the settlement. They're not going to bother to check those crime-scene pictures. So I pinned the theft on Mr. Fortunato. It's fair enough. He took plenty from *me*."

That "plenty" didn't include Dick—only the baubles and figurines thrown into the Hefty bags after he was shot, the gaudy stuff whose value (and then some) she'd recoup from the insurance company.

She saw the disgust on my face, but maintained her own stone-cold expression. "Richard isn't just dead, Matthew. He's dead to *me*."

Dick had turned out to be one more failed venture, another

show unfairly pulled out from under Dolores Gray—not by his murder but by the illusion-killing stuff in his closet.

Devin would be pleased to learn that Dolores was now dead to *me*. I told her I had a piano lesson to give, which I didn't. I got up and left her alone with the check, and I never saw her again.

CHAPTER 33

FEBRUARY 28, 1977

"I am not going to be fucked over by *you*, and I am not going to be fucked over by the Duke of Marlborough's kid brother!" Kallman shouted. He slammed a copy of today's *Times* onto Robert Millman's desk inside the great glass cube of Manufacturers Hanover. He did it with such an exaggerated swoop of his arm that several homebound pedestrians stopped in their tracks at the corner of Fifth and Forty-Third and stared through the window at this agitated man haranguing an apparently hapless banker.

It was already past six, and Millman was almost by himself in the bank's vast ground-floor offices, which looked more like a showroom, brightly illuminated against the dark February evening outside. He tried calming Dick down with humor. "When I became a banker, I thought I'd be working banker's hours." He pointed to a clock showing 6:35 p.m.

"Cut the crap," said Kallman, who had caught up with this morning's paper only an hour ago and decided he would storm down here right away instead of cooling off between now and tomorrow morning. "Augustus has made pots of money for everybody concerned, including this goddamned bank! We hit the sweet spot of every single trend, knew how much formal stuff and how much patterned stuff to do, made exactly the right number of soft-shouldered jackets and padded ones and—" He realized he was sputtering into specifics. "And I have to read about this in the god-damned *paper*? You couldn't even *call* me? I've never even heard of this fucking 'Genesee' outfit."

"It's 'Genesco,' not 'Genesee,'" Millman told Kallman, quietly, as if correcting him on a point of ancient history, which from a business standpoint this already was. The Genesco company had just acquired Augustus.

"'Genesco,'" said Kallman. "It sounds like one of the five Mafia families."

"They operate with the same level of success," said Millman. "But much more respectably, I can assure you. The check that reaches you will be generous, beautifully watermarked, and it will clear right away."

"And what about the checks after that? What's my new compensation going to be? What's my role from now on?"

"There is no role for you," said Millman, like a hundred casting directors who'd once had to turn Dick Kallman down for a part. "You've been bought out. Nutty will remain an active partner, and he'll be the single voice and embodiment of the line. Genesco thinks the two of you together made for a bit of confusion. They want plummy instead of razzmatazz."

"Get him on the phone!" Kallman shouted.

"There is no particular 'him' at Genesco. That's not how a modern conglomerate operates."

"Not Genesco—Nutty! I don't care if you have to wake up his whole fucking castle!"

"I'm afraid you won't find him there. He's off on some boat—that he's just been able to buy," Millman added after a pause.

Kallman reached not for the banker's neck but for his own. He unknotted his necktie, slid it out from under his collar, and flung it, like a snake, onto Millman's desk. "It's an Augustus," he said.

"And I'm happy to have it," the banker answered, "since the Genesco plan calls for discontinuing accessories like this. They want to focus on the essentials: the suits, and Nutty."

A number of people standing on the icy sidewalk on the other side of the window continued to watch the spectacle, wondering if the man who was standing would hit the one who was sitting.

"Sort of like theater in the round," said Millman, pointing to them and keeping his cool. He had never liked Kallman, from the moment the terry-cloth venture turned into the menswear one over that dinner at the Plaza. "I guess you now know how Rae-monde Rahvis feels."

A minute later, Kallman was literally out in the cold, freezing his way up toward the bird circuit, where he had three drinks in two different bars.

Defeat eventually sent him west, though when he got to Hay-market, a hustler bar at Eighth and Forty-Fifth, he decided that ten p.m. was way too early to go into a place whose action didn't really get going until after one in the morning. So he walked around the block between Eighth and Ninth and saw the sign for Brothers and Sisters, a still-new club tonight featuring Dolores Gray, a second-tier star of film musicals that now felt as obsolete as the vaudeville shows Sophie Tucker started out playing. Years ago he'd liked what he heard of Gray—a big voice—on 78s and at the movies, so he paid the modest cover charge to come through the door and kill some time.

"Is that Dick Kallman? *Alone?*" asked Kaye Ballard.

"More than you know," he answered, brightly enough, but with a high degree of actual self-pity.

"May I?" asked the big-hearted, mugging, flamboyantly Ital-ian Kaye, as she sat down in an empty chair at his table. Years had passed since they last saw each other, but the two of them went back decades, to the time of all the old nightclubs that had been so much prettier than Brothers and Sisters.

"What are you doing here?" Kallman asked Kaye.

"Seeing Dolores, of course," she answered, with a laugh. "I think you met her at my old place in the Village years ago, at one of those Sunday spaghetti brunches I used to give. She was always there."

This prompted a hazy, scrimmed memory in Kallman. Maybe it had happened around the time of *How to Succeed*, when he was giving himself a New York weekend away from the tour? Or when he'd just gotten *Hank*? Kaye had had her own NBC flash in the pan, although *The Mothers-in-Law*, her loud comedy with Eve Arden, managed to last two seasons to *Hank*'s one. Then she'd cheerfully gone on, sort of like Carole Cook, to an endless string of roles and gigs, most of them smaller than her voice and comic talents deserved.

"Well," she cried, raising her glass of white wine, "welcome to the ballyhooed revival of cabaret!" She grandly toasted one of Brothers and Sisters' plywood walls. There were multiple theories for the current and probably short-lived resurrection of this old show-business staple: the new gay assertiveness was bringing it back; or it was just the new expense involved in producing and even attending a Broadway show. Whatever the case, people were noting how the skanky new New York had not stopped aspiring toward a wholesale re-creation of Weimar Germany since Liza got her Sally Bowles Oscar.

Kallman sipped his vodka and Kaye asked the waiter if there was still enough time to get a plate of the lamb chops before Dolores came on at eleven for her second show. "Four ninety-five!" she marveled to Dick, when the waiter said yes. "I'm not even hungry. I just want to be able to eat them at that price!" Expounding upon Brothers and Sisters, she informed him: "Barbara Cook really made this place, such as it is."

"Well, it helped *remake* *her*." The cute little ingenue of *The Music Man* had ballooned, along with her figure, into a big new club and concert star.

After Kallman and Kaye exchanged a few desultory reminiscences about old venues like the Bon Soir, she said, with a curious wonder: "You are *not* the young man I remember."

"Well, who's young at forty-three?" He heard himself saying his actual age. He was like some weary suspect who'd waived his right to a lawyer because, really, what was the point in lying anymore?

"Oh, to be forty-three again!" said Kaye. "Or forty-nine. But no, it's not that you're older. You used to be so *pushy*. Tonight you're almost passive. I think I preferred you when you were a pain in the ass."

"I've just had a bit of disappointment," he told her.

"Well, you've come to the right place," she said, eating a lamb chop as fast as she could. "God knows no one's had more setbacks than Dolores. And she takes every one of them on the chin."

"Oh?"

"Now it looks as if she's going to lose *Ballroom* to Dorothy Loudon. After auditioning like hell against her glamour-girl image in order to get it." Everyone was anticipating Michael Bennett's next big thing.

"I'm the only person in New York who hated *A Chorus Line*," said Kallman. *That* was show business now: backstage sweat-stink and poor-me agonizing put out in front of the audience. No more hitting your mark with a big grin and singing, full-out, a joyful lyric.

Brothers and Sisters' manager took to its tiny stage to introduce "Miss Dolores Gray." He recited her mostly long-ago London triumphs, like *Annie Get Your Gun*; extolled her famous "warm brandy" voice; and named the few films she'd made that anyone could remember.

"If he mentioned all her bombs and all the stuff that got snatched out from under her, he'd have been up there all night," Kaye whispered, without malice, to Kallman.

Dolores started off softly, with "Here's That Rainy Day"—*her* song, she told the audience, even if she got to sing it all of six times before *Carnival in Flanders*, the flopperoo it came from, folded. She warmed up the crowd with a few jokes, including a little mockery of Brothers and Sisters' shoestring operation: "We're all working for peanuts nowadays," she said, referencing the new president. Her accompanist had a vase of pink roses (Dolores's signature color, according to Kaye) on top of his piano, and the lighting consisted of two gooseneck lamps, sympathetically twisted away from the singer's complexion. Amidst some anecdotes about her career ups and downs, Dolores mentioned Determine, the horse with which her husband had once won the Kentucky Derby. "If they'd named it after Dolores's mother," Kaye whispered to Kallman, "it would have been Relentless."

"I know a little about mothers," Kallman whispered back.

He regarded Dolores while she sang "The Opposite Sex" from one of her films, a remake of *The Women*. He couldn't recall if she'd played the Roz Russell part or the predatory shopgirl originated by Joan Crawford—who these days was said to be slowly dying in her apartment across town. He could see a resemblance, in fact, between Crawford and Gray: the metallic quality of the jutting cheekbones and jaws; the sharp, surgically-pinched noses. Dolores interpreted lyrics with a keen but narrow intelligence, and told stories between songs in the same way, without any peripheral vision to complicate her perception of things. She mostly conveyed unhappiness.

"If You Hadn't But You Did," the patter song she now did from *Two on the Aisle*, had lyrics even faster and more complicated than the ones in Sondheim's "(Not) Getting Married Today," and although she had them written out on a clearly visible white card atop the piano, she still got tripped up or just plain lost a couple of times, until the accompanist rescued her with prompts.

During the sympathetic applause, Kaye told Kallman, "That's probably why she lost *Ballroom*. Bennett realizes she can't remember lines anymore."

"But she lost it to Loudon? Isn't *she* about to do *Annie*?"

"Bennett thinks it'll flop and that Dorothy'll be available within weeks."

The two of them got shooshed from a male couple behind them. Kallman turned around with a murderous look and Kaye just laughed.

Dolores made a crack about the new show business versus the old. "Annie used to get her gun. Now she's going to come onstage with a mangy old dog."

"That's her shot at Dorothy," whispered Kaye, while Dolores, all over the place mood-wise, settled into a sultry, almost moving rendition of "Willow Weep for Me." Her emotional range might be as tapered as her intelligence, but self-pity formed its deepest part, and Kallman could feel himself connecting with her. Neither of them, he decided, was *against* intense feeling; only aware that occasions for experiencing it had been given too freely to others and not often enough to themselves.

Kenny.

The crowd liked her, and its members *loved* the idea of themselves as sophisticated émigrés from disco. When her set was over, they kept Dolores at the piano signing autographs, then left her in peace when she went over to Kaye's table for a bite.

"Kaysie," she said, "it's so sweet of you to come." She kissed both of her friend's cheeks.

"You still haven't learned to sing that song your mother stole from me," Kaye replied, referencing what had happened during the out-of-town tryouts for *Two on the Aisle*, causing Kaye to leave the show. All of this, which Kallman sort of remembered hearing in 1951, was now cheerily rehashed by Kaye.

"Dolores, do you remember Dick Kallman? I think you met him years ago at my place."

"Vaguely," Dolores replied, her expression indicating that this half a loaf of recognition should be considered a compliment.

"Wonderful set," said Kallman. "Especially 'Willow.' "

"It was all grand," Kaye added. "You're a triumph at Frères et Soeurs."

Dolores looked puzzled.

"She doesn't *understand* French," Kaye told Kallman. "She just pronounces it."

The three of them began reminiscing about the long-ago era when *Seventeen*, *Two on the Aisle*, and Barbara Cook's *Flahooley* were all running in the same season. Dolores then went even farther back, talking about one night in the forties when Billy Rose heard her at the Copa and offered her a spot in a show called *Seven Lively Arts*. Which made Kallman tell her and Kaye about his youthful stint in Rose's office and how he stole money out of the cash boxes to buy a pin for someone special.

"I like how you think," said Dolores. "She was a lucky girl, whoever she was."

Kallman could see Kaye roll her eyes over Dolores's naivete. But if that's what it was, it struck Kallman as naivete of a peculiar, self-willed kind.

He and Dolores were soon gabbing away and finding that practically everything about yesteryear seemed to connect with everything else: she mentioned how in the early days of TV she'd done *The Buick Circus Hour*, a variety show that ran on the one

Tuesday night Milton Berle had off each month; he responded that Berle had put money into *Seventeen*. As ancient anecdotes matched and knit and delighted the pair, Kaye declared, "You two are like a couple of antiques connoisseurs."

"I love antiques," Dolores replied. "I also love money." She told Kallman about a bronze Renoir statuette she'd owned for years.

Kaye turned to Kallman: "You were starting to buy art when you were doing television, weren't you?" Before he could answer, Dolores interrupted: "My husband is a bit of an antique."

"He mostly stays out in California," Kaye explained, as if pandering to the absurd idea of a Dick-and-Dolores fling.

Responding to her fondness for money, Kallman looked at Dolores and declared, "I was good at making moola." He then told the story of the Augustus venture, right up through today's betrayal. Dolores looked at him with continuous interest, this still-handsome younger man who'd been cheated out of what was rightly his, as she'd been cheated out of so many things.

"You should expect a good long run here," Kallman observed.

"Yes, but I don't see it leading anywhere."

"Dolores," Kaye scolded, "get over *Ballroom*. It may never even get off the ground."

Kallman insisted, similarly, "You're too glamorous for a role like that. Dorothy Loudon can be a lonely widow. Dolores Gray can't."

Dolores was liking what she heard from him; Dick Kallman had an ability to console her that Kaye didn't. She asked him how much he thought his show-business career had helped him in the other businesses that had followed it.

"Oh, plenty," he admitted, going on to tell her the origins of the terry-cloth line.

"I'd like to parlay my fame into something, too," Dolores revealed, while handing him her card, MISS DOLORES GRAY, which listed an address only a couple of blocks from his own on East Fifty-Sixth. Once he made her aware of the proximity, she said that she had a car coming any minute to pick her up. But Kallman declined the offer of a lift: "Alas, I'm meeting a friend for a nightcap." His passing up the invitation seemed to increase Dolores's appreciation of his allure. Kaye, noticing the dynamic, prophesied casual corruption: "'I think this is the beginning of a beautiful friendship.'"

––––––––––

After walking down the portion of Forty-Sixth Street that Mayor Lindsay had a few years ago somewhat desperately rechristened Restaurant Row, Kallman turned onto Eighth Avenue and headed one block north. The dinginess of Hell's Kitchen fit his mood; the Augustus betrayal was back on his mind, and he felt a new determination that any dollar he made from now on would be a dishonest one.

He entered the huge dark space of Haymarket. The neighborhood's cheap rents allowed for the establishment's spaciousness, notwithstanding the large Mafia skim required to operate any gay bar. He sat down in a wooden booth so old he could imagine its occupation by a quartet of Irish ward heelers plotting political strategy before he was born.

The boys here were young, and the lighting so dim that a bartender might plausibly explain to a cop, while handing him an extra envelope, that hey, the kid *looked* eighteen. Kallman ordered a vodka with just ice. From the booth he could survey the attitude and physique of any boy at the pool table. He observed one slim blond with long hair who was playing by himself. The face, when it managed to catch the faint overhead light, looked innocent, but there was a mean decisiveness to the young man's moves.

Boys here could typically be had for twenty-five dollars, but Kallman's MO was never to flash or offer less than a hundred. That way what he purchased would prove more cooperative and trainable. The sky-high fee seemed an even bigger bonanza when recipients realized that the man paying it wanted *them* to be rough with *him* instead of their getting roughed up themselves.

He noticed, in a booth on the bar's other side, an Italian-looking guy who while flipping through the *New York Post* also seemed to be checking out the solitary blond at the pool table. Kallman supposed he had some competition, but it would be a short contest if he got the chance to flash the hundred dollars.

Matty the Horse—big, fat Matty Ianniello, the Mob's sex capo for this neighborhood, whose bars were mostly straight and topless—gave the guy in the other booth a hearty greeting: "My man Andy!" They had a minute of loud, ball-breaking laughter and conversation. "It's all the same!" Matty shouted. "Movin' trash is movin' trash!" He was referring to commonalities between the carting business on Long Island and flesh peddling on Eighth Avenue.

Kallman signaled for a second vodka, and once it was delivered he went over to the pool table to ask the kid with the unclean blond hair if he could stand and watch. "You look like you've got great technique. I'm Dick."

"I'm Jimmy," said the kid, without a smile. "I should probably tell you that I'm his." He nodded toward the guy in the other booth.

"Oh, sorry, my mistake," said Kallman.

"With him and me it's personal," Jimmy explained, "but if you're interested, he runs the guy over there." He pointed to a curly-haired kid sitting on a stool near the jukebox, between two much older men.

"Good to know," said Kallman. "Thanks." Careful never to insert himself into already-formed combinations, he went back to his own booth. He realized that Andy, the guy across the bar, had been observing the pool-table encounter, but without apparent hostility. In fact he was now giving Kallman a sociable nod, which made all seem fine—until he stood up and started walking over. With a friendly warning?

"Didn't you used to be on TV?" Andy asked, with a smile.

"A long while ago."

"I remember you! You played a hustler. I don't mean like these guys. But a guy doing lots of jobs to put himself through school—in a fake kind of way. What was the show?"

"*Hank.*"

"I'm Andy Vitale." He sat down after shaking hands.

"I didn't mean to cut in on anything," said Kallman, pointing in the direction of the pool table.

"Not a problem. You still act?"

"No," said Kallman, who before he knew it was telling Vitale about his more recent lines of work.

Andy reached into his wallet, which appeared to contain several different kinds of business cards. He gave Kallman two of them, each with a Dobbs Ferry, New York, address:

ANDY VITALE
REALTOR OF PROMINENT PROPERTIES

ANDY VITALE
DEALER IN FINE ANTIQUES

Kallman looked at the second card and thought back to his conversation with Dolores at Brothers and Sisters. "That's funny," he said.

After one more quick look at Jimmy, Andy smiled and asked: "How so?"

CHAPTER 34

APRIL 13, 1983

I can play the harpsichord surprisingly well. I learned way back in Astoria from a German-Jewish refugee musician who lived there. (Upon his arrival in New York someone had misdirected him to Astoria when he asked the way to Astor Place, and he wound up staying in Queens for the rest of his days.) For a portion of my early life I was even more comfortable with a harpsichord's stops and double keyboard than with the black-and-whites of a regular piano. Alas, you'd be surprised at how few calls there are for harpsichord players in the orchestra pits of Broadway musicals.

But now there was *Amadeus*. It wasn't even a musical, but it had one harpsichordist onstage for the recital scenes set at court and another in the pit to "dub" some of the music supposedly being played by the actors a few feet above.

Devin pointed to the onstage harpsichordist. "Here was your big chance to be a star."

I could sense, even in the dark of the theater, that he instantly regretted the comment, since these days I wasn't up to even my usual inconspicuous work in the pit. Neuropathy was forcing me to get around with the cane that now rested against the first-row rim of the mezzanine we were sitting in. I couldn't complain: so far no KS, no PCP, and no brain fog rendering me unable to concentrate on this Wednesday matinee. I'd seen *Amadeus* on my own a year ago—before David Dukes replaced Ian McKellan as Salieri—and today I'd been able to get Devin to come with me on his day off.

When intermission arrived, he didn't ask if I wanted to stretch my legs; he knew I'd prefer to save any wincing and stumbling for the walk home. So we stayed in our seats with the house lights up and Devin read the "At This Theatre" portion of *Playbill*, noticing that *Seventeen* had made its run here at the Broadhurst. Pointing to the passage, he said: "So this is where your Dickie Kallman had his big debut."

Of course, I didn't need *Playbill* to remind me. At points during the first act I'd start looking at my old spot in the pit, where the dubbing harpsichordist now sat. Over the decades I'd been in the audience here any number of times, but these two trips to *Amadeus* were the only ones I'd made to the Broadhurst in the three years since Dick's murder. Portions of the theater had been reconfigured since the *Seventeen* days, and the changes made it tricky for me to sustain the feeling that I was really sitting in the same place where that season of my youth had taken place. Last year Laurie had taken me and Devin to Ford's Theatre in Washington, and I'd silently marveled—*This is just what it was like that night*—until a guide explained that not a splinter of wood or tuft of fabric in front of me had been there in 1865: the whole interior had fallen in on itself in the late nineteenth century and been scrupulously replicated many decades later.

Still, this afternoon, if only for a few seconds every now and then, I could look at the stage and see all the kids I'd known with their parasols and straw hats, and instead of bits from *The Marriage of Figaro* I'd be hearing them sing "If We Only Could Stop the Old Town Clock."

"You know," said Devin, as the lights went back down, "I thought Mozart, even if he was just a kid, would have been a little more fucking *cultured* than the guy in this play."

"He was a diamond in the rough," I responded. "Sort of like

you." I squeezed his hand for a second, and then compulsively pressed the button on my new digital watch, cupping my palm around its face to shield my fellow theatergoers from its glowing numerical display. Over the last few months the magically changing integers had increased my sense of time's fleetingness. The second hand of my old watch had made its eternal orbits; the new one's ever-changing digits somehow seemed to warn that everything was heading toward an end point.

But I was happy. For one thing, I had never in my life felt the sort of envy that contorts Salieri when he realizes all of the complicated wonders inside Mozart's head. I'd been glad to be quite good at the little thing I did rather than mediocre at something bigger that I *tried* to do. And these days, along with being happy, I was proud: I had my law-school-dean's-list daughter, and my dean's-list (CUNY at night) computer-science-majoring boyfriend, who by day sold clothes at Jos. A. Bank. Devin looked like a million bucks heading off to work in one of their suits instead of the sweaters he used to wear to the 19th Precinct. He was going places, and I just hoped he'd get there by the time I was gone. What I wanted most was for him and Laurie to remain best friends, even after she'd gotten married and he'd found someone else; to be unofficial family, traveling to see each other at Thanksgiving and Christmas.

Sex had cooled down between me and Devin, not because he was fearful—anything but; he was up-to-date and savvy about all the latest safety protocols and techniques. I was the one who these days was either too nervous, about passing something on to him or just too fatigued. As for him going elsewhere for occasional adventure and relief? It couldn't have bothered me less. As far as I was concerned, "adultery" could remain a crisis for straight people; their gay counterparts now had every other kind of crisis to deal with.

Because of Devin I was so well disposed toward the world (which my instincts told me I would soon be leaving) that everything made me nostalgic. The Woolworth Building had gotten landmarked yesterday, making me talk a blue streak about the old five-and-dime in Astoria: the tiny bins with the red quadrangular price tabs; the lunch counter decorated with color photographs of the food that were so much more vibrant than the food itself. Devin, unimpressed, said: "It was like a Rite Aid, no?"

"Way more enchanting," I insisted.

I now looked toward the wing, stage right, from which Dick had emerged several times each night during *Seventeen*. From what I knew of his later life, I imagined that by now he'd likely be sick if he hadn't been murdered. For a second or two I even wondered if this amounted to some kind of satanic "luck," a weirdly merciful escape. But no, I decided. I didn't fear whatever physical agonies lay ahead or how long things would take. I was only, and already, bereft of what I was leaving.

I had lists in my head of the men I knew personally who were already sick. One of those rosters consisted just of guys I'd done shows with: eight names, including one member of the old *Seventeen* chorus. And as we kept getting told, we were only at the beginning of all this. In the last month alone, three Manhattan Plaza tenants—all of them artsy, of course—had started looking iffy. You never knew what the elevator doors would disclose when they opened. One anxious guy two floors below me more or less lived on Valium: he looked so logy and strung out that one couldn't really guess *what* was wrong with him, and maybe that was the point—not just to delude others, but to delude himself as well.

When *Amadeus* ended, Devin and I made the short walk home; the cane doesn't slow me down too much on days when I'm feeling generally okay. Passing the Majestic, right by the Broadhurst, we could see that *42nd Street* was still going strong. The marquee made us miss Carole, back in Los Angeles for well over a year now. We decided to order in Thai, and as I considered the evening ahead I worried about not having the energy to complete my tax return, due in two days. Devin, already finished with his own, had offered to do it for me, but I'd declined, ashamed to let him see my total income for the previous year, no matter that its meagerness was the result of my many ailments. I'd thought of sending my forms and receipts down to Laurie, who could handle them in the space of ten minutes, but asking her would have made me feel even more helpless than I already did, and closer to being officially "disabled."

We picked up the mail as we came through the lobby. "Dessert!" Devin cried, recognizing the little package that Laurie had sent from Washington as a batch of homemade cookies. I then noticed, stuck to the bottom of it, an air-mail envelope from England.

"Oh, God," I marveled, realizing that more than a year had passed since I'd written him. "It's from Kenny!"

Devin, cautious about another foray into what he sometimes called Dickieland, suggested we save reading the letter until after the Thai food and cookies. He was relieved that I'd long since tucked away the scrapbook, but he knew that moments would sometimes arrive when I backslid into the unexpected drama of the murder. After all, now that he and I had been a couple for three years, it constituted our "early history." So once we got up to the apartment he changed his mind and said, "Okay, knock yourself out. Let's hear the letter."

We sat down on the couch, and as I started to read Kenny's neat handwriting aloud, I realized that I was performing a faint mimicry of his gentle southern voice:

"'Dear Matty—'"

"'Matty'?" asked Devin.

"He always called me that back then."

"It's fucking adorable. It's like the *opposite* of 'Daddy,' but I'm now never going to call you anything else."

"Let me read."

Forgive me for being so slow to respond to the letter you sent ages ago. Getting it was a complete surprise, and I have such fond memories of you and Seventeen. *(Am enclosing an old snapshot of a bunch of us standing outside the Broadhurst. No sign of Ann Crowley in the group. She must have taken the picture?)*

I guess the delay in replying stems from the mental block I have when it comes to thinking or talking about Dick. I had it long before the murder (terrible) which I heard about from Carole Cook.

Thank you for the very odd souvenir! That my name should be on that sheet music—very strange. Are we sure it's not another Kenny? "Dance Away the Night" was not in the original Show Boat, *but they threw it into the London version that I did—and then didn't bother recording it on the cast album! But overall the thing was a great experience—the chance to hear Cleo Laine every night was enough in itself!*

I've been pretty busy over here. Keep an eye out for The Lonely Lady, *a movie that will ooze up onto American shores this fall. I play a hairdresser—that's what* Boys in the B. *typecasting will do—in an all-colors-of-the-rainbow shirt and horn-rimmed aviator glasses that somehow make me look exactly like Bill Bixby.*

The picture is a vehicle *for Miss Pia Zadora, bought for her by her sugar daddy the way Michael Jackson might buy himself a life-size toy train. Anyway,* this *train fell off the rails the first day, but the movie's a hoot and I urge you to go see it. As for the size of my part: blink and you'll miss me.*

I hope you're well, though it's hard to be sure what that means these days. I'm part of what they call the "worried well," which sounds like "wishing well." And maybe is. Or wishful *well. Oh, well!*

I'm sorry I can't write more about Dick. I disliked him for all the obvious reasons that most people did—but also because in those days I wasn't prepared to be liked by anyone. And he liked me in a way that really left me spooked. The night the show opened he tried to give me a beautiful piece of jewelry. At first I thought it was the fraternity-pin prop in the play. He said to me, with a weird intensity, "Now we're pinned." But I looked down into my hand and saw what looked like a real piece of platinum with tiny diamonds—and I rebuffed him as if he'd put a scorpion on my palm. Even now I'm embarrassed telling you this story.

From what I heard the murder sounded almost random? There was no coverage of it over here. Our Yorkshire Ripper gets all the ink.

It was nice to hear from you, Matty. I hope you're

happy and taking care of yourself. For all my lateness in replying, your letter made the day I got it.

♪ *"This was just another day, an ordinary day, till you!"* ♪

K.N.

"*Papi*, should I be worried?" asked Devin. "He sounds sweet on you."

"That last line is just from one of the songs in *Seventeen*," I explained, before adding, "We were all sweet on *him*." I somehow couldn't get over the new, candid Kenny—talking about the "worried well," a group I'd already passed out of into the "clearly sick." In my mind he was still a naive, abashed boy, not a man of—what, fifty-three now?

Before going to bed I called Carole in LA. She and her husband had just come back from dinner, and she had a piece of typically effervescent news. "I've gotten the part of Grandma Helen in a movie called *Sixteen Candles*. A comedy for teenagers. Grandma Helen! It makes me feel older than Helen Twelvetrees!" (Even I had to look up that one.) "But how are *you*, darling? How are you *feeling*?"

"I'm doing okay. Carole, I heard from Kenny. After more than a year."

"Oh, my. And I thought *I* was behind in my correspondence."

I read her the letter, skipping over the obvious AIDS fears, though she no doubt knew more about Kenny's situation than I now did from the letter.

"Pia Zadora!" she exclaimed, when I got to *The Lonely Lady*. "God, I've even *seen* her. I think she's been injected with the Munchkins' entire supply of collagen. I don't know where the little ones in the Actors Fund Home are going to find any more for themselves."

I laughed, even as I found myself wondering whether Dick's murder could be *both* "random," as Kenny imagined, and "karmic payback," as Janice Carroll insisted. But what I really wondered was why this pin—so mesmerizing to Dick's killers, and apparently bought all those years ago for Kenny!—had been thrust into *my* hand right before Dick was killed.

CHAPTER 35

SEPTEMBER 4, 1978—DECEMBER 4, 1979

Birds chittered beyond the bathroom window while Dick Kallman rummaged in his Dopp kit. Pausing to look through the half-open plantation shutters, he could see another of the houseguests here in Sag Harbor make a morning dive into the pool.

There was no sign of the Grecian Formula bottle among the rest of his toiletries, so he would have to do without it. As it was, he used the product only sparingly, just over the temples where at forty-five he'd begun to gray. He could stand to hit the gym more often, but on the whole he thought he looked pretty good, slightly younger than his age, which he had continued owning up to except in those rare instances when the person he was talking to actually remembered *Hank*. In such cases he would knock off several years, because the effect of doing so was to make the *other* person feel younger: helpful flattery when you were trying to sell him, or more often her, an expensive antique.

One trick of this new business was to make the individual prospect believe, at the start, that she was in a purely social encounter; don't let her realize that she was attending a show, as an audience of one, and becoming, unsuspectingly, a customer. The lady, or the gentleman, must be made to think that an offhand reference to some fine piece (or when Dolores did the talking, *pièce*) had found its way into the conversation only because the listener's obvious discrimination and taste had brought the choice object to Dick's or Dolores's mind. Then, within a few minutes, the piece would be mentioned again, with the listener beginning to discover an interest in possibly owning it.

By this Labor Day, Possessions of Prominence had officially been in business for four months, ever since Kallman and Dolores finally drew up a handwritten single-page agreement. Only weeks had passed since he'd moved into two floors of the town house he was renting on East Seventy-Seventh Street, a space now filling up with art and furniture, some of the objects actually "fine" and some of them not. Business, thanks in part to enthusiastic word of mouth, was already excellent. Behind the scenes, however, the words that stoked it were often whispered, as when Andy Vitale would offer Dick and Dolores a tip on a piece whose provenance might be a little shaky but which was worth a look even so. Dick and Dolores would then make it their business to acquire the object and resell it at a profit to Vitale, who would sell it once again—to "someone not classy enough for you two to meet"—at an even more daring price. Vitale called himself a "second middleman": the fewer sellers he dealt with directly, the less exposure he felt, and it was worth his while to let "the two stars," as he called them, make a little money before he made a lot more.

During this long weekend near the Hamptons, Dolores never came downstairs before lunch, and on the third and final day, her entrance met with actual applause from the other guests at the dining-room table. She sat down between the wife of a residential real-estate baron and the gay, caftaned owner of a chain of sunglass boutiques in Manhattan. Each was sure to ask her more questions about what Lauren Bacall and June Allyson, neither of whom she'd talked to in more than twenty years, were really like.

Dolores's and Dick's minor celebrity came with minor, and occasionally major, advantages, ranging from a weekend here to a whole week in Morocco, where they'd gone a few months ago courtesy of some Malcolm Forbes manqué, nearly as rich as the original, if lacking the hot-air balloons. Neither houseguest ever arrived with so much as a hostess gift, or left having bestowed even a hollow reciprocal invitation to dinner back in New York. Their *presence* here, Dolores's and Dick's, was to be recognized as their contribution. And as she'd said to him upstairs, just before coming down: "This still beats wasting the whole day just to do ten minutes on that bastard Jerry Lewis's telethon."

Helen, the weekend's hostess, the wife of some big man at Chemical Bank, now turned the conversation away from both long-ago Hollywood and local matters—like where one could find the best sun-dried tomatoes—to the wider world. She remarked upon the various humble touches evident in yesterday's installation of Cardinal Luciani as Pope John Paul. "I love the way he combined the names of his two predecessors—so self-effacing, don't you think?"

"Not even a crown!" added Jerry, the sunglass mogul.

Dick gave Dolores a look, a signal: "Can you spot an opening here?"

"Speaking of crowns and Rome," she said, picking up the cue, "we bought the most beautiful tiara at what was practically a junk shop near the Spanish Steps. A lovely, subtle thing—nothing high and pointy; more like a slightly raised barrette. Early nineteenth century, with the tiniest little emeralds. Helen would look spectacular in it, and yet the thing is so understated that no one will think she's trying to look like goddamned Princess Margaret!"

The eight people around the table all laughed, before Helen's husband, the Chemical executive, rose from his chair to go smoke a cigar outside by the pool. The second he was beyond the screen door Helen began to express an interest in purchasing the tiara.

"Dick will have to show it to you on Seventy-Seventh Street," said Dolores, who now expanded on what everyone had been told over the past couple of days about Dick's transformation of his two floors of the town house. Helen regarded the idea of a home in which everything was for sale as wonderfully clever. She'd love to see it—and the tiara.

While Dick and Dolores had not paid for anything this weekend, not even the town car that brought them out on Friday and would take them home tonight, their shiny if small celebrity profited them in another, particular way. For people like Helen, it added a distinguished element to the pedigree of any item they might be selling. That the object had been briefly owned by, and resided with, a onetime stage-and-screen actress and an erstwhile TV star actually persuaded some customers to pay more than they would have otherwise.

Within two weeks the tiara would go to Helen for six times what Dick and Dolores had paid for it in Rome. And if the emeralds weren't exactly real, Helen didn't know that, and it was still a pretty piece, so why shouldn't everyone be happy?

Meanwhile, as Labor Day wore on, Dolores spent a pleasant afternoon indoors among the living room's hundred throw pillows. She still viewed the protection of her face as an occupational necessity and wouldn't go out even to the shaded patio until the sun began its early-evening descent. Well before that, a pair of bartenders arrived to cater to the six houseguests and the dozen or so people who could be counted on to drop by the pool for cocktails.

Around five o'clock, one of the servers—a young man in khakis, a white shirt, and bow tie—came over to Dick Kallman's chaise longue and asked: "May I get you another one, sir?" The fellow looked like one of the clean-cut college boys who used to work summers at The Balsams, a comparison that Kallman now imparted to the kid, possibly impressing him. He could still impress *himself* by mentioning the old resort and recalling the apex of Torchy's fortunes.

The young man said, "Actually, I'm already out of college. I'm heading into my last year at Columbia Law."

"Really?" said Kallman. "You don't look nearly old enough, though I'm getting to the point where everyone between twenty and thirty-five looks the same: young!"

The boy smiled, and Kallman got the feeling it was okay, maybe even a net plus, that he hadn't been able to cover his patches of gray hair this morning.

"I'm living at home with my folks and brothers for the summer, a few towns over."

"I'll bet they're delighted to have you around."

"Not sure about that!" said the young man, with a laugh. He shook a hand of Kallman's that sported two rings and added: "I'm Steven."

———————

Father duBois called at five minutes to five. Kallman took a peeved look at the clock as he picked up the phone.

"I'm going to have to make this quick, Doobie. I've got a business associate arriving any second."

"Of course," said the Episcopal priest. "I'm just in such a good mood that I had to call *someone*, and I thought of my favorite 'disciple'!"

"What's got you so happy?" Kallman asked, while repositioning an item on a glass-topped coffee table, believing the change might show it off to greater advantage. The coffee table itself, which purported to be from a London furniture maker, circa 1895, had in fact been manufactured in upstate New York around 1940. It was priced (and inconspicuously stickered) at twenty-five hundred dollars, and he was sure it would soon sell.

"It's this new pope that's got me so happy! What a marvel! Honestly, I may just cross the ancient divide and offer myself to Rome. He's standing firm against everything that the spineless Episcopalians keep buckling under to." Doobie referred to John Paul II, who had assumed the papacy when John Paul I died less than a month after his installation last fall. The new pontiff had just announced that Catholic priests would have to remain celibate if they wanted to remain priests. Father duBois, who had not been "familiar" (his word) with Dick since 1975, but who remained ever-hopeful that their hasty intimacies might someday resume, strongly approved of this latest edict.

Kallman jokingly asked Doobie: "Do you think this second

John Paul helped to poison the first one?" Rumors of foul play had abounded after the almost instant demise of poor Luciani, who some believed to harbor liberal sentiments.

"If JP Two was in on it, then thank God he knew to administer a high enough dose!" Doobie, delighted at his own blasphemy, laughed loudly until he changed the subject and asked: "How is your business, Dick? I'm so proud of the success you're making, however much I'd still rather see you and Miss Gray in some big musical onscreen."

"I've got to run, Doobie. Doorbell!"

The bell didn't actually ring for another couple of minutes, at which point it signaled the arrival, right on time, of Andy Vitale. To Kallman's surprise, he was accompanied by the blond from the pool table at Haymarket two years before. The boy might be better shampooed today, but it was definitely him—Jimmy Ingrassia, according to Andy's introduction.

"I'm teaching him the business," Vitale explained. "And when he doesn't behave, I'm *givin'* him the business." Jimmy laughed—a bit uneasily, Kallman thought—at his keeper's joke.

"What can I get you gentlemen?" asked Kallman.

Andy answered that two beers would do nicely. He specified a lite one for Jimmy, whose slender frame he clearly wanted maintained. As everyone took a seat, Kallman chose the yellow-upholstered armchair that was the living room's bright focal point. On the other side of the coffee table, Vitale opened a box he'd carried through the door. He read aloud the label affixed to it: "One ewer (pitcher). Glazed Kashan tiles. Thirteenth century."

"It glows," said Kallman appreciatively.

"Like fuckin' Three Mile Island," Andy agreed. Jimmy looked perplexed.

"My young friend is not a regular consumer of *The New York Times*," Vitale explained. "Or of any other news source. He regards 1010 WINS as a speed bump on the radio dial."

Kallman laughed. "That's okay. He's got other charms, I'm sure."

"You're *sure*? You're talkin' personal knowledge?" Andy asked, with a laugh that betrayed a certain ominous suspicion. Kallman decided it would be prudent to bring the conversation back to the tiled pitcher.

"It's from a private dealer," Vitale explained. "I got it for nine hundred dollars, but I'm betting you and Miss Gray can charm somebody into taking it for four grand. So you two can have it from me for three."

Kallman looked at the pitcher—beautiful, whatever its real age and story might be—and wondered who might be a mark for it.

"You've got that fancy Ivy League boyfriend now," Andy reminded him. Seven months had passed since meeting Steven in Sag Harbor. "Maybe he knows some broke art-history student who can embellish the thing's origins, cook up a little provenance for it."

Kallman decided to buy, thinking that he himself might be able to perform the task Andy was recommending. He was learning fast, thanks to the occasional big buying trip with Dolores—Hong Kong was coming up—and even their quick outings to local antiques shows, like the one at the Mamaroneck yacht club last week.

"So what do *you* have for *me*?" Andy asked. This was a two-way street, after all. If Dick and Dolores ran with people who'd like to boast about having a thirteenth-century pitcher in their apartment, Andy's friends enjoyed flashing big watches, and rings twice as heavy as the pinkies they encumbered. Since Kallman's own attraction to loud jewelry had never abated, he became the obvious man to supply Andy with such items for resale.

"*Here's* what I've got for you," he now said. "Take a look." He opened the snap lid of a velvet case. It contained a gold ring whose square, stippled face was as big as a pat of butter, and a medallion that matched the pattern. This latter item would likely be worn on a gold chain against a hairy chest, the arrangement visible beneath an iridescent, partly unbuttoned shirt.

"Where'd you get it?" asked Vitale.

"From a guy in Philly, for seven hundred. If you inflate the number of carats a bit, I'll bet you can get sixteen for it. Dolores and I will take an even grand." He paused for a second. "If that's okay with you, of course."

"Done," said Vitale. "An excellent five minutes' worth of business." He looked around the large living room and pointed to some framed vintage posters stacked against a table. "You branching out into commercial art?" he asked, sounding disappointed.

Kallman made light of his newest initiative: "You call a poster an 'affiche' and it's worth twice as much."

Andy shook his head. "They're too tearable." He preferred the solidity of pitchers and watches and rings, or at least canvas. "But that's all right. We're branching out a little, too. Okay, Jimbo, it's your turn."

Jimmy Ingrassia began a nervous presentation, like something rehearsed for performance in front of a middle-school class. "Mr. Kallman, Andy tells me you've got a nice respectable boyfriend now, and we're very happy for you. But we imagine there could still be nights when you entertain other guys and might want to be able to offer them some refreshments."

Jimmy looked to Andy for approval. Vitale seemed more amused than impressed with his boyfriend's maiden voyage, at least in this apartment, as a drug dealer, while Kallman tried to decide whether it was a good idea to mix antiquing with this additional activity. He had a perfectly reliable dealer five blocks away and didn't need some kid up in Westchester. But would it offend Andy if he said no?

"Well, sure," he finally answered, keeping it matter-of-fact. He ended up giving Jimmy forty dollars more than the asking price for the two little plastic bags that were now handed over. Kallman checked the time on a nearby ormolu clock, hoping he could quickly finish up with his visitors. But then the doorbell rang and he noticed Andy's eyes dart in its direction; this was a man who didn't like surprises. Kallman put the plastic bags in his jacket pocket.

Steven, living this spring with a roommate over in Brooklyn and studying for his last semester of exams at Columbia, had arrived early. Kallman had plans to cook him dinner for the second time in two weeks. "We're just about done," he informed him, before making introductions to Andy Vitale and Jimmy Ingrassia.

"Good to meet you," said Jimmy, shaking Steven's hand.

Kallman felt relief when Andy and his boy were out the door

and on their way back to Westchester. The evening ahead was important. He was proud and increasingly fond of Steven, this good-looking, preprofessional young man who was reactivating his old craving for sweetness, for Kenny, albeit with a new paternal tingle. Still, the flip side of these needs, the ones requiring Jimmy's colleagues at Haymarket, was growing sharper and riskier. The equipment involved in fulfilling those was stored in a closet feet away from the bureau drawer he tonight intended to offer Steven: a place to keep some underwear and socks and a couple of shirts. A little beachhead of domesticity inside the loftlike bedroom on the duplex's second floor.

―――――――

By the time Thanksgiving came and went several months later, Steven's overnight visits had so increased in frequency that the single drawer became two. He'd also acquired half a hanger rack in a closet on the other side of the one containing the paraphernalia employed on nights he wasn't there.

Tonight, once Steven and Dick settled themselves at a table inside Ted Hook's Backstage nightclub on West Forty-Fifth, the waiter told Kallman that there was no need to start a tab; things would be on the house. Steven was impressed by the clout of his boyfriend. "Boyfriend": was it the word he'd at last bring himself to use (even if he didn't bring the boyfriend himself) when he went home to Long Island for Christmas? In truth, he couldn't yet allow himself to use the word inside his own head. It was one thing to go to the gay dances in Earl Hall up at Columbia—he'd even gotten Dick to come with him on a couple of Friday nights—but it was another to live that life seven days a week.

And yet here in this nightclub, where at least half the patrons must be gay, Steven enjoyed being openly attached to someone, and someone semifamous to boot (though early on he'd had to admit to Dick that it was *The Wild Wild West* he watched as a kid, not *Hank*).

"Tell Ted that this is very kind of him," Dick now instructed the waiter, accepting the comp with a big smile.

"You're the Dolores Gray party, right?" asked the server, who suddenly seemed to feel he ought to make sure.

"Yes," said Dick, smiling a bit less as it became evident who was really being comped. "She'll be here any minute."

"Oh, good," the waiter replied. "Those were my instructions."

Steven could see some of the shine coming off an evening that was supposed to be slightly momentous. Tonight he was finally going to meet Dolores. He couldn't recall even *seeing* her that weekend he'd tended bar in Sag Harbor, and in the year since he'd only heard about her.

"This place is fascinating," he told Dick, as they awaited her arrival.

Ted Hook's club here on West Forty-Fifth had been going strong for six years, Dick explained. Before starting it, the proprietor, a pint-sized former chorus boy, had worked for some years as a secretary to Tallulah Bankhead. "Can you imagine what a wild gig that was?" Dick now asked Steven, who remembered Bankhead as a guest star on one of Lucille Ball's hour-long shows, which he'd seen in reruns growing up. (Over the last several months, when Steven tried to get him to talk about his association with Lucy herself, Dick had usually changed the subject. When the two of them were alone, Dick tended to swing between compulsive showbiz name-dropping and wanting to leave all of that behind.)

Steven may have known who Tallulah Bankhead was, but he required Dick's show-business expertise to make him understand who a lot of the people here tonight were. Rex Reed and Margaret Whiting sat two tables away. "A forties band singer," Dick said of the latter. "Almost before *my* time!" He explained that she, like Dolores, would be part of the entertainment tonight, which worked according to a setup: the knowledge that some celebrities would be at the club drew people in after the shows let out; then, near midnight, one or two of the names would get up and "spontaneously" perform at the piano. "The customers think they're getting a surprise treat," Dick explained, "but it's funny how the piano player always seems to have the right sheet music!"

Steven kept hoping that some of these performers would come over and say hi, since in the past months he'd met only Dick's acquaintances from the clothing industry or the people with whom he did his antiques business.

But on the whole Steven felt happy enough just to look around, and Kallman enjoyed watching him watch, proud to be seen with the handsome, low-key young man, though never losing his awareness that Haymarket was just a couple of blocks away and that half of himself wanted to be there. He *was* there, still, once or twice a week, nights when Steven was home in Brooklyn studying for the bar or paralegaling after-hours to make his rent. On the evenings Steven came to Seventy-Seventh Street, a wholly different sort of sex occurred from what went on with the Haymarket boys, but the absence of shame could never really compensate for the loss of excitement. Cocaine, inhaled in the bathroom where Steven couldn't see (though he surely knew it was involved in the proceedings), helped somewhat. It would be on hand when they got home later tonight.

In the meantime, here at last was Dolores, coming toward them in a peach-colored dress to a smattering of applause from those (less than half the crowd) who recognized her. Tiny Ted Hook rushed out to escort her to the table, and Steven, nicely brought up, rose from his chair to greet her.

"Pleased to meet you," she said, half an octave lower than usual.

Steven was visibly struck by her formality—a manner not exactly hostile, he thought, but definitely reserved. He sensed a star's entitlement and recognized his own probationary status. Dick knew there *was* hostility under Dolores's lacquered veneer, most of it animated by her suppressed attraction to *him*. When that figured into things, he always did his best to hide what would be, to her, the least attractive aspects of his sexual leanings, allowing only the respectable ones to surface in the form of someone like Steven, who had been well rehearsed for this evening. He'd been prepped on Gene Kelly and Comden and Green and brought downtown a week ago to watch a revival-house showing of Dolores's *It's Always Fair Weather*—in case *she* brought it up. Unlike a potential customer, Steven was not to ask *her* about the film's other stars and creators, since to Dolores's way of thinking that implied she was subordinate to them, interesting only because of bigger people she had known. Steven had asked Dick if he should expect her to ask *him* about, say, the bar exam or the beginnings of his job hunt. "Not likely," Dick had answered, knowing that Dolores tended to save that kind of feigned interest for people with whom she hoped to do business.

Looking around the room, the lady herself now gave Ted Hook's place what passed for an endorsement: "Well, it's better than getting crushed to death at a rock concert."

"Wasn't that awful?" Steven responded. Last night eleven people had been fatally trampled outside an arena in Cincinnati. Dick appeared unsure of what was being talked about. "This young man reads the papers. You should try it," said Dolores, ribbing her partner, as if she were Andy Vitale to Kallman's Jimmy Ingrassia.

Dick noticed that she'd called Steven "*this* young man," not "*your* young man," but even so, a grudging approval was apparent. Steven went on to speak of the Iranian hostages and Teddy Kennedy's challenge to Carter, figuring that current events might hold the greatest conversational promise with Dolores.

But her mind soon turned to her role as one of tonight's good-sport, pseudo-spur-of-the-moment performers. Ted Hook had just glided toward the piano to introduce the first of them: "My old boss once said to an aspiring performer"—and here he went into Tallulah's boozy basso profundo—'*Dahling*, if you *really* want to help the theater, *please* don't be an actress. Be an *audience*.' Well, in this club we're lucky that the performers and the audience are often one and the same. And we've got *two* of them tonight, two of the *greats*, who've just now agreed to favor us with songs."

Up stood Margaret Whiting, who went back to her big-band roots for "That Old Black Magic." At one point in the lyrics, perplexingly to Steven, she substituted "Jack" for "black."

"Did she make a mistake?" he whispered to Dick.

"No. She's dating Jack Wrangler."

"The porn star?"

Kallman was relieved to know that Steven wasn't so dewily innocent he'd never heard of Wrangler, but he could spot his not-in-Kansas-anymore expression over news of Jack's involvement with Whiting. He understood how two impulses—wanting to go further into this gay world and wanting to flee it—competed in

Steven, just as these things even now competed, to a darker degree and at a more violent level, inside himself. He tried not to push Steven too hard—for example, he toned down the new flamboyance of his own clothes when they went out together; he'd left his recently acquired fur coat at home tonight.

Dolores pretended to pay appreciative attention to Whiting's phrasing, but her mind was focused on getting up there herself, as soon as Ted Hook gave the signal. Once he did, she walked toward the piano to about the same level of applause that Whiting had gotten—something Kallman measured, knowing that Dolores would be measuring it, too.

She chose to sing "Blame It on My Youth," during which she made a gentle hand gesture toward her own table. A sweet acknowledgment of Steven's presence? Or maybe she wanted the audience to believe that she, like Whiting, had a boy toy—not Steven but Dick Kallman, somebody less outrageously inappropriate than Jack Wrangler. Perhaps she was hoping the crowd would take Steven for a nephew one of them had brought along, a kid making a holiday trip to New York.

It was a clear night, very cold, and when the show ended, the party of three waited a few minutes for their town car to pull up at the curb. Next door to Hook's club stood the Martin Beck Theatre, which *Dracula* would soon be vacating to make room for *Harold and Maude*. Dick and Dolores had gone to a backers' audition for the latter and taken a flyer on it by writing a couple of modest checks. Steven, hoping to show that he could participate in a theatrical conversation, mentioned how much he wanted to see the just-opened *Bent*, in which pink-triangled homosexuals fell in love in a Nazi concentration camp. Dick and Dolores both seemed, by their facial expressions, to find it more distasteful than brave, the kind of grubby political stuff from which show business ought to stay away. Kallman even called it *The Boys in the Camp*.

As the car made its way to the East Side, Steven sat in the middle of its roomy back seat, as if he really were a nephew. Dolores would be the first to get out, on East Fifty-Seventh, and just before she did, Kallman mentioned how Steven might be helpful to the business with his new legal knowledge of contracts. The young man politely protested that this wasn't his specialty, but said that he would gladly, when on the premises, let people in and allow them to browse. Dolores's silence made clear her lack of interest in seeing any third party have such a role in Possessions of Prominence. She said only "Pleased to have met you, Steven," as she exited the car. With her high heels planted on the pavement, she looked at Kallman through the still-open door, as if the two of them were alone together, and declared, "He's a nice young man, Richard."

The driver continued on to East Seventy-Seventh. Arriving at number 17, Dick asked Steven, "Why don't we use your keys?"

The young man laughed. "Because I don't have any?"

"You do now," said Kallman, handing him a set attached to a small chain whose black onyx fob was embossed with a single gold *S*.

Steven's expression mixed gratitude and unease.

"It's ridiculous for you to be paying rent in Brooklyn," Dick insisted. "Come and *live* among all these beautiful things we've got."

For one thing, Steven's daily presence here would add to his own safety, would make it less easy for him to give in to temptation and skip out to Haymarket. He wished, beyond that, to find a way to tell Steven that he *meant* something to him, though if he tried to, he wouldn't be singing "All the Things You Are"; it would be more like "All the Things You Aren't." You aren't show business; aren't a hustler of your body or of merchandise; you aren't *me*.

And if the litany of praise had to stop there—because, alas, Steven wasn't Kenny, either—at least the young man was accepting, not throwing back, what had just been put in the palm of his hand.

Steven smiled, and the two of them walked up the steps of the brownstone together.

OCTOBER 3, 1984

We were coming out of the *Noises Off* matinee at the Brooks Atkinson. Devin pushed my wheelchair down West Forty-Seventh into weather a lot warmer than yesterday's. The sun's autumn orange was so lovely that we decided to have a "walk," a loop that would take us over to Fifth Avenue and then down to Forty-Second Street, before we headed west back to Manhattan Plaza.

I was quiet for the first couple of blocks, worrying over the difficulty I'd had following some of the play's action. Was my brain going, too? AIDS was developing a whole subset of acronyms, including ADC (AIDS dementia complex). But maybe *Noises Off*—a clever, lightning-speed farce—was too much for anyone to keep up with completely.

At the corner of Fifth and Forty-Sixth, a woman passing out Mondale buttons (stickers, these days, actually) offered me one, and I put it on.

"*Papi*," said Devin, his tone voicing the hopelessness of the Democrat's prospects and a sympathy for the incumbent that he mostly kept quiet, "even Ali is for Ronnie."

I smirked, having seen the item about the former heavy-weight champ's approval of how Reagan was supposedly "putting God back into the schools."

We continued south to Forty-Second. Before we made our right turn Devin pointed to the Mid-Manhattan lending library two blocks farther down Fifth. "You want to get a book?"

I looked toward the building and remembered when it was Arnold Constable, the department store, and I'd gone in to buy a velvet party dress for Laurie, barely a toddler. "No, D. Let's go home."

We rolled along the wide sidewalk bordering the New York Public Library proper and Bryant Park. After we pushed our way to the skanky hem of the theater district and waited for a light, I looked up at the street sign and thought not of the actual, scuzzy thoroughfare but of *42nd Street*, the musical. I began singing the bit of "Shuffle Off to Buffalo" that had belonged to Carole during the show's early run:

> *When she knows as much as we know*
> *She'll be on her way to Reno. . . .*

"I'm just amusing myself," I told a puzzled Devin. "Shuffling off to Buffalo instead of shuffling off this mortal coil."

"Whatever."

Devin hated pessimism, and I was glad he didn't know the meaning of Hamlet's phrase.

I went on with the song, picking up the tempo. Devin sped up the chair and jerked it a little from side to side, just for fun, getting us toward the corner of Seventh Avenue a little more wackily than we would have otherwise. But then, suddenly, he tugged the chair to a stop, throwing me forward a bit, enough to make me think I ought to get a seat belt.

"Hey!" he barked at a bike messenger who was up on the sidewalk, riding past us in the opposite direction. Devin could be overprotective, but his agitation puzzled me: the guy on the bike wasn't really speeding or close enough to present much risk. In fact, without a helmet he was probably in more danger than we were.

Looking over my shoulder, I saw him flip Devin off and continue going east. But Devin shouted at him a second time. "Hey, *Jimmy*! What's your fuckin' hurry? You late for a break-in? Or are you just developing your leg muscles to beat the competition at Second and Fifty-Third?"

The guy stopped, turned the bike around, and walked it toward us. My boyfriend, looking strong and confident in his charcoal-gray Jos. A. Bank suit, shot him a steely smile. I now realized that it was Jimmy Ingrassia.

"How long have you been out?" Devin asked him.

Jimmy, appearing confused about who this questioner was, gave his answer in a righteous tone. "I been out a little less than a year. I did my time."

"All two and a half years of it! Wow. What are you now? Twenty-five? Twenty-six? Actually," Devin went on, pointing to the bike, "you're a little old for this, no? Not to mention too old for Fifty-Third and Second."

"What the fuck are *you* so mad about?" asked Jimmy, scrutinizing Devin's face through narrowed eyes. "Wait a minute! I know who you are! You're the guy who went from the corner to the 19th Precinct. The detective's butt boy!"

"Really?" said Devin. "*You're* gonna use that term with *me*?"

By this time he'd turned my chair fully around, so that I was facing Ingrassia—at which point Jimmy also recognized me.

"And *you're* the guy who has the fuckin' pin!" He said this with more wonder than hostility, as if he'd come upon the Wizard of Oz or the man who carved the Rosetta Stone. I recalled the startled look he had three years ago, when he noticed me wearing the pin at his sentencing; the same way This-Here's-Dante had spotted it during the plea hearing.

"So what *is* the big deal about the pin?" Devin asked Jimmy. "*Tell* us."

"Asshole," Jimmy replied, "it's what we came to get that night."

"Oh, *right*," Devin scoffed. "You went there just for *that*. When there was a whole apartment full of stealable stuff."

"'Cause the pin's worth sixty thousand dollars. And because it could fit in somebody's pocket. We'd be in and out."

"What made you think it was worth that?" Devin asked.

"Kallman said so," declared Jimmy, who at this point turned to me: "How did *you* get the fucking pin?"

"Dick gave it to me." I didn't say anything more, just silently recalled the frantic moment when I tried leaving the apartment and Dick insisted I take with me what he suggested was an old prop: "Oh, Joe, your fraternity pin! Your beautiful five-dollar pin!"

Ingrassia pressed the point: "*When* did he give it to you?"

Devin answered for me: "None of your fucking business, actually."

"It isn't worth anything like that," I told Jimmy. "Maybe three thousand dollars."

"Bullshit."

"He could prove it to you," said Devin.

Why "he" and not "we"? I immediately wondered. And how *could* I prove it? Take Jimmy back to the apartment and show him the written appraisal we'd gotten? It was Devin I needed to put these questions to, but I turned to Jimmy instead. "When did Dick tell you it was worth sixty thousand dollars?"

"I'll tell you when you prove to me it wasn't."

Devin said "Come on" to Jimmy and started pushing my chair west. I began to protest, attempting to convince Devin that going to the apartment with Ingrassia was a terrible idea, but he said, firmly, to both me and Jimmy: "Two stops." He then leaned down, as he kept pushing the chair, to whisper "Trust me" into my ear. Jimmy walked his bike alongside us, past the dirty bookstores. I could sense his annoyance but also his curiosity. As it was, he'd probably made his last message delivery of the day.

"Right turn," ordered Devin.

The three of us were soon crossing Forty-Second, going north, with me relieved that we were no longer heading to Manhattan Plaza. Within another minute Devin halted us at a coffee shop near Eighth and Forty-Third. "I'll go *get* what will prove it to you," he told Jimmy. I realized that while Devin went and found the appraisal, I was supposed to wait here, inside the little diner, and buy a cup of coffee for the kid who'd arranged

Dick's killing. Devin had said "he" and not "we" back on Forty-Second to camouflage the fact that we lived together, and to keep Jimmy from knowing where. He now even asked me for "the keys to *your* apartment."

Jimmy chained his bike to a parking meter, and I decided that he wouldn't try to steal my wheelchair or hurt me in front of the dozen patrons in the coffee shop. Once we all entered, Devin folded my chair and stored it near the door. He gave me a reassuring pat, then took off fast; I managed to walk to a booth on my own. But I felt scared for the first time: alone with Jimmy Ingrassia, how was I going to make conversation for the next ten or so minutes?

As I ordered coffee—Jimmy wanted a sticky Danish, too—I realized that *he* was scared of *me* as well, and that it had nothing to do with the murders. When I put down my water glass after taking a sip, he moved his own glass closer to himself, so that he wouldn't pick up the wrong one and catch something—given that I was so obviously sick with you-know-what.

After a first messy bite of his Danish, Jimmy licked his fingers and said "Sorry," as if this offense against etiquette were what might prejudice me against him. He ate ravenously. Didn't Andy feed him? And if he was still with Andy, why was he working as a bike messenger?

"How long have you had your job?" I asked him.

"Since spring." He laughed with disgust. "I'll be lucky if I've still got it by *next* spring."

"How come?"

He made a funny, soft *pop-pop-pop* sound with his mouth. He was imitating the noise of a fax machine, the little roll of thermal paper printing a line at a time and making its infant crawl out of the machine and onto the tray. The device was threatening to put bike messengers out of business.

"You work?" he asked me.

"No. I'm officially disabled now." Until recently I would tell people that I was between shows. These days it was more accurate to say that I was between hospitalizations. "I used to play the piano for musicals."

"Oh, yeah. That's how you knew Dick." He was remembering

the preliminary bits of my testimony at the trial. I was rattled—offended—to hear him use his victim's first name, and it was even worse when I heard him ask: "How do you know Devin?"

A moment of panic buzzed through me. It's true that after Forti and Paulie's plea hearing Devin and I had always tried to sit apart during court proceedings, lest anyone realize we'd met at the 19th Precinct; and I knew that Jimmy had not seen me with Devin the one time I was there to identify the voice from behind the screen. But was he now entertaining some idea of collusion between me and Devin? Was he maybe even feeling an impulse to gather evidence of it, enough somehow to over-turn the verdict or at least get Devin in trouble? But the panic subsided as quickly as it arose. What would Jimmy actually want to undo? The sweetest deal any prosecution witness had ever gotten? I could hear Judge McGinley's words: "In my view, Mr. Ingrassia has literally gotten away with murder."

I also knew that Devin, who generally thinks two steps ahead of me, would already have reached the same conclusion. And the last thing Jimmy would want is for Dante Forti to get out of prison any earlier than forty years from now.

"I met Devin the day Detective Volker had all of us go up to that Collectibles place," I finally lied. "We became friends after the Forti verdict came in. He's been very nice to me since I got sick."

"You got no idea how many guys on the inside have it." For a second Jimmy sounded as if he were offering some weird sort of gay solidarity about AIDS. But he quickly toughened his affect: "I managed to keep that shit far away from me."

I said nothing. And then he suddenly brightened: "Hey, you were in the theater. Ever seen *Cats*? I fuckin' *loved* it. Andy wouldn't let me keep a stray, this calico that I brought home one time. Broke my fuckin' heart. So *did* you? See *Cats*?"

"I did. Twice. I had comps from a friend." This last fact seemed somehow to mitigate the mortifying truth that I'd liked the show. Jimmy, in any case, didn't seem to know what comps were.

There was one thing I found myself wanting to ask him: *When you went back to the apartment to get your coat that night, did you stop to look at Dick Kallman dead in his yellow chair—or at Steven, his head on the carpet, finally motionless?*

But my mind was mostly working to will Devin's fast return to the coffee shop. He did, thank God, make astonishingly good time.

"Slide over, Matthew," he said, getting into the booth. No *papi*: another part of his effort to keep it from appearing that we lived together. He now put on the table what he'd retrieved from the apartment: the pin, wrapped in a pink piece of paper.

Jimmy regarded it with a momentary fascination that gave way to hostility, as if the pin had caused him a lot of grief, duped him into the orchestration of a double murder that had proved to be a waste of time. He seemed averse to even touching its little diamond shape, less than an inch high or wide, fringed with precious stones no bigger than the tiniest seeds. He pointed to the little diamonds and said "They're not real? The ruby neither?"

"Everything there is little, but it's real," Devin informed him, while unfolding the pink sheet of paper with the appraiser's estimate: $2,995. Devin had arranged the paper so that the Delectable Collectibles name and logo weren't visible, but the official-looking form beneath those things, with its boxes filled in, seemed to convince Jimmy that the valuation was true.

"That fucking fake," he said, meaning Dick. I guess he was angry at him for forcing Jimmy and his associates to kill him. We didn't even have to *ask* for the rest of the story. After turning around to make sure the booth behind him was empty, Jimmy just started telling it. "We were there, in the apartment, like three days before it happened. Me and Andy."

Devin, picking up on the passive voice, repeated "'Before it *happened*'"—the killings again made equivalent to a falling flowerpot or a fender bender.

"We came as usual to look at stuff he had to sell. Watches and jewelry. And he was nervous. He'd been doing a lot of blow lately—I'd sold it to him—and I got the feeling that things with the other one weren't going well."

"'The *other one*,'" I said, employing Devin's repetitive sarcasm. "Steven."

Jimmy ignored me. "Kallman also owed Andy a lot of money, and he was worried about it, which he should have been. He was twitching, and he kept fingering something in his jacket pocket, like a whaddyacallit—a security blanket. And at one point he didn't realize he'd took it out. Andy asked 'What's that?' And it was *that*." He pointed to the pin that was now sitting, indifferently, on the Formica tabletop, beside a caddy holding little cups of artificial creamer.

"So how did you come to believe it was worth sixty thousand dollars?" I asked.

"You should have heard the story he told! All of it bullshit, I'm now sure. How this thing had been his mother's, from nineteen hundred or something; how it was the most valuable thing in the house. How she'd gotten it when she was a famous actress. Some shit like that. 'It's so precious to me, so precious to me,' he kept saying. The only thing that was ever precious to him was *money*, so I figured this must be worth a *lot* of it. He saw me eyeing it, and I could see that that made him nervous. He could tell I'd, like, gotten fixated on it, and he actually said 'Some things are not for sale.' Really? Then it was the only thing in that fucking apartment that wasn't."

Dolores herself had probably never seen it.

"So," said Devin. "Not for sale, but okay for stealing. The pin gives you the idea, and then—once you meet Paulie, that Einstein—you come up with your plan."

"Fuck you," said Jimmy, almost jocularly. "You've heard Ehren's whole spiel. You want to believe every word of it? Go ahead."

Something the prosecutor had said in his office now came back to me: "Keep in mind that Mr. Kallman *knew* Ingrassia. Which means that Ingrassia knew Kallman could identify him. There was no way they were going to leave him alive. And they knew that when they pressed the doorbell."

I now knew that Jimmy must have described the pin, in detail, to Dante and Paulie. They never saw it until they were inside the courtroom, but they'd been made to salivate over the possibility of stealing it, and it's what they'd come looking for that night. *That's* why they'd never come with their own bags for carrying out the swag. The little pin was all they were after; stealing everything else and stuffing it into Hefty bags from the kitchen was an afterthought, a consolation prize. A frustrated vision of the tiny pin, this little Grail, had stayed with them, allowing them to recognize the object when they saw it fastened to me.

"Dante went fucking ballistic when there was no sign of it in the apartment. He figured it must be in the safe. And Kallman wouldn't give up the combination."

"It was never in there," I told him.

"You're telling me he *gave* it to *you* that week? Between the Monday I saw it and that Thursday night?"

"Actually, he gave it to me *on* Thursday night. Between your first and second visits to his apartment that evening."

"What'd he give it to you for? Safekeeping?"

"Yes, I'll bet it was that exactly." Dick must have remembered his Monday braggadocio and realized—or been told, during the first visit—that the pin, not the watch, was what they wanted; that the crazy urgency of the phone calls and arrivals indicated they were going to get it one way or another.

"Well," said Jimmy, "he was stupid to get himself killed over it."

"Yeah," said Devin, "and it was real foolish for dead Steven to get his head kicked like that, too. Very careless of both of them. Let me ask you, Jimmy. Why didn't you spill all this about the pin at the trial? Or to Ehren?"

"'Cause Andy and my lawyer told me it was too—what's the fucking word?—*specific*. Sayin' we went in there lookin' for one particular thing would make what we wound up doing look even more 'premeditated.' "

Devin scooped up the pin and the appraisal sheet and put them in his suit pocket. "Let's get you set, Matthew." He helped me out of the booth and toward the folded wheelchair. On the way to it he looked back over his shoulder at Jimmy and said, "Pay the check."

It would have been a nice, small piece of justice if someone had made off with Jimmy's bike while we were inside. But we could see it still chained to the parking meter, as we began to walk and wheel down Forty-Third Street toward Ninth Avenue.

I was never happier to get into the elevator at Manhattan Plaza, just the two of us, and then to be back in the apartment. Devin and I sat down on the couch, where we would have our tasty dinner, on tray tables, as soon as he fixed the plates. But for the moment, while he sat beside me, I took his hand, which actually shook a little.

He'd always tried to dissuade me from obsessing over Dick's murder, but when he saw Jimmy Ingrassia pedal past us this afternoon, he couldn't control his anger, couldn't keep from shouting and stopping him, because Devin Arroyo is a good man.

"I'm glad you did what you did," I told him.

"Yeah. I'm not sure what we got out of it."

I was sure. My brain might or might not be starting to fog, but if I couldn't keep the plot of *Noises Off* straight, I could find an element of truth in what Jimmy said. I now understood this: Dick Kallman had died because of both love and his big mendacious mouth. He had gotten himself killed because the best and worst parts of him were both operating during that last week. Along with the compulsive lying and grandiosity (this absurd, pointless story that made Jimmy lust after the pin) he was exhibiting the one weirdly pure component of his personality: his unrealizable, defeated love for Kenny. He died protecting the symbol of his arrested development, the speck of innocence that had somehow remained alive within him, quarantined from everything else. Knowing, or just sensing, that Jimmy was after the pin because of the hot air he'd blown about it a couple of days before, he tried to save it with another lie, the small, benign one he directed at me as he thrust it into my hand, suggesting it was just the little prop from *Seventeen*. He knew that sentiment would make me take it out of the house before Jimmy and his confederates could come back.

I thought of explaining all this to Devin, but I just held him for a long moment, long enough to feel how none of it would be important to him. *I*—dying me—was important to him.

"I think we should bury this fucking pin." He had it out of his jacket and in his hand.

I pulled back and laughed. "With me, you mean?"

He winced. Where my illness and clearly not-far-off death were concerned, black humor wasn't his line.

I took the pin from his hand, thinking of how, almost thirty-five years earlier, in maybe the only tender gesture of Dick Kallman's life, it had been refused.

"Poor pin," I said. "It never got to do the job it was meant to do. To offer somebody's love and to get it accepted."

I fastened the pin to the lapel of Devin's handsome charcoal-gray jacket.

All my life, I'd needed to hear the words and the music together. It had been my job to make the singer and the piano align. But there was no music playing in the room now, so at this moment I needed the words to be the music as well.

"Will you wear it?" I asked Devin. "For the next fifty years? For me?"

He looked me in the eye, brought me closer, and prepared to speak. And as with everything else he'd ever told me, I knew that whatever he said would be the truth.

He whispered in my ear: "Fucking A, *papi*."